HER ONLY SAFE HAVEN WAS
THE MAN BEFORE HER

"Is this a dream? It can't be true," Kendra said in wonder.

"Why do you say such things?" Brice asked.

"I know you think I'm crazy, but I'm not. I'm from the twentieth century. We have airplanes, and ships without sails that can cross oceans, and cars that don't need horses to pull them. And telephones to make calls from London halfway around the world to Florida. If I wanted to—"

"Hush," he told her, placing his fingers on her lips. "I'll take care of you, Kendra. I won't let anything happen to you."

When he wrapped his arms around her, she started to cry. "I'm scared, Brice," she said.

"I know," he whispered. He kissed her. "I know."

When Midnight Comes

✧ ROBIN BURCELL ✧

HarperPaperbacks
A Division of HarperCollinsPublishers

HarperPaperbacks   *A Division of* HarperCollins*Publishers*
10 East 53rd Street, New York, N.Y. 10022

Copyright © 1995 by Robin Burcell
All rights reserved. No part of this book may be used or reproduced in any manner whatsoever without written permission of the publisher, except in the case of brief quotations embodied in critical articles and reviews. For information address HarperCollins*Publishers*,
10 East 53rd Street, New York, N.Y. 10022.

Cover illustration by Diane Sivavec

First printing: December 1995

Printed in the United States of America

HarperPaperbacks, HarperMonogram, and colophon are trademarks of HarperCollins*Publishers*

❖ 10 9 8 7 6 5 4 3 2 1

To my mother, Francesca, whose love of history inspired Hawk's passion. The terra-cotta fawn is for you.

To the Fabulous Five. You know who you are.

Most of all, to my real-life hero, my husband Gary, who believes in my creativity and intelligence, encouraging me to write even if it means dinner is late or nonexistent.

1

Detective Kendra Browning glanced at her watch as she rushed from the elevator into the precinct lobby where her friend stood waiting. "Sorry I'm late," she said, when she reached the dark-haired woman's side. "The captain called a meeting at the last minute, and I couldn't get out of it."

Frances "Frankie" Wendall smiled. "Let me guess. Another murder, and lunch is canceled?"

"Yes, and not exactly," Kendra answered. Frankie was used to Kendra's hectic schedule, which usually resulted in their plans being curtailed for one reason or the other. "I don't have time for much more than a hamburger, because Jack and I have to go check on a lead that might be related to the Debutante Murders. Hope you don't mind."

"Turkey and sprouts would have been better, but hamburgers are fine."

The two women exited the building and hurried to a nearby fast-food restaurant where they ordered their lunch. After they'd finished eating, Frankie pulled a small gift-wrapped package from her purse and put it on Kendra's lunch tray. "Happy birthday."

"What is it?"

"Why do people always ask that when you give them a gift? If I wanted you to know, I wouldn't have wrapped it."

Frankie, a travel agent, had talked about giving her a weekend getaway for two she'd acquired as a bonus, but when Kendra shook the present, it rattled. Tearing off the yellow paper, she opened the small white box to reveal a necklace. An opalescent moonstone set in a pendant of silver filigree. "So you didn't leave your glasses there after all, you sneak. You went back and bought it!"

"Someone had to. Besides, I thought it a much better gift than a couple of nights at a hotel in Orlando. This will last you the rest of your life."

They'd found the necklace in a small curio shop while hunting for antiques to furnish Frankie's office. Kendra had instantly been drawn to the simplicity of the milky-white stone, but had decided at the last minute not to purchase it. As a cop, she rarely wore jewelry, and buying something like that had seemed frivolous.

Frankie took the necklace from her, unclasped it, then leaned over the table to place it around her friend's neck. "Don't forget what the shopkeeper said. If you wear it, it will bring you adventure and luck."

"A marriage proposal would be better."

"Well, don't hold your breath. You've been waiting for Jack to say the words for how many years?"

Kendra glanced at her watch. "Look at the time. I told Jack I'd be back five minutes ago." Both women stood, and Kendra gave Frankie a quick hug. "Thanks for the necklace. I love it."

*   *   *

Kendra's partner, Jack Sinclair, was pacing back and forth by the elevator when she returned. Upon seeing her, he stopped. "What took you so long?" He raked his fingers through his wavy blond hair.

"Frankie took me out to lunch."

"So what'd the captain say in his meeting?"

"He's upset we had to let our suspect go because we couldn't match his prints to the ones on the murder weapon."

"What'd you tell him?" Jack directed her toward the wide expanse of tinted glass that looked out over the busy Miami street. Outside, though the dead of winter, tourists dressed in shorts and Hawaiian print shirts crowded the sidewalks.

"I told him we held the guy as long as we could without filing formal charges. We have to wait for the DNA tests on the blood samples taken from the knife. But I doubt we'll get a match. I can't picture some dirt-bag picking up on Florida's elite daughters, much less luring them to their deaths in a secluded park. It has to be someone with a little finesse at the least. Definitely someone with money. There's no way any of those girls would follow a two-bit heroin addict anywhere."

"No doubt the captain agreed," he said with sarcasm.

"That'll be the day."

Jack pushed open the smoke-colored glass door, then stopped to look over his shoulder at Kendra. "Was that *all* he wanted?"

"Are you kidding?" She pulled her tan blazer about her, covering the badge she wore on her belt. "We'll both be working overtime 'til this case is solved. The city's in an uproar over the last debutante's death and the captain's taking the heat for it."

"People are funny. Kill a prostitute and no one cares."

"Yeah, well, I'm tired of dead bodies, no matter who they are. I want out."

"Don't tell me you're going back to juvie? You told me you couldn't handle it."

"That's not why I left. I got tired of pulling a kid from a home and having the courts send him back there the next week to get beat up again. At least working homicide you can send a murderer to jail for a couple of years." She looked up at the clear sky. A warm breeze swept in through the door and she found herself wishing she were somewhere else—anywhere else. "I need a vacation. Someplace different . . . where there's no crime."

"Yeah, right. The captain's gonna okay that in a heartbeat. You're lucky we're still getting weekends off."

"Let's go away this Saturday. You know, a date. We could go sailing or to the Dickens Festival."

"Dickens Festival?"

"On that old sailing ship. Jan and Mark are going and so are a couple of guys from property."

Jack laughed, then stepped through the door, allowing it to swing closed behind him. Kendra watched him through the thick glass, wondering when he might notice she'd not followed. He was nearly at the parking lot when he finally turned, his expression one of annoyance. He retraced his steps, then opened the door. "You coming, or what?"

She folded her arms across her chest. "You never answered me."

"About what?"

"Our date."

"What're ya talking about? We gotta date. I ordered sandwiches from Gio's and rented us a couple videos tonight. *Lethal Weapon II* and *III*."

"How romantic," she muttered.

He let the door fall shut once more. Kendra stared at the back of his head through the glass for a moment, then pushed the heavy door open. She caught up with him just as he was descending the steps that led to the parking garage. "You still don't get it, do you?" she called out.

"Get what?" he asked without turning around.

"What happened back there?"

"What're you talking about, Ken? I get an anonymous call from some psycho who thinks another deb's been killed out at the park, and you're asking me if I remember what happened back there?"

Kendra grabbed his sleeve, forcing him to stop and look at her. "I want something more."

"You *do* need a vacation."

"What I *need* is a little romance."

"Browning, what the hell are you talking about? Damn it," he said when she looked away from him. "You're gonna cry again, aren't you?"

She turned to face him squarely. Although she loved Jack with all her heart and knew he loved her, she knew also that police work was his life. He didn't place her second on purpose, it just happened. Especially during a case as important as this, which the press had dubbed the Debutante Murders. When Jack concentrated entirely on his work, she became his partner and nothing more. Somewhere along the line, he'd forgotten that she was a woman with needs. "What I'm talking about is our date, Jack. A *damn date.* You know, candlelit dinner, dancing, a walk in the moonlight."

"You been reading those romance novels again?"

Kendra cursed at herself for bringing the subject up. She knew exactly what he was going to say.

He didn't disappoint her.

"You wanted to be a cop, Kendra. It's a man's job in a man's world." He strode toward their undercover car, a brown Taurus, and unlocked it. "You want me to open the car door for you too?"

"You'll never understand." She opened the door herself and got in. After buckling her seat belt, she turned on the police radio hidden inside the glove box. "Just once," she continued after he got in, "I'd like to be treated like a lady, not one of the guys. I want to be wined and dined on something besides Gio's deli. I want to be told I'm beautiful. I want to have a conversation about something besides police work and what's the best gun to carry. I want to go dancing once in a while!"

"Geez, Ken. Whaddya want from me?"

She took a deep breath and let it out slowly. "Nothing, Jack. Nothing."

"Great. Now call dispatch and tell them we're en route." He started the car, then glanced over at her. "You got a radio?"

She patted the fanny pack she always wore strapped around her waist beneath her blazer. "In here with my gun."

"Good. 'Cause I forgot mine."

A half hour later, Kendra and Jack made their way down a narrow path that led to a man-made lake, where captive flamingoes waded about in the quiet waters.

The two detectives stopped at a stone retainer wall that surrounded the walkway circling the water. Kendra climbed on top of the low wall and, shading her eyes, looked around. On the surface, all seemed peaceful. The dozen or so palm trees scattered around the water's edge swayed gracefully in the gentle breeze. At the far end, a waterfall splashed over an artfully built wall of rocks, indigenous more to the Pacific Islands than the Florida swamps. Hidden just beyond, within the bright green foliage of the two acres of thick tropical growth that made up the park, lay a myriad of walkways, picnic areas, and lovers' retreats—and perhaps a dead body.

The newly built park was mostly deserted. Few area residents and even fewer tourists frequented the sanctuary after the first murder took place over a year ago. But after the second, six months ago, it was all but abandoned to the wildlife.

"See anything?" Jack asked.

"No. We'll have to split up."

He grabbed her hand and she jumped the short distance to the ground.

"See, Kendra? I can be a gentleman."

"Very funny. Let's get this over with. I wouldn't want to chance missing a romantic evening filled with gourmet food and fine entertainment."

"I thought you liked Mel Gibson."

Kendra ignored him and looked around the park. "I hope your anonymous caller isn't sending us on a wild goose chase." She pointed north toward the waterfall. "You take that section over there, and I'll search this one here."

Jack nodded, then left. Kendra started in the opposite direction, scanning the paths leading from the pond.

"Jesus! Kendra, get over here!"

Jack stood on a large rock beside the waterfall. When he waved at her to hurry, she ran down the path, then climbed up to stand beside him. He was staring at a cement park bench hidden in a private alcove of ferns.

She was about to ask him what it was when her gaze traveled to a level, sand-shrouded spot just beyond the bench.

"Oh, God!" The sight turned her stomach. Behind her, the ceaseless pounding of the waterfall matched that of her heart. She turned away for a moment, then looked back at the yellow, blood-soaked blouse. "Where's the body?"

"Who knows. Call a tech. And get 'em out here fast."

Kendra unzipped her fanny pack and pulled out her portable radio. "Sixteen-thirty-seven."

"Sixteen-thirty-seven," the radio crackled back. "Go ahead."

"We'll need an F.E.T. at Paradise Park. Make it code two—three if possible. Also a search team."

"Ten-four."

Fifteen minutes later, the park was filled with a dozen uniformed officers in teams of two, all searching for some sign of the body.

The photographer, a heavyset gray-haired man named Rick Johnson, snapped photos of the blouse. When he was finished with his close-ups, he moved to the rocks above Kendra to take a few shots of the general area. As he bent over for different angle, a canister of film fell out of his top pocket and landed in the rocks at Kendra's feet. "Hey, Browning," he called out to her. "Toss my film up, will ya?"

Kendra looked down, but didn't see the small black container. "Where'd it go?"

"Over there, to your left. I think it fell into that crevice."

Kneeling down, she pulled her penlight out of her fanny pack and directed the thin beam into the hole.

The film canister was wedged about a foot down. A tiny lizard scurried across it and away from the light.

Just as it disappeared, her eye caught sight of something shiny and metal.

"Kendra. You got my film, or what?"

"Hold on. I think I found something . . . a chain." She reached in and pulled it up, surprised to see a heavy, gold medallion hanging from the broken clasp.

Jack, standing beside Johnson, glanced her way. "The girl's?"

"I don't think so," she said, discovering a catch on the perimeter. "It looks like a man's pocket watch." Careful not to touch the smooth metal cover except at the edges, she opened it and noticed the crystal was broken and the time stopped at 12. The pattern on the clock face was unusual. Two half-circles of different sizes: the larger one with the ends facing down, the smaller one balanced on top, its ends facing up. Inside the case, the words, "Do what thou wilt," were engraved upon it.

She held it out. "You better get a few pictures of this, Johnson, before we bag it up and send it in for prints."

The photographer nodded, moved to her side, then took a few photos. Just as Kendra dropped the piece into an envelope, a shout came from the area beyond the waterfall.

The body had been found.

Kendra frowned at the threatening horizon. She shouldn't have sailed this far out on her own, given her limited experience, but the gentle breeze and clear blue sky had lured her farther from shore and the harsh realities of life. She had gone sailing to forget her problems—instead, she forgot time.

As she maneuvered her Catalina 22 toward shore, she was relieved to see that hers was not the only craft left on the choppy waters. A few hundred feet to her right sailed a small yacht, and between it and the Miami shoreline was an assortment of other sailboats all heading in.

She shivered as the spray from the whitecaps soaked her clothes, and she wished she hadn't taken off her windbreaker earlier. And her life jacket, she realized belatedly, spying the vest she'd forgotten to put back on just out of reach near the open hatch. She'd need to put it on shortly, as soon as the wind gave her a break, but for now, she didn't dare let go of the tiller. Overhead, she was dismayed to see that the sky was thick with ominous black clouds.

Why oh why hadn't she gone with the others on the tour of that replica schooner? She had actually started on the tour with several friends who were eager to see the Dickensian celebration taking place on board. But as the men and women in their nineteenth-century costumes and affected English accents surrounded her, singing, "God Rest Ye Merry, Gentlemen," she'd felt suffocated, as if trapped within the confines of the ship.

As she reefed the sails in the midst of the squall, she worried in earnest. The heavy winds tossed her boat around like some insignificant piece of debris. The tiller ripped from her grasp. Waves towered overhead, obscuring the shoreline from sight as her sailboat keeled dangerously, sending her life preserver flying overboard.

Banner headlines flashed in her mind. *Miami Cop Drowns Off Coast: Partner, Jack Sinclair, Mourns Her Loss.*

Without warning, a seemingly endless wall of water crested over her. "Dear God—"

Kendra never finished her prayer. The wave crashed down, swamping her boat and plunging her into the depths of the sea. The brine engulfed her, and she squeezed her eyes shut against the burning salt water. It filled her mouth and ears, and she panicked as the turbulent undertow grasped her in a relentless hold.

The urge to survive spurred her to action. Every muscle burned, but she forced her leaden limbs to continue as she fought for the surface. When she thought her lungs would explode and she could go no farther, her face emerged from the seething foam and she sucked in the salty air.

A sharp jab in her back sent a new surge of adrenaline rushing through her. Sharks! Envisioning a great white, she forced herself to look, at the same time wondering what she'd do if she saw one.

Relief flooded through her as she discovered the source of her terror: the hull of her capsized sailboat. But any expectations of righting it were dashed as it sank below the surface in an eruption of bubbles.

At that moment something shot above the churning waves from the boat's watery grave. Like a welcome companion, an orange seat cushion bobbed just out of reach. Thanking the forces watching out for her, Kendra struggled through the water to the thick square of floating vinyl.

2

"Captain! Man off to starboard!"

Captain Brice Montgomery surely misunderstood his first mate over the roar of the wind. Not that it mattered. It would be pure lunacy, not to mention certain death, to attempt a rescue in such weather. "You are seeing things, Riley," he shouted back. He remembered no ships in the surrounding waters before the sudden storm broke furiously upon them several hours ago, sending them off course. "It's a trick of the storm."

But as Brice looked out over the rough sea, he wondered at the sudden parting of the gunmetal clouds in the midst of such a tempest. The full moon lit the midnight sky and dark turbulent waters. Rubbing his eyes, he stared in amazement at what appeared to be a person clinging to a piece of flotsam. "Bloody hell! There is someone! Throw a line!" he ordered. He pulled off his boots, then his oiled canvas, before starting over the side.

"Ye can't go in there, Captain!" But Riley's warning came too late, for his captain had already dived into the raging sea.

Several harrowing minutes later, Riley and a few men gathered at the side to help their captain and his listless burden up the side of the ship.

Riley lifted the woman from his arms. "What do ye want me to do with her?"

"Take her to my cabin. I'll be there shortly."

As Riley started toward the captain's quarters, Brice turned to survey his ship. Ensuring that everything on deck was in hand, he stayed but a few moments longer before following his first mate.

"'Twas a bloody foolish thing ye did," Riley told him when he finally made it to his cabin.

He purposefully ignored the older man's reprimand, knowing only too well the risks he had taken. "Is she alive?"

"Barely."

Brice moved to the bedside. He touched one small, limp hand. "We've got to get her out of these wet clothes."

Riley shook his snowy head emphatically. "Oh, no. Ye plucked her from the water, ye can bloody well undress her. I'll not be part of—"

"Damnation, Riley! God will not strike you dead for seeing a woman naked. Trust me. I know." Seeing that Riley was stubbornly refusing to help, he said, "Fine. Fetch some dry linens and several blankets. I will play lady's maid."

Riley quickly exited, leaving Brice alone with the strangely dressed woman. Her garb was unlike any he had ever seen before, he thought, while trying to remove the heavy satchel belted around her waist. The buckle, an enigma in itself, stymied him, and just when he considered cutting the strap, it clicked open.

That done, he pulled off the white knee-breeches,

then her sleeveless red and white striped shirt, taking care not to catch it on the necklace she wore: a pearlescent moonstone set in silver filigree upon a silver chain. After tossing her wet things on the floor, he paused at her unusual undergarments, trying to decide if he should leave them on, or remove them.

Her chattering teeth and blue lips served to remind him that he had no time to waste. She was cold, her undergarments were soaked.

He quickly pulled them off, adding them to the pile of wet things. Then, before he had time to mull over her strangely tanned skin, he wrapped the blanket from his bed around her.

A few minutes later, Riley came bustling in the door, his arms burdened down with several blankets and extra linens.

Brice lifted the girl in his arms. "The bed is damp," he said.

"Aye, Cap'n." Riley removed the wet linens from the bed, and made it up anew. Piling several blankets on top of that, he turned them down, then looked away while the captain deposited her on the mattress and covered her up.

"You may turn around now, Riley."

"How do ye figure she got there?" Riley asked, eyeing the girl warily.

"I suppose we won't know until she wakens." Brice tucked the blankets snugly around her before standing to remove his own wet clothes. "She is fortunate to have survived thus far. Whether she lasts through the night remains to be seen."

Riley leaned over her, listening to her shallow breathing. After a moment he rose. "Well, the wind seems to be dying somewhat. If it gentles enough, we might try puttin' somethin' hot down her. Some tea or broth. Ye could use some yerself, sir." Riley started toward the door, then paused. "Ye want me to hang yer hammock?"

"I will manage, thank you."

"Suit yerself." Riley tossed a quick look at the girl before leaving the two of them alone.

Not until morning did the sea calm enough for the cook to prepare any hot meals. By then, the captain had already been up for hours, leaving a rather frustrated first mate to watch over their bedraggled guest. She still had not come around, but then, no one had expected her to. Ever. And so, when Riley saw her begin to toss and turn in her sleep, knocking the covers from her and exposing—much to his puritan horror—one bare shoulder, he ran posthaste for help.

"Cap'n! Cap'n!" he yelled, while running across the deck to where his superior stood behind the wheel of the schooner.

"What is it, Riley?"

"Ye have ta come quick like."

"The girl. She's not—"

"Oh no, sir." Riley's face reddened considerably. "It's not that. But she needs ye. I can't—she's . . . ahem."

A few minutes later, Brice walked in to find his charge partially uncovered. Apparently her fitful sleep had loosened the top of the white lawn shirt he'd dressed her in. But that was enough for Riley, and unless Brice did something to remedy the matter, he would have no peace from his first mate.

Moving to her side, he fastened her shirt and pulled the covers to her neck, but she pushed them away and whispered, "Hot," then grasped at the moonstone at her throat.

"You're awake."

She did not answer, nor did she open her eyes, and so he waited until she was resting comfortably once more before he left her to find Riley.

Kendra dreamed of someone helping her to the toilet, only when she sat down, it felt more like a pot. She tried to flush it, but whoever was with her kept batting her arm down. Thankfully, the bizarre dream faded and she curled up in her bed away from the wavering lamp light. She must be camping somewhere, she decided—in her dreams, of course, since she never went anywhere without running water and electricity.

"How are you feeling this evening?" a richly timbered, most definitely British voice asked her, rousing her from her comfortable darkness.

She ignored whoever it was, turning away from the sound, until she remembered her boating accident. Where was she? The hospital? But no, hospitals didn't roll with the surf. A boat, then? Her hand flew to her waist, feeling for her fanny pack. It was gone, as were her clothes, she soon discovered, for whatever she was wearing was not hers. She lifted her head up slightly, trying to see where she was, then spied her things neatly folded at the foot of her bed, the fanny pack lying atop everything. Immediately, she reached for it, dragging it by its strap to her lap.

"Although I took the liberty of having your clothing rinsed, your . . . reticule has been undisturbed," the voice said.

Reticule? Kendra turned toward the cultured masculine voice. She saw nothing at first, then, as her eyes adjusted, she saw the silhouette of a man. He appeared to be leaning over a chest of some sort. Ignoring him for the moment, she quickly unzipped the bag and saw that all of her things were safe and dry inside their protective plastic bag: her gun, checkbook, credit card, and ID. Thank God for Ziplock storage bags, she thought, grateful that the clerk at the boat rental shop had insisted she put her things in one, though at first she had been offended at his reference that she might be less than competent at sailing.

"I can't believe you never opened this," she told him, "at least to see who I was. It would've been the first thing I looked at."

"The thought crossed my mind. My first mate, Riley, suspected you were carrying gold or jewels, the thing being quite heavy. I assumed, since you had it strapped to your waist when I pulled you from the water, that whatever was in there must be important and rather private. As for your name, I had no doubt you'd tell me in good time."

"Kendra. Kendra Browning. And thank you for finding me." She placed her hand over her eyes to lessen the glare that emanated from the stained glass window of the cabin wall and the lantern that hung above.

Her rescuer was dressed in a pair of dark, form-fitting pants and no shirt. "I hope you're feeling better, Miss Browning. It is *Miss* Browning?"

"Yes."

"I had thought you still asleep when I came in to change for dinner."

"Who are you?"

"Brice Montgomery, captain of the *Eterne* at your service." He gave a slight bow.

"That's pretty formal stuff. How about I just call you Monty?"

"Brice will do, thank you."

"You're British."

"Quite," he said.

"I could tell by your accent. I've always admired English accents. When I was little, I used to try and imitate the ones I heard on TV."

"Tee Vee?"

"Yes. Not that I watched it that much. My mother didn't— Say, do you collect antiques?" she asked abruptly. The warm light from the window colored the mahogany-paneled walls with rich burgundy highlights. But what really caught her attention was the carved mahogany desk he was leaning against. There, on the polished surface, authenticating its aged appearance, lay an unrolled map of thick parchment, its curled edges weighted down by cut crystal decanters that were probably museum pieces themselves.

Kendra stared at the heavy desk, recalling that she'd seen something quite similar to it in an antique store— the same place her friend had bought her moonstone necklace, she recalled, reaching up to stroke the smooth hard stone. "You've got quite a collection here," she said, looking around the room, her gaze resting on a Queen Anne style table with four matching chairs. "My best friend Frankie collects antiques too. Some of this stuff's in great shape."

"As it should be. The ship is only two years old."

"Who owns all this? I know people who'd pay a fortune for it. Frankie for one."

Brice smiled indulgently, no doubt paying little attention to her ramblings. Moving to her side, he sat down on the edge of the bed and placed one large, callused hand on her forehead. "Your fever seems to have broken at last. I took the liberty of having some food brought in for you. Are you hungry?"

It was precisely at that moment that Kendra looked up and really *saw* the man she was speaking to. He was . . . magnificent. And suddenly Kendra knew where the phrase "tall, dark, and handsome" was coined—from the vision before her eyes.

A lock of raven hair fell onto his forehead, and he raked it back with his fingers—strong fingers connected to large hands, connected to muscular arms, connected to broad shoulders, connected to a granite chest, connected to rippling stomach muscles . . .

Flustered, Kendra dragged her eyes away in order to catch her breath. Perhaps magnificent was too mild a word.

Only when he moved away to put on his shirt did she breathe normally again. Glancing at her open fanny pack, she zipped it up. "Thank God, my gun didn't get wet," she said, thinking anything was better than her embarrassed silence.

"A gun?" He raised his dark brows. "Do you mean to say you carry a pistol in your reticule?"

"Yeah, I'm a cop. In fact, so's my boyfriend, Jack. We were supposed to get married, but things never quite . . . worked out." Only when Brice looked at her oddly did it occur to her she was telling her life history to a complete stranger.

As if he sensed her sudden discomfort, Captain Montgomery indicated the table where two places were set. "If you would care to dine with me, Miss Browning."

Kendra sat up, taking care to pull down the overly large shirt she was dressed in, before walking on weak legs across the cabin.

Captain Montgomery pulled out a chair and held it for her as she sat. Unused to such treatment from the male species, Kendra smiled up at him. After returning her smile, he took a seat across from her, then pushed the laden tray containing a dish of stew before her. "I had the cook make yours thinner, more of a soup. I wasn't at all certain whether you would be up to eating yet."

Her stomach grumbled at the scent of the savory meat and vegetables. "Thanks," she said, waiting for the captain to start. But he didn't, and she realized he was waiting for her. Amused, and slightly flustered by his formal etiquette, she picked up her spoon, solid sterling by the weight of it, and took a bite. "My compliments to the chef. It's good." He nodded, then began his meal.

After a few bites, she set her spoon down. "Do you think that after dinner, if it's not too much trouble, you could take me back to shore?"

Brice raised one dark brow, but said nothing.

"I wouldn't mind staying awhile," she continued, "but I signed a rental agreement for that sailboat, and if I don't go and explain what happened, they're gonna charge me double for every hour it's out past the return time. I must owe a fortune by now, especially if that sneaky boat dealer charges me the hourly rental on top of the price of the boat. I imagine it was pretty wiped out by the storm."

"If you mean your boat was destroyed, Miss Browning, I can only assume so. When I pulled you from the water, nothing else remained that any of us could see. Were there no others?"

"No, just me. Everyone else went to see the Dickens Christmas Festival on that big ship." Suddenly, everything made sense. She looked around the cabin, then back at him. "*This* is that same ship, isn't it?"

"What ship do you speak of?" he asked, while pouring wine into two cut crystal glasses.

"The Dickens ship. The replica of the old English clipper, or schooner, or whatever you call it. That's why you're in costume, isn't it?"

He handed one glass to her. "Costume?"

"It's really authentic looking." She took a sip of her wine, a full-bodied red with hints of oak and pepper. "I studied historical fashion in school before I changed from history to criminal justice. You know, my friend is never going to believe this. Frankie loves acting and all that old fashioned stuff. When she finds out I was rescued by a troupe of actors, she's—"

"I assure you, Miss Browning, we are not a *troupe* of actors."

"I'm sorry," she said. "I didn't mean it in a derogatory way. Anyway, I've really enjoyed my stay here, but I really *do* need to be going."

"And just where had you planned on going?" he asked.

"Home, of course. You don't think I'd stay here? I appreciate your hospitality and all, but my friends are probably worried by now."

"Miss Browning," he said, after taking a leisurely sip from his glass, "have you any idea how long you've been here?"

"Several hours?" When he shook his head, she queried, "A day?"

"Times three."

"Oh my God!" She stood up, nearly knocking over her chair. "I'm liable to get fired from my job! Suspended at the very least. You've got to take me back to shore right now!"

"I fear that is quite impossible."

His calmness unnerved her. "What do you mean *impossible*? Just how far out are we? And where the hell are we going in this tub?"

"I'd be most appreciative if you'd not refer to my ship as a tub, Miss Browning. The *Eterne* is the finest—"

"To hell with your boat, Monty. Just tell me what the blazes is going on here?"

"If you would care to have a seat, I'll attempt to answer your questions." When she remained standing, he said, "Did I make mention, Miss Browning, of the fact that your legs are quite charming?"

Kendra immediately sat down, embarrassed. "Like all men, your manners are despicable."

He ignored her gibe. "What, pray tell, would you like to know?"

"Why you can't take me back to shore? Tonight?"

"Because we're nowhere near shore."

"Then where are we?" she asked, trying to keep the panic from her voice.

"About five weeks from England. Even if we were closer, the weather makes it nearly—"

Kendra leaped out of her chair. "England! You've gotta be kidding! I don't even have a passport. You've— what do you mean *five weeks* away?"

"If the winds stay with us, that is precisely how long it will take to reach port in London."

"What is this, a world cruise ship? God! They'll think I'm dead by then!" Kendra started pacing the room, pausing every few steps to toss her host dark looks. "Is there a phone on this tub?"

"A phone?"

"Yes, or a radio?"

"If I knew what they were, I'd tell you," he said in an exasperatingly calm voice. "But since I'm quite familiar with everything on board my *ship*, I believe I can safely say no."

"What is it you people are trying to do? Relive the past by sailing around without any modern conveniences just to see if it can be done?" She stopped to stare at him in dawning horror. "Don't tell me you use chamber pots and all that?"

"The chamber pot is behind the screen if you're interested." He nodded in that direction.

Kendra looked in the corner to see if what he said was true. To her dismay it was, for there behind a large oriental folding screen was the chamber pot. Seeing it brought vague recollections of someone assisting her to use it. "Did you . . . I mean, tell me someone else . . ." His knowing look only brought her further embarrassment.

She sank into her chair. "Just my luck, to be rescued by some relic of the past. Aren't there any modern conveniences on board this thing?"

"Rest assured, Miss Browning, that everything on board the *Eterne* is the finest available."

Kendra surveyed the room. It was lavishly furnished and, all in all, nicer than some of the hotels she had stayed at. The carpet was much thicker and softer than any she was used to, and the mahogany furniture was exceedingly beautiful, and so finely kept that she wondered if they were not antiques, but replicas. A number of exquisite paintings, all nautical scenes, graced the dark paneled walls, and several lamps hung from the ceilings, spreading a warm glow throughout the entire room. On the opposite wall on either side of the stained-glass mullioned window were built-in bookshelves filled with leather-bound books, and below that, cabinets, perhaps filled with more books or even antique nautical instruments, such as those that lay scattered across the large desk that faced toward the door of the cabin.

There was no doubt in her mind as she looked about her that *everything* was the finest money could buy. Still, she couldn't help the feeling that something was wrong.

Sensing his gaze upon her, she turned to him, and

smiled sweetly. "This is all very well and nice," she offered. "You have a lovely boat, and I appreciate your rescuing me, but I really must be going."

"I must ask you to remain inside my cabin. At least for now."

Kendra gave her rescuer a determined, but suspicious look. "Why? Are you afraid I'll see something I shouldn't? Well, I'm not about to let you or anyone else stand in my way when I leave this oversized rowboat." So saying, she moved to open the door.

"Miss Browning!"

The captain's bellow caused her to freeze, momentarily. Purposefully, she opened the door, only to feel his vice-like grip on her arm drawing her back into the room. Unable to pull free, she glared up at him, and her pulse quickened at such proximity to his virile form. "Kidnapping a cop is a pretty serious offense even in England, so you can let go now, Monty."

He did, after he moved between her and the door, which he shut. "There are a few things we must discuss. First, you shall address me properly. Captain Montgomery or Brice, if you so desire. Secondly, when I give an order, Miss Browning, I expect it to be obeyed. Now if you will kindly sit down, I will tell you *why* you cannot go on deck dressed as you are." He looked down at her exposed thighs.

"Don't tell me your crew's never seen a woman's legs before?" she asked. "Or are you worried they'll think you and I have been tumbling around in that bed of yours?"

"I'm certain they're already under that impression, Miss Browning." She was sure her face turned beet red, but he continued as if he didn't notice. "I assure you, had I not been around, they wouldn't have wasted any time in enjoying your delightful body. The only difference between them and me is that I don't share."

"*What* exactly do you mean by that?"

"I mean that as long as they think you and I are . . ." he gave a pointed look toward the bed, before continuing with, "then you'll have nothing to worry about."

"Great! Who cares that everyone on board thinks I'm sleeping with a man I only just met?" The sudden thought that he might follow through with what he said made her eyes narrow in suspicion. "And don't even think about it because it's not going to happen."

Captain Montgomery's eyes held a wicked gleam. His grin sent the heat coursing through her cheeks once more.

"You have my word of honor, Miss Browning," he replied, far more sardonically than she cared for. He leaned against the door, his muscular arms folded across his chest. "The bed is yours, unless you invite me there."

"Well, don't expect an invitation to be forthcoming, your captainship."

"Are you always this charming?" he asked.

"Only when I'm cornered. Now if you don't mind, I'd like to go outside to see if you're telling the truth."

He hesitated, as if unsure whether he should let her out or not. "You will find some breeches in my chest."

Seeing that he wasn't about to move from the door, Kendra opened the sea chest that sat at the foot of the bed. After sorting through the clothing, she pulled out the first pair she could find. "This is it?" she asked incredulously, holding up gray pants styled in similar fashion to the black pair he wore. But what clung to his long muscular thighs like a second skin had no chance of fitting her.

"I'm afraid we're fresh out of ballgowns, my lady," he said with a mock bow. "You'll have to make do with rolling up the legs."

Kendra carried the pants to the bed and sat down to

slip them on. After tucking in her long shirt, she gathered the waist in her hands.

Brice fashioned her a belt from a length of cord he pulled from his chest.

Once she had it securely tied, she said, "I'm ready for the grand tour."

"This way, my lady," he responded. Standing aside, he let her pass him through the door.

The moment Kendra stepped out on deck into the light of the setting sun, and heard the sound of the wind whipping in the sails above, she noticed something was different. Everything seemed crisper, cleaner somehow, but she dismissed the phenomenon as the aftereffects of the storm. Immediately, she moved toward the railing, ignoring the blatant stares from the crew as they watched her pass, while she, in turn, tried not to stare at them. Like the captain, their costumes were extremely authentic.

It was apparent as she looked around that the captain was indeed telling the truth about their not being close to shore. Nothing but water surrounded them as far as the eye could see. The momentary sense of panic she felt was stayed by the thought that if anything was going to happen to her, it would have by now. Surely God hadn't spared her from the sea only to once again place her in danger here? She looked out at a cerulean blue sky that faded into the sea in a splash of deep golds and darker reds. She couldn't help but think that fate had played a small part in placing her in the care of this man beside her.

Glancing at him, she was surprised to see that he too was admiring the beauty of the sunset, and so she took the moment to study him. Her gaze swept over his open white lawn shirt, which billowed in the wind, then moved to his broad chest and shoulders before lingering on the ruggedly handsome profile of his tanned face, with its squared jaw, sensuous mouth, straight nose, and blue eyes as dark as a night sky. "Perfection," she whispered, not realizing she'd spoken her thoughts aloud.

"I beg pardon?"

Embarrassed, she prevaricated, "The sunset—it's beautiful."

His gaze held hers for what seemed an eternity before he answered. "It's the same color as your hair, Miss Browning. Gold, with touches of red throughout."

Kendra's hand flew to what she had always considered unremarkable hair, to brush it self-consciously from her face. His simple words brought a different sort of panic to her—one she was not ready to identify—and she quickly sought to change the subject from sunsets and hair color to one less intimate. Looking around the ship she asked, "Do all your men wear their costumes throughout the entire voyage?"

"They wear what they brought with them, or what they acquire in the different ports we stop at."

"What I mean is, do they always dress in period costumes?"

Brice raised his dark brows in question.

"You know, antique stuff. Like what you have on, and what you gave me to wear. Didn't any of you bring normal clothes?" Seeing he still didn't understand, she added, "For when you reach London."

"London? The men are usually garbed in similar fashion even when not on board ship. For them it wouldn't be practical to dress otherwise."

"Do you mean to tell me they dress that way all the time?"

"Just how would you have them clothed? In formal attire with cravats neatly tied?"

"I think you've gotten a little too far into your role here, Captain Brice."

"Captain Montgomery," he corrected.

"Whatever, Monty," she said, despite his earlier wishes to be addressed otherwise. "You're losing touch with reality. You've certainly lost touch with the twentieth century."

"I've a hard enough time keeping up with the century I'm in, Miss Browning, without adding a hundred or so years to the score."

Kendra's jaw dropped at his matter-of-fact tone. "My God! You're serious, aren't you?" Seeking a way to justify his words in her mind, she suddenly came up with the solution. "Oh! I get it. This is one of those cruises where everyone dresses up in period costumes and no matter what, they have to act as if they're actually in that time span. Kind of like the Dickens Festival at Christmas, or the Renaissance fair near San Francisco. They dress in medieval costumes and act like they're from the Renaissance period no matter how hard you try and get them to break their role."

"Medieval costumes for the Renaissance? How very interesting."

Kendra shrugged at her error. "Now you know why I changed my major to criminal justice." She looked around the ship. "I have to admit, I prefer the more modern appearance of—what would these be, nineteenth-century clothes? More romantic. Do they have anything like that in England?"

"Do we have what in England?" he asked, looking utterly confused. And terribly handsome.

"Where everyone gets together in costumes, pretending to be from another time."

"We have masquerade balls." He leaned against the railing before adding, "Some center around one specific period in time, but for the most part, the guests dress in a variety of costumes."

"Well, then," she said, "I'll do my best to play my part. Only I may need some help every now and then, since I'm sadly lacking in nineteenth-century protocol. But be forewarned. The first ship we pass that has a telephone, I want you to stop."

Captain Montgomery gave her a brief—and rather sympathetic—smile.

When the sun finally set, he suggested that she turn in for the night. "Since there are no other cabins available, you may continue to sleep in the bed, and until the time you say otherwise," he added with that wicked twinkle to his eye, "I'll sleep in my hammock."

Kendra decided to ignore his reference to their earlier conversation, telling herself they had a long voyage together, and it would be best if she didn't make enemies with the man—especially considering that most of his crew members looked as if they'd devour her in a moment's notice were the captain not standing next to her. Then again, maybe it was just their authentic costumes lending them such a hard-core, pirate look.

The next few weeks passed quickly enough, once Kendra got over the stress of having no modern conveniences. The worst moment during the entire voyage, she thought, was the day she started her period and had to approach the captain in an attempt—through her embarrassment—to ask his help. A gentleman to the end, Brice very obligingly and discreetly helped her solve the dilemma by providing several clean shirts which were torn into rags. Although he said they no longer fit him, Kendra suspected he might be sacrificing them to her cause.

Despite her constant worry at not being able to contact Frankie and Jack—and work, she added with less enthusiasm—Kendra found she was actually enjoying herself.

There must be something about not having to worry about telephones, televisions, and time that lends a sense of well-being to one's frame of mind, she thought one afternoon, as she leaned over the balustrade letting the gentle wind caress her face. She had even stopped worrying about missing work—after all, she reasoned, it wasn't as if she'd asked to be dumped into the sea during that storm so many weeks ago. And with no way to contact anyone, it made things a lot simpler.

"Your thoughts are far away, Miss Browning," the captain said as he leaned against the railing next to her.

Kendra pulled her gaze from the endless sea to smile at him. In spite of his insistence to stick with his inane role of a nineteenth-century sea captain, she had come to admire him. Sometimes she found it easier to pretend she was in the same century, only because it was exasperating to have to explain things he pretended not to understand, such as airplanes and microwave popcorn—especially when he looked at her as if she'd lost her mind. And yet, in such surroundings it was easy to imagine that she had somehow stepped back in time.

"I was thinking of my friend again."

"Ah, yes. Frances. Is she as beautiful as you?"

Sometimes Kendra had no idea how to accept his flattery. At times it seemed genuine—when he wasn't grinning his rakish smile and arching his brow in that sardonic way, reminding her of a hero in one of her romance novels. "Frankie's much prettier. A bit taller, with thick wavy hair the color of chestnuts, not straight dishwater brown hair like mine."

"Your hair is anything but brown," he replied softly as he reached out to wrap a strand around his finger. "Burnished gold comes to mind."

Words failed her as she felt his gaze boring into her soul. They had lived in such proximity these past few weeks, and she, for one, found it difficult to ignore his magnetic presence. She sensed that he felt the same way about her, but—true to his word, and sometimes much to her dismay—he remained a gentleman every minute they were together.

But now, as his dark blue eyes stared into hers, Kendra had the feeling that he was going to kiss her—right here on deck in front of everyone. Instinctively, her lips parted as he neared his face toward hers, and then, just as his warm breath brushed her lips, a shout from the crow's nest brought him up short.

"Jolly Roger to starboard, sir!"

A burly deckhand rushed forth and handed Brice a spyglass, and he held it up to his eye to see for himself. After a moment, he lowered the instrument. "Bloody hell!" he muttered, before shouting orders to the men on deck who were already scurrying around as if their very lives depended on it.

"May I see?" Kendra asked. Absently, he handed the brass telescope to her, and she saw a schooner that appeared to be sailing straight toward them. Atop its mast was a flag, its field black, and when the wind whipped it open, a skull and crossbones was clearly visible. After a moment, she handed it back, thinking it was all very exciting. In fact, she was amazed that they would go to such lengths to promote the realism of the voyage. Ever conscious that she was a guest on board and, therefore, not really a part of the acting, she found a place to sit down where she could watch the approaching ship and not be in the way.

Around her, the men worked feverishly, loading the cannons on deck as they prepared for what appeared to be a realistic looking battle. Surprised by the loudness of the first blast which vibrated the entire ship, she jumped from her seat at the noise. It was then that Brice finally seemed to notice her and ordered her to their cabin, not to come out until told.

"I want to watch," she replied.

"That's out of the question, Miss Browning," he answered, all friendliness gone from his voice.

"But—"

"You'll go willingly, or I'll have Riley carry you there."

Recognizing by the look in his eye that he'd brook no disobedience on her part, Kendra relented. But as she sat in the cabin listening to the cannon blasts that shook the very bowels of the ship, her curiosity overruled her promise to obey. She just couldn't miss seeing an authentically played-out battle between the *Eterne* and the supposed pirate ship.

Creeping stealthily out to the deck, she took up a place behind several water barrels, and watched avidly as the ships battled it out with each other. She had no idea that they needed to be so close. Most of the shots landed far short of either ship in a great splash, but occasionally she saw one hit the pirate ship, and wondered how the special effects were managed.

Not until a ball slammed into a nearby water barrel, in an explosion of wood and liquid, did she realize they weren't using props. Scared to death, she jumped from her hiding place just as another ball swept through the railing, narrowly missing her as she stood in the middle of the deck.

"Are you people stark raving mad?" she cried. "Someone could be hurt, for God's sake!"

Captain Montgomery groaned at the sound of her voice. *"God's teeth, but you're an exasperating woman!"* Turning the command over to Riley, he quickly advanced toward her, picking her up as if she weighed next to nothing. He tossed her over his shoulder. "I gave you an order," he barked as he strode to his cabin.

Once inside he deposited her onto the floor and was about to turn and leave, but hesitated. "Don't be afraid, Miss Browning, we'll get through this."

"Don't be afraid? You're as mad as a hatter. They're using real cannonballs."

"As are we," he said.

Kendra grabbed his arm. "You can't mean to go back up there? You could get yourself killed!"

"Miss Browning, my men are dependent upon me." The look he gave her, made her realize *he* was worried. Very much so. But before she could comment, he was gone, shutting and locking the door behind him.

Stunned, Kendra could do no more than stare at the closed door as the walls shuddered around her.

After what seemed an eternity, the blasts from the cannons stopped, and the sound of running feet and shouting men permeated her sanctuary. Realizing that she had an opportunity to see some of what went on around her through the stained glass window, she crossed the cabin and stood on tiptoe to peer through one of the lighter colored panes before she discovered that she could actually open a small section and look out.

The *Eterne*, she saw, was now alongside the pirate ship. A number of the crewmen, including Captain Montgomery, had boarded the enemy vessel and were—very convincingly to Kendra's inexperienced eye—battling each other with lethal looking swords.

It was better than watching an old Errol Flynn movie.

Captain Montgomery was an extremely talented swordsman, as was his most recent opponent, a black-bearded pirate with the typical gold earring in one ear.

"Aye, ye bloody scurvies," she improvised, thinking it quite an adequate pirate imitation. "Ye'll be walking the plank before sunset, which is no more than you deserve for daring to attack—*Brice!*" she shouted suddenly. "Look out behind you!"

Even though he couldn't hear her, it appeared as if he had, for the moment she cried out her warning, he turned to face a man, sword in hand, jumping toward him from an upper deck.

Faster than a heartbeat, Brice raised his sword, stepped back and turned on his attacker. And then, with the flick of the pirate's sword against the captain's arm, what had seemed to be a mock battle only moments before, turned real. Frighteningly real. A dark stain spread across Brice's sleeve, and there was no mistaking the flash of pain on his face as he fought for his life against not one, but two pirates.

Her stomach clenched. "This can't be happening. It can't be." She watched as Brice skillfully battled the two men, disarming one, and then running his sword clean through the other's middle.

On weak knees, she left the window, trying to erase the bloody scene from her mind.

It wasn't possible. It couldn't be. And yet, the event she'd just witnessed would never have occurred in the modern world.

"No. I refuse to believe it," she whispered, as she sank to the bed. "I live in the twentieth century."

About a half hour later, she heard someone unlocking the door. Captain Montgomery stepped into the room with Riley on his heels.

"Mark my words, Cap'n," Riley grumbled. "That bloody pirate Parkston's responsible for this."

"Perhaps."

"Perhaps nothin'. He's been after ye ever since ye established yer shippin' interests in the Bahamas. Half the plantation owners refuse to deal with his men now that there's someone honest. Blames ye for stealing his profits, he does."

"Even so, there's nothing we can do until we have proof."

"And those brigands won't be tellin'. Leastwise, not the ones on the bottom of the sea. Ye want that I should get the truth out of them that's in our hold?"

"No, Riley. Parkston is not fool enough to leave his reputation in the hands of a few pirates. That much I know. Nevertheless, one day, I'll find the means to stop him."

Kendra saw Riley scowl, then soften his expression. "How's yer arm, Cap'n?" he asked.

"Fine. I'll live until the others are tended. Perhaps if Miss Browning is as good with a needle as she is with making up stories, she can tend to me."

Riley cast a dubious look at Kendra, who had sat up in bed. "The lass will probably swoon, but have it yer way. Since I'm needed elsewhere, she's about all ye have."

"Why will I swoon?" she asked, watching Brice pull needle and thread from a cabinet beneath the bookcase and place them onto his desk.

"Riley thinks you might faint at the sight of blood."

She turned her most indignant look onto Riley. "Ha! I've seen a lot more blood in my time on the streets of Miami than what was just poured out there on the deck of that so-called pirate ship. Real blood too," she added with emphasis. When reality was too harsh to bear, denial, she decided, worked wonders. Why, she already felt better. Until she eyed the dark stain on the arm of the captain's pristine lawn shirt.

"And what the hell did ye think *that* was?" the first mate demanded.

"Riley."

"Er—pardon, Cap'n."

"See to the others. Miss Browning will assist me."

"As you wish." With a dark look at Kendra, Riley left the cabin.

Kendra swung her legs over the side of the bed, telling herself that she had not witnessed a real battle, and that the captain's arm was not really bleeding. "I gather he doesn't like me."

"He merely wanted to ensure I was in good hands before he departed."

She hopped off the bed, then strolled toward the desk, eyeing the needle and thread. "What are you planning on doing with that?"

"Not I, Miss Browning—you."

"Me what?"

"You are going to stitch my wound."

3

"You don't expect me to believe all that was for real?" Kendra asked, her expression one of total shock. "Because if you do, I refuse. I've decided that it was all an act."

In answer, he stripped off his shirt, revealing a deep gash on his left arm.

"Oh—my—God! How the *hell* did that happen?"

"I slipped." Despite his pain, Brice grinned in an attempt to lessen her unease. "Now, Miss Browning . . . the needle and thread, please."

Kendra's gaze darted toward the sewing items on the desk. "Sorry, Monty," she said, shaking her head as he removed a decanter of brandy from his cabinet and set it beside the thread. "This is where I draw the line. I've tried to live up to your rules of pretending there isn't a world outside this ship. I've ignored the fact that until we reach England I'll have to live without hot showers, razors and a decent toothbrush, but this—this is going too far! I think it's high time you called a doctor."

Brice hardened his features in hopes of making her see reason. "This is *not* a game, Miss Browning, and the physician, if you care to refer to Riley as such, is tending those whose wounds are far more serious than mine."

"You're damned lucky no one was killed!"

"I feel damned lucky more weren't killed, what with you running around in the midst of it all. Damnation, woman! I was lucky *I* wasn't killed."

"Do you mean to tell me the man I saw you run through with your blade is . . . dead?" When Brice didn't answer, she sank into the chair by the desk. "That's murder." Her face paled. "I—I saw you through the window. You murdered him."

"He was about to murder me. If I had not, it would be me on that deck, not him." Brice wrapped his shirt around his wounded arm to staunch the flow of blood. "You saw them fire on us, did you not?" Kendra nodded. "Our ship is heavily laden. They'd have taken us had we not fought back."

"I don't know what kind of game this is, Mister Montgomery, but I want no part of it. I want off this ship *now*!"

Brice pulled out a chair and sat down before her. Taking one of her hands in his, he looked her in the eye. "As I've said before, it's not possible to leave until we reach port, unless you plan on swimming the rest of the way."

Kendra tried to shake free of his grasp, but he held tight. "Miss Browning. Kendra," he said softer this time. "I've tried to make every consideration where you were concerned because of your plight. But I won't endanger my crew because of your misguided notion as to what's right and what's wrong. I may burn in hell for my past deeds, but I'll sleep tonight with a clear conscience knowing I did everything in my power to save my ship, my men, and even you."

Her pale face held suspicion. "What do you mean by that?"

"Dare you even think about what those men would've done had they taken a prize like you on board?"

"Is that what you think of me in this game of yours? A prize?"

"Of course not," he replied angrily, wondering what had possessed him to try to explain it to her in the first place. The woman was half mad. That much he knew. And yet, there was something about her. "What I think of you has nothing to do with this. What I'm telling you is the truth. Had those pirates won the battle, you'd be better off dead, or at least wishing you were. Now think about it. Was there anything you saw that would convince you we were not fighting for our lives?"

Kendra buried her face in her hands. "This is all a dream. I'm going to wake up and find I'm still at home. God, if I wake up now, I'll never leave my backyard again. I promise."

Brice put his finger under her chin and lifted her face, resisting the urge to pull her into his arms and hold her until she calmed. "If you want this to be a dream, then it is. In the meantime, I need your assistance."

"You'll have to tell me what to do," she said finally. "I've been prepared for most every emergency imagined, but having to do surgery was *not* one of them. And before I get started," she added, "I want you to be aware that I plan on going straight to the authorities about what happened out there just now."

"If you insist, I'll take you there myself."

"It doesn't bother you that I'm going to the police, or Scotland Yard, or whatever it is you call them?"

"No. Now, soak the needle and thread in the brandy and then pour the remainder on my arm. The rest is quite simple, assuming you know how to sew."

"Well, I don't. I didn't become a police officer because of my domestic talents," she muttered as she awkwardly threaded the needle.

When he asked if she needed assistance, she refused, instead saying, "Aren't you supposed to bite a bullet or something?"

"Bite a what?"

"Bite something to keep from crying out."

"Just sew, Miss Browning."

And she did, amazing him with her self-control, even though she had to close her eyes the first few times she pushed the needle through. He clenched his jaw, then told her to make the stitches smaller.

When she was finished, he immediately got up, took another decanter of brandy from the cabinet, and poured himself a drink.

Swallowing it down in one gulp, he eyed Kendra warily, noting her face had turned a pasty white. "You look as if you could use a bit of this yourself." He poured her a small portion of the brandy.

"No, really, I'm fine. I see this kind of thing all the time at work." Apparently, to prove her point, she waved her hand in dismissal, stood up, then promptly fainted.

It was at that precise moment that Riley chose to return. "I told ye she'd swoon."

"At least she had the grace to do it *after* she stitched my arm."

Riley assisted his captain in moving her limp form onto the bed, mumbling something about the hazards of bringing women on board. "Ye better let me have a peek at that arm of yers," he said when they had finished. "I want to make sure it's done up proper like."

"You needn't worry Riley. Her stitches are almost as neat as yours." He showed off his arm and grinned.

Riley, placated over the captain's veiled compliment, turned his attention to the girl on the bed. "Don't ye think we should try and bring her 'round?"

"I seem to have forgotten my hartshorn. Have you any?"

"Well, ah, we can't leave her like this can we?"

"Why not? She is really quite beautiful with her golden hair fanned out such as it is on the pillow."

"When ladies faint, someone's supposed to do something," Riley said gruffly.

Brice looked at Kendra thoughtfully as he sat down beside her on the bed. He meant what he had said. She really was beautiful, lying there so quietly. He could almost pretend that there was nothing at all the matter with her. "Miss Browning?" He tapped her on the cheek. "Miss Browning?"

When she didn't respond, Riley asked, "Is she breathing?"

Brice leaned closer and put his ear to her mouth. Her breath was a feather soft caress against his skin. Forgetting Riley's presence, he kissed her, lightly, on the lips.

"What'd ye go and do that fer?"

"My sister told me that in her storybooks the prince kisses the sleeping princess to awaken her." Kendra's eyes fluttered open.

"She ain't no bloody princess," the seaman grumbled. "And ye ain't no prince—duke or no duke."

When Kendra tried to sit up, Brice stopped her. "You need your rest, princess."

*   *   *

Several days later, Kendra stood upon the deck waiting for her first glimpse of England when Brice came up behind her. "We'll reach port soon."

She knew without turning that his eyes were ablaze with desire—they had been for days now—for they mirrored her own. Each time she'd emerged from their cabin, she found her glance had strayed toward him, watching the play of muscles on his bared, tanned chest as he worked side by side with his men. She imagined the feel of his sweat-glistened skin next to hers . . . And the way he would stop what he was doing for the moment to wipe his brow, his gaze alighting on hers, and she'd look away, but not before she saw him drink in her presence like a man thirsty for water. To make matters worse, the proximity in which they had lived—the intimate meals, moonlit walks on the deck, sharing his quarters but *not* his bed—had taken its toll on her resolve at insisting he keep his distance. Despite this, he'd remained the perfect gentleman, much to her dismay.

And *now* he was telling her they'd be reaching port soon, when what she really wanted was to turn the damned ship around and start over.

She looked up at him, this man who'd rescued her then sent her sensible heart adrift on the sea. "Midnight," she whispered.

"Pardon?"

"Your eyes are midnight blue."

Brice raised a dark brow. "Are they?"

Suddenly, Kendra knew she would miss this man. And his silly charade. "I'd better get my things. I want to call Frankie as soon as we dock," she said, telling herself once again that if she refused to believe she was in the past, it couldn't be true.

She pushed past him to return to his cabin, unwilling to let him see her cry.

Once there, she picked up her fanny pack, unzipped it and dumped the contents onto Brice's desk, and just stared at them, thinking about Brice all the while. Had it been a dream? That kiss he'd given her after she'd fainted? Had she only imagined his lips touching hers? Real or not, she'd treasure the memory. It was all she had, now that they were nearing England.

An hour later, she forced her thoughts from Brice and opened her checkbook, dismayed to see only one check and a few deposit slips left. Just like her to leave home unprepared. Still, she didn't really need any checks, since she had her VISA card tucked safely inside the checkbook cover along with her driver's license. If nothing else, at least her gun was dry, she thought, removing it from the Ziplock storage bag. She pressed the release, allowing the clip to fall to the desk.

"*What* is that?"

Brice stood in the open doorway, staring at her weapon.

"It's a Smith and Wesson 9 millimeter. Normally I don't carry such a large gun off duty, but Florida's dangerous what with all the drugs being run through that state—" She stopped when she realized he wasn't paying any attention to what she said. His gaze was fixed on the gun. Just like Jack, she thought. More interested in weapons than me.

"I've never seen anything like it before. May I?"

"Sure." Kendra emptied the round from the chamber, leaving it open, then handed it to him.

He examined it closely. "How does it work?"

Kendra's first thought was that as usual he was taking this I-live-in-the-nineteenth-century stuff too far. "Surely you've handled a gun before?"

"Not like this." He set the weapon down, then took a small chest from the shelf built into the wall. "These are mine," he said, setting the chest upon the desk before her. He opened the box, then unfolded some oiled canvas and beneath that a velvet covering, revealing two matched pistols.

Kendra, not a gun enthusiast by any means, still appreciated the beauty of the weapons before her. "These must be about a hundred years old."

"They're less than a year old."

"Replicas, huh." She picked one up. "Is it loaded?"

"No."

After examining it for a bit, she set it back inside the velvet-lined case. "Nice."

"But what is this?" Brice picked up the clip.

"That's what feeds the ammunition into the chamber when you pull the trigger." She slid a few rounds out, showing him how the spring pushed each successive round up. "This here," she said, picking up her weapon and pointing to the empty chamber, "is where the bullet goes."

She pushed the clip in, then slid the chamber back. "It's loaded now. After the round enters the chamber," she recited, "you pull the trigger, which hits the primer and causes a small explosion thereby expelling the bullet." Jack would probably shudder at her juvenile explanation, but she didn't care. "Same principle as your antiques there, but a lot quicker and more accurate."

Brice arched a dark brow in disbelief, which made Kendra add, "Accurate as long as you practice, and God knows I've practiced. At least ten hours a week. Jack's a slave driver."

"Jack?"

"My partner. He's a gun fanatic. He gave me this for Christmas."

"A rather unusual gift for a woman, I should think."

"You're telling me. But that's Jack for you. He wouldn't know the first thing about buying a girl a—" The cabin shuddered and Kendra gripped the edge of the desk. "What was that?"

"I believe, Miss Browning, that we have just docked."

Sadness and relief swept through her at once. Sadness that her time with Brice had come to an end, and relief that she'd finally be able to let Frankie know she was safe. Things would be different on dry land. Back to normal. "I enjoyed my stay here, Monty. Or should I say Captain Montgomery?"

"Brice."

Kendra shivered at the intimacy of his rich voice. "Brice," she whispered in return. "I'll miss you." She held his gaze, thinking she'd like nothing better than to stay and play his game with him, especially if it meant he would kiss her again as he had when she'd fainted. "Why don't you think about bringing your show to Florida again? I know there are—"

Before she was aware of his intent, he closed the distance between them, taking her in his arms. His mouth descended upon hers, silencing her as his tongue parted her lips.

Heaven, Kendra thought, pure heaven. Jack had never made her feel like this. Nor had anyone else for that matter. She brought her arms up around his neck and ran her fingers through his thick, dark hair, then melted when he did the same.

Brice stopped kissing her to look into her eyes. "I can't let you go, sweet Kendra. They'll take you from me if I do."

Before she had a chance to comment, he was kissing her once more, and she found herself wishing they were still out at sea. Or stranded on a desert island.

All too soon, he was stepping away from her and moving toward the door. "It would be best if you stayed here until I can arrange to have some proper clothing brought on board."

Kendra looked down at her baggy pants and the soft white, overly large shirt. "These will do. I mean they wear stranger stuff than this back home. Just point me to the nearest shoe store and I'll get out of your hair. I can't hang out at the airport all day in bare feet. I don't even know if they'll let me fly home barefooted. Will they?"

Brice's expression held pity for the briefest moment. "At least allow me to get you proper transportation."

"Do taxis take credit cards? That's all I have. My checks are pretty much gone, and I doubt they'd take one anyway." She held up her checkbook, then impulsively tore a sheet from her register, wrote her address and phone number on it, and handed it to Brice. "If you're ever in Florida again, after this mess is taken care of, look me up."

Brice took the slip of paper from her and set it down upon his desk. "I'll be only a moment."

He left and shut the door behind him. Kendra hurriedly put her gun and checkbook case back into her fanny pack then slung the strap over her shoulder as she rushed to the door after him. She followed him on deck, stopping in surprise at the bustle of activity around her. She had to push her way past several deckhands to reach him near the gang plank.

"Hey, Monty!" she called over the din of men shouting orders, and trunks and casks being carried and rolled about her.

Brice was talking to a man she had never seen before. He too wore a nineteenth-century costume, though much more resplendent than anything Kendra had seen so far. She preferred the simpler look of Brice's ship clothes to the bright lemon satin coat and white pants the other man wore.

The newcomer was slight in build, with receding dark-brown hair, a mustache, goatee and a well-tanned face—with the exception of his jawline, which appeared to be sunburned as if he'd been used to wearing a beard and had shaved it off only recently. And yet despite his tan, he seemed out of place on board ship, with all the lace at his throat and his sleeves. Kendra easily pictured him lounging on a silk-covered French-provincial sofa while he stroked a beribboned poodle on his lap.

As she approached, she realized the two men had started arguing. Several crew members, Riley included, stopped what they were doing and gravitated to the general area in apparent support of their captain.

Kendra's desire to contact Frankie, however, outweighed her common sense, and she stepped up to the two men. "Excuse me, Monty," she interrupted, "but I have to call my friend."

The satin-coated man pulled out a lace handkerchief and held it to his nose as he regarded her thoroughly, and Kendra caught a whiff of perfume coming from the lacy bit of material. The captain, however, seemed to be holding his temper in check. "I shall be with you in but a moment, Miss Browning." Though his gaze never left the other man's face, the look in his eyes—rather murderous now that she thought about it—told Kendra that this was not the time to bother him.

"I'll just wait over here, then." She moved toward the railing to look out upon the docks.

"Now, Parkston," she heard Brice say, his voice tight with fury. "I suggest you leave my ship before I have you thrown over the side. It's bad enough I must fend off your pirates at sea without having to see your gloating face when I return to shore."

"If you're accusing me of piracy, you're mistaken."

"Then why else come to meet me here at port, and risk getting your fine clothes soiled, other than to see whether your pirates were successful in seeing your plot through?"

"I came to discuss what you owe."

"What I owe?"

"For my ship, the *Alastor*. I like to think there is some explanation as to why you sank a simple merchant ship. A fully loaded one, I might add."

Brice laughed. "Merchant ship? I hardly think that a ship flying no colors, with guns at the ready, while refusing to turn away, typical of a simple merchant ship. You must forgive me if I decided not to wait around to see if yours was one of the many pirates that frequent that corner of the world. But then again, you must not have forgiven me, since you obviously ordered your cutthroats to attack the *Eterne* in retaliation but a few days ago."

"I've no idea what you're talking about. How could I, when my other ship arrived in port but yesterday? Unless you're accusing me of being in two places at one time?"

They continued to argue, and Kendra became caught up in the sights as she leaned against the ship's balustrade searching the quays for some sign of a phone booth. "Lord! Will you look at that," she said to herself, wishing she had a camera. Peasants, aristocrats, horse-drawn carriages, even the buildings, were antique looking. At least those close up. Fascinated, she turned to Brice to ask if this was some sort of festival, but stopped suddenly as her mind finally registered the rancid odors wafting up from refuse piles along the quayside. She turned back to the scene before her, realizing that something about it bothered her, only she couldn't quite figure out what. She searched everywhere, high and low, far and near. And then she knew.

"It can't be," she whispered, shaking her head and backing toward the gangplank. "No. I refuse to believe it. It's all a bad dream! It has to be!"

4

WHEN MIDNIGHT COMES

Kendra hit something solid. She whipped around to see Brice watching her with an odd expression on his face. Tears sprang to her eyes. "Tell me this isn't true?" She laughed, her voice panic-stricken. "A festival? Right?"

Brice held out his hand. "Miss Browning."

"Don't call me that. My name is Kendra. Or Browning. Everyone at work calls me Browning. Oh God! I'm going crazy, aren't I?"

She shook her head. "No. It won't happen if I pretend—*believe* everything's fine. I've been telling myself that over and over, you know. Ever since the sea battle. It has to work. It—Where's your friend?" she asked suddenly. "The man you were arguing with?"

"Lord Parkston? He's gone, Kendra."

"He looked at me as if he *knew.*"

"Kendra, please."

"No. I can't do this. Do you know there's not one speedboat out there in the water? We didn't see one the whole trip over here. And another thing. There are no wires. Not one. Look." She pointed dockside. "And no skyscrapers. No cars. Not even a trash can. Not one. It smells like a dump out here. My God! There's not even a telephone pole. I can't even call my friend to tell her I'm alive, because there's not one damned phone!" She covered her eyes to stem the flow of tears, but it didn't help. Vaguely she was aware of Brice's arms coming around her, comforting her. Shaking her head, she pushed him away.

"I have to find a phone." He tried to stop her as she stepped past him, but she brushed his hand away. "No. I've got to find a phone."

"Miss Browning! Kendra! Stop!"

She ignored Brice's command. Once she was on land, she felt as if her legs had hit solid rock. Her knees jarred uncomfortably with each stride, but she didn't care. She pushed her way past all manner of people, many in need of baths, if her sense of smell was any indication. Some were dressed in rags, others in clothes as rich or richer than Parkston's.

When she heard Brice call out behind her, she dodged around a group of men unloading a cart, then between two wagons filled with barrels. Her heart raced wildly. Stopping for a moment, she sucked air into her labored lungs, then screamed when someone tapped her on the shoulder. She spun around, expecting to see Brice, and was startled to see the man dressed in lemon satin. Lord Parkston.

His brown eyes regarded her with open curiosity. "Miss Browning, was it not? Did you, er, call your friend?"

She felt suddenly vulnerable. And then she realized her fanny pack was gone. She must have lost it during her flight from Brice. A cop without a gun. For the first time in her life, she felt truly helpless. "Get away from me."

"Maybe I can find her for you. Let me help." His voice was smooth, lulling, and he took a step closer.

"How can you help?"

"I'll find your friend for you. My carriage is just over there." When he pointed, Kendra's gaze caught on the flash of gold from a ring on his hand. For some reason she couldn't seem to keep her eyes from it, almost as if he were hypnotizing her with it. "Shall we?" he crooned.

The man's voice reminded Kendra of the waves after her boat overturned. Powerful. Far more so than she. She struggled to think.

"What is your friend's name?" he asked moving closer, closer.

Frankie. She could almost hear her familiar voice. She tipped her head to listen. No. It wasn't Frankie, but someone she knew. Brice.

"Miss Browning!" she heard him call out. "Where are you?"

His shout seemed to break whatever it was that held her rooted to the spot, and she tore her gaze from Lord Parkston's ring and bolted past him. She ran into the crowd, oblivious to what was going on around her, her only concern to flee from Lord Parkston, these maddening docks, and Brice and his ship, and everything else that stood in her way.

"There she is, Cap'n!" she heard Riley's voice shouting. "She's headin' fer them casks. I'll go around th' other side."

She almost made it past the barrels when a hand grasped her shoulder. She screamed.

Brice's voice sounded firmly in her ear. "Kendra, you must come with me."

"No." In her panic, every self-defense tactic she'd ever learned fled from her mind as he wrapped his arms around her in an iron grip. "I've got to find my friend Frankie."

"Where does she live?"

"I told you. Florida."

"And you, Miss Browning, are in London." He grasped her face and forced her to look at him. "London. Your friend is an ocean away. Do you understand?"

Suddenly she did. There was no way she could call Frankie. Now or ever. "I've died, haven't I?"

"No, Kendra. You are very much alive."

He picked her up and carried her to a closed carriage with a gold-crested seal emblazoned upon it. A liveried servant opened the door and Brice placed her inside, taking a seat next to her.

Kendra remained silent until the carriage began to move. "I'm dead. Or this is all a dream. It can't be true."

"Why do you say such things?"

Kendra was surprised at how calm she suddenly felt. "I know you think I'm crazy, but I'm not. I've told you a hundred times on board your ship: I'm from the twentieth century. We have airplanes that fly in the air, and ships without sails that can cross the oceans, and cars that don't need horses to pull them. And telephones to make calls from London halfway around the world to Florida. If I wanted to—"

"Hush," he told her, placing his fingers upon her lips. "I'll take care of you, Kendra. I won't let anything happen to you."

He looked at her with sympathy, concern, and something else she couldn't quite decipher. Just then, all she wanted was to let him take care of her. She threw herself against him. When he wrapped his arms around her, she started to cry uncontrollably. "I'm scared, Brice," she sobbed. "I'm scared."

"I know," he whispered. He kissed the top of her head. "I know."

Brice stroked her hair down her back, then held her tightly to him. What was it about this strange girl that made him want to protect her? Ever since he had pulled this golden-haired beauty from the sea, he had wanted to be near her, to touch her, hear her laughter, let her smile lift his heart. There was no question that he wanted her, physically, and that she too wanted him—he could see the need in her eyes when he kissed her. But he could never take advantage of her, not when her hold on reality was so fragile. He told himself he must wait, until she was better, until she had completely recovered from her near drowning, which he was certain had caused her illness. It had to be that, he thought, burying his face in her golden tresses.

He cut off the direction his thoughts were taking, sensing that a woman as strong-willed as Kendra would never consent to being anyone's mistress. And, even should her health improve, he could never marry her. Never would he forget his purpose in life: to marry a woman of impeccable lineage, such as the very beautiful Lady Caroline. That was the only way he could erase the stain his grandfather had placed on the Montgomery name when the fool had married a half-Gypsy. A love match, his grandfather had called it.

Brice was ashamed of his heritage and his grandmother. His *half-Gypsy* grandmother. It bothered him, this less than perfect lineage, one that led to his own father's demise. How many times had he begged his father to stop drinking, and not to gamble what was left of the family fortune? And what had his father always said? "'Tis the Gypsy blood in me that does it. Can't help it at all."

Brice nestled his face in Kendra's hair and whispered soothing words. He was reminded of another woman who had cried in his arms much the same way. His mother. True, he was only nine at the time, but he remembered thinking how strong he must be for both of them. It was right after the creditors had come, one of many such visits, to collect on his father's gambling debts. He heard the pounding on the door as if it were yesterday.

The butler had let the men in and Brice had grasped his mother's skirts, even as he tried to hide his fear. "Do not go this time, Mama," he had pleaded, knowing how she always cried afterward, especially upon walking past one of the newly bare spots where a painting used to hang, or where an heirloom used to sit. He had stood up straight and squared his shoulders. "Let me go instead. I shall tell them to leave."

His mother had smiled encouragingly at him, and tousled his hair. "You're a brave boy. Nevertheless, I must meet with them myself. If I do not satisfy your father's debts, it will bring ruin and scandal not only upon all of Blackmoor, but upon the Montgomery name as well. I cannot allow that to happen."

"Why must we care what others think of us?"

She kneeled down so that he was eye level to her. "Because it is your heritage, Brice," she explained. "Of all things that are important in the world, honor and your name mean everything. You must always remember that. Being the duke of Blackmoor will simply remain an empty title if the name of Montgomery is not respected first. I'll not leave that legacy for my only son. Do you understand?"

"Yes, Mother."

"And as I have done for you, so must you do for your son when you are grown. Promise me that you'll not allow scandal upon your name, nor follow in your father's footsteps."

"I shan't be like Papa. I promise."

She hugged him tightly. "I know," she said as she rose.

"Mother?"

"Yes, Brice?"

"When the time comes for me to go to school, I do not have to go to Eton. You don't have to sell your jewels this time."

"That is sweet of you to worry, son, but truly there is no need," she had said, never telling him that there was nothing left of her jewels but paste.

He had watched her descend the stairs. With regal grace, she had ushered the three men into the salon and shut the doors, and all he could think was that she was alone, with no one to protect her.

With single-minded purpose Brice had crossed his mother's room and opened the door that led to his father's bedchamber.

"Papa?" It took a few moments for his sight to adjust to the darkened room. When he saw the slumped figure in the wing chair before the fire, he realized no help would come from that quarter.

"Is that you, m'boy?"

"Yes, Papa."

"Come here."

He remembered wishing at that moment that he had not come. "You promised, Papa," he had said, once he stood before him. Even in the dim firelight, his father's bloodshot eyes were noticeable. "You told mother to give you a second chance. You promised."

"Promised what?" the gray-haired man had replied, as he stared into the dying embers.

"Not to gamble anymore."

"Can't help it, m'boy. 'Tis the Gypsy blood in me." He'd lifted a wine-filled glass to his lips and took a long sip. "Let that be a lesson to you," he had said after a moment. "Never taint the bloodline. Look what it did to the great name of Montgomery."

"You broke your promise," Brice had whispered, sickened by the smell of port on his father's breath. "I shall *never* forgive you."

"'Tis your grandmother's fault I'm the way I am. Half-Gypsy, she is." His father had drained his glass, then promptly filled it from the crystal decanter on the side table. "Not to worry, though, m'boy. Your mother will buy them off for a time. Always does. Later, I'll get the money back. You'll see."

Brice had fled from the room, and later that afternoon, while he'd held his mother as she cried, he had vowed for her sake that if it took every waking moment of his life, he would erase the tarnish placed on the Montgomery name by his father.

For that reason alone, he had always been careful to do *everything* exceedingly properly. Never would he allow what was left of the Montgomery bloodline to be mixed with anything less than the oldest, most respected of British aristocratic families—not that anyone else in the *ton* would dare comment on his lineage. They did not need to. He knew it was there; his father had reminded him on a daily basis. But, perhaps, after several generations of careful breeding, the Montgomery blood would finally be washed clean.

*　　*　　*

The coach slowed, then eventually stopped. He carefully set her from him, a sad disappointment filling him that he must leave her. Forever.

"Miss Browning." He nudged her away. "We have arrived."

Kendra sat up, and wiped her swollen eyes, then looked around her at the unfamiliar sights. "Where?"

"Home. Blackmoor Hall."

A mild sense of panic filled her, but he allayed it at once. "You're welcome here until arrangements can be made to take you home. I'd put you on my very next ship, but I think you need time to recover from your—" He stopped when a footman opened the door. Brice stepped from the coach, then turned to help her out.

Kendra wasn't sure what she'd expected to see, but knew it certainly wasn't this magnificent Palladian mansion surrounded by lush, green countryside.

Brice took her elbow in his hand and led her up the few wide stairs to the open doorway. "I thought it better to come here, rather than stay in London. After your arduous journey, I rather think the country might be less harrowing."

"I suppose you're right. I don't think I could face—" Her thoughts were lost the moment she stepped into the spacious foyer. The outside was impressive enough with its huge columns supporting the facade. It was nothing compared to the interior. Kendra's entire apartment could fit inside the foyer alone, a circular room lined with doors. At the very center, a wide marble staircase led up to an open landing, divided, then wound up to the floor above that. From there, her gaze was drawn to the high-domed ceiling, painted to match the pattern in the marble beneath her bare feet.

Struck by a wave of self-consciousness brought on by

such opulent surroundings, Kendra glanced down at her toes, dismayed to see how dirty they were. She took a protective step behind Brice, hoping that no one would notice.

A young woman came bounding down the steps. Her elegant hairstyle, chestnut curls pulled up in a knot to cascade down one shoulder, as well as her high-waisted, puffed-sleeved, black silk gown, accentuated the girl's natural beauty. If she were a foot taller, Kendra thought, she would have made a stunning cover-girl model.

"Brice!" the woman shouted in glee. "You're home!" When she reached the bottom of the stairs, she threw herself into his waiting arms and he spun her around, laughing all the while.

"Cecily, you little minx. Shouldn't you be practicing your singing lessons?"

"Oh fiddle! I'll turn old and gray before I'm able to sing well enough for anyone to want to listen. Besides, I—" She stopped short at the sight of Kendra. "Who is this?"

Kendra expected the young lady to turn her pretty nose up in disgust at the sight of her disheveled presence.

"This, my dear, is Miss Kendra Browning, who was shipwrecked near the Colonies. She will be staying with us for a time. And this, Miss Browning," he said, turning to Kendra, "is my sister, Lady Cecilia. Though she much prefers Cecily."

Shock swept through Kendra as she realized the import of Cecily's title. *Lady* Cecily. God! What did that make Brice? she wondered. Somewhere, in the back of her mind, she had a vague recollection of Riley calling Brice a prince. No, it was a duke. At the time, she assumed he was being facetious. But now? Was she supposed to bow or curtsy or what? "How do you do?" she asked shakily.

Cecily's smile never wavered as she clasped Kendra's hand warmly in both of hers. "I'm quite well, thank you. But really, Brice," she said, turning a stern look upon her brother. "You're really very naughty to keep the poor girl waiting like this. She's in need of refreshment at the very least."

Brice patted his sister on her back. "Then I'll leave her in your very capable hands as I have—"

"I know. Important business matters to attend to. It's always the same with him," Cecily said to Kendra. "Business, business, business. But never you mind. We shall do just fine without him. Now do come along. Let us see about getting you a bath. I daresay you must be in want of one, having been cooped up on that ghastly boat for so long."

Kendra, so overwhelmed by everything around her, could do no more than paste a smile upon her face and allow Lady Cecily to lead her up the stairs and into a brightly lit, elegantly furnished room decorated in pale yellows, the same colors in her room at home. The sunlight, she noticed, poured through a large expanse of windows that dominated an entire wall.

Lady Cecily pulled a bell cord hanging in the far corner. "This will be your bedchamber while you're with us. Although it's quite small in comparison to some of the other rooms, the view from this window is exquisite. 'Tis my favorite room, next to my own of course, which is right next door."

Kendra strode across the thick carpet that cushioned her bare feet to stand in front of the window. The view was indeed extraordinary. Trees shaded manicured lawns, and graveled pathways meandered throughout the well-tended though bare flower beds bordered by low hedges. The entire garden was surrounded by a tall brick wall, separating it from the countryside. Just outside the wall, she saw a small chapel replete with its own cemetery. Beyond the magnificent grave markers of cherubs and archangels lay a forest that seemed to stretch for miles beneath the clear blue sky. "Breathtaking."

Lady Cecily stepped up to the window. "Sometimes at night, if you watch very closely, you can see the druids' fire in the woods. They dance around it."

"Druids?"

Lady Cecily shrugged. "Well, maybe not druids, but you can see the fire just the same. Usually around midnight. Druid's Cave is out there, but Brice forbids anyone to go near the place. We think it's haunted."

"Midnight?"

"I've never seen it at any other time."

"How interesting." She searched the woods and saw a curl of smoke rising amongst the trees. "That's not one of your fires is it?"

Cecily laughed. "Goodness no. That's the dower house. My grandmother lives there." Cecily pointed to the left where the trees were taller, thicker. "That's where I saw the fires. If you like, I can wake you if I ever see them again."

They were interrupted from further conversation when a short, pleasant-faced maid with dark, curly hair entered the room and Cecily instructed her to see to Kendra's bath in the adjoining dressing room. When it was ready, Cecily excused herself.

As Kendra slid Brice's shirt off her head, it caught on the chain of her pendant. Carefully freeing it, she undressed the rest of the way, removing all but her necklace. She stepped into the tub and luxuriated in the warm water, trying to remember the last time she had allowed herself to soak in a tub. At home, she rarely had time for anything but a quick shower.

Home.

She brought her knees up to her chest and slid deeper in the water. "God. Frankie must think I'm dead by now. And Jack, too." The thought saddened her. Lifting the chain around her neck, she stared into the cloudy depths of the opalescent moonstone that Frankie had given her on her last birthday.

Kendra thought of her best friend. She missed Frankie, and knew Frankie would miss her. But Jack? Of course he probably was worried now, but had he even noticed she'd gone away for the weekend without him? She had intended the two-day respite to give her time to relax, so that she might think seriously about their stagnating relationship. When she'd last seen Jack, she'd come to the dismal conclusion that she must choose between marriage or a career. With Jack, it couldn't be both. And the way she felt about her job lately—investigating one murder after the other—giving up her career didn't seem so outlandish.

Kendra sighed. Jack was beyond her reach now. There was not much she could do to change their relationship while she was separated by the Atlantic ocean and well over a century. Was she truly sitting in a tub in a duke's mansion?

"It's a dream," she whispered. Men like Brice did not exist in real life. Men like Jack did. "The alarm will go off, and I'll wake up and go to work, and Jack will be waiting."

The water grew chilled and Kendra quickly washed her hair, then stepped from the tub. After she toweled herself dry and put on the robe left for her, she returned to her bedchamber. She stood before the window, her gaze sweeping past the lovely garden to rest upon the forest beyond the wall, where Lady Cecily had seen her mysterious midnight fires. Had they occurred in modern-day Miami, Kendra would guess the fires were started by teenagers holding some sort of satanic ritual. But in the nineteenth-century? Were teenagers that unruly during these times too?

A knock at the door interrupted her thoughts. "Come in," she called.

The maid who'd overseen the drawing of her bath came in carrying a bundle of clothing. "Lady Cecily thought you might be in need of some fresh gowns after your trip, seeing as how all yours were lost in your shipwreck."

So that was what Brice had told everyone. Well, it suited her fine. "Thank you."

"I've brought my sewing things, since you're a bit taller than milady. I thought I could let down the hems on some of these gowns until yer fitted fer yer new clothes."

"New clothes?"

Lady Cecily entered just then. "Of course. You can't be expected to wear my cast-offs forever."

Kendra eyed the fine gowns. "A few more pairs of pants will suit me fine."

The maid looked appalled.

A curious glint entered Lady Cecily's eyes. "Truly?"

"Yes," Kendra answered. "I wear them to work, even out to dinner. Why where I come from, everyone—"

She stopped at the sight of Brice filling her doorway. His expression was grim, though it softened a bit when he looked at his sister.

Cecily smiled at her brother. "Dora was just going to let the hems down on some of my gowns for Miss Browning."

Brice nodded his head toward the maid. "You needn't bother."

"But I can't wear them," Cecily said. "It has not yet been six months!"

"Your period of mourning is finished," he replied curtly. "One or two weeks won't make a difference. Nevertheless, I've sent for the seamstress from the village. Now if you'll excuse us, I wish to speak to Miss Browning."

The maid fled with the gowns, leaving Kendra to wonder if he ran his home much the same as he did his ship. When Cecily hesitated, Brice added, "In private."

"You forget yourself, Brother. We're in her bedchamber after all."

"If you recall, sister dear, she and I shared a cabin together for several weeks. Had I wished to ravish her then . . . "

"Yes, well, that was all very different then."

"*Cecily!*" he barked.

The younger woman tossed an apologetic glance at Kendra. "I'll be right next door, should you need anything."

"You didn't have to yell at her. She was only trying to—" Brice's furious glare stopped Kendra short.

"From this day forward, Miss Browning," he said in a slow and deliberate voice, "you will cease your talk of the future. I will not have my sister frightened nor subjected to ridicule should someone hear your Banbury tales."

"Banbury tales! Everything I've told you is the truth."

"Perhaps you believe it to be so, after your near drowning."

"It is so. You saw my gun. Do you honestly believe that someone in this archaic age could manufacture something of that quality?"

"I'll admit that it's beyond anything I've seen. But certainly not impossible."

"Of course it's not impossible, because *we* have the technology. We've sent people to the moon."

Brice slammed the door, then stormed across the room to grip her shoulders. "Stop it, damn you. Don't you understand? They will put you in an asylum if you continue to speak so."

She was frightened by his anger. "You just don't want to hear the truth. Admit it."

"No, Kendra, I don't. I have no desire to see your lovely body wasting away in some dark cell after your caretakers are tired of using you, which is precisely what will happen if anyone hears you. And I may not always be around to protect you."

"Well, this is *my* dream. I don't need your protection, Monty."

"Be that as it may, my dear," he said, holding her shoulders in a painfully tight grip, "I am all that stands between you and Bedlam. Without me, you have nowhere to go."

The truth of his statement hit Kendra like a blow to the face. Asylums in the twentieth century were no treat, and from her history books, she knew she never wanted to visit their nineteenth-century prototype.

Brice relaxed his grip, but did not let her go. "At no time are you to leave this house without me. Not if you value your life. Do you understand?"

Kendra nodded.

"And you'll dress like a proper gentlewoman. One of good breeding. I'll not have any sort of scandal come down upon the family because of you."

Kendra glanced at the clothes she had worn on board his ship. "Couldn't I wear them around the house?"

"You will not wear breeches. Understood?"

"Ten-four."

"Ten-four?"

"Understood, sir."

"Then I may leave here for a few days without worrying about you?"

"I'm not a child."

His dark gaze locked with hers, and Kendra thought she recognized passion. The tone of his response confirmed it. "I know."

Uncomfortable under his scrutiny, Kendra glanced toward the window. A sparrow flitted about amongst the leaves of an ivy vine that grew up a trellis beneath the second-floor window sill. "In other words, I am to be your prisoner."

"You're not my prisoner."

"Then I can walk in the garden?"

"Don't leave the grounds. And if someone speaks to you, for God's sake, don't say a word. Have a fit of the vapors or something."

Kendra smiled, unable to picture herself as the swooning sort. She'd never fainted before in her entire life—or at least not until she'd had to stitch Brice's arm. Things could be worse. She could only thank providence that when her boat went under, she hadn't been pulled from the water by Vikings, or by those who burned witches. "Don't worry. I'll be a proper lady."

"Not a word about what happened in your life before I fished you from the sea. When I return, we will discuss it all in detail."

Hope welled up inside her. "You mean you'll listen to what I say? About where and when I came from? You believe me?"

He never answered. Instead, he looked about the

light-colored room, then back at her. "This bedchamber suits you. Soft and feminine, like a pale yellow rose." His thumb brushed across her cheek, to the sensitive nape of her neck, then trailed downward, along the collar of her robe. His touch sent her heart racing. He paused in his musings to look at her, as if waiting for her approval to make love to her—and he probably would have done so, too, had she not so foolishly uttered, "Do you? Believe me?"

His lips stilled, just above hers. After a few moments he let her go and strode from the room.

"Oh well," she whispered to herself. "He didn't say he didn't believe me." Kendra remained where she was a while longer, wondering what to do. Her options, at the moment, were rather limited, since the maid had taken the gowns and Brice had forbidden her to wear his clothes. She padded to the window, throwing it open. As she leaned out to breathe in the garden-scented air, voices from an adjoining room caught her attention.

"I'm sorry you feel that way, Cecily," she heard Brice say. "But I was not being uncivilized by ordering you from her room. You simply don't understand the gravity of the situation. Miss Browning is quite ill."

"Then I'll send for the physician, though I don't think she needs one."

"No," he replied curtly. "Just have her stay in her room until the seamstress arrives. But under no circumstances is she to leave here."

"Why ever not?"

"Something happened to her when she fell overboard. A sickness."

Kendra bristled at his words. He thought she was crazy!

"Oh pooh!" Cecily exclaimed. "Anyone can see she is fine."

"I won't be disobeyed in this matter," came Brice's stern reply. "Not even by you. And if I must lock both you and her in your respective rooms to ensure your compliance, then so be it. Now as for this period of mourning for Father you feel you must honor . . ."

Kendra had heard enough. So she was to be kept prisoner here. But for what reason? Surely if Brice cared about her, he'd have listened to what she'd said. Then a horrifying thought came to her. What if he was only trying to placate her until *they* arrived to take her away? No doubt the "seamstress" he sent for was a man in a funny white coat.

"I'll be damned if I let that happen," she muttered as she tore off her robe, then dressed in Brice's shirt and breeches. Unfortunately, she still had no shoes, but she was not about to let a minor detail such as that stop her. She strode to the window then poked her head out to listen. All was quiet.

Kendra glanced down, then swallowed. Though she was generally not afraid of heights, the ground seemed awfully far away. At least the ivy vine growing up the trellis looked strong, and judging from the size of the trunk, ancient. She climbed out on the sill then lowered her feet to the thick, twisting vines. When she found a firm hold with one foot, she lowered herself farther. About halfway down, she heard Cecily's voice calling out from the open window.

"Miss Browning?" Silence, then, "Brice. She's gone."

"What do you mean she's gone?"

"She's not in her bedchamber."

Kendra continued her descent, though trying to be as quiet as possible. She was no more than five or six feet from the ground when Cecily leaned out the window and looked directly at her.

5

Kendra's grip on the ancient vine tightened at the sound of Brice's voice. "Where the bloody hell is she?"

Cecily turned her back to the window, then shrugged her narrow shoulders. "I don't know."

With a sigh of relief, Kendra dropped to the ground. Cecily had not given her up. Unfortunately, Brice's answering shout told her he'd guessed the answer anyway. "Damn it, Cecily. Why didn't you tell me she had climbed out the bloody window?"

"You needn't curse, Brice."

"*Kendra!*" he boomed. "Come back here."

Kendra hesitated as Brice leaned out, a murderous expression upon his face. "I won't let you lock me up."

"You're giving me no choice when you constantly run from me."

"I'll run as long as it takes to make you understand I have no intention of being your prisoner. If you won't listen to me, I'll find some other way to get home without your help."

"Damn it, Kendra . . . Miss Browning. Be reasonable."

"I'm a very reasonable woman." She began to back away when she saw him start to climb out the window.

"There's nowhere you can go, Miss Browning. The garden's enclosed, and the gate is locked."

Kendra looked at the wall. It was at least eight feet tall, and even with her training, she knew she couldn't climb that. Feeling much like a mouse cornered by a cat, she wondered what her next course of action should be. Brice's words decided it for her.

"You there," he shouted to someone behind her. "Mr. Cobbs. Stop her."

Kendra spun on her heel to see a burly man about twenty feet away carrying a rake. He immediately dropped it and ran toward her.

"When you catch her, hold her," Brice demanded as he swung off the sill and onto the vine. She turned her attention to the fast approaching Mr. Cobbs. Just before he reached her, Kendra lunged around him, then ran past. Though he was a large man, he was no match in a foot race. It was Brice she worried about.

Fleeing to the back of the gardens, she hurdled over low hedges and across narrow pathways, keeping to the lawns whenever possible to protect her bare feet. A quick glance over her shoulder told her that Brice had reached ground level and was now in swift pursuit. Before her, the garden wall seemed to grow higher with each step she took. Then, to make matters worse, the gardener, Mr. Cobbs, called out for help from a strapping boy who sat on his haunches near the wall, planting seedlings in the freshly turned upper plot of a terraced garden.

"Catch her, lad! Afore she runs off."

The boy, perhaps all of fourteen, stood and moved toward Kendra, jumping down to the next plot of turned earth. At last, a way out, she thought, noting the upper level of the terraced plot was at least two feet higher than anywhere else. She hesitated only an instant before running straight through the boy's bit of garden, then up four stairs to the next small plot of herbs.

"She's ruined me plants, Mr. Cobbs," the boy cried.

"Forget the bloody plants," Brice shouted from close behind. "Catch her. She can't get past the wall."

Watch me. Kendra raced toward the brick wall, which now, because of the upper level of the terraced garden, stood a mere six feet. She shot forward, placing her foot squarely in the middle of the wall, vaulting herself upward to catch the top of the wall with her hands. Then, before she lost momentum, she swung her other foot to the top, and used it to pull herself over.

She spared only a quick glance back to see the looks of astonishment on the faces of the three men who stood staring as if they'd never seen a woman jump a wall before.

"Miami Police Academy, class of 1987!" she shouted triumphantly before dropping to the ground on the other side to flee toward the cemetery that lay about twenty yards away. She hid behind a massive grave marker set apart from the rest. The feeling that she was being watched caused her to look up. Above her, perched upon the gravestone, stood a tall, marble archangel, staring down his chiseled nose at her as if silently reprimanding her for trespassing upon sacred ground. Wondering whose grave she'd desecrated, she glanced at the marker and read: Jonathan Montgomery, fifth duke of Blackmoor, 23 March 1762–30 August 1829. Brice's father, she realized, moving from the still-soft ground.

The shouts of her pursuers brought her up short, and she forced herself to continue. After circling around the far side of the little chapel that stood on the grounds, she peeked around the corner to see Brice and the gardener running toward the graveyard from the opposite side.

Her only chance was to lose them in the forest, and so she raced toward the woods. Her feet, sore from her trek across the garden and wall, were cushioned somewhat by the bed of dried leaves and moss of the forest floor. Every now and again a sharp rock or twig stabbed at her soles, but she stopped herself, most of the time, from crying out in pain. Shortly, she came to a well-worn path that led away from Blackmoor Hall. Finally, when she thought her lungs might burst, she left the path, walking for several feet before dropping behind the base of a large oak.

When her labored breathing and pounding heart quieted, she returned to the narrow trail. She slackened her pace, and after several minutes, the forest thinned considerably, allowing the bright sunlight to filter through the trees. Above her, birds began singing and a pair of squirrels chattered noisily. Even the air smelled fresher, cleaner, if that were possible.

A moment later, the path led her to a grassy clearing where, in the middle, flanked by two giant oaks, stood what Kendra could only describe as a storybook cottage—well, much larger than a cottage, but storybook just the same. And while everywhere else in the countryside it appeared that winter had not quite faded, here there was no doubt as to the ending of that season. The ethereal beauty of the place beckoned to her, and she wondered if the sun had warmed this particular spot on earth just for the enjoyment of watching it bloom.

A mass of dark green vines covered the brick house. Diamond-shaped mullioned windows glinted like colored jewels in the bright sun, reflecting the reds, yellows, lavenders, and oranges from the vast flower beds that surrounded the place. Near a side door, a large sundial stood amidst a circle of early daffodils, and stepping stones led to a vine-covered arbor where long clumps of purple wisteria hung down through the white trellis work. The fragrant flowers' petals floated gently down, covering the lawn in a carpet of soft lavender, where, sitting beneath the arbor, as if the whisper of falling petals had lulled her to sleep, rested a gray-haired woman.

Kendra was tempted to step back into the shelter of the trees, but upon regarding the figure for a few moments, changed her mind. She decided the woman must be asleep, for she neither moved nor gave any other indication that she was aware of another's presence in her garden.

Could this be Lady Cecily's grandmother? Her dress appeared to be plain cotton, green, with a white apron tied around her waist. Her gray hair was pulled back in a long braid that fell across one shoulder. One finely boned hand held a straw hat in her lap, while a basket filled with daffodils lay at her feet.

Perhaps she was the dowager's maid. That must be it, Kendra decided, carefully approaching the woman across the lawn, so cool beneath her aching feet.

When she was but a short distance away, the woman spoke. "You have come to put out the fires."

Kendra stopped in surprise. "What?"

The woman smiled but did not open her eyes. "Nothing my dear. Just an old woman's prattling. Do come closer." Kendra obeyed, and was surprised again by her next words. "You're hurt."

Kendra looked down at her feet to see dried blood and dirt caked upon them. She looked back at the woman, who still sat with her eyes closed. "How'd you know?"

The woman laughed lightly then opened her eyes, dark as midnight, to look up at Kendra. "Your gait, 'twas uneven."

Kendra couldn't help but stare in amazement.

"What brings you here, child?"

"I'm looking for Lady Cecily's grandmother," Kendra said, though she hadn't realized it until that very moment.

"I am she."

"Oh. How do you do, uh, Lady . . . ?"

"Alethea. You are a friend of Cecilia's?"

Kendra recalled Cecily's kindness, and how she'd helped her by not giving her away. "Yes."

The woman smiled. "Then you may call me Grandmère."

"I'm Kendra. Kendra Browning. Lady Cecily told me about you."

"Did she?"

"Yes," Kendra replied. "You see, I'm not from here."

"Indeed," the old woman replied matter-of-factly. "That is quite an unusual pendant you are wearing. May I see it?"

Kendra unclasped the chain. "I mean, I'm *really* not from here," she said, handing the necklace over. "Not even from this time," she blurted out, unsure why she felt compelled to reveal herself to this woman.

Alethea's dark eyes sparkled kindly as she examined the moonstone, turning it over and over before handing it back. "Yes. I can tell."

Kendra snapped her mouth shut the moment she realized it had dropped open. "You can? How?"

Alethea cocked her head to one side as she regarded Kendra thoughtfully. "There is a clear nimbus about your person not present in anyone else. I noticed it immediately."

"Nimbus?" Kendra turned and looked over her shoulder expecting to see a cloud hovering behind her.

"It is nothing you can see, my dear. Very few can, though my granddaughter, Cecilia, shows great promise. But how can I explain? Perhaps it is more like a light emanating from your soul."

Kendra fingered the moonstone hanging from her throat. "You mean like an aura. My friend Frankie told me all about them. She's into all that hocus-pocus stuff. Has her fortune told once a week, though I didn't think you could tell someone's fortune by the color of their aura."

"I think to call it fortune-telling is a bit presumptuous." A small sparrow alighted on the ground near her feet, and Alethea dug into the pocket of her apron, pulling out a bit of crust. Breaking off a piece, she tossed a few crumbs to the ground. When the bird cocked its head at Kendra before hopping toward the offering, she was suddenly reminded of the sparrow that had landed on the ivy vine, almost as if it were showing her how to get out of the room. I'm losing it, she thought, especially at thinking that this was that very same bird.

Alethea tossed a few more crumbs. "No. Definitely not fortune-telling," she continued, "though learning one's potential can certainly be done given the right opportunity. I'm more inclined to discover what sort of person I meet. I've seen a few with very dark auras. A blackened soul, if you will. Most persons fall in between, however, the colors changing with each individual's various emotions."

Kendra drew her gaze from the precocious bird. "Is that how one becomes green with envy or sad and blue?"

"A rather simplistic approach, but apt."

"What is so different from mine that you can tell I'm . . . from another time?"

"Your aura, if you will, is very bright and completely clear. Or rather, not there at all. I close my eyes and see nothing."

"You see auras with your eyes closed?" Kendra couldn't help the feeling that this woman was a bit on the loony side.

"Look closely at me for a few seconds, then close your eyes," Alethea said patiently. "You should see the reflection or shadow of me in your mind."

Kendra did as she was told, and sure enough could make out a shadowy figure that resembled Alethea's form, complete with arbor and wisteria, minus the finer details, of course. Her eyes still closed, she said, "And?"

"And the difference is that when I see people, I see what you're seeing now, only clearer. 'Tis the best way I can explain it. What I see, I see in each blink of the eye. Very quickly, very clear, and very often. Most people can see but the shadowy reminiscences of what is before them. Not so for me."

"Okay, so you can tell by my aura I'm not from here. Would you believe I'm from the year nineteen hundred and ninety-five?"

Alethea raised her thin gray brows. "So far? From where?"

"Miami."

"Is that somewhere in the Colonies? I would assume as much from your accent. I have always wanted to visit North America, but have never had the opportunity."

"I suppose Florida wasn't quite so popular then—or now, I mean."

"And how did you arrive?"

"On Monty's, er, I mean Captain Montgomery's ship. These are his clothes, you know."

"Brice *brought* you to this time?"

"Not willingly. I was shipwrecked in my own time, and he rescued me in his. Or something like that." She felt much like Alice in Wonderland at the moment—very much in awe, and very confused. "Only I didn't know he was from your time, or maybe it was more that I didn't want to believe it, until I got to London. Does that make any sense?"

When the older woman nodded, Kendra stared at her a moment. "Aren't you even surprised? You don't think I'm crazy? Because your grandson certainly does."

"I have lived on this earth for seventy-three years and have seen many strange things. My mother, and grand-mother, Gypsies both, were gifted as I with a second sight, if you will, theirs being much stronger since full Gypsy blood runs in their veins. Surely even in your time, strange happenings have occurred? Things that no one can explain away? That which legends are made of?"

"I suppose. There are stories of flying saucers, strange men from space. That sort of thing."

"Then why not traveling into time? The Gypsies have long told of legends of such things. 'Tis folk who fear the unknown that refuse to believe."

"Brice doesn't believe me."

"My grandson is a stubborn young man. He'll believe when he's ready and not before. But enough of that. You must tell me about your adventure."

Kendra, mesmerized by the woman's inner power, sat down upon the petal-strewn lawn, inhaling the soft, sweet fragrance of the wisteria. She completely forgot that Brice was looking for her while she described to Alethea her life in Florida and finally the storm that led to her shipwreck and eventual rescue.

Alethea listened patiently, asking when Kendra was finished, "Why did you feel so compelled to leave your home in the first place?"

Kendra thought a few moments. "I just wanted to get away from it all, I guess. Sailing seemed like the easiest solution at the time."

"But what of your family? They must surely be worried?"

"I don't really have any. Unless you count Frankie. She sort of adopted me as her little sister after my mom died. She lived in the house next door with her foster parents."

"And your father?"

"He's been dead about five years now."

By the time Alethea finished asking her questions, the sun had long since dipped down past the trees and a cool breeze stirred the lavender petals from the lawn, blowing them about like snowflakes through the air. "So you see," Kendra said, finally, "all I want is to go home. Unfortunately, there's more than a mere ocean standing in my way."

"That does present a problem. One that I can't easily answer." Alethea reached for her basket, then rose. "The air's grown quite chilly. I fear I've kept you occupied far past tea time. You must come inside and warm yourself, and perhaps we can do something about the cuts upon your feet."

Kendra stood and followed the petite old woman into the house. Alethea led her to a cozy room just off the kitchen where a low fire burned merrily in the grate. She waved to a rose damask armchair before the hearth. "Do sit down, Miss Browning. I'll have Mary Beth bring you a basin of warm water to soak your feet while we take tea."

Alethea had just left when a door on the far side of the room burst open and Lady Cecily ran inside.

"Oh, good . . . Miss Browning . . . you made it here." Cecily dropped into a matching chair opposite Kendra's and took a few deep breaths. "I just left Brice. He's been searching for at least an hour or more and is furious that he hasn't found you. When he came back, he asked me all sorts of questions about where you might have gone to, but I managed to convince him I knew nothing. I told the gardener, Mr. Cobbs, that I saw you running off in quite the opposite direction."

Alethea entered just then, followed by a plump maid carrying a basin of steaming water and a towel hung over one arm. The round-faced servant smiled at Kendra as she set the basin of water and towel at her feet then left the room. The amber-colored liquid smelled suspiciously like tea.

"I'm told by my dear friend, Botolf, that this particular brew will heal your cuts quite rapidly, as well as take away much of the pain, though it will sting at first."

Kendra dutifully plunged her feet in. She had to grit her teeth against the sharp sting of the herbs, but only for a moment, for, as promised, the pain quickly dissipated.

Cecily wrinkled her nose. "Nasty stuff to drink, though. Grandmère recommends it for everything."

Alethea smiled at her granddaughter. "You'll be pleased to know we'll be drinking a more delicate tea. How are you, Cecilia dear?"

"Quite well, Grandmère. Though once Brice learns that I've found Miss Browning and haven't told him, I'll probably be confined to my rooms forever. He's already angered with me for wearing mourning. It's as if he refuses to admit that Papa died."

Alethea shook her head. "It's his method of death that Brice refuses to understand. He only learned of his father's death just before he left for your country on business matters," she explained to Kendra. "Brice has vast shipping interests over there."

Cecily lifted her black skirts, propped her feet up on a small footstool, and stared at her black slippers. "Brice worries that he'll be just like Papa."

Alethea nodded, and there was a deep sadness in her eyes. "That's why Brice works so diligently on estate matters and his shipping business. To undo what his father has done. Brice has spent every moment rebuilding the family fortune, and as a result, he's gone more often than not."

"Brice thinks Papa was insane," Cecily said. "Papa did nothing when he was alive but gamble to excess. And after Mama died, he drank more than ever. And then, . . . then he killed himself," she finished in a whisper.

Alethea broke the silence that followed. "Brice worries that insanity runs in the family. Tainted blood, as he calls it, though never to my face. I fear he blames me, since I gave birth to his father."

"That's why he calls her Alethea instead of Grandmère," Cecily explained.

"Well, Brice thinks I'm insane," Kendra put in. "Lately, I'm beginning to agree."

"*I* don't believe it," Cecily offered. "Even so, I knew there was something about you, Miss Browning, that was . . . well, different from anyone I've ever seen."

The three women were silent as Mary Beth entered again, this time with their tea tray. After setting it upon the cherrywood piecrust table between Kendra's and Cecily's chairs, the maid moved an embroidered high-backed chair from the wall to the fire for Alethea to sit in. "Will there be anything else, your grace?"

"No, thank you, Mary Beth," Alethea replied. After the maid left, she said, "I believe I'll take Miss Browning to Botolf's."

Cecily jumped up from her chair. "To Hawthorne Woods? Might I go, Grandmère? Please?"

"No, dear. Not this time." Grandmère poured three cups of tea. "Do you take milk or sugar?" she asked Kendra.

"Neither, thank you." Kendra took the proffered cup. "Who's Botolf?"

Cecily, appearing somewhat dejected, took her teacup, then sat. "A druid wizard. Hawthorne Woods is the forest where he lives. Grandmère took me there once when I was very young, but never since."

"He is *not* a wizard, dear," Alethea corrected gently.

Kendra couldn't help but notice that she didn't say he was not a druid. "Can Botolf help me get home?"

"Perhaps," she answered, picking up a plate of delicate looking teacakes, which she offered to Kendra. "We shall leave for Hawthorne Woods on the morrow."

Cecily was just reaching for a cake when a loud crash sounded from the front of the house. "Oh dear," she said. "Brice must have found us."

6

Alethea rose from her chair. "I shall speak to my grandson in the salon."

The moment Grandmère left, Cecily jumped up and strode across the room. She motioned for Kendra to do the same, before pressing her ear to the door.

Kendra started to rise, until she remembered the basin of tea. The herbal water had soothed her feet so much, she'd nearly forgotten that she was soaking in it. She pulled her feet from the water, then dried them upon the towel before following Cecily and putting her ear, in similar fashion, against the door.

Kendra heard Brice's familiar deep voice. "Where is she?"

Grandmère sounded calm despite his curt tone. "Do sit down, Brice. Would you care to take tea?"

"Where is she?" he repeated.

"If you are speaking of your sister, she's with me."

"You know damn well who I'm speaking of."

"Miss Browning is quite safe, if that's where your concern lies. Now please sit down before you wear a hole in my beautiful Persian rug. Your grandfather brought that home for me on our fifteenth year."

"Alethea," he said, coolly. "I don't believe you understand. Miss Browning could be in danger should she let her wild imagination and loose tongue get the better of her."

"I quite agree, dear boy," Grandmère replied, giving Kendra cause to wonder whether the woman had merely been placating her until Brice's arrival. Cecily, however, did not seem in the least disturbed by her grandmother's affirmative reply. Kendra had to trust Cecily and Grandmère, for there was no one else.

"What has she told you?" Brice asked.

"Everything. Which is why I've decided she must stay here with me."

Cecily clasped Kendra's hand in hers and smiled.

There was a short pause before Brice said slowly, "You cannot mean it, Alethea."

"I do," she replied.

"But you're—"

"Old? A Gypsy?"

"That's not what I meant."

"Brice, you must remember I see things that you choose not to see."

He said nothing.

"Is there anything else you wished to converse with me on?"

"Just keep Cecily away from her," he said.

Cecily narrowed her eyes at that.

"You're a touch late," Grandmère replied.

"Cecily!" Brice yelled.

Cecily, not in the least perturbed by her brother's anger, smiled at Kendra, then opened the door and stepped into the other room. Kendra peered in, and, taking one look at Brice's angry countenance, decided she was not budging from her safe haven.

Brice crossed his arms and narrowed his eyes at Cecily. "It seems you've disobeyed me once more."

Cecily's smile faltered for the briefest second before she replied, "It's not quite how Grandmère said, Brice. I really had no way of knowing if she actually *came* here or not."

Brice glanced in Kendra's direction. He glared coldly at her, and she stepped from her shield of wood to face the full force of his anger. It was not fair to let Cecily take all the blame.

"It's true," Kendra offered. "She couldn't have known I'd come here for certain."

Brice stared at Kendra a moment longer, then turned back to Grandmère. "For now, she may stay here at Briarwood with you, Alethea. Perhaps 'tis best. More out of the way. I'll have the seamstress, who's been waiting this past hour, sent over." He looked back at Kendra. "And don't repeat your tale to anyone. Not to Cecily, not to me, not to Alethea, *not to anyone.* Is that clear?"

Kendra nodded.

"What tale?" Cecily asked, turning a suspicious eye toward her brother.

Grandmère, a Mona Lisa smile upon her face, cocked her head at Brice, waiting for his answer.

Kendra, hoping to alleviate Brice's fears, for his sister's sake, replied, "The circumstances surrounding my rescue, and the fact that I was . . ." she looked up at Brice, "unchaperoned for so long a time," she finished.

He nodded. "Her reputation will be torn to shreds, not to mention the scandal on our family, should anyone learn of what occurred."

Cecily crossed her arms and stared at Brice in disbelief. "Is that why you told me she was sick? In case she let slip

that she was unchaperoned? You already told me that,
Brice. Besides, Grandmère said she was taking her—"

"I see no reason," Grandmère interrupted, "to take
Miss Browning to *town* if Brice has already sent for the
seamstress. And as for any gossip that might start, we'll
tell everyone that Miss Browning is our very dear cousin
Kendra, come to visit from the Colonies."

Cecily looked as if she was about to say something,
but apparently thought better of it upon seeing
Grandmère's placid look.

Brice strode toward the front door, opened it, then
looked back over his shoulder at his grandmother.
"Assuming she told you everything, then you're well
aware of the danger she might be in?"

"Quite," Grandmère said. "I shall take every precau-
tion to ensure that nothing untoward occurs while she is
in my care."

He nodded, then after a quick glance at Kendra, left
without another word.

"What did he mean?" Cecily asked. "What secrets are
you keeping?"

Kendra felt a twinge of guilt, but she could not break
her word to Brice. Thankfully, Alethea answered for her.
"We would certainly tell you if we could, Cecilia dear.
But you heard Brice. He forbids us to speak of it. If you
want to find out what is going on, you must pay extra
attention and discover it on your own."

Cecily crossed her arms and regarded Kendra thoroughly. "There's something about you. I noticed it
immediately. But I haven't Grandmère's skill."

"You have," Alethea answered. "You simply have not
yet discovered how to use it. Just be patient, it will come.
Now let's finish our tea before it grows chilled, and
before the seamstress arrives. It will take hours to fit

Cousin Kendra for an entire season." She ushered the women back into the sitting room.

"Season?" Kendra repeated.

"Yes. It lasts through the summer."

Winter was barely over. "I hate to disappoint you, but I plan to be long gone before then."

"And perhaps you will," Grandmère replied, taking her seat by the fire. "But what if you are not? We still don't know why you're here. Fate is very strange at times. Even so, 'tis best to be prepared. That's why we'll tell everyone that you're our dear cousin, and why you *must* remember to call me Grandmère. Do you dance?"

"I learned to waltz in cotillion, but as far as any other nineteenth-century dances, I'm lost."

"Then we'll have to make certain you're instructed in all the latest steps," Grandmère said. "At least if we want you to have a proper come-out."

Kendra picked up her cup of tea, but found it had grown cold. She set it back down. "Don't you think I'm a bit old?"

Cecily shook her head no, apparently pleased by the prospect of having a companion for the season. "Surely, you're no older than I? A year or two at the most?"

Kendra eyed Cecily, noting the lack of any detectable laugh lines. "What are you, seventeen? Eighteen?"

"Eighteen next month. This will be my second season."

"Then I'm only ten years older."

Cecily's jaw dropped. "Twenty-eight? And not married? Grandmère," she said aghast, "she's on the shelf! Whatever shall we do?"

Kendra smiled politely. "Twenty-eight is not so terribly old where I come from."

Alethea rubbed her chin thoughtfully. "I believe that's a fact best left to ourselves. Your age, that is. Your marriageability is an asset we'll take advantage of. No one would think to question that, since why else would you come to visit us but to find a suitable husband?"

"Why else indeed?" Kendra replied. "God knows I wasn't doing well in that respect back home. Even so," she added cheerily, "they say distance makes the heart grow fonder, and I'm certainly far away."

"Oh dear," Grandmère said. "There *is* someone at home? You failed to mention any betrothal."

"Only because there wasn't any. And I suppose if you get right down to it, he was one of the main reasons I went sailing by myself. I love Jack dearly, but sometimes I think we weren't meant to be. The man's married to his work." That was it, she thought. If he weren't so wrapped up in his job, they'd definitely have had a chance.

"What a quaint way of saying it," Cecily commented. "Why, Brice is married to his work too!"

Alethea poured fresh tea into Kendra's cup. "What was the other reason, dear?"

"My job. Too many murders, too depressing."

Cecily gasped. "Murders?"

Kendra wondered if she'd said too much. Grandmère, however, apparently didn't think so, since she answered, "Cousin Kendra, of course, will never speak of this outside this room, but she investigated murders in the Colonies. Much like one of our Bow Street Runners."

"But she's a lady!" Cecily cried.

"To be certain, dear. But things are done differently in America, which is why one must never mention it. Not even in front of servants. They would never understand."

"Besides," Kendra added, "not many people knew exactly what I did. If I were walking down the street, you'd think me perfectly ordinary, just like any woman of my age."

Cecily looked at Kendra with renewed interest. "I shall enjoy discovering this mystery about you, Cousin. You're becoming more intriguing by the second."

"But," Grandmère warned, "you must take care not to let anyone know what you've learned. As your brother mentioned, it may be dangerous for Miss Browning."

"Why?" Cecily asked.

"There are many who'd never understand. Though Brice may not believe all he hears, he's quite aware of what might occur should others hear. And of course, you mustn't tell Brice anything you've discovered on your own."

"But Brice already knows," Cecily pointed out.

"Do you care to stir his wrath?"

"No, Grandmère."

"That's a dear. Now drink your tea, and we'll talk of the coming season. Brice will want to ensure when you return home that we've not poisoned your ears."

The seamstress came and went in a flurry of colorful swatches, shears and pattern cards. To Kendra, the experience was exhilarating, yet tiring. She worried about the expense and thought Alethea was ordering far too many gowns, but Grandmère simply shook her head whenever Kendra mentioned anything. "Brice can afford it, dear," she told her each time the seamstress showed them a new pattern.

Shoes were a different matter entirely. It had not occurred to anyone that Kendra did not have any. Grandmère's were too small and Lady Cecily's too large. Grandmère, however, came up with the idea of putting a bit of cloth in the toes of a pair of Cecily's slippers until a visit to the cobbler was made.

By the time Kendra was shown to her bedchamber, she was more than ready for sleep. She barely noticed the thick carpet beneath her bare feet, or the warm fire that crackled in the hearth. She was too intent on stripping off her clothes and slipping between the covers of the large four poster bed. Within minutes, she was fast asleep.

The next morning, Kendra dressed in one of Cecily's altered gowns. She stood before the long mirror, studying her reflection. The gown, pale green silk trimmed with cream lace around the bodice and wide puffed sleeves, complimented her coloring, and she wondered what Brice would think of her if he saw her now. The gown gave her a distinctly feminine appearance—one she had not been familiar with since becoming a police officer over seven years ago. On impulse, she pulled her hair up to allow the soft waves to cascade over one shoulder much like the hairstyle that Cecily wore. The effect was nice, but she couldn't figure out how to make it stay, and so ended up tying it back with a length of green ribbon.

After stifling a yawn, she put on the matching kid slippers, but finding her feet were still sore from yesterday's trek through the woods, kicked them off before going downstairs to hunt for coffee or anything that might be remotely caffeinated.

He did not miss her. Brice pushed open the garden gate, then strolled across the soft lawn toward the side door of Briarwood. Behind him, the shadows of the surrounding forest mirrored his present state of mind—although he told himself his dark mood had nothing to do with the fact that he could not sleep last night. That was simply because he was no longer on his ship. His bedchamber had been too quiet. Too still. But it was not the rolling of the waves that he had missed, nor the swing of his hammock. It was the gentle, even sound of her breathing as she slept but a few feet away from him in his cabin.

No, he did *not* miss her. This urge to see Kendra had nothing to do with this being the first morning after they had slept apart—even though they had never actually slept *together* in the same bed. He was merely concerned. That was it. She was ill and he was merely looking after her welfare. His lack of sleep had nothing at all to do with it.

The tantalizing scent of fresh baked goods welcomed him into the house and he was reminded of the mornings when, as a child, he and his mother used to come and breakfast with his grandmother in her cozy little room, with its splendid view of the garden just off the kitchen. It had been years since he had let himself in by the side door—not since he was a lad in short pants—as his father had forbidden him to spend any time alone with his grandmother once he was out of the schoolroom. After that, his visits with her had always been in the more formal setting of Blackmoor Hall.

But as he stepped into his grandmother's breakfast room, he felt as if everything had stayed the same in the many years of his absence. The same teapot she had used year after year, the same lace coverlets on the table, the same flowers from her garden, the chirping of the birds outside, and her presence at the table all added to the feeling that here, if nowhere else on earth, time had not passed.

The comforting and familiar surroundings eased the ache and frustration that he had nursed throughout the solitary hours of the night. Until he saw *her* enter the room from the salon. Pausing in the doorway, he simply stared. He had never seen Kendra in anything other than the breeches and shirt she'd worn on board the *Eterne*. Dressed in one of his sister's gowns, its color matching the green of her eyes, Kendra looked as magical as the unseasonably early flowers in his grandmother's garden.

"Good morning, Lady Alethea," Kendra said, apparently not noticing him standing there.

The older woman lowered her newspaper and smiled. "Good morning, dear. And do remember to call me Grandmère. We must keep up our appearances. As for proper titles, we shall address that subject later as you seem to be lacking in that respect."

"Yes, Grandmère," Kendra replied.

"I trust you slept well?"

"Pretty much." She rubbed her temples. "I've got a killer headache. Other than that, I had a few strange dreams last night, mostly of my voyage here, and being late for work. It was all rather confusing."

"Have a cup of tea, dear," Alethea offered. "'Tis really quite soothing. And there are fresh muffins, of course. Breakfast here is very informal, unlike at Blackmoor Hall. I usually take a light meal in the morning, but if you care for something more, you need only ask."

A plate filled with large berry muffins was set on a lace doily in the center of the table. "This looks great. And tea will do, unless you have some black coffee?"

"I can have Mary Beth make some, if you wish."

"Tea's fine." She sat down opposite Grandmère. "So what's up for today?" she asked picking up a muffin and breaking it in two.

"What's . . . up?" Alethea repeated, raising her brows in question.

"Um, what are your plans for today?"

Alethea poured two cups of tea. "We'll journey to Hawthorne Woods—" She looked up just then. "Why, Brice. What a pleasant surprise. I didn't hear you enter."

"Good morning, Alethea. Miss Browning." He stepped into the room, and said, "I gave explicit instructions to Miss Browning that she was not to leave here without me. Now where did you say you were going?"

"Going?" Alethea echoed, while pouring first milk, then sugar into one of the teacups, and stirring it briskly. She lifted the delicate cup to her lips, and looked up at him with her dark eyes, so very like his own.

He knew his grandmother too well to ignore that she was trying to hide something. "What are you doing?"

"Why, whatever do you mean?"

"You never take anything with your tea."

She hesitated but the slightest of instances before saying, "Why, of course not. I was pouring this for dear cousin Kendra."

She passed the cup to Miss Browning, who announced, "I *like* my tea this way."

He crossed his arms. Kendra tossed him a smug look, then took a sip. A very *small* sip, he noticed.

Alethea cleared her throat gently. "You were asking about our itinerary?"

"Yes," he said, turning his attention back to his grandmother.

"Kendra has no shoes. I thought a visit to the cobbler was in order."

He looked down at Miss Browning's feet, and she lifted her gown exposing one trim ankle before wiggling her slender toes in confirmation. "See, Monty. No shoes. I can't dress like a woman of good breeding if I have no shoes."

"Was there anything else you wished to discuss, dear?" Alethea asked.

Brice looked from one woman to the other, and at that moment realized he hadn't the slightest idea why he was even here. "No."

Alethea poured herself a fresh cup of tea. "Well, I have something I wish to speak to you about. I had thought about engaging a dance master. Kendra knows but one dance. The waltz."

"A dance master?"

"Yes. She *must* know how to dance before the season begins."

"Season? For Miss Browning?" He glanced at Kendra, who looked as surprised as he. Had Kendra remained with him at Blackmoor Hall, such a ludicrous thought as introducing her to society would *never* have entered his mind. "We'll discuss this matter at a later date. As it is, I must depart for London. I expect to return some time tomorrow afternoon if you wish to discuss it then."

"As you wish, dear."

Brice stayed a moment more, then after a pointed look to Kendra, turned and left through the door he had entered.

Kendra watched Brice's retreating figure, wondering how she was going to find a way to get home if he didn't allow her any freedom.

"Drink your tea, dear," Alethea offered, apparently noticing her distress. "It really is soothing."

Kendra looked down at the sickly sweet concoction Alethea had passed to her. "Do you mind if I dump this out and pour a fresh cup?"

"Set it aside and I'll pour you another." Alethea took a clean teacup from the tea service, and filled it to the brim before handing it to Kendra.

Steam rising from the delicate porcelain cup wafted up in a soothing scent of cinnamon and herbs. She breathed in deeply, suspecting that this was another concoction of Alethea's that was more than a simple beverage. Her suspicions were confirmed when after several sips, her headache did not seem quite so noticeable.

"Is this one of Botolf's recipes?"

Alethea smiled. "My grandmother's."

"Oh," Kendra drained the cup and poured herself another. "Since Brice came and ruined our plans—"

"Nonsense, dear. He didn't ruin anything. Botolf lives at the very northernmost tip of Hawthorne Woods, half of which Brice owns. We'll never actually be leaving the estate on our journey, therefore we shan't be disobeying Brice in the least. And while he's in London, he'll never even notice we're gone."

Kendra sipped the hot tea. "Do you think Botolf will be able to help me get home?"

"'Tis difficult to say. Even so, as I said last night, we must prepare you should that not be possible."

"Like how?"

Alethea opened her mouth as if to speak, was silent for a moment, then said, "I believe proper use of the King's English will be the place to start. If I hear you say something . . . amiss, please don't take offense if I correct you. For instance, 'what's up' and 'like how' *shall not* be used in the future. Do you think you can remember to . . . "

At that moment, Kendra realized this masquerade was going to be much tougher than she thought. Her entire English vocabulary, one that she thought was perfectly adequate in her day, had to be completely revamped. "Don't worry. My feelings aren't hurt too easily."

"I didn't think so. Still, you must take care how you speak in front of others. One's speech is what separates the classes, and we must be able to convince society that you're a lady of quality. Additionally, despite Brice's objections, I'll engage a dance master, and—"

"Whoa! Dream or no dream, hiring a dance master is going a bit too far. Why don't we just wait and see what your friend Botolf has to say before you decide my whole future? After all, I may not be here for that long."

Grandmère smiled pleasantly. "As you wish, dear."

Hawthorne Woods, Kendra discovered later, was a little section of the same forest that surrounded the dower cottage, named for the earl of Hawthorne's estate, which was situated nearby.

Grandmère pointed out the earl's large mansion, set on park-like grounds dotted with stately oaks, as they drove past in their carriage. "The earl," she said, "is Brice's closest friend. They were inseparable as boys, and even went to Eton together. Hawthorne's estate borders Blackmoor."

Kendra looked back through the trees of the forest and could just make out the roof line of Blackmoor Hall. "I didn't realize there was any other place so close, with the exception of your house."

"It is about a twenty minute walk, from Hawthorne Manor to Blackmoor Hall, and another five to mine. And, even though Hawthorne's lands extend much farther north than Brice's, the forest is divided nearly evenly."

"Is the forest very big?"

"It is so vast that neither Brice nor Hawthorne can keep watch of all that goes on within the confines of the trees. Brice has forbidden us to venture too far from Blackmoor Hall without an escort."

"Why?"

"It is far too dangerous. Which is why we are taking the long road that leads around the edge of the woods instead of traveling through them."

Kendra shivered as she glanced over her shoulder into the bowels of the dark woods, her vivid imagination picturing all sorts of bandits and ruffians. Leave it to her to lose her gun, then end up living on the edge of a nightmarish forestland that was beginning to sound more and more like some seedy part of Miami.

After traveling northward along the deserted road for nearly an hour, the driver finally turned their carriage onto a well-worn track that led back into the forest. Several minutes later he stopped their conveyance before a small thatched-roof cottage set amidst the shade of the trees. To Kendra's eye, the cottage, from the outside at least, appeared more suited for the likes of a woodcutter than a man reputed to be a wizard or druid. The inside was a different matter entirely. They were let in by a handsome boy, perhaps aged ten or so, with white-blonde hair. The magician's apprentice? Kendra wondered.

The lad looked up at Grandmère and smiled widely before remembering his manners and giving a slight bow. "Your grace. We didn't know you'd be calling today."

"I didn't know myself until last night. Is your grandpapa ensconced in the dungeon?" Grandmère asked with a twinkle in her eye.

The boy giggled. "Yes, milady." He led them through the front room and then down a short hallway. The cottage was furnished much as Kendra expected it to be, with plain wooden chairs, a small rug before the hearth, and a cheery fire that eliminated any chill from the continual shade of the forest. At first Kendra thought the boy meant to take them into one of the rooms they passed, but instead he led them straight to the end of the narrow hall where a bookcase filled the wall.

Curious, she watched as the boy pulled out a book from the middle. A moment later the entire bookshelf swung silently open, revealing a narrow winding staircase that led into the depths of the earth. Torches hanging upon one wall lit their way as they followed the boy down. At the bottom, he pushed open a wooden door that, indeed, reminded Kendra of something one would see in the bowels of a castle. On the other side, a wide dungeon-like chamber opened up, revealing that which the seemingly ordinary cottage hid so well.

The first thing Kendra noticed was the smell: a faint mustiness mingled with the aroma of exotic spices. Three walls were lined with a multitude of shelves, most containing ancient-looking books all covered with dust. Several shelves displayed jars and bottles set in neat rows, each labeled in a fine spidery script in a language Kendra couldn't even begin to guess at. Most of the containers appeared to have ordinary herbs within, but some seemed less innocuous in that solid things were floating around in a clear yellow-greenish liquid.

The fourth wall was filled with a large hearth where a giant caldron bubbled away, giving the place a definite wizard-like atmosphere. What magic concoction was this Botolf brewing?

In the center of the room, a heavy table, its wood scarred and battered with years of use, took up a good portion of the room. And, next to that, before a tall bookstand—the type that Bibles or very large dictionaries are usually set on—stood a man, dressed in long, flowing gray robes and white hair that fell to the middle of his back. He seemed engrossed in whatever he was reading, for he did not indicate in any way that he had heard them enter. He turned a large vellum page and traced his fingers down it as if searching for something written there. After a moment, he closed the heavy tome, sending a cloud of dust into the air, then looked up to see who had entered his domain.

His eyes crinkled at the corners the moment he saw Grandmère. He appeared to be smiling, though Kendra couldn't be sure since most of his face was covered with a waist-length snowy beard and mustache.

"Alethea, what a pleasant surprise. And who have we here?" he asked as he regarded Kendra with open curiosity.

Grandmère drew her forward. "Good day, Botolf. This is Miss Kendra Browning, come to us these past few weeks from the Colonies. My grandson had the pleasure of bringing her to us after rescuing her from the sea."

Botolf waved to a pair of sturdy wooden chairs at the table. After Kendra and Grandmère sat, he turned to his grandson. "Randolf, have you finished your chores?"

The young boy shook his head.

"Then off with you." Botolf's eyes held a fond look as he watched his grandson run up the stairs to do his bidding. After a moment, no doubt waiting for the lad to be out of hearing, he asked, "And there is a reason, then, that you seek me out, Miss Browning?"

"I want to go home."

Botolf raised his bushy, white brows. "Oh?"

Once again, Kendra found herself relating the strange circumstances of her journey. Like Grandmère, Botolf did not seem at all shocked to hear her tale. When she finished, he merely asked, "Nineteen hundred and ninety-five?"

"Yes," Kendra replied, thinking this man looked more and more like a wizard the longer she sat there.

He stood and approached the bookstand. "Might you be able to show me just where it was that you were shipwrecked?" He opened the large volume, then started flipping through the pages until he stopped somewhere near the back of the book.

"I can try," Kendra said as she moved to his side. After studying the page he had turned to, she recognized a fairly accurate, though old, illumination of North America. "Right about here," she said, pointing to Florida's southeastern coastline on the map.

"I see." He stared at the map for a moment, then turned a few pages, read something there, nodded, then turned to a different page showing a map of England. "You've accomplished quite a journey."

"Tell me about it. I keep thinking I'm going to wake up and find it's all a dream, like the Wizard of Oz or something."

The druid shook his head. "I assure you, you're not dreaming, though I can't answer for this wizard you speak of. Perhaps he's the one that's helped you through the portal?"

Kendra had to smile. "No. He's merely a fictional character in a story where a girl got swept up in a tornado and was dropped in the Land of Oz. I was nearly drowned and ended up on Brice's ship."

"That's what I find most intriguing," Botolf said, stroking the length of his thick, white beard. "I've never heard of this occurring in such a manner . . . through the sea . . . I find it rather interesting that you came through under water. Most unusual. Unless that area was once dry land."

"You mean you *have* heard of this happening before?"

"Oh yes. There are several such places scattered

throughout the world that allow journeying through time."

"Then all I have to do is get Brice to take me back to where he picked me up and *poof!* I'm back in my own time."

Botolf shook his head. "I'd certainly not want to risk it."

"Why not?" Kendra asked, willing to try nearly anything to get home.

"Because there were more forces at work than just a simple 'poof' as you call it. The storm, the wave that thrust you under the water, the time of day, the object that led you to this particular time. Everything must be aligned just so. Should you jump back into the water whence you came, you might find yourself drowned, unless you are a strong swimmer."

"But when can I go home?"

Botolf closed the great book with a thud, and Kendra stepped back to avoid the dust cloud. "Not until the time is right," he answered. "Such an event happens but twice a year, and then for only a few nights at a stretch. On those three nights, one at the waxing moon, one on the full, and one on the waning, the portal stays open but a few hours past midnight."

"There's got to be a way back home without all this waiting," Kendra said. "Everyone's sure to think I'm dead by now. You said there were other places where this phenomenon occurs? Can't I at least try one of those?"

Botolf regarded Kendra thoughtfully. "There are a few such places here in England. Stonehenge is one."

Hope welled up inside her. "Stonehenge?"

Botolf nodded solemnly. "That, and one or two others I know of, one being very close to here. An old druids' cave situated not too far from Hawthorne Manor and Blackmoor Hall."

Kendra jumped up. "Then why can't I just go there?"

"As I said, things must be lined up just so. Unless you have somehow broken through the barriers that keep all things in the universe aligned."

"Can't I learn?"

"You could, but it's considered a black art."

Kendra wasn't sure she liked the sound of that. "Is that similar to black magic?"

"Precisely. Powers far greater than yours and mine would have to be called forth in order to use it and travel through time at will. To unleash something of that nature would be to risk losing one's soul and mind to the blackness that pervades."

"Oh." She fell back into her chair, her hope deflating once more. "There has to be a way," she said, fingering her moonstone necklace.

"There is," he told her. "As I said, you must wait for what fate has in store for you. Twice a year, on the first full moon after the winter and summer solstice, the portal is at its widest. Then, and only then, at midnight, can you travel back to your own time, or to ours as simply as if you were stepping into the next room."

"You make it sound so easy," Kendra replied, unable to keep the sarcastic tone from her voice.

Grandmère cleared her throat in gentle reprimand.

"If it were too convenient, there'd be naught to keep people from passing from one time to another whenever the whimsy struck. Then again, they lack the one item you possess to step into the next realm of time. The Druid's Light."

Kendra couldn't imagine what that might be and said so.

Botolf approached her, holding out one gnarled finger as he pointed to her throat. "This stone you wear around your neck. Ancient legend tells of the Druid's Light showing the way into the next time. I am curious as to how you came to be in possession of one."

Kendra held up the necklace to stare into the opalescent stone. "I found it in a little shop in Miami." She recalled the day with sudden clarity when she and Frankie had spent an afternoon antique shopping. Kendra was drawn to the curio shop upon looking in the window and seeing mountains of knick-knacks in a low-ceilinged room, where cobwebs had hung from the ceiling much like wispy shawls of the most delicate fairy lace. When they had entered, the shopkeeper, a wizened old man, showed them the necklace.

She looked up at Botolf, suddenly remembering what the man had told her. "He said it would bring me adventure and luck as long as I always wore it, and my friend Frankie went back and bought it for my birthday. I've never taken it off, from that day on." Kendra sighed deeply as she looked at the necklace once more. "So far, I could do with a little less adventure and a lot more luck."

Grandmère leaned over and patted Kendra's hand. "It seems to me, dear girl, that luck most certainly was on your side when Brice was there to rescue you. You'll no doubt experience that type of fortune again."

"One can only hope."

Botolf stared at the necklace a moment, then asked, "May I see it?"

Kendra turned the chain and unclasped it, then handed it to the old man.

He examined it carefully, paying particular attention to the chain and finally the clasp before handing it back. Then, without another word, he moved to the far wall, where he picked up a small wooden box that had sat unnoticed amongst the rows of dusty books. When he stood before Kendra once more, he opened the box, and there, in the center of the black velvet lining, lay a perfectly shaped moonstone, set in filigreed silver.

"This," he said holding the box down so Kendra could see, "is one such stone. Not many exist. And, although you believe you found yours, it is more than likely quite the other way around. It found you."

"Me?" Kendra stared in awe, then looked at her own with renewed interest. "This little thing lets you travel in time?"

"It can, if as I said, all nature's forces are in alignment."

"Without messing around with any of that black magic stuff?"

Grandmère answered her. "Nature's force is crystal clear, white so to speak. The black magic you speak of works against nature."

Botolf closed the lid to the box and took it back to the shelf. "Which is why he who's involved in the black art can step through time far easier than you or I, though not necessarily at will. The druids, who once possessed these stones, learned to work with nature, not against it. You must guard yours well. I once had two in my possession, but one was stolen a few years ago. I was careless and left it above stairs."

"Stolen?" Kendra repeated.

"Yes. 'Twould not surprise me at all if this were that stone."

"I thought you just said my moonstone found me? If they really have that sort of power, how could one become stolen? And how did I end up with your stone?"

"The Druid's Light is owned by no one. It's difficult to explain. They are, after all, merely inanimate objects. Anyone might pick one up, should a careless soul leave one lying about. If yours were to become lost, your chance to return home diminishes greatly." He pointed to her necklace. "I noticed that the clasp on your chain appears to have weakened. You should have it mended, perhaps put on a stronger chain."

Kendra gripped her necklace tightly, not realizing until then its true value.

Grandmère stood up. "We must depart now, Botolf. I'm pleased that you were able to help us, but I must see to hiring a dance master for Kendra, since it appears she'll be staying on. Brice fears that she'll be endangered should anyone learn of what we've discussed this afternoon—about her past, that is—and so we're most anxious that she blend in with society."

"A wise decision. Never let others hear her discussing such matters as what the future holds." He laid one hand on Kendra's shoulder. "People are afraid of change, and so afraid to listen to something they know nothing of. Do be careful."

"I will," Kendra promised.

A loud hiss startled her and she spun around, almost expecting a dragon to materialize in the corner. With a mild sense of relief, she saw it was only the caldron on the hearth, which had boiled over. Botolf ran over to stir the brew in an attempt to slow the mass of bubbles spilling over the side.

"What's in there?" Kendra asked, imagining it must be a magic potion of some sort. Dragon's tongues and eyes of newt at the very least.

"My supper," Botolf said. "Venison stew."

Disappointed to discover it was something so normal, Kendra followed Alethea to the stairs, stopping only when Botolf called out.

"Don't worry about knowing where to go when the

time is upon us. I'll come to you on the first night the portal is open after the summer solstice."

"What if—"

"I shall be there when midnight comes," Botolf affirmed gently. "I shall await you at the garden gate that leads to the chapel."

"Shouldn't we meet a little earlier?" Kendra asked, watching him stir the thick liquid. "What if something happens?"

"If necessary, I'll await your presence at the gate on the second and third nights if for some reason you don't arrive as scheduled. 'Tis the best I can offer."

"Well, rest assured, I'll be there on the very first night you're there. Day number one. I want out of this place as soon as possible."

"Time and deeds will tell," he said.

Alethea started up the stairs, but Kendra, still not at ease, said, "What if something happens to you? What if *you're* not there?"

"When the time comes to leave, whether I'm there or not makes little difference. The Light shall lead your way. I am merely, like you, a keeper and you will find yourself in the right place at the right time."

Botolf's parting words remained in Kendra's mind long after she and Alethea had departed, and she wondered if what he said were true. She recalled the strong feelings that had led her to rent the sailboat the afternoon she was shipwrecked. Was that what he meant?

By the time they reached the dower house, Kendra's mind was so befuddled with all she'd learned that afternoon that she again wondered if she were insane after all. Many a police officer had succumbed to the pressures of their jobs, and God knew that investigating homicides in a city like Miami was stressful in itself, especially that last case she'd worked on with Jack before she went sailing. The Debutante Murders. The senseless and brutal killings of those young girls in the prime of their lives was more than she could bear. She wondered if Jack had solved the case in her absence. A few leads had been found at the scene of the last murder, such as the partial prints they had lifted from that pocket watch with the strange symbol and the words "Do what thou wilt" engraved upon it.

Well, one good thing came out of this time travel business, she thought that night as she readied herself for bed. At least she would not have to investigate any more murders. If nothing else, she could use the time until she found her way back home to get the rest and relaxation she needed without the added stress of knowing there was a pile of cases waiting for her on her desk at work. Assuming, she thought sleepily, as she climbed into bed, that she still had a job when she got back.

Fragments of strange dreams weaved through her subconscious. Ships flying through tornadoes, landing in the nineteenth century. Druids dancing around fire rings on a beach in Florida. A knife-wielding man dressed all in black, chasing after her as she raced for Brice's ship and safety in his arms.

Kendra sat up in bed, her heart beating wildly, slowing only when she realized it was just a dream. All around her was dark, but worse yet, in her mind, was that *something* had wakened her, and whatever it was, was not part of her dream.

7

Nothing moved in the room, and there was no sound, save Kendra's own breath. She held it and listened. Whatever had awakened her was not here. Nevertheless, her instincts were seldom wrong, and so she knew better than to ignore the thought that something was amiss.

Rising from her bed, she padded across the thick carpet to open her door. All seemed quiet, and so she shut it, before moving silently to the window to pull open one heavy drape. A single moonbeam fell to the floor. Kendra stood to one side of the pale light and peered out the second story window.

Outside, the stars sparkled brightly against their black velvet canopy, while the full moon lit the treetops that swayed gently in a soft breeze. She scanned the forest, unable to see much, and was just about to turn away when in the midst of the trees a flicker of something bright caught her eye. A fire.

Could this be one of the druid fires Cecily spoke of?

Kendra strained to see, but could not tell if anyone was dancing around it. Not from this distance. The mystery must remain unsolved, at least until morning, since she was not about to go traipsing through the woods in the middle of the night.

After several moments, she looked across the silver-lined treetops in the direction of Blackmoor Hall. What was Brice doing at this moment? With a sigh, she closed the drapes, shutting out the bright moonlight, before climbing into bed. After a deep yawn, she was soon fast asleep.

———

The coach lurched forward sending Kendra sprawling back against the thick squabs. "These guys are worse than Miami cab drivers," Kendra muttered as she righted herself and looked out the window onto the crowded streets of London.

"These guys?" Grandmère replied archly, her expression one of disapproval.

Kendra cursed to herself. She had to remember to talk as if she were one of the Vanderbilts, or a visiting dignitary to the Oval Office at the least. "I was merely expressing how very similar your driver is to the many cab drivers we have in Flor—er, in the Colonies."

"Much better, dear. You must remember to guard your tongue."

"Yes, your grace."

"And *do* call me Grandmère. If we are to successfully accomplish this ruse, you must remember you are our cousin. 'Tis bad enough that Brice calls me by my given name."

Kendra took in the sights of the inner streets of London and wished she had a camera to capture all that she saw. It was one thing to read about the past in history books, or see it in a painting. Not even her vivid imagination could do justice to the actual experience. Everything around her was real: the crowded buildings, dingy from soot, towering over the quaint cobbled streets below. Vendors calling out to sell their wares. Peasants dressed in dull shades of autumn scurrying out of the way of finely dressed lords and ladies, out for a stroll. The various carriages and horse-drawn carts that ambled down the lanes. The sharp stench reeking from dark alleyways, where whisper-thin children dressed in rags played or sifted through refuse heaps looking for scraps to eat.

Kendra closed her eyes at the sight.

A light touch on her hand caused her to look up. Alethea's face held concern. "Are you feeling ill?"

"No, Grandmère. I was just thinking about those children digging in the trash. Someone ought to do something about it."

"A part of life, I fear. One cannot help every soul, though we do try our very best."

"We?"

"Yes. The Ladies' Charitable Society. We meet every Wednesday afternoon for tea." Patting Kendra's hand, she added, "Perhaps you'd care to help? You might consider—"

Kendra shook her head. "No way. I'm not planning on being here that long, remember?" Feeling a bit of remorse at her callousness, she added, "Just tell me who to give my donation to." When Alethea said nothing, her guilt magnified. "All right, I'd love to go to a meeting."

Alethea smiled her Mona Lisa smile, and Kendra wondered just what she'd gotten herself into.

For the remainder of the afternoon, Grandmère and Kendra visited one shop after the other to put the finishing touches on Kendra's wardrobe for the coming season. All in all, Kendra enjoyed herself, even finding it easier than she expected to act with the graces of one born to the crème de la crème of society. She had never been to England in her own era, and to see it from the privileged aristocratic viewpoint of the nineteenth century was a truly rewarding experience—once they had reached the fashionable part of town, that is. Everyone treated Kendra as if she were visiting royalty, due of course to the dowager duchess of Blackmoor's presence.

It was late afternoon when they entered the last shop, the jeweler's, where Kendra's necklace was repaired while she looked on.

Grandmère, who was seated in the front of the shop, stood suddenly. "I nearly forgot to pick up a few things at the apothecary's." She hesitated at the door, as if trying to decide whether or not she should leave Kendra alone.

"Don't worry. I won't be going anywhere without my necklace. I'll wait here for you. "

"I shan't be but a few minutes, dear," Grandmère said. "'Tis just up the street. I'm certain Mister Bright will not mind if you wait here until I return."

The jeweler, a balding man wearing spectacles, shook his head, though never taking his eye from the setting he worked on. "Not at all, milady," he told Kendra. "You're perfectly welcome."

Kendra waved to Grandmère as she left. "I'll be fine. You'll see."

After just a few minutes, the necklace was finished, the silver filigree cleaned, polished and repaired, and the old chain replaced. "Here you are, Miss Browning," he said as he held it up for her.

Kendra, inspecting his work for any flaws, tugged on the chain, put it on and then pulled on the pendant.

Nothing gave, and so after thanking him, she left the shop to await Grandmère's return.

Outside, Kendra looked up and down the shop-lined street to see if she could spot Grandmère's coach. Believing she saw it not too far away, she decided to walk the distance, rather than wait.

As she strolled along, she couldn't help but notice a few odd stares tossed her way from some of the women passing by. After the fourth glance in her direction, she was struck by a lack of confidence in her ability to blend into her surroundings and so checked her reflection in the glass of a shop. Nothing appeared wrong with her peach walking gown. The neckline was modest, the lace trimming tastefully applied at the sleeves and bodice, and no spots or tears to be seen. Nor did her hair seem to be mussed, still pulled back in a simple chignon.

All in all, she thought she looked much the same as any other woman her age, a bit taller than average, perhaps, and minus a maid or—or chaperone, she realized belatedly. Oh well, she thought. Let them stare. They could think whatever they wanted about her and her reasons for walking down the street alone. It wasn't as if she was going to see any of these people again in the next one hundred and fifty years or so—she hoped.

As she continued up the street, the sight of a filthy urchin carrying a small knife at his side caught her eye. The boy sidled up to a young lady caught up in an animated conversation with an older woman wearing a ridiculous looking hat with a bird's nest in it. Neither woman noticed the lad until he very conveniently appeared to trip and fall against the younger lady's skirts. Immediately, he rose, apologized profusely, even going so far as to tip his grimy cap to the pair before casually skipping away from them.

Curious, Kendra watched as the young woman, more worried about the state of her gown than the boy, began brushing her skirts. Suddenly she started screaming. "Thief! Thief! Come back. My reticule."

The boy's carefree gait turned into a dead run.

Kendra stepped in front of his path thinking to block his escape. "Hey, kid! Drop the purse."

He slowed only an instant to assess this latest obstacle, then darted around her into an alley. Without thinking, Kendra hitched up her skirts and ran after him, yelling, "Stop! Police!" He led her on a merry chase, with a distinct advantage, since he was not wearing a gown nor flimsy kid slippers. Still, Kendra refused to give up, following as best she could through narrow alleyways and unfamiliar streets, until too late she discovered that not only had she lost the boy, she was thoroughly lost herself. After cursing at her foolishness, she retraced her steps in hopes of finding *any* familiar landmark, when a sudden high-pitched scream pierced the air.

Kendra thought the cry came from across the street. She raced to the other side just in time to see a fat man pulling her young thief by the scruff of his collar toward one of those dark, dank alleyways she had seen earlier. The boy, thin as a rail, struggled vainly against his attacker, who backhanded him across the face. Wailing, he tried to cover his eyes, as the man hit him twice more.

Although several people, men included, stopped to look at the disturbance, no one made a move to help the boy as he was dragged farther down the alley.

Incited by the blatant abuse, she pushed past several well-dressed gentleman and followed the pair into the stinking back street. At the sight of the man raising his hand to deliver yet another blow, she rushed forward and grabbed his thick arm. "Stop it! You're hurting him."

He yanked his arm away. "A bit far from Covent Garden, aren't ye?" he asked, rubbing his unshaven double chin. "Too bad I got pockets to let. Might enjoy a quick tumble with a fancy piece like yerself."

"You're calling me a whore? You'll have to do better than that."

The boy, a dirty-faced urchin of perhaps five or six, looked up at Kendra with something close to awe in his wide, frightened blue eyes. The man, however, was clearly not amused. "I'll call ye a lot worse 'an that, if ye don't get yer bawdy nose outta my way." He jerked the lad against him as if to show he meant business. "Now get, afore I forget yer not 'ere to offer yer wares."

Kendra held her ground. "Let the boy go."

"Don't worry yer pretty face, duchess. I'll be lettin' 'im go as soon as 'e he gets the beating 'e deserves, and not a moment sooner. 'E'll be lucky 'e can still use 'is arse fer sittin' after wot 'e did."

"And just what was that?" Surely, the man had no knowledge of the stolen purse? She spared a quick glance at the boy, unable to tell if his face was bruised beneath the layers of grime.

"What'd 'e do? Ye mean besides runnin' off this mornin' after complainin' of bein' too ill to go to 'is chimneys that need sweepin', or spillin' his gruel on the floor and 'elpin' 'imself to more without thought that there might be others wot's as 'ungry? Did 'e stop and think how 'is own greed would cause me to starve?" He turned his cold blue gaze on the boy and gave him a shake. "Did ye?"

"No, Papa," he whispered. "But I brought you this." He held up the reticule in his fist. His father grabbed it and shoved it into his own pocket.

Kendra, ignoring the stolen purse, eyed the man's

heavy girth, doubting that she could take him on in spite of her training.

"As if you were close to starving," she taunted. A glance over her shoulder told her that the curious spectators had no interest in helping her or the boy. The few that remained soon went their separate ways.

Things hadn't changed over the years. Here, as in the twentieth century, no one wanted to get involved. She turned back to the man, wondering if she could somehow get him to let go of the boy or at the very least redirect his anger.

Her surly aggressor scratched at his protruding belly. "Wot I'm starvin' fer is a bit of wot yer hidin' beneath yer skirts." His leer sent a frisson of cold fear coursing through her. Unfortunately, her cop's instinct, which had sent her racing to the boy's rescue, had surfaced faster than her recollection of the oh-so-minor detail that she was no longer a mere radio call away from help.

He took a menacing step forward, dragging the child with him. When she edged back, his bloodshot eyes darted to the side, resting briefly on a nearby trash heap. A sickening smile spread across his face, and Kendra watched in dawning horror as he leaned over to pick up a long piece of turned wood, probably the remnants of a broken chair. Letting go of the boy, he advanced again, slapping his makeshift club in his free hand. The child, taking advantage of the situation, pushed the cretin from behind. In anger, he raised his stick to strike at the boy, but stumbled on a loose paving stone as he turned. His feet flew out from beneath him and he landed in the pile of refuse, splattering Kendra's gown with the gray-green muck.

She nearly gagged from the stench, but seeing her chance grabbed the boy's hand, pulling him from the alley, and, she hoped, to safety. A loud curse echoed through the narrow lane, accompanied by the sound of his pursuit. Despite their head start, his father caught up with them just as they reached the street. Quickly, Kendra shoved the boy behind her skirt and faced the man. "I'm warning you. Back off, or—"

"Or what, duchess?" he sneered.

"Or you'll be sorry." She glanced up the road, hoping to see anyone who might help. It didn't look promising. With one hand glued on the boy's shoulder, keeping him firmly behind her, she inched her way into the street, stopping only when she heard the sound of a carriage passing behind her.

"Sorry? Not as sorry as ye'll be fer in'erferin'." He lunged forward and grabbed her arm, but when she tried to kick at him, her leg became tangled in her long skirt. The man laughed as he flung her to the ground. His large, dirty hand raised for a blow, and Kendra closed her eyes against the pain she knew would follow.

"I would think twice before striking the lady," a deep voice boomed from just behind her.

Kendra's eyes flew open at the heavenly sound, and she turned to see Brice towering over them.

"The wench deserves a beatin'," the odious man said, his fist still poised in the air.

"To be certain," Brice answered, sparing Kendra a quick glance to ensure she was unharmed. "But not by you."

"Now, wait a minute," Kendra interjected after scrambling from harm's way, while the soot-covered lad clung to her skirts. "If *anyone* deserves punishment here, it's this lout for beating his own son."

The foolish woman was actually championing this street urchin? He turned a stern eye to her, then nodded toward his coach a few feet away. "Into the carriage before you cause further mishap."

Kendra shook her head. "Not without the boy. If we leave him here, this man will beat him."

How had he forgotten what a stubborn chit she was? She would be the death of them all yet. He assumed a bored expression, as if it were all a great nuisance. After brushing an invisible speck of dust from his shoulder, he asked, "How much for the lad?"

The heavy man glanced quickly at the coach, no doubt doubling his figure at the sight of the ducal crest emblazoned upon the door. "'E's me own flesh and blood, 'e is. I won't be sellin' 'im to no one. Ain't right."

"How much?" he asked again.

"'E's all I got since I 'urt me back. Without 'im, I'd 'ave no means."

"I sincerely doubt it. What is your name, sir?"

"Grimly."

"Your given name."

"That's it. Just Grimly."

Brice produced a small bag heavy with coins from his pocket and tossed it on the ground where it slid with a clatter before the portly man's feet. "Well then, Mister Grimly. If you invest this wisely, there should be more than enough to compensate for your son's loss."

Grimly scooped up the bag, opened it and poured out several coins that shone silver in his dirty palm. Then, as if he thought Brice might change his mind, he pocketed the money and fled down the alley, never stopping to spare a parting glance for his only son.

With that threat removed, Brice strode to Kendra's side. Wisely, she remained silent as he lifted the child into the carriage.

He turned to assist her, unable to keep his anger

dimmed now that she was safe. "Where is Alethea and why the bloody hell aren't you with her?"

She bravely met his gaze, although he could tell, from her pale visage, that the event had frightened her a great deal. Hell, she was lucky she wasn't hurt! Damned lucky.

"Your grandmother is at the apothecary's," she told him. "I think it's on Bond Street."

"You are nowhere near Bond Street, Miss Browning."

"I know. It's just that I caught this boy stealing. Oh, hell," she said, her eyes glistening. He resisted the urge to take her in his arms and comfort her. The streets of London were no place for a woman like her, and much like a child, she needed to be taught a lesson.

"He was stealing?" he prompted, a bit gentler than he should have, considering the fright she had given him.

"The kid stole this woman's purse and I tried to stop him. I didn't even think about it, it just happened, and before I knew it, here I was. Besides, the jerk should've never—"

"We'll discuss this matter later, Miss Browning," he said, deciding that the sooner they left this part of town, the better.

Her lips thinned in indignation. "I'm not a child, Monty. Besides, I was dutifully staying put at the jeweler's until—well, until this happened."

He helped her into the carriage, his hand gripping hers tightly. "You could have gotten yourself killed or hurt or worse." He held on to her hand for several long moments, trying not to decipher whatever it was that his heart whispered so insistently to him.

"I'm sorry to worry you, really. But the man was breaking the law! That was out and out child abuse and he deserves to be in—in Newgate at the very least."

Brice let go of her hand, his anger returning. He had half a mind to take her over his knee if it would cure her of her headstrong impulses. How could he possibly protect her from the world if she continually jumped into the middle of things—dangerous things—that she knew nothing about? "You forget yourself, Miss Browning. You are not the magistrate. You would also be hard-pressed to find anyone that would imprison a father for merely disciplining his son, especially one who had committed the crime which you have just mentioned."

Kendra climbed into the coach without his offered assistance. "That wasn't discipline, and you know it." The boy scurried into her lap the moment Brice entered and she wrapped her arms about his small form. "I can't imagine anything worse than seeing this poor child beaten by that pitiful excuse of a man. And that he could sell him at the drop of a hat!"

She began stroking the lad's hair. "Thank you," she said. "For helping him . . . and me."

"It was a very foolish thing you did," he said, thanking providence that he had chosen to take that particular street to avoid the heavy traffic on his way out of town.

The door snapped shut, and the child bolted from Kendra's lap. "Hey!" She grabbed at him, but missed.

"Let me out!" he cried, trying to open the door, even though the carriage had started moving.

Brice caught him around the waist, having to use two hands to keep him from squirming free. "Here now! What do you think you are doing? Sit and behave."

"Let me go!"

Kendra grasped the boy's shoulders. "The duke's only trying to help, you know."

The lad calmed at her soothing voice, after glancing quickly at Brice with renewed interest. Brice could almost see the wheels of the boy's mind working, when he quietly took his seat once more. Suspicious, Brice kept an eye on him, but he did nothing to cause further doubts as to his character.

When they reached the apothecary's, Alethea's carriage was still there, and Brice left to inform Alethea that he was taking Kendra home. The remainder of their journey passed in silence. He was too busy berating himself for leaving Kendra's safety and care to a foolish old woman.

Kendra, apparently lost in her own thoughts, stared out the window. Finally, as they neared Blackmoor Hall, she said, "I'm sorry."

Her apology surprised him. "That was a very dangerous part of town. Had I not chanced to be passing by—" He turned away without finishing.

Kendra did not try to talk to him again until the coach stopped before the front doors. "Do you want me to wait here for your grandmother? Or do you trust me to walk back to Briarwood on my own?"

"You're not returning to Briarwood." The words were out before he knew it.

"You mean not until Grandmère returns."

"I mean not at all."

Kendra looked as if she wanted nothing more than to jump out of the coach at that instant and flee to Briarwood herself—until she apparently remembered the sleeping boy in her arms.

Brice looked down at the boy, then back up at her. "It seems I've finally found the means to keep you from running off, Miss Browning, as you seem wont to do when all is not as you like. The boy will remain at Blackmoor Hall, until I can arrange a suitable home for him. If you want to be with him, you'll remain as well."

"I'm not going to run off. At least not for several months."

"Be that as it may, you shall stay here."

Kendra hugged the lad to her breast, and he was at once envious. "Why?" she asked.

"Today has proved that I can't trust Alethea to watch over you."

"You still think I'm crazy, don't you?"

"After today's performance, Miss Browning, I find I'm hard-pressed to think otherwise." With that, he turned his back on her and left her in the coach, just as a footman appeared to assist her. Kendra handed the sleeping boy over, then hopped out herself.

Brice thought to take refuge in his study, but before he made it through the door, she stopped him.

After a small, rather insolent curtsy, she asked, "What should I do now, oh master?"

He looked from her to the footman holding the grubby child in his arms, noting just how thin the boy actually was. "I suggest you give the lad a bath and then, if there's anything left of him after all that filth's removed, feed him."

"Whatever you say, Monty."

Ignoring her anger, and, once again, the way she massacred his family name, he stepped into his study, believing that at last he would have some peace, until Kendra poked her head in the door and asked, "Was there any particular place you wanted me to give him a bath? He's kind of dirty, and everything upstairs is—"

"There's a room just off the kitchens."

"How about a tub and some soap?"

"You'll find everything you need there."

"What about his clothes? He—"

Apparently the look he gave her was sufficient, for

she immediately shut up and backed from the room, closing the door with a firm click.

He sat down behind his desk to go over the stacks of ledgers from his various estates. Though he tried to bury himself in his work, his mind kept picturing Kendra lying on the ground with that ogre standing over her, ready to strike, all because she felt the need to champion a street urchin. He tried to picture Lady Caroline, the woman he hoped to make his wife, doing the same, but could not. Though she was a virtuous young woman, Caroline was no different from the rest of the *ton*. She would have pretended not to see what was before her eyes, or at the very most, expressed a word of pity for the poor boy's fate. But not Kendra. She was different from any woman he'd ever met, and somehow, even had it been a fire-breathing dragon and not some slovenly mortal after the boy, he didn't doubt for an instant that Kendra would not have hesitated to save the lad again.

Reminding himself that he had work to do, he turned his attention back to the ledger, pushing all thoughts of jade-colored eyes from his mind. When, after several attempts to add the same column of figures resulted in a different answer each time, he realized it was not visions of Kendra's eyes that kept him from concentrating. It was the racket coming from somewhere in the back of the house. When the cacophony of noises continued without any indication that it would ever let up, he decided to investigate.

The source was not difficult to find, nor did he have any doubt about Kendra's involvement. She had turned his life inside out from the moment he had dived into the sea and rescued her, and so it came as no surprise to discover she had done the same to his normally smooth-running household. Nevertheless, he did not expect to see the kitchen in such a condition. Though he could not recall the last time since childhood that he had set foot in the cook's domain, he was certain that the place was not usually in such disarray—no, disaster was a more apt description. A near empty sack of flour lay hanging from the table, what little remained of its contents spilling forth. Flour covered the floor, table, walls, and—he glanced up, almost afraid to look—yes, the ceiling.

As he crossed the floor, clouds of white powder poofed up from beneath his shoes with each step. In no way was he curious as to how any of this came to be. He knew. The shouts and screams and the sound of running feet from the room beyond told him he would find the culprits in there, one of which was sure to be a green-eyed enchantress.

He paused at the doorway. Cook—at least he thought it was Cook beneath her snowy-white dusting—ran from the room with her hands raised in defeat, swearing in French. Kendra, his sister, and her maid, Jenny, all doused with a liberal coating of flour, were chasing the lad around the filled tub, to no avail. Several rings of white footprints circled the bath, telling him that this had been going on for quite some time. Finally, the three women cornered the urchin, then herded him toward the water.

Kendra, her hands held out as if to keep him from slipping away, asked, "What's there to be afraid of?"

Jenny cocked her head to one side, examining the child. "He's probably never had one before."

Kendra laughed at that. "You won't die from a bath, you know." The youth's look told her he thought otherwise.

Jenny, not about to be undone by a mere slip of a lad, tried a different tactic. She got down on her knees and faced him. "What's yer name?"

"Tommy," he whispered.

"Well, Tommy," the maid said, "why don't you just take off yer clothes and hop in the water before it grows cold."

Tommy shook his head. Jenny reached out to stroke the boy's head, but he flinched out of the way.

"No one's going to hurt you, Tommy. We're all your friends. Now *please* get into the tub," Kendra said.

Tommy eyed the water, then the back door, as if deciding to make a run for it. Kendra, however, was quicker and grabbed him by his dirty shirt, nearly ripping it from his back. "Not so fast, little guy," she said, pulling him toward the tub. "I know you don't understand, but you're much better off here."

Once again, he started screaming, and Lady Cecily said, "You would think we were trying to beat him, not help him."

The three women were no match for the boy, however, and soon, flour aside, they were all nearly as filthy as he and had made little progress. Just when Kendra looked as if she were about to give up hope that they would ever get Tommy into the tub, she noticed Brice leaning against the door frame.

"Are you here to help?" she asked, from her position on the floor, while trying to keep a firm grip on one of Tommy's squirming legs.

Brice crossed his arms, trying hard not to smile. "Help? Actually, no. My intention was to stop this infernal noise."

Kendra, who was fast losing her grip, said between gritted teeth, "We're trying to give Tommy a bath."

"Ah, then that explains it. Have you ever thought that you are going about it all wrong?"

Tommy scissor-kicked his way free from Kendra's and Cecily's grasp. Only Jenny remained, her arms wrapped about his chest. It was apparent, though, that she would soon be losing her grip as well.

Brice took a step forward and picked Tommy up by his grubby arms until he was eye to eye with the youth, whose feet were now dangling about three feet off the floor. "Get into the bath," he said slowly, "and not another word until you're clean. Is that understood?"

The youth nodded frantically.

Brice lowered him to the ground and gave him a gentle push toward the tub. "Afterwards there'll be scones and anything else you might fancy, but only if you're clean." At the mention of food, the boy ripped off his clothes and nearly jumped into the tub of water.

Brice tossed Kendra a look meant to express his anger at having been interrupted. It was lost at the sight of her pert flour-tipped nose, and, once more, he had to resist the urge to smile. He must try to remember that he was displeased with her, a task made difficult when all he wanted to do was brush the flour from her face, her neck, her breasts . . . And not with his fingers, either. Only when he turned away to stare at the child in the tub did he recall exactly why he was angry with her. "Now, Miss Browning," he said, "I wish to speak to you in my study."

"But the bath."

"Jenny and my sister will manage quite well, I assure you."

Kendra looked at Cecily and Jenny, both women working furiously to scrub the boy clean. "But it's not right, your sister working—"

"As you can see, Cecily is quite content, and, much like you, she has a mind of her own. Now, Miss Browning, if you have no further argument?" He waved his hand toward the door and gave her a mock bow.

Kendra preceded him through the door and down the hallway to his study. When she reached for the door to open it he gently brushed her hand aside, then pushed the door open, allowing her to enter first.

She had never been in Brice's study before, but the moment she entered, she knew she was in a man's domain—the epitome of an English study, she was sure. Hunter green wallpaper combined with the rich, golden oak of the wall panels set off the room, giving it a warm, yet masculine look. Paintings of horses and fox hunts graced the walls. A large desk, situated in one corner, faced the length of the room and was surrounded by several comfortable chairs, no doubt for any business transactions made within the confines of this private world.

Brice shut the door behind them. "Please, be seated." His polite voice held an undercurrent of anger, and Kendra cringed at the thought of facing him alone in his territory.

She needed a place of advantage. "I'm kind of dirty from all the flour."

"Sit down."

Two wing chairs, in rich burgundy, were set before the lit hearth, and she immediately moved toward them, deciding she did not like the idea of confronting him across the wide space of his desk, nor seated beside him on the sofa situated on the opposite side of the room.

After she sat, Brice said, "Would you care for a drink, Miss Browning?"

"Must you always call me that? I've got a first name, you know."

"Was that a yes or a no, Miss Browning?"

Kendra thought him the most stubborn man she had ever met. "Fine," she said. "What do you have?"

"Brandy."

"No, thanks. It's too early for something that heavy."

A few moments later, he stood before her, holding his drink. Kendra waited for him to sit down, but he seemed perfectly content to stand before her, swirling the amber liquid in his glass.

"Well?" she asked, uncomfortable beneath his scrutiny.

Brice sipped his brandy, then set the glass upon the mantle. "About today—"

"Look, Monty," she said, hoping to head off another lecture. "I realize what I did today was foolish, but I couldn't just stand there and let the poor child have the daylights beaten out of him." When he was about to speak, she added, "I understand your concern and I won't do it again. I promise. So just let me return to Briarwood with Grandmère, and I'll stay out of your way."

"No."

"Why not?"

"Apparently Alethea's been unable to watch over you as she should."

"It wasn't her fault."

"On the contrary, Miss Browning. Any woman of her age should know better than to leave a young lady such as yourself unchaperoned for even a moment."

"Unchaperoned! Really, Monty, I'm not some innocent virgin who's never been around the block. Trust me. I've seen what goes on."

"You may have no concern for your reputation, but I do. At least as long as you're abiding under my roof, masquerading as part of my family. And since Alethea's been unable to properly escort you about, then you'll remain here, unless I personally accompany you. I'll not have you bring scandal and ruin upon—"

"I know. Upon the Montgomery name. I've heard that

lecture before." Kendra slumped back in her chair. "You're being totally unfair."

Brice seemed not to care.

"What about another chance?"

"I do not give second chances. Ever." It was said so quietly, she'd almost not heard it.

"On anything?"

"Never."

"Then you're losing out on something, your royalship. Everyone needs a second chance now and then, and one day you'll regret not giving it."

"I sincerely doubt it."

Kendra wondered what she could do to change his mind. After living with him on board his ship, though, she knew better. Still, she had to win his confidence somehow, if she was to have any sort of freedom. How could anyone so handsome be so damn stubborn? "All right, Monty, you win. What do I have to do to remain in your good graces?"

"You need only stay in this house until such time as I can make arrangements for your passage home."

"And just when might that be?"

"I've promised Alethea that I'll stay until the end of the season."

"You're out of your ever loving mind, Mister Duke, if you think I'm going to stay cooped up in this mausoleum until then. That's months away."

"However," he continued, as if never having been interrupted, "I shall endeavor to send you home earlier, if you feel you can't wait. Two of my ships have just arrived in port."

Great! That was *all* she needed, to be sent back home in the wrong century! "No thanks. If you can't take me, then I stay here." That would at least buy her the time to await the first full moon past the summer solstice to get her back to her own time.

"Under my rules."

"Fine. As long as you let me out of my cage once in a while."

"As I informed you earlier, Miss Browning, you're not a prisoner. However, you're not to leave this house unless accompanied by me personally. Is that clear?"

"Funny how our definitions of prisoner differ," she grumbled under her breath.

"I beg your pardon, Miss Browning?"

"Nothing." Kendra couldn't let her emotions get in the way. She must learn to conduct herself as a proper debutante—well, maybe not quite the debutante—if she was to find the way back to her own time, even if that meant following Brice's rigid rules and ignoring his incessantly formal use of her surname. "What else do you expect of me, my lord grace."

"Nothing more than what I've asked. I'll be very busy for the next several weeks attending to estate matters too long neglected. You will, of course, abide by all rules set forth."

"What is it you're worried about?" she said, without thinking. "That I'm going to spout off about motorboats and television?"

Brice closed the distance between them in one step. Placing his hands on the arms of her chair, trapping her beneath him, he leaned down, his face level with hers. "I thought it understood between us, that you would *not* repeat any such nonsense again."

Kendra's mind refused to function with Brice's mouth so very close to her own. The only clear thought in her head was the remembrance of the kiss they'd shared on board his ship. It had seemed so long ago and worlds away. Forgotten was any concern over what century she was in. Now, she wanted nothing more than to feel his mouth upon hers while his arms wrapped around her, holding her tight, never letting go. She wanted to tell him, to let him know, but she could only stare numbly while he gazed at her with barely leashed fury.

Brice took a slow, controlled breath. "Well?" When Kendra did not answer, he gripped her shoulders and lifted her from the chair until she was standing before him. "Answer me, Miss Browning."

Kendra moved her mouth to speak, but no words came forth. She felt hypnotized by his mouth and had to forcefully draw her gaze up. His midnight eyes flashed anger, fear and . . . was that passion? Suddenly, she heard herself speak, as if from a distance. "Kiss me."

He did. His mouth came down upon hers, forcing it open, allowing his tongue to mate with hers. It was not a gentle kiss, but Kendra didn't care. She slid her hands up, around his neck and pulled him closer, reveling in the feel of his arms as they wrapped tightly around her, one strong hand moving to her hips, pressing her against him. His desire was evident, and she wondered if he would make love with her, here in his study.

"Kendra," he whispered.

"Don't talk, Monty. Just kiss me."

Surprisingly, he kissed the tip of her nose, brushing his lips across it, soft as a feather. "Did I mention how fetching you look in flour?"

"No."

He ran his fingers through her hair and kissed her mouth once more. Then, when Kendra thought her blood was on fire, she felt his thumb caress her breast. An instant later, he had lowered the shoulders of her gown, and began kissing a trail down her neck. She cried out softly as she felt his mouth cover her, suckling gently. She wanted more. All of him. "Please, Brice."

He moved to the other breast, and Kendra knew she was melting the moment she felt his tongue teasing her. As her knees started to buckle, he reached down and scooped her up in his arms, carrying her to the sofa. He had not even set her down yet, when through the pounding of blood in her heart, Kendra heard someone knocking.

"Brice! Kendra! Come quick!" Cecily called from the other side of the door.

He cursed softly, then set Kendra on her feet, brushing the flour from his dark blue jacket while she straightened her bodice before he answered.

Kendra felt heat creep up her face when he strode to the door. Thankfully, he did not open it wide, allowing her a moment of privacy. His voice was curt when he asked, "What is it?"

"It's Tommy," Cecily replied. "He's run off."

8

Kendra ran to the door, all passion forgotten. "What do you mean he's run off?"

Cecily tearfully explained how they'd dressed him in the clothes borrowed from the cook's son, then left him in the kitchen for a moment. Cook apparently caught him stuffing something down his shirt and yelled at him. "He ran from the room," Cecily cried.

Kendra tried to push past Brice. "We've got to find him before he gets too far. He could get lost, or hurt. God, what if he tries to return to his father?"

Brice stopped her from leaving. "He's more than likely in the house, hiding. We'll arrange a search party. Cecily, you inform the housekeeper and have her assign a few servants to assist. Do the same with the outside help, in case he made it out without our knowing it. Make certain the gates are watched. Kendra and I will start on the top floor with the attic and work our way down."

Cecily left at once. As Kendra started out the door, Brice said, "One moment, Miss Browning."

"What now?" she asked, instantly regretting her angry tone.

"About what we were speaking of."

Kendra knew at once that he meant her talking about the future. "Oh, that," she said lightly. "I was going to tell you before we . . . um, well, anyway, when I said all that stuff about that other time, I realize now that it was all caused by a—a blow to my head. You see, it's all coming back to me now, slowly but surely, that I was on a little boat at the same time and day as you. I think that I was confused because . . ." She looked away, her eye straying to the book-lined walls. "Because I was reading a story—a fairy tale," she added smugly, meeting his gaze to give emphasis to her words. "It took place in the future. All those things I told you about were figments of some author's imagination."

Unfortunately, he looked as if he thought it was all a figment of *her* imagination. Even so, he surprised her by saying, "I'm pleased to hear you're coming to your senses." Perhaps he believed her after all. "Now about the other matter of what happened, I apologize for my ungentlemanly behavior. I should never have let things get so out of hand."

Kendra, dismayed, said, "But I asked you to kiss me."

"Nevertheless," he replied, once more his cool and reserved self, "what happened is something that should only occur between husband and wife. And since neither of us intends to marry the other, it will not occur again."

"Are you saying that you've never made love to someone you weren't married to?"

"Of course not. Gentleman of my station take mistresses, Miss Browning."

Although he did not exactly say he *had* a mistress, the

sudden thought of Brice making love to someone else sickened her. "How convenient."

She knocked his hand off her shoulder and stormed past him through the door, heading toward the stairs. Once again, he prevented her from continuing. "It will be easier if we take the back stairs," he said, guiding her down the hallway toward the rear of the house.

Brice lit a candle and led the way up the narrow staircase, opening several doors on each floor along the way but finding nothing. When they finally reached the attic landing, she said, "Look, Monty. If I should be offended, I want to know now."

"Offended?" He pushed the door open. The candlelight wavered in the musty draft.

"About what you said, in your study."

He turned to stare at her. "Might I inquire as to the direction of your thoughts?"

"About taking a mistress. I want to know what you meant by that."

"I don't follow."

She felt ridiculous for even bringing the subject up, but it was too late now. "You said a man of your station would take a mistress. Does that mean I'm not good enough? To be your mistress? Is that why you won't make love to me?"

A light flickered in his gaze, but she dismissed it as being the reflection of the candle's flame. "No, Miss Browning, it isn't." He turned away without clarifying his answer, and she followed in frustration.

After several minutes of traipsing through the dust-filled room, Kendra sneezed. "I don't think he's up here," she said.

"He's here, as I thought."

"Where?"

"He's hiding behind that chest over there," Brice replied in an amused voice, pointing across the room.

She sneezed. Through watering eyes she looked past the assorted pieces of furniture, statues, trunks, and paintings scattered about the attic. Although she didn't see him, she heard a distinct shuffling sound, too loud to be made by any rats, and, after wiping her eyes, noticed the distinct tell-tale footprints that marred the fine layer of dust across the wooden floor. "How did you know he'd be up here?"

"It's precisely where I would have hidden at his age."

"I refuse to believe you were *ever* his age," Kendra replied, miffed because his detective work far outshone hers.

"After the little incident in the study, Miss Browning, I can't picture *you* as a little girl."

Although Kendra knew he was teasing, she blushed just the same, and so, to keep him from seeing her embarrassment over her earlier forward behavior, she moved toward the chest.

"Tommy!" she cried. "What are you doing up here?"

The boy peeked over the top of the chest at Kendra, his now clean face pale with fear. "I'm not sorry I took the silver, and I ain't gonna come out. Never."

"But Tommy—" Kendra eyed the few pieces of silver flatware and one candlestick strewn beside him "—we only want to help you. You didn't have to steal these things."

"It wasn't fer me. I was savin' it fer someone."

"For who?"

"My sister, Bonnie. 'E's sure to send 'er out to the chimneys now I'm gone. And she's not big as me. I 'ave to go back."

Brice sat gently down beside him, leaning his back against the wall without care that he was sitting in the dust. "If I promise to get your sister for you, will you stay where you're told?"

Hope flooded the boy's face for an instant, then he shook his head.

"You can't help your sister by running away, young master."

"I ain't coming with you."

"Tell me, Tommy," Brice said, scratching his chin. "I thought I might return for your sister and bring her here. But with you up here . . ."

"I won't let you send me an' Bonnie to no orph'age. We'd run away, just like before."

"If you have a father, what were you doing in an orphanage?"

"'E ain't really our papa. 'E just makes us call 'im that so's they wouldn't take us back to the orph . . ." He looked up at Brice in question.

"Orphanage?"

Tommy nodded. "We didn't like it there and runned away. Mister Grimly found us. That's why I was cleanin' chimneys. At first 'e was nice, but when 'e ran out o' whiskey and there weren't no money to buy more, 'e blamed us, 'e did. 'E 'it my sister, 'e did."

Kendra moved closer and Brice waved his hand at her for silence. "Has he ever done this to Bonnie before?"

Tommy nodded. "But this time 'e was real drunk and passed out. She 'id in the alley 'til I got 'ome. That's why I stole that purse. There weren't no money to buy no whiskey or gin. And I didn't take the gruel fer me. It was fer Bonnie, only I lied so 'e wouldn't 'it 'er again."

"That was a very brave thing to do, Master Tommy. But now, we must get your sister. And to do that, I need your help."

Tommy's thin chest puffed out a bit. "You want *me* to help?"

"I'll need you to tell me exactly where I can find your sister. I assume it's in the same alley we found you?"

"Yes, sir."

"Then you and I must meet in my study where we can talk about this further. I need to know certain things about Mister Grimly that are better not mentioned in front of any lady's delicate ears. Things that only we men should know."

Tommy looked at Kendra, then nodded. "Men things," he repeated.

"Now do you think you can come with me to my study?" He stood and held out his hand. The boy grasped it and together, they left the room.

Kendra gathered up the silver and followed. "I'd like to get my hands on that Grimly fellow," she muttered to herself as she went to find Cecily to call off the search.

"I wonder what Brice will do?" his sister asked when Kendra found her.

"I don't know, but I intend to find out."

Kendra stood guard outside the study door, waiting for the two "men" to emerge. Several minutes later, Tommy appeared, looking as if the weight of the world had been lifted off his shoulders as he ran out the door heading toward the kitchen. Kendra entered. "Where's he going?"

"To apologize to Cook."

"I've never seen a boy so eager to apologize before."

"I told him if he was very nice, he might be able to coax her into making bread pudding for supper."

Kendra had to admire his skill at dealing with children. "So what was all this secret stuff you talked about away from my delicate ears?"

"I merely wanted to know if there were any weapons in Grimly's house."

"Are there?"

"A knife, but that seems to be it."

"Well, take my word for it, pretend there are guns in the house and act accordingly."

Brice cocked an eyebrow at Kendra. "Why, thank you, Miss Browning."

"I want to go with you when you pick up Bonnie."

"You'll remain here."

"But you can't go there alone. It's not safe."

"I'm quite aware of the dangers that may exist. And I don't intend to go alone."

"Well, at the least, after you pick Bonnie up, let the authorities know. That man deserves to be thrown in Newgate."

Brice strode over to his desk, and after unlocking a drawer, pulled out a small pistol. "Justice shall be served, Miss Browning. I promise you."

"You're not going to kill him?" she asked, watching him stuff the pistol into his waistband.

"I don't plan on it. Now if you'll excuse me. I have an appointment to keep."

9

The somber-faced butler showed Brice into the study of Hawthorne Manor, then backed out and shut the doors behind him. Brice strode toward the fire. The earl was seated nearby in an armchair, his legs stretched out before him. Beside him on a small Queen Anne table, laid out in precise neat rows, were tiny, dirt-covered artifacts: bits of terra-cotta, a few pieces of tarnished jewelry and coins with emperors' heads crowned in leaves. Several other tables in the large room displayed similar fare, all evidence of the earl's great passion in life: history.

"Hawk," Brice greeted, noting the earl's state of disarray from the tip of his sandy brown head to the toes of his once shiny Hessians. "Take a tumble from your horse or out digging for more lost civilizations?"

Lord Hawthorne looked up, his brown eyes showing fatigue. "If that were all, I'd feel infinitely better. How was your voyage?"

Brice helped himself to a glass of brandy from one of the crystal decanters on the table between them, then took a seat near his friend. "Other than a storm that threw my ship off course for a while, smooth sailing 'til the end."

"The end?" Hawk queried. "It's true then, what I heard? That the *Eterne* was set upon by pirates?"

"By Parkston, you mean." He watched closely for Hawk's reaction, as Parkston was considered a close friend of the earl's family.

Lord Hawthorne did not look the least bit offended. "It's hard to believe a man as spineless as Parkston capable of piracy. Still, I've long told my mother that he's nothing more than a knave. She, however, insists on maintaining her friendship with him because of his wife. She refuses to believe that sweet Cousin Anne would have married him if he were naught but a scoundrel. You must admit that Parkston dotes on her."

"True."

"Even so, because of Mother's misconstrued beliefs, I'm forced to face him at every social event she hosts."

"The hazards of being a dutiful son, my friend," Brice said, lifting his glass in a mock toast.

"Have you seen Lady Caroline?" Hawk asked abruptly, his brown eyes flashing with something akin to anger. But then, upon second glance, they were calm once more, and Brice thought perhaps he had imagined it. Hawk well knew of Brice's intentions concerning Lady Caroline, and would never overstep the boundaries of their friendship by furthering his own relationship with her.

"I haven't," he answered. "Now, about the reason you summoned me?"

Hawk drained his glass of port, then after pouring himself another, said, "You should really try some. It's excellent."

Brice eyed the heavy wine in his friend's crystal goblet with distaste. "No, thank you," he said, thinking that even after all these years, he still could not stomach the stuff his father had drunk day after day. "You were saying? About your missive?"

"Ah, yes. I've tried to go at this alone, but it's too much. Why, just this afternoon, I found the remains of another fire. Couldn't be more than a day, maybe two, old. You've seen nothing since you've been back?"

Brice shook his head. Nothing but a green-eyed siren each time he closed his eyes. "I was in London last night."

"Damn. If there was some sort of pattern, we might be able to discover something. Set a trap at the least. But as it is, on the rare occasions my men have noticed the fires, naught is left but ashes. It's almost as if they're forewarned, or perhaps able to disappear at a moment's notice."

"Nothing unusual about this one?"

"There was no murder, this time. Not that I could tell, and believe me, I searched every bloody inch of that place. Perhaps, though, you'd better have a look yourself."

"I'll do so come morning."

Hawk was silent for a moment. "Maybe it won't happen again."

"We can't count on that."

"I know. It's just so damned frustrating." He drained his glass as if to wash away whatever thoughts he had pictured in his mind. "If it were only those damned occasional bonfires, but I've counted three murders since you've been gone. All the same: young girls, all gently bred, the last one being a squire's daughter. Radcliff."

"Radcliff's daughter, Sabrina?" He pictured the sweet yellow-haired girl, recalling the last time he had seen her, several months ago at a soiree in London, flirting outrageously with Lord Hawthorne until her mama dragged her away, fearful that Hawk's rakehell reputation might sully her daughter's chances for a husband.

"Yes. Sabrina. It just doesn't make sense. The Runners I've hired have turned up nothing. And the men I've posted refuse to stand guard for fear that the place is haunted."

"Perhaps the murders aren't related to the fires?"

Hawthorne shook his head. "There's no doubt in my mind. All in the Circle near the Druid's Cave. You'll see for yourself. Can you go tomorrow?"

"Of course." Brice sipped his brandy, then set his glass down. "Not to change the subject, but I have a favor to ask of you tonight."

"Oh?"

"I need your assistance in town." He told his friend about the incident involving Tommy and the discovery of the boy's sister still in London, while very neatly skirting the issue of Kendra's involvement. There was time enough later to explain how she came to be situated at Blackmoor Hall.

"Why are we waiting? I've a fair amount of frustration that can be put to better use than drowning it in a bottle of port."

Brice smiled grimly. "As do I, my friend. As do I."

A few hours later, Brice lifted the sleeping child into his arms and carried her from his carriage into the house. He and Hawk had little trouble retrieving her from the ramshackle hovel Grimly lived in. Brice rubbed his bruised knuckles, thinking at the time that Grimly had deserved far more than the simple blow Brice delivered in his moment of anger at the sight of little Bonnie, bruised and dirty, hiding in a corner of the dingy room. The man put up little fight, though he was angered at Brice's suggestion that he work to pay off the money he wrongfully acquired for Tommy. But that was over now, and Grimly would receive his just reward and more for all his sins, past and present, by working on one of Brice's ships. One bound for China.

Brice handed Bonnie to a servant, with instructions to bathe her, then to put her in the same bed with Tommy. A moment later, he and Hawthorne shut themselves in his study.

Hawk immediately sank into one of the wing chairs facing the hearth. He stretched out before the fire while Brice poured their drinks.

"So tell me about this chit you so gallantly rescued."

Brice handed him his brandy snifter, then sat in the matching chair. A vision of Kendra flashed in his mind as clearly as if she were seated before him. "Sometimes I don't quite know what to think of her. One moment she's as sane as you or I, and the next, she's short one sheet, spouting off about strange and unusual things."

"Is that so very different from any female you're acquainted with?"

"You have a point. Still, she's easily the most exasperating woman I have ever met. Her notions of right and wrong are ludicrous and she refuses to listen."

Hawthorne smiled at his friend over the rim of his glass. "Are you trying to convince yourself or me?"

"Quite simply, I don't know. One moment I want to kiss her senseless, the next I want to strangle her."

"True love."

Brice laughed. "Hardly, my friend. You have only to meet her to understand. Perhaps you can tomorrow after I ride out to inspect the latest fire at the Druid's Cave. Besides, I want your opinion on her. My aunt insists on introducing her into society with Cecily in tow."

"Is that so very terrible?"

"I believe so. The *ton* will flail her to shreds. She has absolutely no concept of how to conduct herself in polite society. I don't want to see her hurt."

"Perhaps you merely don't want to share," his friend offered shrewdly.

Brice said nothing, wondering if, indeed, his friend might be correct.

After Hawk left, Brice stepped from his study, intent on retiring for the night. The thought died as he glanced into the open library door and saw Kendra asleep on the sofa. She looked so fragile lying there, and that unfamiliar surge of emotion swept through him again. True love? He scoffed, recalling Hawk's taunt. Absolutely not. He had no need for such a trivial emotion.

Still, as he regarded her sleeping form, with her burnished-gold tresses fanned out upon the damask pillow, he knew there was something about her that made him want to shield her from all harm. He couldn't explain the terror he had felt the moment he had recognized her lying on the ground at Grimly's feet. It had been all he could do not to kill the man then and there.

She stirred, her green eyes lighting up when she saw him. She smiled drowsily. "Hello, Monty."

Her sleepy voice warmed him—the tug on his heartstrings scared him. "Bonnie's safe upstairs with her brother."

At the mention of the little girl's name, she pushed herself up, then rubbed her eyes. "Thank you, Brice."

Kendra threw her arms around him, surprising him by the force of her hug. "I knew you wouldn't let me down," she whispered in his ear.

The overwhelming urge to wrap his arms around her, pulling her tight, consumed him. He was fighting a losing battle.

He leaned back to look into the eyes of this woman who infuriated him so. On impulse, he reached out and stroked the softness of her cheek. "Sometimes, Miss Browning, I do not quite know what to make of you."

She looked surprised by his show of tenderness. "Why not?"

"Do you not know, sweet Kendra?" And then he kissed her. From the moment his lips touched hers, fire exploded in his heart, burning a path to his loins where it pooled like molten lava, fighting for release. He wanted to bury himself within her, to match his heat to hers, but dared not act upon his desire. Even so, not until he had drunk his fill of the honeyed sweetness of her mouth did he let her go, and then, only because the library door was standing wide open. When he set her from him, ignoring the strain of his manhood against his breeches, it was to see that she was just as affected by their kiss. Her breasts rose and fell in rapid succession with each breath as if she had run a great distance. Her eyes had turned a smoky green, and he longed to stoke the fires within.

"Brice?"

Her soft voice shook him to awareness. What was he thinking? Had he not just promised that very afternoon he would never allow himself to kiss her again? She was his guest, after all, and deserved to be left alone, despite that he wished otherwise. "Yes, Miss Browning?"

"Miss Browning?" she repeated. Several seconds passed by as all passion fled from her now narrowed eyes. "*Miss Browning*? Why is it that I'm beginning to notice a pattern here?"

"Pattern?"

"Yes. This Miss Browning stuff's gone too far. My name is Kendra. Capital K. E-N-D-R-A. Ken-dra. Get it?"

"Get it?" he echoed, more confused than ever.

"You're as bad as Jack, sometimes." She folded her arms across her chest, her expression one of pure obstinacy.

Brice recalled her mentioning Jack before. Her beau, if he remembered correctly. "You're comparing us?" The thought astounded him.

"Compare? What's there to compare? You're both pig-headed men!"

"You needn't shout, Miss Browning, or need I remind you that there are children sleeping above now."

Kendra stood, then stalked past him to the library door which she slammed shut. "There. Is that better, *your dukeship*?"

"I believe you mean your grace?"

"Whatever."

"Perhaps, you'd care to enlighten me as to this grave offense I've committed?"

"By all means," she said, returning to stand before him. "You call me Kendra when you kiss me, then Miss Browning when the fun's over and you're ready to play *formal* friends. For instance," she clarified, "you kissed me, then obviously thought better of it, so you stood up and called me Miss Browning. You do it every time you want to distance yourself from me. Next time, try running away. It's less obvious."

"There is, of course, a point to all this?"

"The point?" She turned away from him, but not before he saw the glisten of unshed tears upon her dark lashes. "No, I have *no* point."

He hesitated, unsure. How had he let this slip of a

woman wrap herself so tightly around his emotions? He knew now, what she meant. He *had* been doing exactly what she said. For the most part. But he could not let himself get involved any more than he already was. Not when she had been so adamant on being returned home at the first opportunity. "One of my ships is leaving tomorrow for America. If you so desire—"

She crossed her arms tightly about her. "Forget your ship, Monty. I'm staying 'til the end of the season."

"You have changed your mind then?"

"Yes."

He refused to acknowledge that small voice in his head that said he was glad she was staying—the same voice that whispered of the opportunity for an illicit affair. Although not an aristocrat, she was a respectable young lady, and as such, deserved an offer of marriage— if such liberties were taken—something that *he* could not give her. But how then could he possibly live in the same house with her, when simply to look at her from across the room caused not only his heart to ache, but his loins as well?

"My apologies, Miss Browning. I didn't mean to offend you. As I mentioned before—"

She put her hands over her ears. "Stow it, Monty. I don't want to hear it."

"What don't you want to hear?"

She spun around to face him, the tears spilling over her lashes. "Admit it. You don't want me here!"

"Want you, Miss Browning?" He closed the distance between them, grasping her shoulders and pulling her close until her exquisite face with those liquid green eyes was mere inches from him. "Not a minute of the day goes by when I don't think how much I want you. And whether I call you Miss Browning or Kendra makes no difference. The desire's still there. It refuses to go away, no matter how I try to convince myself otherwise."

Brice brushed the tears from her cheeks, before reluctantly letting her go. Then he strode toward the door. As he opened it, he turned to her and added, "The question is, Miss Browning, if you knew me at all, would you want me?" With that, he left the room.

10

Kendra stared at the empty doorway. Of course she wanted him! That was the point. Or was it? Truthfully, she couldn't think of one valid reason for her sudden outburst just a few minutes ago. Who cared if he called her Miss Browning? It certainly beat Ken, or even just plain Browning, as most of her fellow officers called her. In fact, when she thought about it, "Miss Browning" was really kind of cute. It was just that he was so damned formal, so unlike the dashing captain aboard the *Eterne*. Wanted him? Hell, yes, she wanted him! Almost as much as she wanted to go home. If only she could have both.

An impossibility, she thought, deciding there were more important matters she needed to deal with, such as figuring out if what that old druid had said was true. Would the door to her world really open on the first full moon after the summer solstice?

An outlandish thought struck her. What if this time-travel business was not as accidental as she'd once thought? She twisted a strand of hair around her finger as she stared into the fire. Botolf did say that the moonstone found her, and not the other way around. What if she was meant to come to this time to accomplish something that couldn't be done by anyone else? And how was she ever going to do this monumental task if she had to make everyone believe that she was from the nineteenth century? Worse, yet, what if, when the time came, she'd not accomplished this task, and her Druid's Light decided to find someone else?

Things had been a good deal easier for Dorothy Gale of Kansas, she thought, falling to the sofa in a very unladylike manner. Everyone knew Dorothy was from another place and time. "Hard to miss with a house dropping from the sky," she muttered.

"A house from the sky? Whatever do you mean?" Lady Cecily peeked in the doorway, then drifted across the room in a light silk wrapper and sat down next to her.

"Nothing. What are you doing up so late?"

"I thought to find a rather boring book to read, in hopes it would put me to sleep. But since you're still awake— Is aught amiss?"

"Hmm? Oh, no. I was just trying to figure out why I was brought here. You know, kind of a fate thing. If Brice hadn't saved me, I wouldn't have been there to save Tommy, who in turn led us to save Bonnie." The thought bore merit.

"Well, then. The only one left in need of saving is Brice."

"His *immortal* soul?" Kendra quipped.

"No. His heart. 'Tis quite in need of saving."

"Assuming your brother had a heart."

"Oh, he does. He's merely forgotten it exists. Within a day or two Brice will be so involved in all his business pursuits that he'll scarce remember we exist. He'll either lock himself in his study to conduct estate matters, or leave on another voyage, all for the sake of money." She fingered the silk of her wrapper. "It's quite nice having wonderful things, but it would be much nicer to have Brice at home instead."

"Well, you still have Grandmère."

A bittersweet smile turned up the corners of Cecily's lips. "Dear Grandmère. If not for her, I'd be ever so lonely. I only wish Brice—well, sometimes he can be rather cool toward her."

"I'd noticed. You were saying the other day that that's why he calls her Alethea and not Grandmère?"

Cecily nodded sadly. "It's his way of refusing to acknowledge his heritage, as if somehow doing that will erase all of Papa's mistakes." She sighed and looked into the fire. "Grandmère does not blame him though, for when you're raised to be a duke, you're taught at birth that the family name comes first, and honor is everything. I, for one, would never want to be a duke or a duchess. Not if it meant living without love."

"Neither would I," Kendra agreed, "want to live without love, that is."

Much later, as she readied herself for bed, she realized that she wanted Brice more than she cared to admit. She loved him and every starkly formal bone in his body. Her lips still ached from his kiss, leaving her wishing for more. Somehow, she'd have to remedy that. She'd seduce him. Tomorrow night. *An easy enough prospect*, she thought.

An impossible prospect, she discovered the next morning. At breakfast, Alethea informed her that Brice had set sail. For America. An unexpected trip, she'd said. Kendra suspected otherwise. He did *not* want her at all.

Why else would he take off on a voyage expected to last for several months? She hid her hurt even as the remembrances of the days they'd spent together on board the *Eterne* lingered in her mind like a cherished dream. Instead, she concentrated on her purpose for being in this time. And tried to determine exactly what that purpose was.

The passing days drifted into months, and the warming weather coaxed the flowers from their spring pastels to riots of bold summer blooms. The nights, the nights were all the same: hours of loneliness with only the dreams of the softness of the sea beneath Kendra's bed, gentle waves lapping against the sides, rocking her to sleep with the whispered memories of the sound of Brice's voice, the vague recollection of the fire in his touch . . . . And then morning always came, and with the warm light, the cold reality that she would probably not see Brice again before she left.

Despite the depression that usually overtook her in the early hours of the day, she looked forward to her lessons on how to conduct herself in society. Under Grandmère's careful tutelage, Kendra learned everything from curtsying to the proper forms of address. Visitors came and went as she practiced her newfound manners at tea, and, as promised, every Wednesday Kendra attended the meetings of the Ladies' Charitable Society with Alethea. It was there she actually learned some of her best lessons, sitting quietly and listening to the aristocratic ladies discuss the latest *on dit*, as Alethea would say. "Did you hear that Lady Rosewood was seen coming from Lord Stantford's carriage? One wonders what her husband would think," one matron said.

"The gown Lady Edwina wore to the opera last night was *quite* beyond the pale," another would comment.

Occasionally, however, the meetings were actually used to encourage charitable acts from the ladies present, and it was during these times that an idea of what Kendra might do to help London's destitute children formed in her mind. She wanted to start a shelter so that other children would not have to suffer what Tommy and Bonnie lived through.

Not just any shelter would do, however. Hers must be run by people who cared, and there were many who cared in the Ladies' Charitable Society. All they needed was guidance, Kendra realized after only a few meetings. Guidance and access to money, for though several of the women were from exceptionally wealthy families, or married to wealthy men, they had no control of the purse strings.

What Kendra needed to do was to convince their very rich family and friends to donate money to so worthy a cause. Unfortunately, time had swept by and she had little left to her. The summer solstice was nearly upon them.

"I must have a season, or part of one, since I'll be gone before it's over," she told Grandmère one afternoon as they took tea in the salon. Kendra and Cecily had spent the morning riding, and it was Cecily who had pointed out the necessity of expanding her social standing to increase any expected donations. Unfortunately, Brice had left explicit orders that *she* was not to attend any social functions without him. Before, the restriction had not bothered her, and Cecily and Grandmère had seemed quite content to stay at home with her. But now, having been at Blackmoor Hall for several months, she had a purpose. "If my shelter's going to succeed, I have to have the support of more than just the ladies in our group."

Cecily nodded. "The Seftons' ball is tonight. I thought it the perfect place for our dear cousin to make her first appearance in society."

"A commendable idea, my dear," Alethea replied. "I shall bring up the subject to his grace this very moment."

"He's home?" Cecily cried.

Kendra, almost afraid to hope, looked to Grandmère for confirmation.

"I just spoke to him not five minutes ago."

As if on cue, Brice appeared in the doorway. Kendra feasted her eyes on the beloved sight of his tanned face. Was it her imagination, or was he looking at her with the same hunger in his eyes?

"Cecily. Miss Browning," he said, nodding his head in greeting. "I trust you fared well during my absence?"

She wanted to scream. If dreaming about him every night for weeks on end, wishing he'd materialize in her bed, in her arms, meant she'd fared well. "Yes, I did. Too bad you weren't around—"

"As you know, Brice," Grandmère interjected, "anyone who's anyone will be at Lord and Lady Sefton's tonight. I'm certain you wouldn't want Miss Browning to miss such a wonderful opportunity."

"No," Brice replied succinctly, and Kendra wished she'd not been so curt—maybe he wouldn't have turned her down so fast. "Excuse me, Alethea, ladies, Hawk awaits me in my study." With a slight bow, he quit the salon, leaving Kendra, Grandmère and Cecily staring at the vacant doorway.

"Well, hell," Kendra muttered, breaking the silence at last, "the least he could do was stick around and let us convince him. Now I'll never get to know enough people to solicit donations for my children's shelter." That wasn't the full reason for her disappointment. She'd missed him and he didn't seem to care.

Cecily looked ready to do battle. "We'll just have to

change his mind. Better yet, we shall go without him. He'll never notice you in the crush."

"If the way he notices me around here's any indication, it's almost guaranteed." In her heart—now that it had calmed since seeing Brice after so long an absence—she yearned for his acceptance. She'd not toiled over lessons in etiquette, dance and other niceties of society merely in hopes others wouldn't think her insane. She did it for Brice. She wanted to see his midnight eyes shine with approval. She'd pictured him returning from his voyage, seeing her across a ballroom floor, surprised by her transformation. He'd ask her to dance. She'd accept. . . . Kendra stared at the vacant doorway, wondering what excuse she might come up with to interrupt his meeting. With so little time left in this century, she wanted to spend each moment in his company despite his indifference to her.

"And in the future," Cecily continued, drawing Kendra's attention back to the matter at hand, "Grandmère could make it a point to go over each and every invitation with Brice to determine which he plans on accepting. Once we know which he's chosen, we'll be certain to steer well clear."

Lady Alethea, however, shook her head. "That will simply not do, my dears. Kendra must have his grace's support and introduction if she's to succeed at all with her plans for the children's shelter. I'd hoped he might capitulate on this evening's entertainment. To be accepted by the Seftons would all but guarantee admittance to the highest circles even if we were not sponsoring you."

Kendra dropped onto the sofa, earning a disapproving look from Grandmère. "Sorry," she said, mentally reminding herself that *ladies sit gracefully, and never give in to their urgings for comfort.*

Grandmère smiled. "You'll remember in time. You're a very adept student, Kendra, and other than your charming accent and the occasional slip of the tongue now and then, one would never guess that you were not brought up in high society. No one from the Ladies' Charitable Society suspects that you're not what you seem."

"Then why does it matter if I have Brice's approval? I'm only a house guest."

"Even so," Grandmère answered, "should Brice arrive at a ball, see you and, given his misguided notions of protecting you, drag you out, or worse yet, give you the cut direct—"

"I get the picture. I *mean*," Kendra amended, "I understand completely. But how do you intend to change his mind? Besides, there'll be other balls besides the Seftons' tonight. The season's not ended yet." But her time was nearly up, she thought sadly.

"Dismiss it as the prattling of an old woman, but I can't help but feel strongly that you must attend tonight," Alethea informed her. "As for how *you* intend to change his mind, I'll leave that in your very capable hands. Brice has a visitor, Lord Hawthorne. Since you've been unable to charm Brice into allowing you to go, not that it's your fault, you must simply charm his friend, Hawk. The two are extremely close, and Brice will undoubtedly capitulate under his friend's pressure."

"You want me to go in there, right now, and flirt with his friend? An earl, no less?"

"Of course not!" Alethea responded. "We'll let them relax for a short while, take some refreshment perhaps." Her Mona Lisa smile appeared. "And then, you shall do exactly that."

*   *   *

The earl of Hawthorne was seated in one of the chairs, one booted foot propped casually upon an andiron, when Brice entered his study.

"I'm assuming you came to see the ring?" Brice asked.

"Yes."

Brice strode to his desk and opened the drawer. After rummaging beneath a few papers, he pulled out a large gold ring, then returned to Hawk's side and handed it to him.

"You say you found this the day after I told you to search the Druid's Cave?" Hawk asked, examining the ring closely. "I scoured the area myself and found nothing." His eyes narrowed as he looked up at Brice. "Why didn't you tell me of this before you left on your last voyage?"

"There was no time." If he hadn't left when he did. . . . Christ, but he'd been a fool. To think that by sailing away, putting a mere ocean between himself and that green-eyed siren would lessen his desire for her. "Like you," he said, shaking such useless thoughts from his mind, "I searched the area in vain. Even so, I was in a hurry to make it to my ship, and only discovered it by accident."

"Assuming that it truly belongs to the murderer, what is your opinion?"

"Judging from the crack in the band, I'd hazard a guess that its owner did not intend to lose it. In spite of the minor defect, the ring's quite well made, and heavy with gold."

"Which would lead you to believe that its owner had the funds to commission such a piece."

"Quite so. And my intuition tells me our man's not of the merchant class, which leaves only us."

Hawk tensed visibly, then shifted in his chair. "Us?"

"The nobility, my friend." Brice moved to the fire. "Those individuals who have nothing better to do than waste their time on meaningless pursuits that feed their appetites for debauchery. Surely, even at the tender age of thirty-two, you can recall the scandal of the Hell-Fire Club many years back?"

Hawthorne nodded slowly, as if what Brice said were finally sinking in, but then he shook his head suddenly. "No. Even they'd not murder."

"Who'd tell on them if their victims were dead?"

"But surely that heinous association hasn't been revived?"

"I sincerely doubt it," Brice said, "unless its members have risen from their graves. But perhaps the murders committed in the midst of our woods have been fashioned after it. Someone who's very much aware of the history of the Club. You're certain you found no additional clues? The Bow Street Runners have turned up nothing?"

"Merely a peasant caught poaching in the woods. He recalled seeing a black-hooded figure, voices chanting, and the fires of course."

Brice paced the room. If only he had not stayed away so long on that last voyage, just after his father committed suicide—or, at the least, if he had not dismissed that first incident just before he left as one isolated murder— things might have been different. But for some reason he had felt compelled to make that voyage.

The compulsion had stayed with him up until the moment he received Hawk's letter calling him back. Or was it when he found Kendra? He was not certain, nor was he sure whether he wanted to examine the issue too closely. Especially after the ridiculous notion popped into his head that he was somehow *meant to find her*.

Such thoughts accomplished nothing. He'd spent the past few months trying *not* to think of her, to no avail. Frustrated, Brice looked down, realizing he still gripped the ring, the only solid piece of evidence to this mystery. Opening his hand, he saw that the face of the ring had pressed against his palm, leaving its mark embedded in his flesh: two semi-circles, one large, one small, balancing one atop the other.

After tossing the ring onto his desk, he rubbed his palm with the thumb of his other hand until all traces of the strange symbol vanished into one red mark. "Just before I set sail, my sister mentioned seeing a fire at the ruins, certain she'd seen *druids* dancing around it. I dismissed it as her childish imagination. I had no idea it was related."

"I, too, am to blame. After the first few incidents, I tended to think it nothing that couldn't be stopped simply by putting a few men to stand sentry in the woods. Despite my efforts, the murders happened just the same. But for now, it seems to have stopped."

"Let's hope it remains so."

Kendra knocked upon the door, her stomach fluttering much like it did when she was called into the captain's office at work—only the man behind the door was not her captain, and she had committed no violation of departmental procedures. Why then was she feeling so nervous about a simple flirtation? Because she was not the flirting kind, and Brice was bound to see it for what it was, a lie.

Just as she thought to turn away, having talked herself completely out of such a foolish venture, Brice called out, "Enter."

Dismayed to see her hand tremble, she opened the door and stepped into his study. Brice was standing before the fire, while in the chair beside him was, she presumed, the earl of Hawthorne.

"Your grace," she said, grateful for Alethea's endless lessons, although she was still a bit confused as to exactly *why* Brice wasn't addressed as my lord. "I thought I might have a word with you about my children's shelter. Would it be an . . ." Her voice trailed off at the sight of his tense features. This was not the relaxed atmosphere Grandmère had thought it would be.

"Excuse me." She realized that this was not at all an opportune time to try to charm Brice or his friend into anything. "I'll come back later."

The man in the chair rose. He stood nearly as tall as Brice, and he brushed back a lock of sandy blonde hair that fell upon his forehead, just above slightly darker brows. His expression, every bit as stern as Brice's, softened as his piercing brown eyes regarded her with interest. Strikingly handsome, he reminded Kendra of Jack, and she decided it would not be so very difficult to flirt with him after all.

Ignoring Brice completely, she shut the door and moved into the room, then turned her brightest smile on the man beside him. She dropped into a curtsy. "You must be Lord Hawthorne."

"Yes." Hawthorne smiled back, while quickly closing the distance between them. Kendra allowed him to take her hand in his.

Brice moved forward, almost possessively. "Miss Browning, permit me to introduce Henry, Lord Hawthorne. Hawk. This is Miss Kendra Browning."

Hawthorne looked stunned, all the while keeping his gaze glued to Kendra's face. "This charming creature's the girl you so valiantly pulled from the sea? You must take me on your next voyage, Brice, for I vow that no lovelier mermaid exists." He bowed over her hand, bestowing a chaste kiss on the back. "Miss Browning, are there more of you swimming around to lure sailors into the murky seas?"

"You're far too kind, my lord," she said demurely, searching her mind for something—anything—old-fashioned to say. "I vow, I'm unused to such flattery. 'Tis almost overwhelming. And me without my hartshorn."

Hawthorne drew her to the settee where he positioned himself next to her, still grasping her hands in his. "Rest here, Miss Browning, and let me drink in your beauty."

And Kendra thought that *she'd* overdone it! Sparing a quick glance toward Brice, she saw he looked anything but pleased. A trill of pleasure curled through her at the thought that he might be jealous. "My lord," she said, returning her attention to the earl, to look at him through lowered lashes. "You embarrass me with such talk."

He laughed, as if sensing that she toyed with him. "Nonsense. A woman as lovely as you should be told so every moment of every day. I'd wager you never lack at hearing such things."

Kendra looked directly into his smiling brown eyes. "I assure you, kind sir, were that the case, I might think your words true. But, alas, you're the first who's ever commented on such a thing as my alleged beauty."

Hawk raised one of her hands to his lips, where he allowed it to linger for a moment before saying, "I see now why Brice has conspired to hide you from the rest of the world, allowing only himself the pleasure of your company. I'd certainly do the same if I thought I might get away with it."

From the corner of her eye, Kendra saw Brice's

expression darken. He took one step toward them. "I have *not* conspired to keep her all to myself."

Kendra leaned toward Hawthorne. "He won't even allow me to have a season," she whispered loudly.

"What?" Hawk demanded, as if appalled. "A crime that must not continue, I say. Why, I myself will remedy the situation at once. Lord Sefton's giving a ball this very eve, and I'd be most honored if you were to accompany me."

"My lord, you must not tease me so."

"I tease you not, Miss Browning. Tell me, do you care for things historical?"

"What?" The sudden subject change confused her.

"Forgive me. But history is something I'm very fond of. What think you of digging and traipsing around the countryside looking for artifacts?"

"I suppose I've never given it much thought."

He appeared crestfallen. "It matters not. Even so, Miss Browning, I'd very much like to escort you to the Seftons' tonight."

"It would be an honor, my lord."

Brice's words cut short the victory that seemed so close. "But quite impossible."

Hawk stood up. "And why is that?"

"She has absolutely no idea how to conduct herself in society."

"Why, Miss Browning's manners are impeccable," Hawthorne defended. "So much so that I begin to wonder if you don't have ulterior motives. If so, then speak up, for I wouldn't want to tread in dangerous waters."

Brice remained silent, apparently uncomfortable with whatever his friend implied. What that might be, Kendra had no idea, since it was clear that Brice was not the least bit interested in her. In the back of her mind, she knew he was merely worried that she was, at the least, slightly mad with her tales of the future, and as such, likely to bring ruin upon the great name of Montgomery.

Hawthorne's fists clenched at his sides. "Are you saying that you're no longer considering the possibility of a betrothal to Lady Caroline?"

Betrothal? To Lady Caroline? Who the . . . the bloody hell was that? She tried to remember if she'd met a Lady Caroline at any of the Ladies' Charitable Society meetings. Her mind scanned the names and faces of the women she remembered: Lady Winterowd and Lady Burlington. Oh God! Wasn't there a Lady Throckmorton with a niece named Lady Caroline? There was, she remembered, and worse yet—assuming this was the *same* Lady Caroline—she was a beautiful and very petite brunette. And nice too, she recalled with dismay, holding her breath as she awaited Brice's answer.

"Well?" Hawk asked. "Do you intend to cry off?"

"I mentioned nothing of the sort," Brice replied sternly.

Kendra looked down, not willing to let either man know she was hurt by this sudden turn of events. Opening a children's shelter was her first priority, and getting home her next. And to do the former, she needed to be introduced to society, Brice's betrothal be damned!

"Well, then," Hawk demanded. "What reason can you possibly have for denying Miss Browning the simple pleasure of a London season?"

Kendra felt Brice's gaze upon her. "Miss Browning?" he asked. She stared at the thick Aubusson at her feet. "Kendra?"

At the sound of her name, she looked up at him, careful to keep the hope from her eyes.

"Do you desire Hawthorne's company at Lord Sefton's ball?" A knock on the door prevented her from answering. "Enter," he called out, without taking his gaze from Kendra's.

Alethea poked her head into the room. "Brice?"

He ignored his grandmother. "Do you want Lord Hawthorne to take you?"

Somehow, Kendra knew she was doomed no matter what she said. "I do."

"Alethea?" Brice asked, without the slightest indication he was upset.

"I had just wondered if Kendra might be in here," she replied brightly. "Cecilia and I were about to take tea, and wanted her to join us. We'd thought to discuss the latest news on a building we inquired about for the children's shelter." Turning to Lord Hawthorne, she asked, "You recall little Bonnie and Tommy?"

"Yes. What happened to them?"

"They are being cared for by the sister of Cecily's maid, Jenny, and are doing quite well, thank you. Anyway, after that incident, dear *cousin* Kendra has joined the Ladies' Charitable Society and come up with the splendid idea of opening a shelter for children."

The earl glanced at Kendra with renewed interest. "But there are already workhouses and orphanages for such a thing."

"Not just orphaned children," Kendra explained, "children who need a second chance at life, a helping hand to escape the misery of beatings and abuse suffered at the hands of parents or caretakers."

"I see," Hawthorne said. "And how do you propose to start this?"

"I'd hoped to solicit donations. In fact, I'd thought about speaking to some of the guests at Lord Sefton's tonight on that very topic."

Brice strode over to the hearth and slammed his fist

upon the mantle. "Now do you understand, Hawk? Can you imagine the horror? Soliciting donations at the Seftons' ball? I shudder to think what others will say."

"What I see," his friend said, "is that she's brave enough to speak out for a worthy cause, and I shall be first in line to write a draft."

"Why, thank you, my lord. You're more than kind." She curtsied politely to the earl, then added, "It was a pleasure to make your acquaintance."

Hawthorne, having stood when she did, bowed slightly. "And yours. I'm looking forward to an evening filled with your delightful company, Miss Browning, and shall call for you at nine. I assume Lady Cecily will be accompanying us, as will her grandmother?"

Kendra nodded, quite regally she thought. "Of course."

Alethea smiled. "There *is* one thing that I ask of you, if you are to escort Kendra tonight."

"Anything at all," he replied enthusiastically.

"I insist that you introduce Kendra as our dear cousin visiting from America. That way no one will think to comment on her long *unchaperoned* voyage with Brice, should that ever be discovered."

"A brilliant idea," Hawk said.

"Then we shall expect you at nine," Alethea replied just before she left.

After a small curtsy, Kendra followed Grandmère from the room, grateful to leave the tension-filled atmosphere behind.

Kendra kept watch on the study door, waiting for the earl to leave. Several minutes later he did, and Kendra made her way into the study, not bothering to knock. Brice stood staring into the fire. She closed the door silently, then waited for him to acknowledge her presence.

After an interminable silence, Brice turned to her. "Was there something you wished to discuss, Miss Browning?"

"Yes." She moved toward him, stopping when he turned back to the fire. She stood in the middle of the room, feeling alone and foolish. "I wanted to apologize for going against your wishes."

"A bit late for that, don't you agree?"

"I know you meant well. It's just that I feel very strongly about going tonight, despite your fears that society will rip me apart."

"Not that I've decided to let you go."

"Even so," she continued, "someday you'll understand my motives, I hope." When I am light years and lifetimes away, she thought sadly.

"Just what are your motives?"

"To get home, of course."

He looked at her as if he doubted her word completely. "And you don't trust me to take you?"

"It's not that, I assure you." How could she explain something she barely understood herself?

Brice's smile was grim. "I fail to see how charming another man into escorting you to a ball will get you home any quicker. If anything, it'll land you in a lunatic asylum."

"I'm not crazy, and I don't expect you to understand."

"My apologies. That remark was uncalled for. It's just that on our return voyage, you said things that gave me cause to worry. You must forgive me for thinking, because you now say differently, that the leopard has changed its spots. I don't want to see you hurt. Many of the people you'll meet tonight are . . . relentless. They strive only to ensure their own pleasures, caring about nothing but themselves."

Kendra felt a tug on her heartstrings. He did care. "The things I told you on board the *Eterne* are things I've promised not to repeat. You must trust in me."

"I shall endeavor to do so."

"Thank you." It seemed as if they'd come to a sort of truce. Feeling more at ease, she walked about the room admiring the masculine furnishings.

"Would you care for a glass of brandy?"

"Sure." She admired his heavy oak desk, tracing her fingers across the distinctive grain of the desktop. "Just a splash, though. I'm not a heavy drinker."

Brice poured two glasses, then handed one to her. She leaned against the desktop, taking the proffered drink. "Thank you."

"You're quite welcome."

Kendra raised her crystal glass. "To your betrothal. May your marriage be a happy one."

Brice clinked his glass to hers. "My thanks, but there's nothing to toast, since I'm not yet betrothed."

Kendra ignored the spark of hope that flared to life. She *was* going home. Who cared if he was or was not engaged? "I apologize. I was under the impression when Lord Hawthorne mentioned it, that, well—"

"I mentioned the possibility to him before I left on my first voyage eight months ago. I have not yet spoken to Lady Caroline, though her father's most anxious for the match."

"I met Lady Caroline and her aunt, Lady Throckmorton, at the Ladies' Charitable Society," she said, trying to sound light. "I imagine Lady Caroline must be thrilled."

Brice shrugged. "I have not seen her since my return.

Nor does that signify, since she has no say in the matter. It's her father who must give his approval."

"You mean you'd marry her even if she didn't love you? Do you love her?"

"Love?" Brice laughed. "We're speaking of marriage! All that matters is that Lady Caroline's bloodline is impeccable. More importantly, not a trace of madness runs in her family nor any taint in her bloodline."

"Your father may have taken his own life, but he wasn't mad, Brice. He was an alcoholic with a gambling problem. And there's no reason you should be ashamed of your grandmother's heritage. *Your* heritage. Something you'd realize if you'd simply take the time to think about it. Besides, she's a wonderful woman who loves you very much."

Brice sat down behind his desk, propping his boots upon the desktop. "Perhaps. But my father wasn't a wonderful man, and *she* gave birth to him."

Not wanting to ruin this rare moment of peace between them by arguing, she examined the items on his desktop while sipping at her drink. Several sealed letters lay atop a ledger of some sort to the left, and a stack of papers were neatly piled beside pen and ink to the right. Then her eye caught the flash of gold from a ring lying on the blotter and she picked it up.

"This yours?" she asked, noticing several things about it at once. The gold was heavy, the band was dented and cracked, and there was something engraved upon the inside. Turning it, she examined the insignia upon the top and was struck by the sudden memory of having seen something very similar before.

"I found it in the woods near here."

Kendra barely heard him as the memories of her former life flooded swiftly back. She felt the blood drain from her face at the recollection of where she had seen such a symbol. "The Debutante Murders," she murmured.

"What do you know of murders?" Brice asked, his voice tightly edged.

"This ring has nearly the same symbol as that of a pocket watch I found at a murder scene back home." She inspected the ring closer this time, taking note of the engraving inside the band. The words *fay ce que voudras* were spelled out, though worn nearly smooth from constant wear, or age. "What does this mean?"

"It is Old French, meaning *do what thou wilt.*"

"*What* did you say?"

"Do what thou wilt."

A seed of excitement festered within her. Was this the reason she'd been transported into the nineteenth century? To discover a new clue in an unsolved murder case that happened in the twentieth century? "What significance does that saying have?"

"It was the motto for the Hell-Fire Club."

"Was? You mean there's no such thing now?" Nor one hundred and something years from now?

"In the seventeenth century, the Hell-Fire Club started out with a group of aristocrats who conducted orgies in a deserted cellar. While many of the young men grew up to lead somewhat productive lives, a few continued on with their bouts of debauchery, raping virgins as part of their satanic rituals."

Kendra thought of the evidence she had seen in Paradise Park in Miami: the obvious signs of cult-like doings left behind by someone confident that they would never be caught. "Is it possible that after many years, and from an ocean away someone might have had knowledge about such a thing, perhaps thinking to reenact such a crime?"

"I'm afraid I don't follow you."

"What I found wasn't a ring, but a pocket watch." Kendra described the murder scene at the park, as well as the earlier murders that occurred under similar circumstances but a few months previous to that.

Brice listened intently to all she said. When she finished, he removed his feet from the desktop, then stood up and paced the room. "You're certain of all you've told me?"

"Positive. But don't get so worked up about it. After all, it happened well over—oh, a good several months ago. In fact, I'd hazard a guess that whoever committed the crime merely got the idea out of a history book. They must've read about the Hell-Fire Club." *Could the Debutante Murderer have read about the murders of Hawthorne Woods in a book?* she wondered. The idea had merit.

"The Hell-Fire Club's hardly the thing one reads about in the schoolroom. At least it was in none of the books I was privy to."

"Then they got the idea through the gossip chain," she prevaricated. "Who knows? Either way, it doesn't matter at this point. America's miles away, and so's the murderer. Trust me. We're dealing with two very separate crimes."

"You don't seem to understand. This ring," he said, unable to keep the anger from his voice, "was found alongside a murdered girl in very much the same circumstances as you've described to me."

Kendra almost dropped the offensive piece of jewelry after hearing his words. "What do you mean?"

Brice told her of the murders. This time it was Kendra's turn to sit amazed. By the time Brice finished, she began to have the suspicion that she had learned the true reason that she was called to this time. It was not the children after all. She was a homicide detective, albeit a reluctant one. And Brice needed her help.

"Take me to the murder scene," she said. "I can assist you in solving this."

Brice shook his head. "Absolutely not." As if sensing she was about to protest, he added, "The matter's *not* open for discussion. It's far too dangerous."

Kendra set the ring upon the desk, knowing from past experience that he was not about to change his mind. She'd just have to help in ways he was not likely to notice. Infiltrating society was her best bet for discovering something that might turn up any new leads, especially if, as Brice suspected, and she was likely to agree, the main suspect was indeed a member of society, one who could easily influence the young ladies of quality into following him to their deaths.

Hours later, as Kendra readied herself for the ball, she thought about all she had learned about the mysterious fires and murders. Glancing out her open bedroom window—as she did each night now that the longest days of summer were upon them—she searched for the moon and discovered it rising over the treetops. The pale orb seemed fuller than ever, although Grandmère had assured her she had weeks to go. Even so, the constant ticking of a clock lingered in Kendra's subconscious. Anything she was to learn about the murders of Hawthorne Woods would have to be discovered in the next few nights. She was going home soon. She could feel it. Without Brice. And tonight she was going to attend her first ball. Did she really think she could pull this off? Pretending to be from this time, remembering all the my lords and your graces, while trying to look for a murderer, as well as soliciting for her children's shelter, all the time realizing that soon, oh so very soon, she'd never see Brice again?

"I'll never be able to do it," she said, pacing the empty room. Halting, she turned abruptly to the mirror to stare at the reflection of what appeared to be a genteel nineteenth-century woman, and she was certain at that moment she knew exactly how Eliza Doolittle must have felt in *My Fair Lady*.

Downstairs, Brice did his own pacing. What the deuce was he about allowing Hawk to sweep Kendra from beneath his very nose? What had happened to his now erstwhile intentions of protecting the girl from the cruelties of the *ton*?

Now that he had a moment to reflect upon it all, he realized his intentions were perhaps not quite as honorable as he had led himself to believe. He had never believed her wild ramblings of her life before the shipwreck, nor did he now believe she was insane. In truth, he realized, it was the latter belief that led him to become her protector, but once that fear was diminished, assuming she was not up to something—and he could not help but think she was—he no longer had any worthy reasons to deny her entrance into society if that was what she wished. And to his dismay, she did. With Hawthorne at her side.

It was with that last bitter thought that he came to the conclusion that, perhaps, just perhaps, he had refused the alluring and strangely complex Miss Browning a place in society as a means of keeping her to himself.

Impossible, he decided on further reflection. And to prove it, he felt the only choice left to him was to attend the boring affair, showing not only Kendra, but Hawk, that he was not in the least affected by their presence together. Besides, he had been somewhat remiss of late in paying proper court to the girl he hoped to make his wife: the very blue-blooded Lady Caroline.

11

When Kendra had disembarked from Brice's ship so many months ago, she knew she'd stepped into a different world. She knew she'd see things that would surprise her, even shock her, but nothing—nothing—could have prepared her for the vision before her eyes: lords and ladies dressed in satins and silks of every imaginable hue, some dancing to the strains of a lively country melody, others milling about the highly polished dance floor, while liveried servants waded through their midst carrying silver trays of champagne that reflected the lights from a thousand candles in the chandeliers overhead.

"Close your mouth, dear."

Not until Alethea's gentle whisper permeated her dazed senses did Kendra realize she was standing at the top of the ballroom stairs with her mouth hanging open. She snapped it shut, and attempted to assume a look she hoped was the perfect mixture of boredom and self-confidence, her intention to make others think she was used to such affairs.

She allowed Lord Hawthorne to take her arm and lead her down the stairs, while Alethea and her granddaughter brought up the rear. Only when she reached the bottom did Kendra allow herself to relax. All for naught, it seemed, as Lord Hawthorne leaned toward her and whispered, "Quite impressive, is it not?"

"It shows?"

He laughed. "If you mean that you've never had a season, yes. But not to worry, my dear lady. The amazement shall wear off soon enough. About the time your feet begin to ache from dancing all night, too soon you'll think that you've been here your entire life."

"You sound quite the expert."

"I escorted my sister to her first ball when she came out not too many years ago. Her expression was not unlike your own when we first entered. And you, being as beautiful as she was on her first night, will undoubtedly not lack for any ardent suitors all vying for your attention."

"You're too kind, my lord."

"Not at all. I am merely stating the obvious. I was not so enraptured by my first glimpse of this ballroom that I failed to notice half the male population present watching your entrance."

Kendra studied Hawthorne's serious countenance, again noticing his strong resemblance to Jack. Not just his looks, but his manner—much like Jack's had been before he was assigned to homicide—pleasant, carefree, and attentive to her feelings. She smiled at the memory. If only Jack had not been promoted, there might have been a chance for their relationship. Perhaps, when she returned, she might discuss his asking for a transfer to another division. Perhaps.

Two hours later, Kendra was certain she knew what

Hawthorne meant when he said she'd soon feel as if she had been there her entire life. At once she was bombarded by offers of monetary and voluntary assistance for her children's shelter, thanks to Lord Hawthorne's assistance in casually bringing the subject up whenever he introduced her to anyone new. Later, when she commented on how surprised she was by everyone's easy acceptance of such an idea, he remarked that most of it had to do with the simple ruse of pretending to be Brice's cousin. "Many here would do anything to ingratiate themselves with so powerful a duke as Blackmoor," he explained just before she was swept off by another eager young swain to the dance floor.

Though her eyes pleaded to Hawthorne for rescue, he merely grinned, and mumbled something about going to the card room where Lady Luck awaited him.

Unused to so much dancing, Kendra wanted nothing more than to sit down. So for the first time that night, despite her unexpected popularity and the *ton* wanting to meet Brice's cousin from America, she skipped a dance, leaving a sad but understanding baronet to fetch her a glass of lemonade instead.

As she waited, she found herself searching the ballroom for Brice. He had arrived shortly after her. He offered a polite greeting and immediately disappeared into the crush of people. Kendra saw him two or three times on the dance floor, always in the company of a beautiful woman. Lately, however, she had not seen him, and she couldn't help but wonder where he might have disappeared to.

When the baronet failed to return directly, she took a seat near one of several open veranda doors overlooking the formal gardens. In all the excitement, she'd forgotten that she was looking for a murderer, and she scanned the sea of faces looking for anything that seemed out of place. It was then she heard the sound of laughter coming from outside, rich laughter that warmed her heart and fed her soul. She turned to see Brice strolling from the moonlit garden, arm in arm with none other than the Lady Caroline.

He led the young woman up the veranda steps, then pulled her into a darkened corner, half hidden by a vine-covered trellis, before lowering his head to kiss the girl upon her mouth.

It was only a short kiss, but to Kendra it seemed to last an eternity as all warmth fled from her body. A few seconds later, Brice and the girl stepped back into the light and moved sedately toward the ballroom doors.

"Miss Browning?"

Kendra drew her gaze from the advancing couple to see the baronet standing before her, holding a glass. Not only did the man's name escape her, but she couldn't even remember why he had approached her. "My lord?" Or was it sir? God! Is that how you addressed a baronet? What was it that Alethea had told her about titles? Sir. It most definitely was *sir*.

"Your lemonade." He held out the glass.

"Oh, yes. Thank you." She tried to sip the proffered drink, but it caught in her throat. The poor baronet looked stricken as she coughed on the sour liquid.

"Miss Browning! Do sit down. Oh dear. Is there anything I can do?"

She shook her head. "No," came her hoarse whisper. "Just point out the direction to the necessary room, and I'll be fine."

"Would you like me to escort you?"

"I'll be fine. Please."

He insisted on taking her to the hallway at least, apologizing profusely on the way for her discomfort. When she was finally able to rid herself of his company, she fled in the direction he had indicated, then passed up the room in search of a place where she could find some privacy. She needed to think about what she'd seen, think about why seeing Brice kiss another woman had affected her so. True, she admitted that she loved him, but did it matter when within a few short weeks she'd be going home? Brice was entitled to his own life, after all.

Kendra tried to open the first door she came to, but found it locked. She was just about to open the second one when she heard laughter coming from within. Passing it, she followed the long hallway around the corner, all the while telling herself she should be happy for Brice and that it would be unfair to start something with him when she had so little time left in his world. Nevertheless, she couldn't help but think that not once tonight had Brice asked *her* to dance.

She jiggled another door. It too was locked.

Brice had made it perfectly clear that he did not want sex without marriage, and she knew he most definitely did *not* want to marry her. She wondered if she should be grateful or hurt—grateful that he was attracted to her but respected her, or hurt that she was not blue-blooded enough to marry.

She approached a set of double doors, and expecting those to be locked as well, she turned the knob and almost fell into the room.

The brightly lit chamber was filled from floor to ceiling with books of all sizes. Several wing chairs, a small desk and a few settees were placed casually about, belying the formal style of the palatial library. Twin hearths, in the rococo style, burned at opposite ends of the room, though little heat reached the middle where she stood still holding the door ajar.

Brice's vast library held no comparison, Kendra thought as she shut the door, and strolled down a book-lined wall. She stopped before one particularly old look-ing tome, its familiar title catching her eye. She traced her finger along the spine reading the gold-leafed title: *The Kama Sutra.*

Here was a book she'd heard of, but never read. Her curiosity about the supposedly erotic works of its long ago author piqued her interest and she started to pull the volume from the shelf.

"Astounding. Don't you agree?"

Kendra's hand flew to her side as she spun around to see a man dressed in a cranberry waistcoat with white satin breeches. He sat lounging in a high-backed wing chair, not ten feet away from her. His familiar face struck a chord in her memory, and she recalled him arguing with Brice on board the *Eterne.* Lord Parkston.

She felt her cheeks burn slightly at the thought that he might have witnessed her interest in such a book. "Astounding?" she echoed.

"Why, all these books, Miss Browning." He waved his lace-cuffed hand across the wide room. It was then she noticed the small side door near his chair. The faint sound of music drifted in from that direction and she guessed the door to be one of the many that opened off the ballroom.

She smiled at him. "Oh?"

"Only think how much knowledge is contained in such a place." Parkston rose and approached the shelves near-est her, removing a thick volume which he opened. "History is quite fascinating. To merely imagine the possi-bilities if only Socrates here, or even Aristotle had had the advantage to read what's contained in this room. Why it staggers the mind. What think you, Miss Browning?"

"I think they'd be very flattered to see their names in print."

Lord Parkston raised his brows, then burst out laughing. "Right you are." He replaced the heavy volume, then searched her face. "Actually," he said after a moment, "I'm glad I've found you."

"Why?"

"My lovely wife, Anne, has told me all about your philanthropic work with the Ladies' Charitable Society. I daresay you're ages ahead of your time with such an idea as opening a children's shelter such as she describes."

She recalled meeting the sweet-natured Lady Parkston at a few of the meetings. "Thank you."

"Pray tell, Miss Browning. What brings you here?"

She tried to remember that Parkston was nothing but a pompous fool and that his bland inquiries were merely a means to facilitate a simple conversation. "Why, probably the same reason anyone would come to a library. I love to read," she told him.

Parkston laughed again. "That's not what I meant. But somehow, I gather you knew that."

Kendra pulled out a book and opened it, pretending great interest in what she was reading, even though the text was obviously some foreign language. French, she thought. "Whatever do you mean, my lord?" she asked, flipping a page.

He walked up and took the book from her hand. "I meant, quite simply, that you knew I was in here. Alone."

"Alone? How could I know that?"

"You obviously saw me come in here. That's how it's usually done." Parkston tossed the book to the floor, then moved closer, cornering her between the bookshelves on her left and the door to her right.

"You don't really think I came in here just to be with you?" She edged back, until she hit the door. Reaching behind her, she discreetly felt for the handle.

"But of course, my dear. I saw your interest in that most esteemed of volumes. *The Kama Sutra.*"

Kendra prayed the door opened out. Slowly, she turned the handle and leaned against it. Nothing.

Bloody hell, she thought, surprised by the simple comfort of using one of Brice's favorite expletives. There was nothing left to do but try to pull the door open, then slip out before Parkston could stop her. She laughed out loud. "You're obviously imagining things, my lord."

Kendra gripped the handle, took a step forward, nearly running into him, then pulled the door, but Parkston's hand flew over her shoulder, holding it shut.

"It's impolite to leave in such a rush, Miss Browning."

"What is it you want?"

"Merely to get to know you better, my dear." Then, before she had a chance to react, his arm shot about her waist, pulling her against him. His hot breath on her neck sent a shiver of disgust racing down her spine.

"Let go of me," she demanded.

"Of course." He stroked her cheek with a finger so soft, she doubted he'd ever done a day's work in his life. "But let us talk about your philanthropic charities. I can be persuaded to make a very large donation."

"A large donation?" She smiled her sweetest smile and allowed him to lead her from the door.

His brown eyes gleamed with lust at her apparent cooperation. "But first, let us find somewhere more private. This room's entirely too close to the ballroom. You wouldn't want to bring scandal upon that pristine Blackmoor reputation. Not that you need worry, though, I know the perfect chamber."

The moment they reached the center of the room, Kendra took a small practiced step to the side, reached up, and flipped him over her shoulder. He landed flat on his back, the loud thud echoing throughout the room.

She looked down at his pale, shocked face. "Oh! My *dear* Lord Parkston, a pity I can't accompany you. It's just a shame that no one ever mentioned to you how *impolite* it is not to ask a lady's permission."

He grimaced in apparent pain, but said nothing.

At precisely that moment, the door to the ballroom flew open. A brightly dressed dandy stood in the doorway. When he saw Kendra, he said, "I thought I heard a noise—" He looked down. "I say. Whatever is that fellow doing on the floor?"

Several other people peered into the room past him, Hawthorne amongst them. She looked down at Parkston, wondering if he was glad she was caught alone with him for causing him pain.

"I heard the same noise," she said putting her hand on her breast in concern. "When I came from the other door, I found this poor man lying here on the floor. I thought perhaps he'd fainted."

Quelling her distaste for the viscount, she kneeled beside him and placed her hand on his shoulder in a sympathetic gesture. "Are you very much in pain, my lord?"

Several men rushed into the room. "Here now," the dandy said. "Are you all right?"

Parkston groaned as the men helped him to rise. Kendra, barely concealing the smile that crept to her face, quietly backed toward Lord Hawthorne's side, who, as opposed to everyone else present, seemed more interested in her than in Parkston's condition.

"Poor man," Kendra offered as Hawk escorted her

back to the ballroom. "I do hope he recovers from whatever it was that struck him down."

"Indeed," Hawthorne said, his tone wry.

Thankfully, he did not ask her what happened, and she took the moment to enjoy the dancing before her, until Brice swept past, with Lady Caroline in his arms.

Although in the past jealousy had been a foreign emotion to her, Kendra was beginning to recognize its effects. "Is that the same Lady Caroline that Brice intends to marry?"

"Yes. Lovely woman, isn't she?"

Kendra stared at the couple, then pretended disinterest. "Lord Hawthorne?"

"Yes, Miss Browning?"

"Would you care to dance?"

Hawthorne regarded her closely, his brown eyes holding a solemn expression. "I think not."

"Why not?"

"We've already danced twice. A third time would be deemed most improper."

"I never thought you'd be one to care what others think."

"About me, no. You're a different matter entirely."

"I don't care a fig what others—"

Hawthorne shook his head, almost sadly, then placed a hand on Kendra's arm. "Miss Browning. Dancing with me will not make Blackmoor notice you if he chooses not to."

"Am I that obvious?"

He smiled but said nothing.

"I'm sorry. I didn't mean to lead you on, having you bring me here tonight."

"Don't apologize. Where the heart's concerned, the head's not always thinking properly. Unlike Brice, I wasn't fooled by your little charade in his study this afternoon."

"And yet you still brought me?"

"Let us say," he said, watching Brice and Lady Caroline dance, "that I had reasons of my own."

"Even so—"

"I certainly hope that just because your heart lies elsewhere, Miss Browning, we might still remain friends?"

The earl took her hand in his. After kissing it gallantly, he said, "Then I remain your faithful servant. As for another dance, you shall simply have to wait until next week."

"Why?"

"Mother's giving a ball. You and your dear cousins are, of course, invited."

"I wouldn't miss it for the world, my lord."

Much later that night, after Hawthorne had seen Kendra, Lady Cecily and Alethea home, he returned to town, to St. James Street and his favorite club. He found Brice sitting in his usual chair in a quiet corner of the room. He took a seat opposite him.

"Quite a crush at Sefton's, eh Blackmoor?"

Brice merely nodded.

"You're not still upset that I took your cousin along, are you?"

"Whatever gave you that idea?" Brice picked up a decanter of brandy and splashed some into his empty glass.

"Because in the two years you've been contemplating the betrothal of one Lady Caroline, you've never so much as paid her a moment's notice. Until tonight."

"Perhaps my conscience has been bothering me." He tossed down his drink.

"Perhaps." Hawthorne poured some brandy into a

glass, but sipped it more leisurely. "Then perhaps you were jealous."

"I think not." He stood up and turned to leave, apparently in no mood to be friendly.

"She's in love with you, you know."

His shoulders tensed. "Lady Caroline?" he asked without turning around.

"Miss Browning."

Brice sank into his chair. "Bloody hell. She told you that?"

"She didn't need to. It's as obvious as there are stars in the sky. Incidentally," Hawthorne added, after a moment, "something strange happened tonight."

Brice stared through his empty glass. "What was that?"

"Miss Browning seemed to have a bit of a mishap involving Parkston. She deftly avoided a scandal, but I fear her role in it wasn't quite as innocuous as it seemed."

At the mention of Parkston's name, Brice narrowed his eyes. "How so?"

Hawk related the incident as he had seen it, starting off with the thud that alerted him and the others that something was amiss in the library. "Perhaps it's nothing, but this noise that was supposed to be the sound of Parkston fainting, or whatever it was that he was said to have done, was heard by those of us near the doors over the sound of the orchestra as well as the hundreds of guests all chattering at the same time."

"Go on."

"If it was a fainting spell, as Kendra claimed—which I find rather hard to believe—I think he'd have fallen to the ground in a more genteel manner. Quieter, if you will."

Brice leaned forward in interest.

"The noise I heard was more the sound of— Well, it was bloody loud, echoing off the walls. That's all."

"And you think Kendra, er Miss Browning, had something to do with this?"

"Precisely. She couldn't have gotten into the room any faster than I, and yet she was standing over him when we opened the door."

"Tending him, you said."

"That was how it appeared at first."

"At first."

"I could be wrong, but it seemed to me, just for a moment, that Miss Browning wore an expression that positively gloated at the viscount's condition. As if she were glad he was lying there on the ground. No one else seemed to notice, since they were too wrapped up in helping Parkston off his back. What do you make of it?"

Brice rubbed his chin, then leaned back in his chair. "I don't really know. But if it involves Parkston, it bodes ill."

"Speaking of Parkston, do you still think he's responsible for the attack on your ship? Or have you learned anything else?"

"Nothing that helps. I'm sure Parkston ordered those pirates to attack in retaliation. I just can't prove it. He would've had no way of knowing when I was returning, unless he has some way of seeing into the future. You didn't tell him, did you?" Hawk looked offended that he would even ask such a question. "No. You'd never do that. But perhaps he got wind of it somehow."

"Impossible."

"Then there's no way I can prove it was he."

"Does that mean you're going to apologize to him?" Hawk asked, incredulously.

"What do you think?"

"That, knowing you, you'll find a way to prove he's guilty. Of something."

Brice grinned. "Precisely. That man's soul is as black as your Hessians. Blacker maybe. And while I can't prove he's involved in piracy yet, I haven't given up. One day he'll slip."

"In the meantime, perhaps you'll learn more about him from the lovely Miss Browning. Maybe he really does have a weak heart. We can scare him to death."

"Perhaps," Brice responded, his mood sobering at the thought of what might have occurred in that library. What if Kendra said or did something that gave Parkston the means to use against her, to believe she was— No. He refused to think about it. Kendra was not mad. Her imagination was slightly overactive, but she was not mad. Of that he was certain.

And she loved him. At least Hawk seemed to think so. But what did it matter? He was nearly betrothed to Lady Caroline. He need only sign the betrothal contract and make a formal announcement. So what was holding him back?

He decided not to dwell on the matter. He left his club and rode home at a leisurely pace, concentrating, instead, on what to do with Kendra. He had promised to take her home at the first opportunity, and yet he was reluctant to do so.

She loved him. He could ask her to stay. But to what purpose? He knew his duty lay with marrying Lady Caroline. Her background was impeccable. Not a trace of madness to be found in her bloodline, one that dated back to Charles I. He owed it to his future heirs.

But Kendra loved him. The thought echoed in his mind as he trudged up the wide staircase, then down the hall toward his room.

At the sight of Kendra's bedchamber door slightly ajar, he stopped. A delicate stream of light escaped into the hallway, beckoning him in. He followed it, pushing the door just far enough to see in. The light, he discovered, was a single moonbeam dancing through the open window, and illuminating to perfection the figure that lay sleeping upon the bed.

Not wanting to disturb her, he started to leave, when a slight breeze wafted in, bringing with it the fresh scent of the garden below. The gentle wind riffled the soft moonlit curls that framed Kendra's face, giving her the allure of innocence.

He wanted to feel the silken strands, brush them away from her face, run his fingers down the nape of her neck, touch her lips . . . with his.

Stepping into the room, he shut the door, waited a few seconds while his conscience warred with itself, then moved cautiously to her bedside. He would not touch her.

All resolve wavered when she turned toward him in her sleep.

Soon, he found himself sitting on the edge of the bed, telling himself that he would only look, but somehow his hand crept out of its own volition, to caress the softness of her full lips. And although he meant to leave, her mouth parted as if in invitation. Then, before he knew it, his lips touched hers while he slipped one hand beneath the nape of her neck, bringing her closer. His other hand found its way to her cheek, caressing softly.

Even though he knew she still slept, her tongue sought his, and he pulled her to him, deepening his kiss, reveling in the knowledge that she wanted him even in her sleep.

"Kendra," he whispered. "My sweet Kendra."

"Brice," came her sleepy reply as she wrapped her

arms around him, so that with each quickening breath he felt her undeniable presence.

Leave, he ordered himself, before it is too late. Instead, he kissed her again while his hand drifted down from her shoulder to her breast, caressing until she pressed herself against him. A soft moan escaped her lips and her eyes fluttered open as he kissed his way ever so softly along the sensitive curve of her neck down to where his hands kneaded the warmth of her breasts through the sheet.

"If this is a dream," she whispered, "don't ever wake me."

Grasping his face in her hands, she pulled him down until his mouth covered her breast. He caught at her through the fabric, biting and nipping ever so lightly until she sat up.

He drew back, his breath catching at the sight revealed to him as the sheet slipped from bare shoulders. Wrapped only in moonlight, she wore nothing beneath. Belatedly, he remembered the promise he had made to her that he would never let himself behave in such an ungentlemanly manner again—the most difficult promise he had ever made, and one that kept him apart from her out of necessity. As his house guest, she deserved better than what he was offering.

"I'm sorry," he whispered.

"Sorry?" Disappointment sounded in her voice, confusion clouded her sleepy face.

"For waking you. I saw your door open. I thought you were awake—" Burying his face in her hair, he inhaled its clean scent. "I'll leave. I'm sorry. I'm— Oh, hell." His mouth sought hers in a searing kiss. He was not sorry. He wanted her. She wanted him, and the moment her tongue sought his, he knew he was lost. There was no turning back.

Kendra undid his shirt, then worked at his pants, wanting to feel him next to her, skin to skin. The moment he apparently discovered her intent, his fingers fairly flew to remove the extraneous clothing.

She admired his taut body as he stood before her holding out his hand. Curious, she took hold of it, surprised when he pulled her from the bed until she stood before him.

"You're so very beautiful," he told her as his gaze caressed her entire being. "I want to see you. To touch you, if you'll let me."

"Yes," she whispered in return, feeling suddenly shy.

He brushed the hair away from her shoulders, then took a step back, to look once more. "Do you know what I want to do to you?"

She shook her head, unable to speak.

"First I want to touch you, everywhere, run my hands along your skin until I know every curve of your body, every hidden pleasure."

Kendra's racing heart was about to spin out of control.

"Then I want to taste everywhere that my hands have touched, teasing you with my tongue, my lips, my teeth."

She wet her suddenly dry lips. "And then what?"

"And then," he whispered as he moved forward until she could feel the heat of his body near hers. "And then I'll take this," he grasped her hand and wrapped it around his erection, "and worship you as you were meant to be loved."

Strong masculine fingers sought out every nuance of her face before moving to her neck. With every feather-soft caress, each nerve ending in her skin seemed to come alive as never before, and what he had not touched began to tingle in anticipation as he ran his fingertips in slow, agonizing circles.

When he touched her breasts he did not linger and she longed to call him back, to rub them against him, but he continued on, seemingly oblivious to her need as he traced a path down her stomach past her navel. He threaded his fingertips through the thatch of hair that covered the most sensitive part of her, rubbing ever so lightly, and she had to bite her lower lip to keep from crying out. One finger found its way inside her, but when she pressed herself against him, he moved it down her thigh and she felt a trail of moisture in its wake.

Onward he continued, down her legs to her toes. When she tried to move, he stilled her. "I have not finished," he said, rising to do the same to her backside as he did to the front.

The moment his hand touched her shoulders, she cried out, her skin was so sensitive, and by the time he had traced a final path to her heels, she did not think there was anything he could do to make her want him more.

She was wrong. For true to his word, he began kissing her in every region of her body, his tongue flicking into places that his lips could not reach.

"Please, Brice," she said, every nerve in her body crying out for fulfillment. Lacing her fingers through his hair, she tried to pull him to her. "I can't even stand." It was true. Her knees nearly buckled under his relentless touch and she had to hold onto his shoulders to keep from falling.

He stopped to look up at her, his eyes mirroring the passion she felt. "Very well. We shall finish this on the bed." He scooped her up in his arms, laying her face down upon the mattress, then proceeded where he had left off, moving lower, lower still until Kendra squirmed shamelessly beneath him, her fingernails raking the bed linens waiting for the agony to stop but praying it wouldn't.

Tears of pleasure mingled with frustration stung at her

eyelids when she finally felt him press his arousal against her, and she lifted her hips against him, waiting for him to enter, to take her. But he didn't. Instead, he slid his length against her back, while his mouth found her earlobe.

"You're driving me mad," she managed.

"Am I, my sweet? I should, now that I know you so intimately." His hot breath caressed her ear. "I'm familiar with every sweet spot upon your body, and every tiny area that will drive you to distraction." Gently, he nipped at her neck while his hands caught hers, holding them over her head. And still he did not enter her.

"I love the way you move beneath me, sweet Kendra," he said, his voice thick with passion. "Do you want me as much as I want you?"

"Yes," she said. "More."

He loosened her hands, then rose just enough to turn her onto her back so that she faced him. "More?"

Kendra wasted no time with words. Instead, she grasped his hips and tried to pull him into her.

"Not so fast, my love," he said, lowering himself just enough so that his erection pressed against her belly. "I'm not finished with you."

Then, when she thought she would die for wanting him, he poised himself at her wet entrance.

"Look at me, Kendra." She did, just as he slid his shaft to the hilt.

"Brice," she cried, as he pulled out, then took her again and again. When she convulsed around him, he too found his release, and Kendra realized that somewhere along the way, time stood still, or perhaps it had sped up, merely to pass them by as they lost themselves in an endless night of passion.

*   *   *

Somewhere in the distant countryside, a rooster crowed. Though Brice knew he should leave, he remained where he was, staring thoughtfully out the open window at the coming dawn. Beside him, Kendra stirred, and he pulled the linen sheet over her to ward off the early morning chill.

Belowstairs, the faint echoes of servants moving about reminded him once more of the necessity to depart. Should he be seen here in Kendra's bedchamber, much less her bed at this hour, he would not be able to alter the course of events. No choice would be left them but marriage.

Would that be such a bad thing? he wondered, reaching out to brush back a lock of burnished gold from her face. No, he thought. It would not, despite her sometimes hoydenish ways.

Perhaps that was one of the things he liked best—her unconventional manner. Life would never be dull with Kendra as his wife.

But what of Lady Caroline? His intent had been to make a formal offer for her hand in marriage once he returned from his voyage.

He stared up at the ceiling. That was what he wanted, was it not? Then why had he not asked for her hand last night at the ball as he'd planned? Or spoken to her father at the very least?

A soft sigh escaped Kendra's lips and he raised up on one arm to look at her. "Ah, my sweet mermaid," he whispered. "What spell have you cast over my heart?"

The temptation to let the servants discover them thus overwhelmed him. The choice would be made, taken from their hands. Kendra would have to marry him then. But even as the thought crossed his mind, he knew he could never do it. She deserved better than to be forced into marriage simply to prevent a scandal.

12

When Kendra awoke, Brice had already left. Not that she'd expected him to stay—Brice would never do anything that might be interpreted by the servants as improper, and sleeping with a house guest would, in his opinion, be most improper. "Bloody fool," she whispered to the ceiling.

"Beg pardon, Miss. Did you say something?"

The sound of Jenny's voice caught her by surprise. "Oh! Jenny. I didn't see you."

"Just thought I'd come in and see if you'd be wantin' a bit of cocoa this morning after yer late night."

Heat flooded Kendra's cheeks. "Late night?" she echoed, shocked at her own embarrassment. She was a twentieth-century woman, for God's sake! Who cared if she'd been caught sleeping with a man? She'd be leaving soon anyway, so what did it matter what any of these people thought? But, she knew, somehow, it *did* matter. Greatly. Somewhere along the way, she had come to love everyone in this household.

Thankfully, Jenny was busy throwing open the drapes

and did not see Kendra's discomfiture. "I imagine that after all that dancing, you'd be a wee bit tired this morning, much as Lady Cecilia. I thought some cocoa might be just the thing."

"Oh. Yes. Cocoa," she managed, once she realized Jenny wasn't talking about her late night escapade with Brice.

Jenny gave her a quick smile as she crossed the room, then paused in the doorway. "Her ladyship asked me to tell you that you should be ready to leave this afternoon fer London."

"London? For how long?"

"A week or so, she said. Something about looking at buildings."

At once, she dressed to seek out Alethea. The thought of spending a week apart from Brice when she had so very little time left with him unnerved her. She'd slept every night these past few weeks with her curtains open just to watch the moon's progress, and as much as she'd wished for time to slow, it marched onward while the moon grew fuller. And now, when Brice had finally let down his aristocratic sense of duty and made love to her, she was forced to leave?

Alethea was in the morning room, sorting through a basket of colorful skeins of thread when Kendra found her. "Good morning, dear," she greeted Kendra.

"Jenny says that we're going to London. Today. For a week." Her voice sounded frantic, even to her own ears.

"Yes. This *is* what you wanted, is it not? To open a children's shelter. Lady Winterowd has asked that we assist her in looking for a suitable establishment in which to house the children. She's graciously invited us to stay with her as Brice has chosen to remain at Blackmoor Hall this season, and therefore has decided not to open the townhouse."

"But—"

"Is aught amiss, dear?"

How could she tell her that she'd slept with her grand-son, and that she wanted to stay here, near him? "No."

"Good, then we'll leave just after luncheon. I think a week's time is sufficient for us to find what we're look-ing for. Brice felt it would be silly to skip off to town each morning, spend the day, come back here, only to return to London again to attend a ball or soiree."

"He did?" It seemed that whenever he got too close or let down his guard for even the slightest instance, he did his best to insulate himself from Kendra's presence.

"He did. He's changed his mind about your shelter and doesn't seem to think it so outlandish to approach anyone. If the charity's good enough for the duke of Blackmoor, you can be certain others shall follow suit."

"But what about the little time I have left?" Kendra asked, grasping at any excuse not to leave.

Grandmère cocked her head to one side as if she couldn't understand Kendra's reluctance to go along with some-thing that was so important to her—not that a children's shelter was any less important than before—but after she stepped through the portal, she'd never see Brice again.

"Do you want to stay here at Blackmoor Hall, or go to London and help open the shelter? There's plenty of time before the full moon comes," Alethea said, digging through her basket once more, seemingly unaware of Kendra's devastation. "Where *is* my red twist?" When she found the bright thread, she said, "By my calcula-tions, we have two weeks left. I worked it all out months ago, just after we returned from Botolf's cottage. I think a week in London to fulfill your dream, then a week at Blackmoor Hall in which to say good-bye ought to be sufficient. Cecilia has decided to stay here with Brice."

A week didn't seem like nearly enough time to her in which to say good-bye to the man who held her heart captive. But Alethea was right. The important thing was to get this shelter off the ground and make it a reality. "Of course," she acquiesced. "I'll go pack."

"That's a dear," Grandmère replied absently, as she threaded an embroidery needle with the red twist.

By the time they'd arrived at the countess's home, Kendra had resigned herself to the fate that she and Brice were not meant to be. If they were, he'd have been there when she'd left, to say good-bye at the very least. But as usual, he'd remained conspicuously absent— away on estate matters, Alethea had said.

That evening, as she helped Jenny unpack, she couldn't help thinking that it was probably best that Brice was not with her now. It would make leaving him and his world that much easier.

"This is strange," Jenny said, as she pulled Kendra's nightclothes out of a portmanteau. "I don't remember puttin' this in here." She lifted out a narrow wooden box, a few inches longer than her hand, and gave it to her mistress for inspection.

"It's beautiful," Kendra said, running her finger along the finely crafted marquetry lid of a rose set against a diamond-shaped background. "I'll bet Cecily put it there."

Springing the catch, she opened it, then caught her breath at the sight of what she found within. A single yellow rosebud.

Lifting the flower to her nose, she breathed in the fresh scent, recalling the words that Brice had told her so many months ago, how her bedchamber suited her. "Soft and feminine, like a pale yellow rose," Kendra whispered, his remembered words curling warmly inside her.

"I beg pardon, ma'am?"

"Oh, nothing," Kendra said, her heart swelling with love as she replaced the flower in the box and set it on her bed. It would be the last thing she looked at tonight. And the first thing tomorrow.

The following week was spent with Alethea and the stout, gray-haired Lady Winterowd, searching London for a suitable home to be used as a shelter. After much debate, they finally settled on a mansion situated in a not so very fashionable part of town. The house, abandoned by its bankrupt owners for nearly a year, was small, as mansions went, with only twenty or so rooms in it, but it had a large garden in the back, once very formal, now very much overgrown, and a small yard out front filled with weeds, some as tall as the iron fence that surrounded the place. Paint was peeling from the window sashes, but the building was sound, made entirely from brick.

Inside, the place had reminded Kendra of a haunted house, filled with cobwebs, and a thick coating of dust— marred only by the tiny prints of rodents that had ventured from the woodwork. While the place was not quite what Kendra had in mind, the countess assured them it could be made habitable in no time at all.

On the morning of Kendra's and Alethea's departure from the countess's home, Lady Winterowd announced, "I thought we might call the house Blackmoor Children's Shelter." Alethea told her that she was sure Brice would be honored and promised to tell him.

When they reached Blackmoor Hall, Kendra ran inside, eager to find Brice and thank him for the rose. Disappointment washed through her when Cecily met her in the hall and said that Brice had left with Lord Hawthorne that very afternoon, and was not due back until tomorrow.

Why had he left when Alethea had sent word that

they were returning today? Surely he wasn't running away again, because of his misguided sense of aristocratic duty. Not after sending her the rose?

No. She refused to believe that he didn't want her as much as she wanted him. A man did *not* make love to a woman the way he had, only to dismiss her from his mind at a later date.

Nevertheless, his absence dampened her spirits, and she found herself having to muster up a facade of contentment as she and Alethea sat down for tea.

Alethea picked up a plate of teacakes, then mentioned to Kendra, quite casually and with that cryptic smile of hers, that she'd had a visitor.

"Who?" Kendra asked as she poured their tea.

"Botolf. I regret to say that I have miscalculated the time. *Tomorrow* is the full moon. Not next week, as I thought."

The spout of the teapot clanked against the delicate porcelain cup, nearly knocking it over. Hands shaking, Kendra set the teapot down. "What do you mean tomorrow?"

"The portal is open but three nights. He wanted to forewarn you so that you might make preparations for your departure tonight."

Kendra's mind reeled with the news. "Tonight?"

"When midnight comes. If you recall, the portal is open on the last waxing moon, the full moon, and once more at the waning moon."

"So soon?"

"I thought you were most anxious, dear."

"I was—I mean, I am." *Tonight!* Unexpected tears sprang to her eyes. "It's just that there are so many things I'd hoped to do before I left." *Like talk to Brice.*

"Such as?"

"The children's shelter, for one."

"It's coming along quite nicely. I expect your dream will come to fulfillment after you depart. It will be your legacy to our time."

"And the murders. What about them? Brice told me about them the night of the Seftons' ball. Maybe that's why I was called to this time. To help him solve the murders. I only wish I'd known sooner."

"Oh dear. I'd never even thought of that. It is what you used to do, is it not?"

"Yes," Kendra said thoughtfully, recalling that long ago day she'd initially told Alethea about her past. She tried desperately to remember what it was that Alethea had said upon first meeting her, and she regarded the older woman who was busily stirring milk into her cup of tea. Alethea always drank her tea straight. "*You* told me I was here to put out the fires the day we met. The fires at the Druid's Cave. That's what you meant, wasn't it?"

"Fires at the Druid's Cave? What a silly thing to say to someone one has only just met. I certainly recall *nothing* of the sort. Would you care for a teacake?"

"You knew all along why I was brought here. And I'd suspect Botolf knew as well."

"Nonsense, child. Botolf has no way of knowing what the future brings."

Kendra narrowed her eyes in suspicion. "And you? Do you know?"

"*Me*? A little Romany blood does not a soothsayer make."

"I'd warrant that your Gypsy blood conveniently omits the truth when necessary." Kendra tried to keep their conversation light despite her heart crying out for Brice's return. How would she ever know what to do if

he didn't come back? Should she stay? More importantly, would he want her to, if he knew the truth?

"You cut me to the quick, child." Grandmère placed
her hand on her breast for emphasis, but the twinkle in
her dark eyes belied her words. "Even so, you have little
time left, and had best use it wisely," she added. "There's
so much work to be done on your shelter, and I'm certain
there are other things you'll want to attend to."

Although Kendra suspected that Alethea had some ulterior motive for her change of subject, the woman was right.
There was not enough time to do all the things she wanted
to accomplish before she left. She had to face reality. She
belonged in the twentieth century, and Brice belonged
here. Out of necessity that evening, she took some time,
alone, to prioritize what she wanted done after she was
gone. Despite the seriousness of the murders, there was
little she could do with what information she had.

Deciding to dwell on a more pleasant subject for the
time being, she thought of all the work to do on her shelter. She'd already decided that whoever was in charge of
running the place must be educated, and well paid. It
would be worth their money to hire a Bow Street Runner
to investigate the background of any who worked at the
house. They might not have automated criminal histories
and fingerprint files in the nineteenth century, but that was
no reason to take a chance and hire anyone who might be
in a position to harm the children or take advantage of the
naivete of the women of the Ladies' Charitable Society.

It was for this very reason that Kendra sat at the
escritoire in her bedchamber and began writing everything down. With so little time remaining, there was no
room for errors!

As her list grew longer, she couldn't help but think how
what she was doing was very much like writing a last will

and testament. Depression swept through her as she realized what one must feel like to have a terminal illness. And although she was not going to die, it was much the same thing, for she knew she'd never see her loved ones again.

At least with the opening of her children's shelter, she had left behind something that would bring some good to the world. Tommy and Bonnie were growing into plump, happy children, living with Jenny's sister. But there were so many more who needed help. She thought of all the Tommys and Bonnies—children who would benefit from the generosity of the women in the Ladies' Charitable Society. And perhaps, with the success of this one home, others would be opened.

But even that hope could not erase the loneliness that overwhelmed her. There was so much she'd never know once she left. Would Cecily meet the beau of her dreams this season? A rich and powerful lord who would give her all she wanted in life, or perhaps a younger son who would love her till the end of time? Would Grandmère find her heart's desire: to win back the love of the grandson who was too foolish to realize what he had in his own backyard? And what of Brice?

Brice. How could she possibly live without seeing him again? Dare she remember the one night they'd shared? Instinctively, she knew nothing would ever compare with that singular moment in time. Never would any lover bring her to the heights of passion as he had done over and over again, until all that remained of the night were the faint traces of dawn coming unbidden and unwanted through the window to lull her to sleep in his arms.

The tip of her pen slipped from her grasp, and she looked down at her list as a spot of ink grew at the bottom of the page. Mindlessly, she lifted the pen from the paper, and set it down. *A few hours.* That was all the time she'd have to say good-bye to Brice—if he were to suddenly show up right now. And she knew that even had she all of eternity to say her farewells, it would never be long enough.

On that melancholy note, she forced herself to finish her list so that she might at least enjoy what little time she had left with her surrogate family.

When she came down to dinner, she gave the list to Alethea. "This is everything, so far," she said.

"I shall read it to the ladies at next Wednesday's meeting," Alethea told her solemnly, carefully folding the letter and propping it against the candlestick on their table. "You're ready then?"

Cecily, apparently sensing all wasn't right, looked up from her plate. "Are you going away again?"

Kendra met Alethea's gaze across the table, wondering what she should say. The older woman raised her gray brows, and gave a regal nod, as if telling Kendra that whatever she said would be fine.

"Well," she began, "I—" And then she recalled Botolf's assurance that if something happened, and she didn't make it tonight, he'd be waiting for her on the last two nights that the portal remained open. "No. No I'm not."

Later, after Cecily had excused herself for the night, Alethea took Kendra aside. "Are you certain this is what you want? There are but two nights left after tonight."

She took a deep breath. "I've decided to stay one more night. I can't leave without saying good-bye to Brice."

But Brice did not return the next day either.

When midnight came, if she didn't leave, she'd have only twenty-four hours left. But would he return in time? Or should she leave without saying good-bye?

That night, Kendra, ignoring the tears that threatened, strolled out into the garden, trying to come to a decision. Alethea joined her. The older woman took

Kendra's hand in her own, and in companionable silence, they watched the moon as it rode across the night sky, bathing the garden in shimmering silver.

"What have you decided?" Alethea asked after several minutes.

"If only I knew how he felt. I can't keep making excuses, because time's running out. But if I knew . . . just one word from him and I'd stay in a heartbeat."

Alethea reached up and brushed a tear from Kendra's face, allowing her hand to linger comfortingly. "You must not depend upon my grandson, for he does not know his own mind yet. The decision must be yours. From here," she said, touching Kendra's temple, "and from here," she added, placing her fingertips over Kendra's heart.

"I can't go tonight," Kendra said past the lump in her throat. "I need more time."

"Of course. You must decide in the morning. Still, that leaves you but one night."

"Oh, Grandmère." She threw herself into the older woman's comforting embrace. "I wish you could all come home with me."

"I know, dear," she said, patting Kendra's back. "I know."

Sleep did not come easily, and morning arrived with the speed of a Concorde jet as she awoke to the sounds of Jenny pattering about in her dressing room. The curtains were still drawn tight against the sun, and Kendra, needing all the cheering she could get, rose to let the light in.

The moment she pulled open the drapes, sunlight poured in, and her heart lifted the tiniest fraction. Until she turned toward the dressing room and saw Jenny's bruised face.

"My God, Jenny!" Kendra said. "What happened?"

13

Jenny touched her swollen cheek. "'Twas nothing." She wiped her tears on her sleeve. "I went home and . . . and fell down the stairs last night."

Kendra had seen Jenny's home only once, from a distance, Grandmère having pointed it out to her as they drove past in the carriage. It was a small single-story cottage.

Grasping the younger woman's shoulders, Kendra examined her face. "Who did this to you?" The maid's lower lip trembled, and Kendra, seeing the fright in her eyes, drew her into her arms. "It's all right."

"I— It was my fault. I shouldn't have argued with him. He told me not to be late, but my sister was ill, and the little ones needed feedin', and she's been workin' so hard since she took little Bonnie and Tommy in, so I cooked the poor mites some supper, and then went straight home."

"Your husband did this to you?" Kendra wanted to kill the bastard right then and there.

When Jenny nodded, Kendra's heart went out to her.

Now she understood why the maid had insisted the children go to her sister's when it was so patently obvious that she'd wanted to care for Tommy and Bonnie herself. Jenny, who was as sweet-natured as God ever made a person, obviously didn't want them raised around violence.

"You've got to leave him," Kendra announced with barely leashed fury, even though she'd lived in the nineteenth century long enough to know that such things were even more difficult than in her own time.

"But he's my husband," Jenny said with finality. "We were married in the church. I took a vow."

"So did he. Wasn't part of it to honor and protect?"

Jenny made no reply, and Kendra realized that unless something was done, the maid would return. "I'm going to tell Brice."

"Oh, no! Please—"

"He's the only one who can do anything."

"He'll dismiss me!"

"For what?" Kendra asked incredulously.

"For bein' disobedient to my husband!"

Kendra would have laughed had the situation not been so serious. "Don't worry. It'll be alright."

Unlike Jenny, she had every confidence in the world that once Brice was apprised of the maid's predicament, he would immediately set things to rights. He was a duke, after all. Once again, though, Brice was nowhere to be found. But at least he'd returned, she discovered later from the butler.

"Unfortunately," the somber-faced servant told her, "you've just missed him. His grace said he had to leave on a matter of some importance."

"That figures," she muttered to herself as she sought out Alethea instead, who of course agreed at once that Jenny must leave her husband and stay with them.

At Alethea's suggestion, Jenny was ensconced at the dower house, so that she need not suffer further humiliation at having to face the other servants until she was healed. Most of the morning, and quite a bit of the afternoon had slipped away by the time Kendra settled Jenny comfortably at Briarwood. Once back at Blackmoor Hall, she joined Alethea and Cecily for a nice relaxing cup of tea.

"How is Jenny faring?" Cecily asked with concern.

"Not bad, considering," Kendra informed her. "I think that once her bruises are gone, and she comes back to work, she'll soon be her old self. I only wish I'd known of her troubles earlier. I'd have done something about it long ago."

Alethea shook her head. "I don't know what, if anything, you could have done, my dear. Especially if her husband went to such pains to ensure that his atrocities were not discovered. Brice was just telling me that—"

"He's home?" Kendra asked, setting down her untouched tea. "I have to talk to him. Where is he?"

"Where else?" Cecily put in. "He's in his study."

Excusing herself, Kendra rushed to the study. As she stood there, poised to knock, she thought about her true motive for wanting to see him. Granted, she wanted to discuss the incident involving Jenny and her husband. But what she really wanted to know was how he'd react to seeing her since they'd made love. He'd sent her the rose, and she desperately needed to know his intentions. Tonight was the last night the portal would be open. How did he feel about her? More than likely, judging from his prolonged absence, he'd apologize for his lapse of etiquette, much as he did on that long ago afternoon when he'd kissed her.

On that depressing note, she pushed open the door, without bothering to knock. The sight of him sitting behind his desk, bent over an open ledger, one of many stacked beside it, rankled her nerves. How could he sit there so calmly, when for the past three days, she'd been left wrestling with a decision that could change her life forever?

Brice rubbed at his temples, thinking if he ignored whoever had impolitely entered, they might go away. Upon further thought, he decided a harsh command to leave would work faster. The words, however, died upon his lips as his gaze feasted upon the sweet but stubborn-looking vision before his eyes.

"Come in, Kendra," he said, standing.

The use of her Christian name apparently took her by surprise. "Kendra?" she repeated. The determined tilt to her chin disappeared.

"Forgive me. Miss Browning."

"No! I mean, Kendra's just fine."

He waved for her to take a seat. She crossed the room to his desk, but did not sit, and so he remained standing.

"Was there something you wished to discuss?" he asked, when what he really wanted to discover was if he'd only dreamed about the way she felt in his arms. He had not been able to think of anything else, and he wanted to hear that Kendra had felt the same way, that this was why she had sought him out. Had she found the rose he'd left for her?

"You know about Jenny's husband." Her unexpected words were like a bucket of cold water thrown on his face. It was not a question but a statement. And it had nothing to do with love—lovemaking, he amended.

"I've been made aware of the matter."

"And?" she demanded.

"And what?" he asked, mildly surprised when she looked offended by his response. Why did a simple maid mean more to her than what had happened between them?

"The bastard broke the law!" she said, her voice rising. "He beat Jenny black and blue, and I want the authorities notified at once. I want that bastard to rot in Newgate!"

"Unfortunately, he's broken no laws except perhaps in the eyes of God. Disciplining his wife for whatever sins he feels she's committed is fully within his power as a husband. He need only—"

"I don't believe I'm hearing this! Jenny committed no sin. She went to help her sister who was too ill to care for Tommy and Bonnie. Why, the poor woman couldn't even get out of bed, much less care for two young kids! Jenny was only trying to help."

"I realize that, but you must have faith—"

"Faith? How can I have faith in a system that allows a man to beat his wife because she's considered nothing but chattel?"

"And what would you have me do, Miss Browning? Drag him to Tyburn and hang him myself, all because your tender sensibilities were hurt? You must learn to be reasonable."

"Reasonable?" Kendra's eyes glistened. "The bastard *should* hang. But only after someone has beaten him so that *he* can see what it's like to be picked on. And if you're not going to do it, I will."

"He's dangerous. I forbid you to go near him."

"I don't give a damn what you forbid." She stalked to the door and pulled it open.

"I have not dismissed you, Miss Browning."

She paused at the threshold to stare daggers at him.

"Dismissed me? Oh, that's rich. Well, I have news for you, your grace. I'm not one of your loyal subjects who can be ordered around at your every whim. I may only be a commoner, and not good enough to commingle with your blue blood, but I do know one thing for certain: I could never marry a man who doesn't believe in the same values that I hold. My God! I can't believe I even slept with you!" she cried, just before she slammed the door.

Kendra stood outside the study. Men, no matter what century they were from, were all the same—despicable. And Brice topped the list. Not that anyone would ever mention such a flaw to him. No one would *dare* for fear of angering the almighty duke.

Bloody hell, she thought, turning around and throwing the door open. It bounced against the wall as she stormed back into the study. Let him get angry. After all, she was leaving for home soon, and there was nothing more he could do to hurt her at this point.

Brice, seated behind his desk, a stack of papers in his hand, looked up, his expression one of cool disdain as if he could not care less that she'd almost knocked a hole in the wall with the door. "Was there something more you wished to discuss?"

"As a matter of fact, yes." She shut the door behind her, a bit more gently this time. "Since I'm on a roll, I thought I'd get a few things off my chest."

"If you need assistance lifting something, then I suggest that you summon a footman."

"I don't need anyone's help, Monty. What I need is to tell you something. Something that should've been said a long time ago."

"Proceed, then," he said, rising.

"First—"

"First? If this will take awhile, then perhaps we should both be seated," he told her, sounding anything but polite. When Kendra remained where she was, he moved to the front of his desk and sat on its edge. "You were saying, Miss Browning?"

His cool manner incensed her further. "First off, I think you treat Alethea like dirt. No matter how hard you deny it, she's still your grandmother. Her blood runs in your veins."

"That is none of your concern," he said quietly.

"It is when I see how much you hurt her. Especially when you refuse to acknowledge in your own little way that she's *your* Grandmère. Do you think anyone cares if she's half Gypsy? Her friends don't care. And anyone who does is certainly no friend of hers *or* yours."

"You're in dangerous waters, Miss Browning."

Kendra's laugh sounded shrill to her own ears. "What do I care? I'm not the one who'll wake up one day only to discover that time's passed me by, leaving nothing but an empty shell of a life because I was too busy to take notice of all who cared about me."

She approached him—quite bravely, she thought, judging from his murderous expression. "If you'd stop being a duke for one damned day, you might notice what's going on around you. It doesn't take a brain surgeon to realize how your sister's grown into a woman while you were off gallivanting around the globe on one of your ships. Or that she'll find a beau and marry soon, leaving you behind. Or that *someday* your grandmother will die, leaving you wondering when she'd aged. Not that you'd ever notice."

Too angry to think clearly, Kendra ripped the papers from his hand and waved them before his dispassionate face. "How could you notice when you're holed up in this damned study of yours, taking care of business matters that just can't wait? Well, one day you're going to step out of those doors there, Mister Duke, and discover that the people who love you most in this world are gone." Her throat constricted at the truthfulness of her words. "Damn you," she managed, finally. "At least you'll have your damned *business* to keep you warm at night." As she tossed the papers in the air, the feeling that she might have gone too far intensified when she caught sight of his eyes, cold blue-black diamonds, sparkling with fury.

Still angry, but a bit more rational, she backed to the door as the papers fluttered to his feet. He made no move to pick them up or even come after her. He simply stared at her with that chilling gaze. When she paused at the door, he said, very calmly, "Are you quite finished, Miss Browning?"

Always the perfect duke, she thought. "Hardly. But where to begin? There are so many things you do that *drive* me up a wall—like your bloody perfect manners. Try loosening up a bit. Say something off the wall. In other words, Monty," she clarified when she saw him glance at the study walls in confusion, "do something *unproper* for once in your life."

"Improper," he corrected, turning his gaze back to her once more.

"Who cares? There're more important things in life to worry about. I only hope you figure it out before it's too late."

Kendra grasped the knob, her hand shaking with rage. "Oh, yes. There is one other thing," she said, glancing over her shoulder at his aloof figure. "In case the twentieth century doesn't mean anything to you, it just so happens to be the one I'm from, and the one I'm going back to. Tonight. I only wish I hadn't spent the last couple of days agonizing about whether or not I should stay, so I guess I owe you my thanks for helping me make up my mind so quickly. But either way, I'm glad, because I *never* want to see you again. I wish to God I'd never even met you."

Opening the door with a flourish, she stormed from the room without bothering to shut it, and was about halfway across the wide foyer when she heard the soft click of the study door closing. She would have slammed it, but not he. Brice would never resort to anything so ordinary.

Kendra wiped her eyes, before fleeing from the house to order a horse saddled. The groom, however, refused, still being under the orders of his grace not to allow her off the premises without proper accompaniment.

"Fine," Kendra said, heading toward the gardens. When the groom had gone on about his business once more, she slipped into the stables, grabbed a halter from the tack room, and put it on Cecily's horse, a well-mannered but spirited bay. She didn't bother with the saddle, having no time to waste, then, leading the horse to a mounting block, she hitched up her skirts.

No sooner had she mounted astride when the groom reappeared. "Hey!" he shouted. "You can't—"

"Sorry, bud," she said, urging the bay onward, past the worried groom. It had been years since she'd gone horseback riding without a saddle, and although she was quite adept, she knew she'd pay with sore muscles later.

Nevertheless, within twenty minutes, she found herself in front of the small single-story cottage that had, up until today, been Jenny's home.

Dismounting, she tied the horse's reins about a shrub, then walked around to the side, where she saw a broad-shouldered giant of a man leaning over a bundle, wrapping it with twine. His stringy brown hair hung in his face, hiding it from view, but she didn't need to see it to guess that this man was Jenny's husband. He looked the cowardly type, she thought, with his rough dirty hands and unkempt appearance, all very much the opposite of Jenny, who was fastidiously neat. After a moment, the man tossed the bundle onto the back of a wagon, and leaned down to tie another.

Kendra advanced toward him. "Are you Jenny's husband?"

Ignoring her, he continued what he was doing.

"Are you?" she demanded.

"Aye," he grunted as he knotted the twine tightly about the bundle of goods.

Kendra stepped closer, and without bothering to think, she slugged him in the face.

First shock, then anger, swept across his features. "What the hell was that fer?" He touched his lip, tensing at the sight of blood on his fingertips, and for a moment, he looked as if he'd strike her. Apparently, he thought better of it, and wiped his hand on his shirt, instead.

Even so, she took a cautious step back. "That was for hitting Jenny. And if you ever do it again, I swear, I'll kill you."

"Bleedin' woman's got a damned army defending 'er," he said, rubbing his mouth once more as he stood up to his full height, taller even than Brice, she realized belatedly.

"Army?" How was it that she'd failed to notice his black eye, or that ugly bruise running along his jaw? She took a step back. "I, uh, take it someone else was here before me?"

"If yer meanin' his grace, then yer right."

"Monty did that?"

"Monty?"

"Blackmoor." A sinking feeling began to tug at her conscience as she tried to recall all the hateful things she'd said to Brice before she left. The thought crossed her mind that even though she couldn't quite recall everything said, it would be just like Brice to remember everything with terrible accuracy. "The duke did that?"

"'E did. That and told me if I ever 'it a woman again, it'd be the last thing I used me 'ands for." He leaned down in obvious pain to pick up the bundle and tossed it onto the wagon with the others. Then, after checking the harness on the horse, he gingerly climbed aboard. "You a friend o' Jenny's?"

Kendra nodded, too dumbfounded to speak.

"Tell 'er I'm sorry. I didn't mean to 'urt 'er. Just sometimes, I can't 'elp it like." After casting a wistful glance at the cottage, he shook the reins, and the sway-backed horse plodded down the dusty road.

Kendra watched for a few moments, then returned to her horse, her heart heavy with guilt. She had to get back to Blackmoor Hall and apologize to Brice. Before it was too late.

Alethea intercepted Kendra upon her return just as she was about to see if Brice might still be in his study. "Lady Winterowd has come to see you," she said, ushering Kendra from the foyer into the parlor just as Kendra chanced to see a familiar looking, snowy-haired man disappear into Brice's study.

"Wasn't that Riley?" she asked, craning her neck around to get a better look.

"Riley? What an odd name. I don't believe I know any Rileys," Alethea responded as she pulled the doors shut.

"The first mate from the *Eterne*. I'm certain it was him."

Before Alethea could answer, Lady Winterowd interrupted. "My *dear* Miss Browning. I've just finished speaking to most *every* member of the Ladies' Charitable Society, and so I thought I simply *must* come personally with the news. You'll be pleased to know that they've all agreed wholeheartedly upon the house. Of course there were a few suggestions, and I thought . . . "

Smiling wanly, Kendra sat down to listen to the ideas that a few of the other ladies had passed on.

Finally, about a half hour later, Lady Winterowd rose. "I really *must* be going. I shall be certain to pass on your idea of possibly including unfortunate women in the shelter as well. I can't think any would object, especially when one realizes that these poor women might have children of their own with nowhere to go."

"My thoughts exactly," Kendra said, moving to the door to ensure that the countess was truly leaving.

But when after several minutes Lady Winterowd made no move to depart, Alethea said, "Oh my! Look at the time. There's so much to do before Lord Hawthorne's ball tonight. You *are* going, are you not?"

"Of course!" Lady Winterowd answered as she rushed to the door. "I'd quite forgotten. How very foolish of me, and I must yet drive to town."

"Thank you for dropping by," Kendra called out as the countess left. Then, after excusing herself to Grandmère, she went to the study, wondering if perhaps she might not arrange to ride over to Hawk's with Brice. A moonlit carriage ride would be the perfect place to apologize, she thought, after knocking on the door.

When Brice called for her to enter, she hesitated before pushing the door open.

Brice was seated before the fire opposite Riley. "Ah, Miss Browning," he said without any trace of anger. "I'm pleased you're here." He and Riley stood as she approached.

"You are?" she asked, feeling much like a naughty child about to escape punishment.

"Absolutely," he replied, almost cordially. "It seems that one of your wishes is about to be granted. I was unable to do both."

Perhaps she'd been a bit hasty on deciding he might forgive her. Suspicions aroused, she sat. "What wish?"

"That you get to go home."

She shot up. "What?"

"Riley's consented to take you home on the *Eterne*."

"Riley?" Kendra glanced at the aging seaman. "Four months ago, you told me *you* were going to do it." Not that she wanted either of them to, but she had to stall for time.

Brice strode to his desk and sat down. Turning to Riley, he said, "There is no need for you to stay and listen, unless you care to."

"Not particularly," Riley answered moving toward the door. "I'll be expectin' to set sail at dawn. Ye'll have her on board then?"

"She will be there," he replied as Riley left.

Brice returned his gaze to Kendra, and she realized how foolish she'd been to think she could waltz right in and apologize. How had she forgotten his adamant statement of so many months ago that he never gave second chances to anyone?

It was quite apparent, once she really looked at him, that the reason he wasn't angry was because he'd closed her out of his heart. And now he intended to shut her out of his life.

"You were saying, Miss Browning?"

"I thought you said *you* were going to take me home."

"I would have, but for your marked distaste for my presence. I can't grant your wish that we never met, but this, I think, is the next best thing."

"Well, I won't go!"

"Damnation, woman!" He slammed his fist on the desktop. "From the moment I had the incredible misfortune to pull you from the sea, you've begged me to take you back. And *now*! Now that the opportunity's finally presented itself, you insist otherwise! Well, I think not, Miss Browning," he said with finality.

"Can't it wait for two weeks?" she asked timidly, surprised by his sudden and rare loss of temper. He almost reminded her of the sea captain she had come to know and love—and miss, once he hit dry land. That Brice was different. Full of emotion. He had laughed, teased, and yes, even stormed at her. Brice, the duke, was entirely too proper, too cold. "I liked you better on the *Eterne*," she muttered, when he failed to answer her.

If he heard her, he gave no clue. Once more he was his usual calm self, and said, "Riley must leave on the morrow. His itinerary is such that he can't delay, even for a day. Therefore, I suggest you begin packing at once. I'll take you to the *Eterne* myself, this very night."

She couldn't let him send her home in the wrong century! "What about Hawthorne's ball?" she asked, grasping at straws. "You certainly can't expect me to leave without saying good-bye to all my friends."

"Then I suggest you start gathering your things at once. Perhaps, if you're not too late, Alethea and my sister won't mind waiting for you. I had intended to take them with me as chaperone for Lady Caroline, but—"

Awash with jealousy, she blurted, "You're taking Lady Caroline?"

Brice ignored her question as he pulled open his desk drawer. "I had meant to give this back quite some time ago," he said, lifting out her fanny pack by its strap. "Riley found it and locked it in my cabin on the *Eterne* the day you ran from the ship." She crossed the room and he handed the heavy pack to her. As she started to unzip it, he said, "You needn't worry that anything is missing. I trust Riley implicitly, which is why I've asked him to take you home."

"We don't have to part like this."

For the briefest of moments, she thought she detected something different in his gaze. Almost a longing. But before she could tell, he picked up some papers from his desktop and began to look over them. "As I said, I'll take you to the *Eterne* tonight, myself. Only then will I know that you're safely on board. I hope you don't mind that you must depart from Lord Hawthorne's ball earlier than expected. Now, if you'll excuse me, I have work to do."

"Sure thing, Monty." Refusing to let him see how much he hurt her, she fled from the room to seek Alethea's comforting embrace.

Thankfully, Alethea didn't mind that Kendra soaked the shoulder of her new rose-colored silk gown. "There, there, my dear," the older woman said, patting her back. "You mustn't worry."

"How, when Brice insists I be on that bloody ship this very night?"

"Are you certain that's all that's worrying you? After all, it can make little difference since you shall be leaving tonight anyway."

Kendra knew that was the least of her worries. Brice had broken her heart. That was it, plain and simple. "Even if I wanted to stay, how can I if he forces me to sail to America?"

"You want to stay?"

"I did." Kendra dried her eyes. "But I can't stay now." She tilted her head back and bit her bottom lip. It was no use. The tears came anyway. "I love Brice," she whispered. "But he made it more than obvious the feeling's not mutual. If I stay, I'll only be miserable."

"Are you certain you want to go to Hawthorne's tonight? Cecilia and I would be more than happy to spend the evening with you at home, until it's time to meet Botolf so that he may show you the way."

"No. Let's go. I'll take my things in the carriage with me, and leave from Hawthorne Manor. It won't take that long to get back here to meet him."

"As you wish."

"I only hope Brice doesn't take it on himself to get an early start for the ship."

"I'll find a way to detain him if he does. Now off with you. You must pack whatever it is you need for your trip home. We don't want to arrive too late at the ball. Not tonight."

14

On the way to Lord Hawthorne's, Cecily was much too excited to notice Kendra's preoccupation. In a flash of insight, once they alighted from the carriage and Kendra shook off her somber mood, she determined that Cecily was looking forward to meeting someone there.

Her suspicions were confirmed when a young buck, as she heard Alethea and even Brice call many of the less mature men, approached them. Lord Peter Rothingham bowed politely, then swept Cecily away with a promise of refreshment.

Alethea excused herself as well, and left to make arrangements for Kendra's escape. While Kendra waited, she noticed Lord Parkston, decked out in his usual lace-frilled ballroom attire, heading her way. Having no wish to relive their past confrontation, she moved to the opposite side of the room, grateful that he appeared not to have seen her. Only when Alethea found her several minutes later was Kendra able to relax. The older woman motioned her to one of many small alcoves around the dance floor set up for tête-à-têtes. Each was surrounded by red velvet curtains, the front of which was tied back and opened to the ballroom. Potted palms were placed on either side of a settee, where the two women sat to watch the dancing.

"Everything is ready, dear." Although Alethea whispered, her voice echoed loudly off the marble floor and low ceiling of their tiny space despite the heavy curtains that surrounded them. "I've asked Brice's coachman to return to Blackmoor Hall, telling him that Brice shall be going home with us."

"What good will that do?"

"By itself, nothing, except that I've done the same with ours, telling our driver that we're going home with Brice. That was right after I had your things put in Lady Winterowd's coach. I told her our driver had suddenly taken ill, and asked if she could give us a ride home. As it stands now, Brice will have to borrow a coach if he wants to leave for London, and that's bound to take several minutes. More than enough time to spirit you back to Blackmoor Hall to meet Botolf at the gate by midnight. We'll have to leave here by half-past eleven at the latest."

"I hope nothing goes wrong."

Alethea patted her hand. "I know things will turn out to everyone's satisfaction. Except Brice's perhaps."

Long after Alethea left to visit with some other acquaintances, Kendra remained seated in her private alcove. At the moment, she had no desire to join in the festivities, and turned down several offers to dance. Right now, she wanted only to watch and remember on this, her last night with the Montgomerys.

Just then, Cecily danced past in the arms of her beau, pausing long enough to offer a brief wave before Lord Peter whirled her away. Dear, sweet Cecily. How she would miss her and Alethea. And Brice.

Searching the ballroom, Kendra spied him dancing with Lady Caroline. They were well suited, she thought, watching as the couple stopped beside a pair of matrons, Lady Throckmorton and another whose name Kendra could not recall.

Kendra leaned back in her seat. Life, she decided, was very unfair. Not one man in the twentieth century could compare with Brice.

Still, there was Jack. How was it that she'd forgotten so easily the man she once would have given her very soul to marry? Surely Jack's finer qualities were comparable to Brice's? Minus the nineteenth-century gallantry, of course.

Desperately, she tried to remember what Jack's qualities were, but was continually distracted by the annoying echo of whispered voices nearby. Recalling how her and Alethea's conversation was magnified, she hoped whoever was speaking did not care if they were overheard, for every now and then a snatch of whispering, louder than the rest, floated crystal clear to her. Glancing about her, she spied the heel of a muddied boot to the left beneath the gold tassels of the red velvet drapes.

When the hushed conversation took on a more fevered note, she couldn't help but listen, especially now that the music had died, allowing her to hear better.

"Tonight," came a deep emphatic whisper.

"No!" the second voice, raspy and low, shot back. ". . . dangerous . . . "

It was two men. *Dangerous*? Her interest was piqued.

"As scheduled," the first voice said, his tone brooking no argument.

"Very . . . my lord."

"The girl? You've taken care . . . "

It must be a lover's tryst, Kendra thought, with the servant arranging everything for his master, who was probably married, and worried about the dangers of getting caught. Kendra had discovered during her time in England that affairs were common practice in the nobility, as long as they were conducted discreetly. She wondered, vaguely, if that was how Brice thought of their one night together. As a discreet affair, never to be revealed.

". . . forest, waiting . . ." This certainly aroused her curiosity, since meeting in the forest was a bit odd. Especially as dangerous as Hawthorne Woods was reputed to be. ". . . robed and ready . . . midnight at . . . "

Unfortunately, the remainder of the conversation was covered by the chattering of several women all descending on Kendra at once. She recognized one of the women, Lady Burlington, who had agreed to assist with her shelter. The other three, she did not know.

"Miss Browning!" cried Lady Burlington, a plump woman dressed in a deep blue gown. Her light brown hair fell in ringlets off one shoulder. "Lady Winterowd and I have been discussing your philanthropic charities with my friends, and they've *all* agreed to help."

Kendra immediately forgot about the whispered conversation as the next several minutes were spent in a lively discussion of the benefits of having a children's shelter run by trained professionals. The four women agreed wholeheartedly with Kendra's views, and promised to meet the following week at the London site that Kendra and Lady Winterowd had chosen. Thankfully, Lady Burlington's friends were wealthy, and eager to volunteer their time and money.

Their plans all set, the women launched into a conversation about the latest scandal, the hasty marriage of the earl of Levington's daughter. Feigning interest, for she dared not offend such wealthy benefactresses of so worthy a cause, Kendra smiled politely, agreeing in all the correct places—she hoped—then breathed a sigh of relief when a masculine voice penetrated through their chatter—although she did not at first hear what was said to her, because of the strange acoustics of the curtained chamber in which she sat. She looked past the women that stood about her, her heart racing as she regarded Brice's handsome visage.

"Miss Browning. Might I have the pleasure of this dance?"

"Dance?" she uttered foolishly. The women moved aside and she stood. Brice bowed politely, and Kendra curtsied in return. "I'd like that, thank you," she said. Perhaps he meant to make amends with her. Maybe she wouldn't have to leave at all.

The first notes of a waltz drifted from the orchestra, as he led her to the floor then took her in his arms. "Lady Caroline felt I'd be remiss in not dancing with you."

The joy she felt faded as he spun her around in time with the music. "How very thoughtful of her," she managed. "But you needn't trouble yourself." Though she tried to pull away, he held her tightly, the strong hand at the small of her back refusing to give.

"'Tis no trouble. Since after tomorrow—"

"I'll be out of your hair."

"Since I may never see you again," he said quietly.

His reply brought an all too familiar sting to her eyes. They danced in silence for a few moments, and Kendra had to look away until she was certain she wouldn't cry. Finally, she dared a glance. For the briefest of moments, she thought she detected anguish . . . and longing in his obsidian-blue gaze, but before she had time to analyze it, someone called out his name and he looked away.

"Your grace!" It was Lady Caroline, her expression bordering on frantic. Kendra wanted to smash her.

Their steps slowed as he brought her to the lovely brunette's side. "Is something amiss?" he asked.

"Yes. Oh, dear. Yes," she said, wringing her delicate hands together. "Luci's still missing."

"Who's Luci?" Kendra asked, putting her jealousy aside in the face of the girl's apparent distress.

"My cousin. Her mother asked if we'd seen her while I was dancing with his grace. And that was nearly an hour ago. She last saw her walking in the gardens, but no one's seen her since."

Brice did not appear overly concerned. "Perhaps she's found a secluded corner with that young dandy. What was his name?"

"Robert. Lord Fulsom."

"Ah yes, Fulsom. No doubt if we find him, we'll find her."

Caroline appeared more distressed. "He hasn't seen her either. At least not since shortly after they arrived. Nobody seems to know quite when she disappeared."

Brice placed his hand comfortingly on Caroline's shoulder. "We will find her. Won't we, Miss Browning?"

"Of course."

"There, you see. Now you'd best go and comfort your aunt, and assure her that we'll locate her daughter at once. We wouldn't want her to overset herself."

"No," Caroline replied absently, as she left in search of Lady Throckmorton.

Although Kendra had hoped Brice might resume their waltz, it was not to be. He remained steadfastly at the edge of the dance floor, consumed in his thoughts.

"Is something wrong?" she asked, when after a few moments, he still had not moved.

"I sincerely hope not."

A nagging suspicion tugged at Kendra's consciousness,

and she thought of the conversation she overheard. Suddenly, the murders of Hawthorne Woods came to mind. "What do you mean?"

He didn't answer. Instead, he pulled her from the ballroom to the veranda doors, away from the crush of people. "I didn't want to say anything in front of Caroline. She's not strong like you." Kendra, uncertain whether that was a compliment or not, did not have time to dwell on the matter. "You recall the murders I told you about some time ago?"

How could she forget? But for one being a hundred and sixty-four years apart, they could have been done by the same madman who had killed three of Florida's elite daughters. "Yes," she answered. Without warning, one fragment of the whispered conversation she overheard earlier came back to haunt her. *Midnight.*

She grasped Brice's arm. "You don't think . . . "

"I can't be certain. It's been so long, I'd hoped they'd stopped. And the girls found were never— Well, they were gently bred, but . . . Luci's a viscount's daughter. When I first heard she was missing, I naturally assumed that she had run off with that young upstart she's taken a fancy to. But that was several hours ago. And if he's not seen her . . . "

"This is a big house," Kendra pointed out. "And the gardens, as vast as they are, she's got to be around somewhere." She wanted so hard to convince him, and herself, but one word kept coming back to mind. *Midnight.* "All we have to do is search the grounds and every room," she offered in desperation. Numbness crept slowly through her veins, keeping her from thinking clearly. *Midnight. The fires at midnight.*

"Of course, you're right. No one would dare harm a viscount's daughter. I'll get Hawthorne and arrange a search party at once. Perhaps she's wandered off the grounds, gotten lost in the woods. If you'd organize a search of each room in the house," he said as he headed toward the ballroom.

Just as he stepped on the threshold, Kendra was able to shake off her stupor of fear. Maybe it was nothing, this thing she overheard in the alcove, but her cop's instincts told her differently. "Wait," she called out. "What time is it?"

Brice stopped, looking mildly annoyed. "What does it matter—"

"A great deal. I think."

He crossed the wide porch to stand before her as he pulled out his pocket watch. "Nearly half-past eleven. Why?"

Kendra breathed a sigh of relief. "Thank God. We're not too late."

"What are you talking about?" he asked, grasping her shoulders.

"I think you're right."

"Right?"

"About the murders. That this is one. I overheard a conversation. Well, bits and pieces of one. At first, I thought it was just something harmless. A simple lover's tryst in the forest."

"Lovers don't tryst in Hawthorne Woods, Kendra. Especially, not since—well, go on."

She told him all she remembered. The moment she completed her tale, he rushed toward the doors.

Just before he disappeared into the ballroom, he stopped to issue one last order. "Under *no* circumstances will you, Alethea or Cecily leave this place until Hawk and I return—assuming I can find him. I haven't seen him for the last hour," he said more to himself.

Then to her, he added, "I will not have you traveling through the woods until daybreak. Is that understood?"

He was gone before she could answer.

It took Kendra a moment before she stopped blaming herself for not seeking Brice out sooner to tell him what she'd overheard. She couldn't have known what was going on until after Luci had been discovered missing anyway. With that small bit of consolation, and a quick prayer that Brice was not too late, she went in search of Grandmère to organize a quiet but thorough search of Hawthorne Manor and to let her know that she was not going home tonight after all. Although it meant she'd have to stay for another six months, how could she leave in the face of such tragedy?

At once, Alethea took charge of the search, organizing several level-headed women, including Hawthorne's mother, into pairs at Kendra's insistence.

Only after that was done did it occur to her that she might be of more help to Brice than to anyone inside. Her gut instinct told her Luci was in danger, somewhere in the woods. *At the Druid's Cave*, she realized. *Where the fires were.*

Without a care for decorum, she abandoned the search to seek out Lady Winterowd's carriage. Packed discreetly inside was a bundle of her things she had intended to take with her to meet Botolf tonight. She arrived at the coach, the last in line, and pulled her fanny pack from the bundle, slung it over her shoulder, then put on a dark-colored pelisse, since her pale blue ball gown would be much too visible, before walking casually around to the back of the house. A drop of moisture hit her face, and she glanced up to see the once starry sky thick with clouds. There was no time to worry about the coming rain or the lightning that flashed far off on the horizon. Storm or no storm, she must reach the cave in time.

Snapping her fanny pack around her waist, she raced across the wide expanse of lawn past the summerhouse and gardens and on to the edge of the woods. From there, she knew it was only a short distance to the ruins, perhaps a ten to fifteen minute walk at the most. Guessing that time had slipped past faster than water through a sieve, she ran, slowing only when she could see the shadow of the great dolmens that surrounded the cave entrance looming up before her, their square outline silhouetted by a large fire that burned in the center.

Where had Brice gone? she wondered as she crept forward, ignoring the larger drops of water that now fell from the sky. A twig snapped beneath her feet, sending her heart racing with the fear that she might be overheard. She stopped, crouched and listened, at first hearing nothing, then, gradually, the faint sound of someone chanting.

What a foolish thing she'd done by coming out here. And where were Brice and Hawk? Seeing nothing, she continued in the direction of the eerie stone circle, pausing only long enough to draw her gun from her pack. The familiarity of the cold steel in her hand gave her some small comfort as she moved closer, closer, until she was separated from the large stones by a few feet and some thick shrubbery.

Crouching behind the bushes, she was able to see between the base of two stones that leaned together at the top, forming an upside down V.

The sight beyond caused her blood to run cold. There, upon a slab of granite, lay a girl dressed in a stark white gown. Bound and gagged, she struggled vainly against her bindings. Luci. It had to be. Before the girl stood a hooded, black-robed figure. Two others, shorter in stature, on either side of him were also robed completely in black.

The taller figure looked up to the sky, nodding and

chanting as the rain came down harder, though not hard enough to douse the great fire that burned in the center behind the altar.

Somewhere in the distance, Kendra heard the low rumble of thunder. Damn it all, where was Brice? Finally, it dawned on her that he must be on the opposite side. A slight movement in the shadows on the far side of the circle confirmed her suspicions and offered a small amount of comfort. At least she was not alone.

Cautiously, she crept closer, until she was nearly between the two leaning stones. A large bush growing beside one offered her some cover, as did the shadow of the other stone. Gripping her gun with two hands, one finger on the trigger, she sidled around the bush until she was hidden in the shadows between the two stones only ten or so feet away from the macabre scene that played before her.

The chanting grew louder, and the two men positioned on either side began circling the dais and fire, adding unintelligible words to their chant. The center figure turned and at the same time held up a long knife that glittered deadly cold in the firelight. Raising his other hand, he ran the blade across his palm. At once, dark liquid oozed from the cut, which he held over the writhing girl, allowing his blood to fall drop by drop upon the virgin-white of her dress.

After a moment, one of the other hooded figures stopped beside him, held out a black cloth, then bound the man's hand. A jewel-encrusted goblet was produced by the other figure, from which the man drank when it was held to his lips. Then he lifted the knife over his head as his chanting took on a fevered pitch.

Kendra's pulse raced with alarm and the world tilted crazily, then slowed nightmarishly as he lowered the knife down, down toward the girl's heart.

Adrenaline rushed through her, a thousand pins and needles converging through her veins to her wrists and she aimed her gun and fired. All of a sudden she was slammed to the ground, and her head struck rock as she fell. As if from a distance, she heard someone cry out, then everything faded around her. The last thing she remembered before total darkness engulfed her was her weapon flying from her grasp and a gray-robed arm reaching down to pick it up.

Kendra opened her eyes slowly and looked around, finding herself in the midst of a quiet darkness. Faint, unidentifiable sounds filtered through the trees into her consciousness. She rubbed her temples to ease the ache, wondering who had hit her on the head. She pushed herself to her knees, then stood on shaky limbs, using the side of the great stone to keep herself steady. The slight dizziness she felt cleared as she breathed in the fresh night air. Not until she moved into the circle of stones, a slight drizzle misting her face, did she recall what had happened.

Kendra peered into the night, but saw no sign that anyone had been in the pagan fire-ring. Moving into the center with infinite caution, her pulse pounding in her ears at the memory of such a macabre event, Kendra looked around for any clues that might explain what had occurred. Had the girl been murdered? Or had Kendra's aim been true? But with those questions came more. How was it that she had escaped anyone's notice after firing her weapon? Unless Brice had drawn them off. That must have been it, she decided, returning to pick up her gun in case the suspects returned. Unfortunately, she could not find it anywhere. A vague memory of someone picking up her weapon after she fell came back. The murderer, perhaps? But no, whoever it was had worn gray, not the black of the cultists. Who then?

And what had happened to the girl? Kendra moved toward the stone altar, seeing no sign of bloodshed. Of course the rain had probably washed it clean. She circled the massive granite block expecting to see the remains of a large fire on the opposite side. But there was nothing. Nothing except foot-high weeds, battered down by the rain, but still rooted firmly in the ground. Not even a singed blade of grass remained to give testament to the fire she knew had burned there. Moving from the circle, she walked to the cave entrance just beyond. All was dark within, and without her gun, she was not about to step into that lair. She returned to the circle of stones.

Perplexed, Kendra stood in the midst of the dolmens looking for any sign that she had truly seen what she believed she had seen. As she stood there, a loud roar rumbled across the sky. More thunder she thought. But the noise did not fade as thunder should. It roared. Her heart slammed against her chest, as the sound grew louder and louder until it nearly deafened her.

As she stared at the sky, flashing red lights emerged from the clouds, descending in a steady path toward the horizon. A jet?

She raced from the circle toward Hawthorne Manor, stopping only when she exited the woods to see the mansion, its windows aglow from the thousand lights illuminating its interior and the party held within. The familiar sight calmed her. She couldn't have been knocked out for too long, for it was apparent that Lord Hawthorne's ball was still in full swing.

As she stared at the mansion, however, Kendra could not shake off the eerie feeling that it seemed much smaller. Or was it that everything around it seemed larger? The oak trees dotting the park-like grounds seemed to dwarf the building, and the yew maze behind the summerhouse appeared twice as high as she remembered. And how was it that she had never noticed the great stone wall surrounding the premises? A trick of the moonlight, she decided. Except that the moon was hiding behind the clouds. Pressing on her aching temples, Kendra decided that the blow to her head had shaken her senses. What she needed right now was a good steaming cup of Grandmère's herbal tea.

Concerned that Grandmère and Cecily must surely be worried about her by now, she hurried toward the house. Suddenly two bright lights, side by side, moved swiftly down the drive—illuminating the sleek sides of . . . car after car parked along the road leading to the mansion. Her steps faltered, as her senses were overwhelmed by the brightness of the lights and the cacophony of noises of the modern world.

"It can't be."

But it was. Somehow, some way, she had made it back to the twentieth century.

Who fired that shot? Brice wondered as he fingered the small tubular piece of brass he had found in the ruins. At first, he had believed that Hawk was responsible for that fine piece of marksmanship. It had knocked the knife from the murderer's hand, allowing Brice to rush in and rescue the girl as the black-robed figures fled. But Hawk had assured him he was not responsible. And when they had searched the ruins later by torch light, looking for further clues as to who their murderer might be, all they had found was this tiny brass cylinder with "WIN 9mm LUGER" expertly engraved on the bottom.

It looked suspiciously like the strange objects he had seen in Kendra's pistol, minus the copper mounted on the top. Had Kendra fired the shot?

But no, she couldn't have, for Alethea was positive that Kendra had been searching the house for Luci. But Luci was safe now. And Kendra was missing.

The door to Hawthorne's study opened, and Alethea stood in the doorway. "Shall we go home now, dear?" Cecily appeared behind her, yawning widely.

Brice barely noticed them. The *Eterne*. Of course! Kendra had promised to be on the ship at dawn. "You shall have to leave without me. I am going to the *Eterne*."

Cecily's sleepy yawn turned into an "oh" of dismay. "But you promised to take us home."

"Even so, I must leave you in Hawk's good hands." He had to get to his ship before Kendra was gone from his life forever. The feeling that if she sailed away he might never see her again spurred him to action. Rushing past Cecily and Alethea, he said, "I intend to bring Kendra home. Where she belongs."

"Dear, there's something you ought to know," Alethea called out. "Kendra's not on the *Eterne*."

He stopped cold. "I want to bring Kendra home."

"But you can't, my dear," Alethea responded. "For Kendra's already home. In the twentieth century. Botolf has told me so."

Kendra approached the mansion, wondering how the current occupants would greet her. Men in white coats coming to take her away came to mind as she looked down at her gown. The hem was covered with mud as was the dark-colored pelisse she'd grabbed before leaving the party. Thankfully, it had covered up most of her gown, keeping it fairly clean. Music and laughter drifted from the open windows as she took off her outer wrap before hurrying to the front of the house.

As she rounded the corner, she saw a taxi parked by the front steps. The cabby appeared to be waiting for his passengers. Kendra hurried to the driver's side. "Excuse me. Can you take me to the airport?"

The driver, a balding, round-faced man, tossed his cigarette into the drive. "You the one that called for a cab?" His accent was decidedly American.

"No. But I do need a ride."

"Don't much care who I take, long as I get my fare. Where you from?"

"Miami."

"No kidding. Used to live in Fort Lauderdale myself. Stationed here in the service. Married a pretty English girl, and never went back."

"I was born in Fort Lauderdale," she lied, wondering if she could convince him to take the single check she had left.

"No kidding? Used to live just behind the library. That old bakery still there?"

How would she know? "Yeah. Great place."

"Used to hang out by the back door waiting for—" He stopped and whistled. "Must be some costume party."

Kendra looked down at her clothes. The fanny pack buckled around her waist seemed comical in comparison to the rich silk of the dress. "Yes. It was some party."

"Pretty authentic looking dress," he said as she climbed into the back seat and shut the door. "I seen some like that in the museum at Blackmoor Hall."

"Blackmoor Hall's a museum?"

"Yep," he said, starting the engine. "Most of those old places are like that, you know. Need the money to keep up the repairs. Even Hawthorne Manor, here, gives tours a few times a day. Used to be the old earl would let folks come in and use his park for picnics and the like. Nice lands, you know, been on a picnic there once myself. But not the new earl. He charges folks."

He turned his cab around and headed away from the mansion. "Lost his fortune in some bad investments, posted guards around and started charging. If you want to go on a picnic, you got to pay for the tour first. And take it too. They don't let no one on the lands 'til after the first tour is over. Then everyone is ushered off the grounds by four. You'd think people would protest having to pay for a picnic, but they come in droves. Mostly Americans, like ourselves, though."

The cabby chattered on, but Kendra barely heard him. "Is Blackmoor Hall really a museum?"

"Well, not the main house. The dower house. Briar something, it's called."

"Briarwood," Kendra supplied.

"Yeah, that's it. But if you're interested in seeing it, they're only open for tours on Wednesdays. Went there last week with the kids. My daughter's doin' a report for her history class. Nice place. Don't even charge you. All you have to do is sign their guest register. Got a man that reads every name, greets you and shakes your hand as you come in. And once a year, they open the main house up for a tour as well. Why, I don't know, since the young duke has more money than he knows what to do with. No telling about the rich, though. But I guess you know that, having hobnobbed with a few tonight. Good party, huh?" he looked back at her in the rearview mirror.

"Yeah. Had the time of my life."

At Heathrow airport, Kendra convinced the cabby to accept her last check—the least he could do for a fellow

American, he'd told her, although Kendra thought it had more to do with the considerable bonus she'd added to his fare.

The terminal was a bustle of activity, even at this early hour, with people of every nationality tugging luggage, children, and babies around to their various destinations. Cameras flashed as Kendra walked past a line of Japanese tourists, no doubt interested in her ballgown. She ignored the most blatant stares, but smiled at the children as she stood in line at the British Airways ticket counter. Thankfully, there were only a few people before her, and she did not have long to wait before the clerk asked if he could help her. And then promptly sent her on her way because her credit card had expired.

She'd thought that all she needed to do to get home was return to her own century. But now, as she stood in the middle of the airport, facing the daunting task of calling someone for the airfare home, she realized it was not as easy as she'd first thought. Who would believe her story? She stared at the pay phone, realizing that there were only two people in the world she could consider calling: Jack and Frankie.

If she told Jack what had happened, he would drop her in a straightjacket faster than a jackrabbit crossing a highway. That left Frankie. *Frankie would believe her.* They were best friends. They'd practically grown up together. Kendra had rented the furnished apartment over Frankie's garage for years. Frankie had even told her she'd never consider renting it out to anyone else—it wouldn't be the same, she'd said time and time again. Never in a million years, Kendra thought as she picked up the phone, would Frankie think her crazy.

*   *   *

"Oh my God, you're crazy!" Frankie got up and paced the room. It had taken Kendra nearly a week to get up the courage to tell her, and she did so only because Frankie wasn't convinced by the amnesia story she'd concocted. After having listened to Kendra's unbelievable tale for more than an hour, Frankie still didn't look like she believed her. "I mean, you're talking science fiction here," Frankie continued. "Time travel without the machine."

"Maybe I dreamed it all."

"For six months? No way. Besides, you have the dress."

"Well, what other explanation is there?"

Frankie stopped her pacing to stare at her friend. "My God! Do you know what this means? The Bermuda Triangle!" she announced with aplomb. "God! That means that all those stories are true! Sort of like *Close Encounters of the Third Kind,* without the aliens. All those pilots and stuff who were lost—they're probably wandering around in some other century!"

"I wasn't sailing in the Bermuda Triangle."

"General vicinity counts."

"Come off it Frankie. You know as well as I—"

"That it's not true? Take a look at yourself."

"I knew it. I'm crazy."

"No, you're not," Frankie replied vehemently. "There has to be an explanation. I just don't know what it is yet."

"Do you believe me?"

"I wish I could say yes, but it all seems too fantastic. I do believe, though, that you honestly believe it. And I think, given the time to think about it, I will. Well, maybe not. But I know you're not crazy."

Kendra sank back into her chair and sighed. "What am I going to do?"

"Go to Disney World?"

"Very funny. About the shrink. Thanks to Jack, I've

got an appointment with the department psychiatrist. It's this afternoon. I can't go back to work until he okays me for full duty just in case I'm still suffering from amnesia."

"Well, stick with the amnesia story you told Jack. Trust me. It'll go over better than the one you told me."

"You don't believe me."

"Would you?"

Kendra looked around at all the boxes stacked around her apartment. It would take days to unpack everything. Frankie had thought she was dead, and after the memorial service had been in the process of emptying her apartment, except that her overly sentimental feelings had gotten in the way. When it had come time to put everything in storage, Frankie couldn't force herself to remove the last of Kendra's things.

"No," Kendra said, "I'd think I was crazy."

Later that afternoon Kendra drove to the department psychiatrist.

She walked into the stark office, and took a seat near the window. Picking up a magazine, showing the latest in police safety equipment, she thumbed through the pages, then tossed it back on the table. Perhaps she should have brought her ballgown. Maybe he'd believe her. Then again, the amnesia story was the safest route. But what if she wasn't crazy and it really did happen? No, she knew she wasn't crazy. Crazy people did not dream up men like Brice. Did they?

She could always leave. Did she really want to be a cop anyway? But before she could decide, she heard her name being called.

"Kendra Browning?" Her heart stopped when she looked up to see the doctor, a graying man in his forties, standing at the door. "Good afternoon, Kendra. Come in."

15

The psychiatrist had told Kendra that her lapse of time was a delusion caused by her boating accident. A delusion!

Instead of going straight home, she drove to the pier, bought some crackers to feed the gulls that crowded the docks, then stared out over the water. Not until the sun dipped below the horizon did she drive the few blocks home. Once there, she locked her door, turned on the classical music station, lit a candle, and watched as its flame flickered. After several moments of quiet contemplation, she went into her room and took out her ballgown from the closet. Bringing it back into the living room, she draped it over the coffee table, then sat on the couch, fingering her moonstone pendant while she watched the reflections from the candlelight dance across the pale silk of her gown. Then as the chill of the evening crept into the room, wrapping its icy fingers around her heart, she cried herself to sleep.

The ringing of the doorbell cut swiftly into her dreams of waltzes and moonlit carriage rides. Kendra forced an eye open, but then closed it against the bright sunlight that flooded through her windows. When the persistent and annoying bell tone continued, she pushed herself off the couch to answer the door. She'd slept there the entire night and her shoulders felt stiff.

"I'm coming," she said, as she undid the deadbolt and chain.

Frankie stood on the threshold, holding a cardboard tray. Steam swirled up from two Styrofoam cups on either side of a white bakery bag. "I brought us coffee and croissants."

"I'm not hungry," Kendra said, shutting the door once Frankie stepped inside.

"That bad, huh?"

"I guess that all depends on your point of view. I did get my job back. And the transfer to juvenile." Kendra lifted her ballgown off the table so that Frankie could set their breakfast down.

Kendra, clutching the gown, sat on the couch.

"So tell me, what did the shrink say?" Frankie asked, handing her a cup of coffee.

"He asked me what I did in England, and so I told him. And then he said that what *I* thought had happened was merely a delusion." She resisted the urge to lift the gown to her face. "Very common in amnesia patients, but not the sort of amnesia you get when you just plain forget. He told me that my mind was just filling in the blanks."

"With what?"

"A book. A movie."

"Did you mention that you were gone six months?"

"Of course. He said they'd probably be able to check into my whereabouts somehow. People don't just wander around a foreign country for that long without someone discovering them." Kendra lifted the gown and buried her face in its folds, closing her eyes against the burn of tears. "I *don't* have amnesia. *I can't.*"

"Hey, Ken," Frankie said, moving to her side and putting her arms around her. "He's only a shrink. What could he know?"

"Maybe I'm destined to live out my life with a man like Jack."

"We both know that Jack's not the right man for you."

"You—"

"*You* can never be yourself around him."

"Jack has nothing to do with the way I am."

"Oh?" Frankie plucked one of Kendra's paperbacks—a spy novel—from a box of unpacked books and returned to her seat.

"Leave it alone." Kendra tried to grab the book from her friend's hand.

"No way." Frankie read the blurb on the back of the cover. " 'Even though the cold war with Russia is over, Interpol agent Michael Lewis has one last mission: to retrieve vital papers from the basement of the Kremlin before they are discovered by the new regime. Papers that could start World War III.' "

"So what?" Kendra retorted with an air of nonchalance.

"So what?" her friend repeated. She easily slipped that cover off to reveal the book's true cover. One showing a man and woman embracing beneath a tropical sunset. "You want me to read what's really in here?"

"Okay. You've proved your point. Jack hates it when I read romance novels."

"It's more than that, Ken. You're a romantic at heart. Your bedroom's pale yellow with frilly white curtains. You like to take long bubble baths on your days off and only dream of the ballet because Jack will never take you. You like to have the door opened for you when you go out on a date, and you're looking for Prince Charming."

"Jack's not the romantic sort. He's more . . . overprotective."

"You think he is now. Just wait and see if he gets wind of what you just told the shrink. My God! Did you really tell the doctor everything?"

Kendra nodded. "It . . . just slipped."

"*Slipped*? How does a little thing like time travel just slip?"

"I told you. He's good at his job. Besides, he had a perfectly plausible explanation."

"And you believe it? The doctor's explanation, I mean?"

In her heart, she wanted to believe what had happened to her was real. In her head, she didn't know what to believe. "After retracing my actions, starting with my relationship with Jack, and the fake covers I use for my romance novels, the doctor has determined that I had filled my head with the storyline of whatever historical romances I had read just before the accident."

"I thought you only read contemporary novels."

"Normally, yes. But I did buy one right before I went sailing."

"And?"

Kendra hesitated. "And there were definite similarities, like the time period, a ship . . . the heroine falling in love with the hero . . . "

"In love?"

Kendra closed her eyes. After a moment, she asked, "Could I actually have fallen in love with a storybook character?" She rubbed the hem of her gown against her cheek. "I miss him so," she whispered. "I want him back and I can never have him. He's a figment of my imagination. Someone I dreamed up as the perfect foil for Jack. Or at least that's what the doctor told me."

"Well, if that's true, then what on earth were you doing for the last six months? Wandering around England without a clue? I, for one, have a hard time believing someone wouldn't have noticed you and *insisted* the men in the long white coats come and take you away to the funny farm."

"Who knows? The doctor says until I recover from my amnesia, I won't remember what really happened."

"I don't believe it," Frankie stated firmly. "Do you?" she asked, a little less convincingly.

Picking up her cup, Kendra took a sip of the lukewarm coffee, then stared at the carton of books. "His explanation sounds perfectly plausible, and yet . . . Oh God! I just couldn't have imagined a man like Brice."

"Forget what the shrink told you. Listen to your heart. What's it telling you?"

Kendra, her ballgown clutched in her hand, stood and moved to the kitchen window. Outside, past the palm trees in the yard, she could just make out a sliver of the ocean between two Mediterranean-style houses across the street. The last of the late summer sunlight lit the water into a million shimmering fragments. Overhead, in the cerulean sky, a gull flew by then disappeared from sight.

She heard Frankie pull out a stool at the kitchen counter. "So," her friend prompted, "what's your heart telling you?"

"It's telling me that it's going to be a long, lonely summer."

*   *   *

Kendra's life had settled to a comfortable routine. She started back at the precinct, working juvenile, and spent the remainder of her time in her apartment or downstairs at Frankie's, avoiding contact with Jack. Although she'd seen him at work, she just couldn't face him alone—not after Brice—and she'd used every plausible excuse and many implausible ones whenever he'd called to ask her out.

His persistence bothered her, and despite that he'd sent her more red roses in the past few days than during the entire three years they'd been dating, she couldn't get past the feeling that *if* she did go out with him, she'd be unfaithful to Brice's memory. But could one be unfaithful to a delusion? A delusion that fully intended betrothing himself to another woman?

Such thoughts kept her from sleeping soundly at night. And if that wasn't enough to disturb her sleep, the nagging idea that she should be remembering something terribly important was. Whatever this revelation might be, it continued to elude her—until the morning she sat reading the paper at a sidewalk café a few blocks from her apartment.

Kendra nodded at the waiter who poured her tea, then picked up the paper and started to read. The headline jumped out at her. "Debutante Murderer Strikes Again." The subtitle chilled her through. "Florida Debutante Found Slain in Cult-Style Murder."

How was it that after her return to Miami, she'd barely spared a moment's thought to the case she and Jack had been investigating before she went sailing? Kendra scanned the article, her stomach twisting at the thought that after so long the suspect still hadn't been caught. Suddenly, she recalled the crime scene and the pocket watch she'd found with its strange symbol and the words inscribed inside.

"Of course," she whispered. "Do what thou wilt."
Somewhere within that simple phrase lay the key to the
murders. Throwing a couple of dollars on the red and
white checked tablecloth, Kendra rushed from the café
and drove to the library.

Once there, she asked the woman at the reference
counter to bring her anything and everything pertaining
to the Hell-Fire Club and nineteenth-century murders. If
her hunch was correct, she'd have to have something
tangible to show to Jack. He'd never take her seriously
unless she had something, anything, to back up her wild
theory. Kendra pored over each of the books and articles, until she was as familiar with the cult as a day's
research in a well-stocked library could make her. One
book in particular, *Famous Ritual Murderers of the
17th, 18th and 19th Centuries*, had a small section on
unsolved murders.

Of course the infamous Jack the Ripper was written
about in some detail, but more importantly the murders
of Hawthorne Woods were listed as well. While it was
only a two-paragraph entry, someone apparently thought
the murders worth mentioning, down to the exact nature
of the cult-style slayings, which resembled the Debutante
Murders in every way except the century and country
they were committed in. Could someone have read this
and copied the murders of Hawthorne Woods?

After checking the book out, Kendra went to the local
FBI office to speak to an agent about the possibility of
entering the facts of the Debutante *and* Hawthorne
Woods Murders into their computers to see if they came
up with any similarities. She was careful to include the
message inscribed on the medallion, both in English and
in Old French. After leaving a number where she could
be reached, she headed for the precinct, her next task to

have a teletype sent to every agency across the U.S. to locate any murders with similar M.O.s.

Only when that was done did she seek Jack out. He was sitting at his desk talking on the phone when she entered his office. Looking up, he smiled and pointed to a nearby chair. He covered up the mouthpiece and asked, "Something wrong? You look out of breath."

"Nothing. I've been running a lot of errands."

"What's up?"

"I have to talk to you. It's important."

"I can't right now, sweetheart. Another homicide last night."

"I know. I read about it in the papers. That's why I want to see you. I just remembered something about the last case before I left. The murder where I found that pocket watch."

"Well, make it quick. I have to be at Paradise Park in twenty minutes to interview a witness." He uncovered the mouthpiece. "Hey, Madison, something's come up. Can I put you on hold for a minute? Good." He covered the receiver up again, but didn't put the phone down or even press the hold button. "Okay. What is it? One of your delinquents come up with something?"

Jack had never thought highly of the juvenile division. "Do you recall the timepiece I found? What was written inside of it?" Kendra asked.

"Yeah."

"Well, when I was in England, I saw something similar. *Fay ce que voudras.* It's Old French, and means, 'Do what thou wilt,' which is what was on the pocket watch, except in English."

"And?"

"It's from the Hell-Fire Club."

"The what club?" Finally, he sounded interested.

"Hell-Fire-Club." Kendra explained briefly about the meetings of debauchery that parodied the Church of England. "It started in the seventeenth century, but there've been offshoots of it branching out over the years. Copycat clubs, I guess, some worse than others. I thought if you were to do a check on anyone with ties to something similar, you might discover a lead. Some psychotic history buff trying to recreate the club."

"Look, Kendra, I don't have time for this. How about you just leave a message with the secretary, and I'll look it up later. In the meantime, you get some rest. You're probably still tired from your accident."

He didn't believe her. Setting her copies of the teletypes on his desk, she watched as he scanned them over, then slammed the phone in its cradle at the realization of what she'd done.

"You put *my* name on these?"

"You're working homicide. Not me."

"Dammit, Kendra! You should've asked first. They're gonna think I'm crazy!"

"Everyone already thinks I am, so what the hell," she said, rising. "It wasn't anything less than I would've done, had I *still* been your partner. I just thought I'd save you the trouble. If it doesn't pan out, you can blame me."

She left him, and taking the rest of the afternoon off, returned to her apartment. Two hours later, he was at her door.

Jack moved past her into the apartment, shoving a dozen red roses into her grasp. "I can't believe it!" he said, excitement filling his voice. "You were right. Where did you get it?"

"Get what?" Kendra went into the kitchen and took a vase out of the cupboard. She filled it with water and set the roses in, then closed her eyes and breathed in the scent.

A single, yellow rosebud came to mind, and she wondered how it was that in all the years she'd known Jack, he'd never caught on that yellow roses were her favorite.

"That lead. Simmons just called from the Bureau. He thinks he's got a suspect in our case. Boston P.D. had an old homicide with those very same words in it. 'Whither thou willest.'"

"Do what thou wilt," she corrected, ignoring the ache in her heart. She put the roses on the far side of the room.

"Yeah. That." He sat at the counter. "It was painted over the doorway inside this temple of sorts where they found this murdered woman a couple of years ago. They arrested a suspect, a Sean Parker, but could never pin it on him and had to let him go. Then he disappeared without a trace. The thing's still unsolved."

"You want some coffee?" she asked, even though she didn't really want him to stay.

"No, thanks. They faxed us his prints. The lab's comparing them right now with a partial they lifted from that pocket watch you found last winter."

"Who's this Parker guy?" Kendra asked, not recognizing the name.

"Some rich antiques dealer from Great Britain. Immigrated over a couple of years ago, started an import business, but disappeared right after the case. And you'll never guess where he disappeared to?"

"Here?"

"You got it, sweetheart. Right here in good old Miami Beach. I've got the lab doing DNA tests on some hair samples we found the other night at the latest murder. And if the prints match up, and the DNA matches, we've closed our case. He can't be too far from here. I'll let you know as soon as I find out. Okay?"

"Sure, Jack."

"You haven't lost your touch, judging by the job you did today tracking that information down."

"It was just a lucky guess."

"Yeah, right. So when you coming back?"

"I'm not. I like working juvenile. I've decided kids are more important."

"Sure could use your help. There's a mountain of paperwork."

He hadn't changed. "Oh, God. Look at the time. Frankie will be here any moment and I still haven't vacuumed." She grasped his arm and ushered him to the door. "Let me know how your investigation goes. Okay?" When he tried to kiss her, she turned her cheek.

Disappointment shone in his brown eyes, and she smiled at him to lessen the impact of her actions. "Bye, Jack."

"Bye," he said as she closed the door behind him.

16

The taxi lurched to a stop and a dark-haired man in blue jeans and an off-white cable-knit sweater got out. Before he started up the street, he pulled a piece of paper, worn from constant handling, from his pocket and read once more what he knew by heart.

"Bloody hell." Kendra laid her paperback over the arm of her chair to answer the telephone.

"Good afternoon, sweetheart."

"Oh. Hi, Jack."

"Missed me that much, huh?"

"No. It's not that. I was in the middle of a book. And I'm a little tired. It was a long week."

"So, how's it going in juvenile?"

"It's all right. Kind of depressing at times, especially when a kid you've worked particularly hard at saving denies he was ever abused—right in front of the jury."

"Jeez. I'm sorry. I forgot your case came up in court this week. How'd it go?"

"Good. Even though the kid lied, the medical evidence spoke for itself. Thank God the jury was competent. The father got eight years, and the mother got one for failing to protect."

"Too tired for dinner?"

Kendra hesitated. In spite of Jack's new leaf, they'd not been on a real date since her return. "Tonight?"

"Yeah. A celebration of sorts. You'll never guess who was just arrested, flying in from Heathrow. Parker. Sean Clyde Parker, the Debutante Murderer."

"You're kidding? How? I thought he'd disappeared again. Without a trace you said."

"He did. Right after the last murder. But for whatever reason, he came back. Maybe the guy doesn't read the papers. I mean, once the prints matched up and the DNA tests confirmed it was the same suspect in all the murders, the press had a field day. From what I understand, Great Britain made a bigger show out of it than we did. Nearly wiped the coverage from the royal family. Guess they haven't had a murderer that famous since Jack the Ripper. The guy must have fallen off the face of the earth not to have known he was the main suspect. Either that or he wanted to get caught."

"So what now?"

"He's exercising his right to a speedy trial. Arraignment's first thing in the morning. But in the meantime, we have some celebrating to do."

Kendra could hardly spoil his enthusiasm by refusing, although she wanted to do just that. Like a veritable prince charming, Jack had wooed her continuously, once she had told him she wasn't coming back to homicide. When she'd commented on how considerate he'd suddenly become, he merely told her that it was different from when she was his partner. She was no longer one of the guys.

In short, he was the Jack she'd fallen in love with so many years ago. And yet, something always held her back, keeping her from giving herself completely to him. Visions of midnight eyes and raven hair swirled into her mind, reminding her that true love would never be hers. Wistfully, she wondered each day if it had been a dream. Never. A dream would have faded in intensity. Besides, how could she imagine someone as complex as the duke of Blackmoor? On the *Eterne* he had seemed almost carefree, unfettered by the restraints that society had placed upon him. At Blackmoor Hall, he was ever the aristocrat, even behind closed doors—with the exception of one night, one passion-filled night that she'd remember for the rest of her life. With her eyes closed, Kendra relived each touch, and within moments, she was in agony, wanting, needing to feel his skin next to hers. But her unbidden erotic thoughts served only to remind her of what she could never have. Even if he was not a figment of her imagination—a thought that seemed more probable with each passing day—he was still well over a century in the past.

"Well, sweetheart? What about it? Dinner tonight?"

Jack's voice swept her into the present. "Tonight?" she echoed. Why not? She'd never find anyone else like. . . . Who was she fooling? "Sure."

"Great. I'll pick you up around seven."

"Seven," she echoed as she hung up the phone, wondering why her memories were so easily explained away, and yet so hard to forget. It had been a long summer and promised to be an even longer winter. And lonely. Wandering to her bedroom, she opened the closet to run her fingers, as she had so many times before, across the pale blue silk of her ballgown.

A soft knock broke into her thoughts, then a cheerful, "Kendra? You here?"

"In here, Frankie. I'll be right out." Kendra took one last wistful glance at the gown that held all her secret longings, before shutting out the past by closing the closet door and stepping into the living room.

Frankie tossed her sweater onto the sofa. "It's freezing outside. Must be in the low sixties. You got any hot chocolate?"

Kendra eyed Frankie, who, like her, was dressed in a cotton shirt and jeans. "Sure," she said, moving into the small kitchen to put a cup of water into the microwave. "Jack just called. He asked me out to dinner."

"Again?"

"This time, I told him I'd go." The microwave beeped and Kendra pulled the cup out, then dumped the chocolate in, before stirring it briskly.

"I thought you'd sworn off men. That one in particular," Frankie commented, as Kendra handed her the cup.

"It's not like a date. It's more like a celebratory dinner. He finally arrested the Debutante Murderer. He's in custody at the county jail until his arraignment tomorrow. Besides, Jack's worked so hard on the case, I just couldn't let him down."

"He's worked hard on it? What about your part? Without you, they'd never have caught the guy."

"Let him have his glory. Homicide's his forte now, not mine. Besides, he really has changed, you know. Why just last week he sent me two tickets to the ballet."

"I know. I got to sit next to you for the third time in as many years. How many times can you watch a swan die, for God's sake?"

Kendra grinned, knowing Frankie would much rather have spent the night watching the football game on television. As Jack had done that night. "I love *Swan Lake*."

"I know. But we're talking about dinner. You're really going?"

"Really. He's picking me up at seven."

"Wait a minute. We're talking about Jack Sinclair, here. The man who has carte blanche credit at Giovanni's deli? The same one who thinks if it's not barbecued at home it's not worth paying for?" Frankie took a sip of her chocolate, then said, "I've got it! He's asking you to go Dutch. Right?"

"He didn't say anything about who was paying."

"Seems to me that something's up if Jack's going to all that trouble just over dinner."

"He just wants to celebrate," Kendra said, running water into the sink to start the dishes. "Nothing more."

Frankie finished her chocolate, then handed the mug to Kendra to rinse out. "Whatever you say, Kendra. But don't let a little thing like your pining away for the past few months make you do something stupid tonight. Jack's not the last guy on earth, you know."

"Very funny. Was there a reason for this visit?" Kendra asked, filling the sink with dirty dishes.

"Yes. To see how your case went yesterday."

"Fine. We won, but barely."

Frankie's interest was sincere, since her own childhood was lived under similar circumstances. "Is his foster home good?"

"Yeah. And his father won't be getting out for at least eight years. The kid'll be nineteen then."

"Good."

"How's the travel agency going?" Kendra asked, deciding to change the subject to something less depressing.

"Fine. Business is booming, considering it's the dead of winter. Colorado's pretty popular. A lot of skiing vacations, although I did book a few flights to Mexico, which is where I'd rather be right now. Who'd want to go where it's cold?"

Kendra laughed. "Try spending a winter in England."

"I can't function in anything below fifty. And that's pushing it." Frankie glanced out the window. "Does that look like storm clouds coming up? I was thinking of having dinner tonight at the café."

"You could stay here. There's turkey and sprouts in the fridge."

"What? And witness the touching scene when Jack arrives to take you out? No thanks." Frankie grinned as she slid off her barstool. "But don't forget to tell me how it goes in the morning. All right?"

"In your dreams, woman. Now get out of here, before I make you dry," she threatened, holding up a dish towel with one suds-covered hand.

"I'm out of here." Frankie grabbed her sweater. "Not that I don't want to help, but I do have to get back to work. See you."

"Bye, you rat," Kendra said, tossing the towel on the counter to pick up the scrub brush. The door shut with a soft click, but after a few seconds, opened again. "Forget something?" she asked without looking up.

"Yes, Miss Browning," came the smooth, masculine response. "You."

The dish brush slid from Kendra's wet hands into the water, causing a waft of suds to fly up into her face. She hardly noticed, absently brushing them off with the back of her hand as she stared at the figure in the doorway. "Brice," she whispered, unable to move.

Frankie swept in behind him. "Sorry, Kendra. He asked if you lived here, and I couldn't stop him. He just ran up the stairs and— Hey, Kendra? Are you okay? He said he was a friend . . . from England," she finished lamely.

Kendra scarcely heard her as she rushed from the kitchen, soap suds and all. "You came!" she cried. "You came." She threw herself into his arms, holding tightly, afraid to let go.

He brushed the suds from her cheek, then the tears from her eyes. "Did you think I wouldn't?" he asked tenderly, kissing the tip of her nose.

Kendra stared into his eyes. "No. I didn't. I didn't think it was possible. I—" He silenced her with a kiss.

Frankie gave a discreet cough to let them know she was still there. Kendra pulled away and looked at her friend, then smiled. "He's here."

"So I see," Frankie said. "But who is he?"

"Brice. The man who rescued me."

Frankie's jaw dropped. "From you know *when*?" she whispered after a moment.

Kendra nodded, grinning, her arms wrapped tightly around Brice's neck. He gently disengaged himself from her grasp, then turned toward Frankie, taking her hand in his. He gave a gallant bow, then kissed the back of her hand. "And you must be the lovely Miss Wendall?" he asked.

Frankie, turning bright red, nodded.

"Miss Browning spoke very highly of you. I feel as if we're old friends."

"Likewise, I'm sure," Frankie managed, staring at the back of her hand, then up into his dark eyes, only to blush once more. "Are you really from the nineteenth century?"

Brice glanced at Kendra before answering, as if to see if Frankie could be trusted with their secret. What he couldn't know was that Kendra, too, waited impatiently for his answer, although in her heart, she had always known he existed.

"I am. Though, at times, it's difficult to believe any of this is possible."

"I told you you weren't crazy," Frankie said, before returning her gaze, one of pure adoration, back to Brice's handsome features.

"Weren't you on your way back to work?" Kendra asked, wanting nothing more than to have Brice all to herself.

"You invited me to have dinner here, tonight. Remember?"

"Dinner's hours away, and you turned the invitation down. Now get out," she said, smiling to lessen the bite of her words.

"I'll be downstairs if you need anything," Frankie told her, giving Brice one last heartfelt look before slipping out the door.

Kendra shut and locked it, then turned to stare at the man who had been the mainstay of her dreams every night since her return from England. Here he was in her century. Wearing jeans! Leaning against the door, because her knees were suddenly weak, she asked, "What brought you here?"

"You," he replied, his voice deep velvet.

"I mean, how did you get here?"

He held out his hand, and she grasped it. "We can discuss that later," he replied, drawing her to him.

His mouth descended on hers for a long, searing kiss. Every nerve in Kendra's body came alive. He looked into her eyes for a long moment, then said, "I want you so much, my dear, sweet Kendra. Night after night, I've dreamt of one thing. Seeing you again. And now, now that I have you in my arms. . . . Let me love you." This last was barely a whisper.

Kendra nodded, and months of longing and unfulfilled nights were suddenly swept away as he lifted her in his arms.

"My lady," he said between the kisses he rained upon her face. "Might I ask where your bedchamber is?"

"Straight ahead," Kendra replied.

He carried her into the bedroom, and set her gently upon her bed. Lying next to her, he ran his fingers through her hair, stared at her for several moments, then drew her mouth to his for a deep kiss.

Slowly, they divested themselves of each other's clothing, until they were skin to skin, mouth to mouth, heart to heart.

The room, cool when they'd entered, had warmed considerably as they took turns exploring each others' bodies, remembering the sight, the scent and the taste of each other. As Brice teased the tip of one dusky breast into a tight bud, the fleeting thought that she had to be dreaming came to mind. She didn't care. How could she when his tongue wrought such exquisite feelings from her? And if it was a dream, she thought as he slid one finger inside her, it was the best damned dream she'd ever had.

Slowly, he withdrew his finger, rubbing it lightly against her until she writhed beneath his touch on her most sensitive spot, the center of her desire. She pressed herself against him, feeling the moisture grow between her legs.

"Brice," she said, closing her eyes. The pressure within her mounted, while her awareness of all else dimmed in comparison. His touch brought her close to a sweet, elusive sensation, and she concentrated on it, bringing it closer, deeper within her. Then, without warning, she slipped into the vortex, too late to stop the tumult of sensations that swirled through her. At that moment, Brice slid his shaft into her, and time was lost as they came together in their ageless dance.

*   *   *

It was nearly five in the evening when Kendra awoke to the feel of feather-light kisses upon her cheek. Opening her eyes, she saw Brice's midnight gaze fixed upon her. "If I am dreaming, don't wake me," she said, contentedly.

"I recall you saying that once before," he told her, tapping her nose playfully with his finger. "At the time, I had no idea how significant your words were."

"How do I know I'm not dreaming now?" she asked, half afraid it might be true.

"Because I'm here, and I didn't suffer the near insurmountable fright of flying through the heavens in a horseless carriage just for a dream."

Kendra grinned. "Scared of flying?"

"I was terrified. But I'd do it again if need be to find you," he said, his voice filled with tenderness.

She stroked his whisker-shadowed cheek. "How *did* you find me?"

"Botolf. And this." He reached over the side of the bed, picked up his blue jeans and removed a tattered slip of paper from his pocket, which he handed to her.

Kendra propped herself up on one elbow to unfold and read it. "My address," she said. "I'd forgotten that I gave it to you."

"Thankfully, I did not."

"But how did you get here?"

He stroked her cheek, his dark gaze holding hers. "The night of the ball, when I went to look for Caroline's cousin. I couldn't find you—" His voice cracked, and he turned away for a moment. "You saved her," he said after awhile. "I thought it was Hawk who fired that shot. It was you."

Kendra nodded, but didn't interrupt.

"Very impressive," he continued, his eyes sparkling once more. "I'll think twice before angering you in the future. I wouldn't want you to challenge me to a duel with such a deadly weapon."

"Never fear," she told him. "I lost it. All I have now is a little revolver, which I carry in my purse. I—"

He silenced her with a kiss. "There's time to talk later. Now I want nothing more than to love you as I've dreamed of doing for all the sleepless nights we've been apart."

One long satiated hour later, Kendra asked Brice to tell her what happened the night of Hawk's ball.

"After you fired your shot," he began, "I rushed in and grabbed Luci before she was harmed. The murderer ran off with the other two before Hawk or I had a chance to stop them."

"Did you ever find him?"

"No. He disappeared without a trace. Much as you did, my dear. At first, I thought you'd gone to the *Eterne* as I had ordered. In fact, I was on my way there to fetch you back when—"

Kendra's heart swelled. "You went there to get me?"

"No. Alethea informed me you returned home with the help of Botolf."

"Botolf?" Kendra said, sitting upright, not realizing the sheet had fallen to reveal her breasts, until Brice's gaze told her otherwise. Grabbing the sheet to cover herself—not because she was embarrassed, but because they'd never be able to have a normal conversation if they were busy making love—she said, "He wasn't even there. I found the portal on my own, even though he promised to show me the way."

"So Botolf tells me. But he was there, nonetheless, for he brought me the pistol you left behind when you passed through the portal. He said he stayed just long enough to ensure your safety."

A vague memory of someone picking up her weapon

just before the blackness overtook her came back. "That's who I saw," she whispered. "He was wearing a gray robe. At first I thought it was one of those men."

"It was the druid. And he bade me guard your weapon well. To let others see it might change the course of history, the outcome of wars, he said."

"But what of the murder suspect?" Kendra asked, changing the subject. "Could Luci tell you anything that might help?"

"A description of the men that grabbed her in the garden. It matched that of two dead men we found in the forest."

"So apparently he knew they'd be recognized and killed them."

"My thoughts exactly. Unfortunately, we're no closer to discovering who this madman is. Although at one time Hawk and I thought he must be a peer and was present at Hawk's party, we're not so sure now. Luci was certain she'd have recognized the man if she'd seen him at Hawk's that night."

"Did she remember anything that might help?"

"The only thing she remembers was being led from the garden."

"Then how does she know the suspect wasn't present at Hawk's ball?"

"I don't know, but she's adamant about that fact." He twisted a strand of her hair around his finger, then drew her to him for a light kiss. "In the months since I've seen you, we've discovered nothing further. Perhaps, in part, because I've thought only of a pair of green eyes and burnished-gold hair." He kissed her again. "And now that I've found you, I don't intend to let you go. I want you to come back with me."

Closing her eyes, Kendra breathed deeply while

dropping her head back as he rained kisses down her neck. Until that moment, it had not occurred to her he might leave. Or perhaps she'd just refused to see the truth. Still, she was not ready to make such a decision. "How'd you get here?" she asked instead.

"Botolf gave me his moonstone."

"I see that. But surely you didn't manage this all on your own? The flight, the clothes, money . . . finding me."

"I take offense, dear lady, that you hold me in such low esteem."

"Very funny. You know what I mean."

"As did Botolf. He instructed me to return to his cottage, once I stepped through the portal, and show the moonstone to whoever answered the door. They would know what to do, he said. His descendants live there still.

"Once there, I was taken in hand by a man, Erling his name was. He looks remarkably like Botolf, only several years younger. He accompanied me to the various establishments to obtain my clothing and necessary items for my travels. A good thing, too, since I found myself in awe of my new surroundings. Did you know that Hawthorne Manor is open for tours?"

"I'd heard," Kendra said, recalling the taxi driver's words when she'd returned to this century.

"Erling told me that upon my return, the easiest way into Hawthorne Woods and the Druid's Cave is to take the tour of Hawthorne Manor and use Hawk's secret passage."

"Lord Hawthorne has a secret passage to the woods?"

Brice grinned. "How do you think he steals all of his mistresses into his chambers past that domineering mother of his?"

"Lord Hawthorne has a mistress? But he's such a gentleman!"

He laughed out loud. "Hawk? A gentleman? My dear

sweet Kendra. That *gentleman* has more women parading through his bedchamber than I can possibly count."

"Then this secret passageway must not be much of a secret," Kendra said.

"Oh, it still is. I learned of it as a boy, when Hawk and I played together. His father told him. The only other person aware of it, I'm sure, is Hawk's valet, for he's the one who meets the women and brings them to Hawk's bedchamber. Blindfolded, of course. His secret's still safe."

"And yet, this Erling knew it?"

"Suffice it to say, it was secret in my time. Apparently it's no secret in yours. According to Erling, Hawk's rakish reputation has survived to this day, for that's one of the more popular tours of the nobility's homes. Hawk's bedchamber, and his secret passage, of course."

"How very interesting. And yours? Is there no such attraction in the tour of your home?"

"My home? I never thought to ask. I came—I should think not," he answered in mock horror. "My reputation has always been . . . "

"Yes?" When he didn't answer, Kendra supplied, "Spotless?"

"Yes."

"No wonder your descendants chose only to open a museum in the dower house."

"A museum? Does anyone visit?"

"Occasionally, I've heard."

"A museum is commendable, I think. Why a museum, though?"

Kendra smiled at his serious expression. "Because your descendants did it to share their knowledge of the past with the world. Unlike old Hawk's relations, yours are apparently well off. They don't need the money."

A smug smile lit Brice's face. "Of course not."

They talked about the sights and wonders that Brice had seen on his journey. When Kendra offered to show him the rest of Miami, he declined, saying it was enough that he was there, with her.

Their shower together produced more steam than the hot water, which eventually ran out, reminding them both of the passing of time. It was almost seven when they emerged. Kendra, wearing a light cotton robe, with a towel wrapped around her wet hair, led Brice, dressed once more in his jeans and cable-knit sweater, to the living room, where she introduced him to the television set. "The bane of society," she told him as she handed him the remote. He ignored it at first, more interested in dimming and brightening the table lamp from a wall switch. "Brice. *All* men are interested in remotes." He looked up, and Kendra turned the TV on, then showed him the basics before she returned to the bathroom to dry her hair.

After several moments, Kendra opened the door and poked her head out, almost afraid that he'd disappear again. She could see through her bedroom into the living room where Brice sat before the television. He wasn't watching it—at least not in the sense that any other person would—he was unplugging it. Over and over. Just looking at him staring at the screen as it faded and lit up again brought a sense of fulfillment to her. And relief. It was not a dream. Life had been so empty, before. And now, now he had come back to be with her! For how long, she didn't know. She was afraid to ask.

Brice looked up just then, to see her staring at him. His smile sent a trill of joy racing to her heart, and she turned off her hair dryer and went to him.

He pulled her onto his lap, then ran his fingers through her damp tresses. "This television is interesting, but I'd rather watch you."

Before she could reply, someone knocked at the front door. "If that's Frankie," she muttered, getting up to answer it, "I'm going to personally drag her to the pier and push her off." But it wasn't Frankie. It was Jack, dressed in a dark suit and tie.

"Hi, sweetheart. Aren't you going to invite me in?" he asked.

"Sure." Kendra stood aside for him to enter. "I was just getting ready," she lied. How could she have forgotten he was coming to take her to dinner?

Although Brice could not see the man at the door, he guessed from Kendra's demeanor that all was not to her liking.

The man, a tall blond fellow, stepped into the sparse entryway and said, "We still have plenty of time. Reservations aren't 'til seven-thirty. I thought we'd go check out the restaurant on top of that new hotel they just built." He gave her a light peck on the cheek, then moved into the room. "I— Oh. Hello," he said, seeing Brice for the first time. Brice stood to greet him, but the man turned to Kendra.

"An unexpected visitor," she offered. Brice wondered to which of them she was referring. "Jack, this is Brice Montgomery. Brice, meet Jack Sinclair, my former partner at the police department."

Brice held out his hand. "A pleasure to make your acquaintance, sir."

"You're from England." His tone was accusatory, confusing Brice until he recalled that Kendra had talked about Jack before. A former lover, if he remembered correctly. Had they resumed the relationship? he wondered.

"Brice is the man who rescued me when my sailboat overturned. He just happened to be visiting this part of the country and came by to see me."

Jack took Brice's hand and shook it. "Then I owe you my gratitude."

Most definitely her lover, he decided. "Not at all."

"When did you get in?" Jack asked.

"This afternoon," Brice said.

Kendra backed slowly from the room. "I'm going to finish drying my hair, and throw on some clothes." He sensed that she was distinctly uncomfortable with their combined presence.

Jack waved her off. "So, Brice. How long are you staying for?"

"Until tomorrow. Though I'd like to stay longer, I leave behind a grandmother and a very young sister to whom I must return." A soft click at Kendra's bedroom door told him she had waited to hear his answer before she moved on about her business.

"Oh. Well," Jack said, his voice taking on a more relaxed note, "perhaps you'd care to join us for dinner? We've got some celebrating to do. I reserved a table for two, but we should be able to change it easily enough." Although Jack's invitation seemed sincere, there was no doubt in Brice's mind that the other man did not want him here at all, much less through dinner. Even so, Brice accepted. He was not about to let Kendra out of his sight.

Jack spent the remainder of their wait pressing the buttons on the television box, and talking about some poor soul that was murdered in the park. Thankfully, he did not expect much of a reply. It was not long before Brice came to the conclusion that there was no redeeming value in such an invention as television, since, before one had a chance to understand what was happening, the picture would change to a new scene at the press of a button. For some reason, Jack found it extremely entertaining. Out of politeness, Brice pretended interest as well.

Thankfully, Kendra emerged from her bedchamber shortly thereafter, wearing an unadorned knee-length black dress that accentuated the graceful curves of her figure. The dress suited her well. Her hair was drawn back in a simple chignon, and he longed to stroke his finger across the nape of her exposed neck. In spite of her smile, her somber eyes told him that if given the opportunity, and a shoulder, she was likely to cry.

"Sweetheart," Jack said, rising. "You look fabulous! That a new dress?"

"No," she answered softly. Immediately, she crossed the small room to the television box and pressed a button. The picture faded to black.

"Well, it looks great. Don't you think so, Brice?" Jack looked at his watch. "We'd better get going. I invited your friend along since he'll be leaving in the morning."

"Great," Kendra said. "My car, or yours?"

"I'll drive," Jack said, picking up a sweater off the rack and tossing it to her. "You better take this. You always get cold in restaurants."

"Thanks." As she started to put it on, Brice grasped the sweater and helped her into it, his touch lingering on her shoulder to let her know how sorry he was for putting her in such an awkward predicament. She turned to look up at him for the briefest of moments before following Jack out the door.

17

The three walked toward Jack's car, parked beneath palm trees that swayed in a gentle breeze like giant fans. In the distance a ship's foghorn wailed its melancholy call.

Brice glanced over his shoulder as if trying to discover the source of what, even to Kendra, sounded closer than it actually was. She looked up at him, about to laugh until she was struck by how uncomfortable he must be in these strange surroundings. Kendra put her hand on his arm. Before she uttered a word, Jack said, "Crazy old man. He blows that foghorn every night on the hour as if there were some chance a ship would be dashed on the rocks without it."

Kendra smiled to counter Jack's sour comment. "The man's an old eccentric from Maine and feels his foghorn gives the harbor a more nautical feel." She looked up at Brice. "Kind of like what I thought you were when you pulled me onto that antique ship of yours."

"Old eccentric?" His eyes held the glimmer of a smile.

"Not old, just eccentric."

The balmy air fairly crackled when Brice placed his hand on hers, and for a charged moment their gazes locked. Until Jack became a sudden gentleman and opened the car door, waiting for Kendra to settle herself within.

It was a short drive to the restaurant, with Jack, thankfully, doing all the talking. Kendra could almost feel Brice watching her from the back seat, and she longed to turn around and look at him as well. Why had he not told her he was leaving in the morning? When she'd overheard him telling Jack, she was angry and confused. Later, as she had dressed, she recalled Botolf telling her that the portal only remained open for three nights every six months.

Brice had too many business interests in his era, she knew, to remain here for that long. And although she selfishly entertained the thought of asking him to stay with her, she also knew that he couldn't leave his grandmother and sister behind. But could she just drop everything and go with a man who'd promised her nothing in return?

Jack's normal erratic driving drew Kendra from her thoughts. "Slow down! It's too crowded to be driving this fast. We probably should have walked anyway."

"Don't worry, I know these streets like the back of my hand," her former partner replied nonchalantly, as he came to a screeching stop before a multi-story parking garage at the base of a high-rise.

"It's not you I'm worried about. It's the tourists out there who don't know these streets that scare me."

"You worry too much, sweetheart." He opened his window and grabbed the parking ticket, then handed it to Kendra. "Don't forget to get this validated before we leave."

Kendra absently shoved the ticket into her purse. "There's a place over there," she said, pointing to the end of the building.

Jack drove up to the stall, but hesitated. "Pretty narrow. I don't want any door dings."

"Since when are you worried about a department car anyway?"

Jack ignored her, driving to the next level where he found a place more to his liking. Kendra heard Brice fumbling with the door. She quickly exited and opened his door for him. "My turn to be chivalrous," she whispered as he gave her a grateful nod.

Their footsteps echoed across the garage. After stepping into the elevator, Jack pressed the button for the top floor, then stood near the front, tapping his foot impatiently. The doors closed with a swish and as they sped upward, Brice moved back against the wall. His expression seemed outwardly calm, but a glance at his white-knuckled hands frozen to the handrail told her he was anything but. Discreetly, she reached out and set her hand atop his, and he gave her a crooked grin at her offer of comfort.

As they entered the restaurant, they, or rather Brice, was carefully scrutinized by the formally attired maître d'. Not until then did Kendra realize from the man's almost disdainful expression that Brice might be dressed too casually for such a place.

"May I help you?" he asked in a thick French accent.

Jack, oblivious, said, "I have reservations for two at seven-thirty under Jack Sinclair, but we had an unexpected visitor and now we'll need a table for three."

The maître d' ran his fingers down the list, then looked over his shoulder at the only unoccupied spot in the restaurant, a small table situated against the floor-to-ceiling window overlooking the ocean. When he turned back to them, he gave a pointed look at Brice's attire. "I'm sorry, we won't be able to accommodate you."

Kendra, embarrassed by such a rude reaction, bristled and stepped forward to give the snobbish man a piece of her mind. A firm hand on her shoulder stopped her, and she looked up to see Brice, his eyes sparking with controlled anger. In spite of his twentieth-century surroundings, he was, she knew, very much in his element. A restaurant was a restaurant, no matter what century, and Brice, at that moment, was every inch a duke.

Giving her a subtle shake of his head, Brice advanced on the unsuspecting maître d'. "You are French, sir?" he said, calmly.

"*Oui*," the man answered, already a shadow of doubt entering his eyes at Brice's stern expression.

At once, Brice broke into rapid French. The maître d's face broke out in a sweat, and his eyes darted back and forth as if worried that someone else might understand what was being said to him.

Finally, the poor man put up his hands. "My apologies, monsieur! Please accept them. It's just that we're so full, and I didn't want to crowd you at such a *petite* table. But if you like, I'll have a chair pulled up. Yes? Or if you care to wait, we'll accommodate you at the first opportunity."

Jack impatiently glanced at the only empty table. "A chair'll be fine. I'm too hungry to wait."

"A chair it is, monsieur," the maître d' said, bowing slightly before leading the way.

Jack followed at once, but Kendra lingered behind to speak to Brice. "What'd you tell him?"

"Nothing much."

"You had to have said something. The man's scared out of his wits."

"I merely mentioned that I'd hate to be in his shoes on the morrow should any learn who it was he turned away at the door."

"Very clever," Kendra said as Brice took her elbow to escort her to their table. "What did he say when you told him you were a duke?"

"I never mentioned it."

"If you didn't say, then how was it he became so submissive?"

"Apparently the thought that I *might* be someone important was enough to make him recall how easily he can be replaced."

Jack was already seated when they arrived at the table. The mâitre d' held Kendra's chair for her. As usual, Brice remained standing until Kendra had taken her seat.

As soon as the mâitre d' left, a busboy set a basket of bread on the table, along with the extra place setting, then filled each of their glasses with ice water. Their waiter arrived shortly thereafter, handing each a menu while reciting the daily specials.

The two men looked over their menus silently, while Kendra ignored hers in favor of the spectacular view from their window. Below them, lights bobbed merrily against the velvet black of the sea. The sight reminded her of when, as a very young girl, her mother had taken her to work with her. Although Kendra always took a book to read, she usually ended up gazing out over the water, dreaming, even then, of heroes and dragon slayers until her mother had finished her duties, sometimes very late at night.

Lost in thought, Kendra sighed, unaware that Brice was watching her. "What are you thinking of?"

"My mother, before she passed away. She used to clean office buildings when I was young," she said, looking directly at him to gauge his reaction. When he gave no indication that it bothered him in the least, she continued, "She couldn't afford a baby-sitter and so took me along. Every time I look out a high-rise window at night, I'm always reminded of the nights we spent together. I remember the first time she took me up in one, I looked out at all the lights and thought I must be up in heaven."

Brice smiled sincerely, then looked out the window.

"Heaven?" Jack asked.

Kendra felt foolish for mentioning it, and picked up her menu. "I was very young," she answered, pretending to scrutinize the selections.

"I think," Brice said, "that if I were a child up in a building this high for the very first time, I'd think that an angel must surely have dropped several of the brightest stars from heaven, just so I might admire them."

The way he was looking at her made Kendra feel as if she were one of those stars, and she made a show of perusing the list of entrees to hide her blush. "Rack of lamb sounds good," she said after several moments.

"That's what I was thinking of having." Jack set his menu down. "So tell me, Brice. How was your flight over?"

"It was an experience I won't forget. Unfortunately, I'll have to experience it again all too soon."

His words reminded Kendra that there was so much about him she still had to learn. So much she would never know unless she left with him tomorrow. But how could she just leave everything she'd known her whole life? And what of Jack? He'd stood by upon her return, never forcing her to make a decision about their relationship, yet still willing to wait for her. Besides, she belonged more to Jack's world than Brice's, didn't she?

The conversation during dinner was light, mostly about the sights in Miami that Brice should see if time permitted. When coffee was served, Jack offered to take him on a quick tour before his flight left. "Thank you, no," Brice said. "My flight leaves early afternoon, and I was warned by . . . my friend in England, that I must leave much earlier than that if I hope to avoid the crush."

"That's too bad," Jack said, not seeming at all disappointed. "Perhaps the next time you visit, then."

"I don't know if I'll ever have the opportunity to do so again," Brice answered. With a meaningful glance at Kendra, his eyes almost pleaded with her to go with him. Not for the first time that evening, Kendra felt as if the two men were fighting a silent battle over her. Where other women might have been pleased, the thought did little to cheer her.

In the adjoining room, open to the main dining area, a band started playing a popular song, and Kendra feigned interest in the couples that gravitated toward the dance floor. Tapping her heel to the lively beat, she was taken aback when Brice asked, "Do tell me they are *not* dancing?"

She smiled, knowing how odd the gyrating couples must look to him. "They are. Would you care to try it?"

Brice shook his head. Jack, however, took advantage of the moment, and held out his hand. "I'll dance with you."

Kendra rose from her seat, allowing Jack to lead her to the crowded dance floor. As they twisted and turned to the beat of the music, Kendra made the mistake of looking at Brice. His gaze riveted to hers and she suddenly felt naked and foolish. But then, she decided, this was her world, and she didn't care what he thought. Even so, the way he watched her, Jack and the other couples seemed to fade and she felt as if she were dancing solely for Brice. As her cheeks heated, she turned away so that she no longer faced him. Noting that Jack, too, eyed her intently, she tried to concentrate on his presence, smiling up at him as they danced.

Jack spoke loudly over the music. "I gather from your friend's comment about dancing that he's not used to the night life?"

"Oh, he's used to it, all right," she answered, thinking of all the balls and soirees Brice must attend night after night during the season. "It's just that where Brice comes from they dance a little more conservatively. I think this sort of dancing makes him feel . . . well, uncomfortable."

When the song ended, Jack escorted her back to their table. There was, she decided, a definite mischievous glint in his eye, and she wondered if perhaps he counted himself one point ahead. His next words confirmed her suspicions. "Kendra tells me you don't know how to dance."

Thoroughly embarrassed, Kendra told him, "That's not what I said, and you know it." Looking at Brice, she explained, "I mentioned that you might find this sort of dancing uncomfortable. I didn't think you'd ever been exposed to it before."

Jack refused to let the matter lie. "Then take him out there and show him how."

Kendra threw Jack a murderous glare, then smiled at him through gritted teeth. "He's already said he doesn't want to dance, so lay off."

"He's right," Brice said to Kendra while meeting Jack's triumphant stare. "I'd very much enjoy it if you were to dance with me."

She wanted to scream. Brice would look an absolute idiot out there, and yet he didn't seem to care, so intent was he to accept Jack's obvious challenge. "You don't have to do this."

"I insist," he said, rising to pull her chair out for her.

Kendra was half tempted to walk out on the two of them—Jack for starting this dance nonsense, and Brice for following it through. Just as she was going to decline, for Brice's sake, he smiled that arrogant and very aristocratic smile. Let him flop around like a fish out of water, she decided. "Fine. Let's dance."

The second song ended and, as they approached, the dance floor emptied, killing Kendra's hopes that she could draw Brice into the middle where he'd be less noticeable by those sitting at their tables, Jack included. She was not that heartless after all and regretted her hasty decision. She stopped Brice from drawing her onto the floor. "If you're doing this because of Jack, don't bother. He's only trying to show you up."

Brice didn't answer. Instead, he drew her to the front, closest to the band. "I'll admit to a certain jealousy in the matter, but that's not why I asked you to dance."

"It's not?"

"No. Will you excuse me a moment?" He left her standing alone and approached the musicians. A few quiet words were spoken between them, and Brice reached into his pocket and handed the leader something before returning to her side.

He gave a slight bow, then held out his hand for hers. Kendra was certain the entire restaurant grew silent. Or perhaps it was just that her heart started beating a little louder.

When she placed her hand in his, Brice bestowed a gentle kiss upon it, then asked, "Might I have the honor of this dance, Miss Browning?"

Kendra, feeling her cheeks heat up, was certain she heard several ladies sitting nearby sigh. "Yes, your grace," she whispered. He led her to the center of the dance floor, and as if on cue, the moment he took her in his arms, the band struck up a waltz. Holding her closer than she knew was proper, at least in his day, Brice whirled her around the dance floor. They were soon joined by a few older couples, but neither seemed to notice. They might as well have been dancing on the moon.

Heart to heart, they moved to the music, and Kendra dared not close her eyes, even to blink, for fear if she did, he'd be gone when she opened them. She was reminded of their last waltz. The last time they'd danced, she'd left him. Unwillingly. Suddenly, she wished she hadn't let him bring her out here. She didn't want this to be their last dance.

Brice lowered his lips to her ear, brushing them against her as he whispered, "Would it be improper, Miss Browning, if I were to kiss you, here on the dance floor?"

Kendra's pulse leapt to feel his warm breath against her skin. "Yes, your grace, it would."

"Would you mind, so very much?"

No, she wanted to cry out, but the sight of Jack, from the corner of her eye, reminded her of the game these two were playing. Her former partner, she noted, looked none too pleased with the outcome, although he certainly deserved what he'd gotten so far.

A change of subject, she decided, was the safest course to take. "How'd you know they'd even be able to play a waltz?"

"I could only hope."

"And what would you've done, had they not been able to play one?"

Brice grinned. "We'd have looked rather foolish dancing a waltz to the music they were playing earlier."

Kendra laughed, but sobered as the last strains of lilting music brought their time to an end. Time fled so quickly when she was in his arms, no matter what century. As he led her back to the table, she said, "You never told me your other reason for asking me to dance."

"If you recall, our last waltz was interrupted."

"I thought that last time, you danced with me only because you were forced to . . . by another party," she finished, unwilling to mention Lady Caroline's name.

"You have yet to learn, my dear Miss Browning, that I never do anything I don't want to do. I wanted this," he said, his voice a caress. "We never finished our last dance."

His dark eyes held hers captive, and she sought some way to break the spell. They were in the middle of a restaurant. And Jack was present, she reminded herself. "How much did you pay the band leader to play that waltz?" she asked, as they neared their table.

He shrugged. "All the bills I was given by Erling have ones and noughts on them."

Noughts? Oh yeah, zeroes. "Well, how many noughts?"

"I believe the majority have two."

"Did you even check?" Kendra asked, aghast that he seemed so nonchalant.

Brice gave her a stern look. "I do have some rudimentary knowledge of your monetary system," he said, helping her into her seat before taking his own.

Jack, scowling, reached into his pocket. When he pulled out a small black velvet box and said, "Kendra. There's something I want to ask you," she knew the evening could only go downhill from there.

She had waited years for Jack to ask her to marry him. And he had chosen now. *Now!* With Brice sitting at the same table! Picking up her water glass, she took a long drink.

"Yes, Jack," she said carefully, wondering what she'd do if he really *did* ask her.

He opened the box, revealing a solitaire diamond ring. "What's that?" she croaked.

Jack grinned as he lifted the ring from the box. The diamond, at least a carat, sparkled brightly as he held it up for all to see. Taking her glass from her left hand, he slid the ring onto her finger. "It's an engagement ring."

In spite of the water she drank, her throat felt dry. "Engagement ring?" she whispered hoarsely. "This is all so unexpected. I don't know what to say."

"Say you'll marry me."

Kendra glanced at Brice. Had *he* asked her to marry him this afternoon when he'd asked her to return to his time, she would have immediately said yes. But Brice never mentioned marriage. His duty, she knew, lay in marrying a blue-blooded aristocrat such as Lady Caroline. But then why had he asked her to return? To be his mistress, perhaps? A kept woman, such as one of the many Lord Hawthorne was professed to have?

Looking at the ring once more, then at Jack, she said, "I don't think this is the right time and place to discuss this."

Jack shrugged. "We can talk about it later. Perhaps over breakfast? That is, unless you've already made other plans?"

Brice smiled benignly. "I had hoped Miss Browning might accompany me to the airport, in the morning."

"Why?" Jack asked, his eyes narrowed. "So you can talk her into going back to England with you?"

"If I can, yes."

Jack slid his chair back and gripped the table edge. "I'll be damned if I let you whisk my fiancée off to another country where you can brainwash her again. She damned near had a nervous breakdown when she got back the last time."

Kendra started to speak, but Brice held up his hand. "Be that as it may," he said in a cool, reserved voice, "I shall be damned if I let you decide what is right for her. If Miss Browning wants to accompany me back to England, then so be it."

Jack, his fists clenched, looked as if he might jump across the table and strangle his rival. Brice remained calm, only the ticking of his jaw revealing that he was in the slightest way disturbed.

Kendra was furious. How dare these two fight over her as if she were some trophy for their shelf?

As the two men stared daggers at each other, she slid her chair back. "Did it occur to either of you, the decision's mine?"

Jack never looked at her. "She's going to marry me."

Brice ignored her as well. "Not if she is coming to England with *me*."

Kendra rose, nearly knocking her chair over in the process. Brice, following the etiquette ingrained into him since birth, stood automatically, though his gaze never left Jack's.

"I can't believe you two are arguing over my fate as if I weren't even here." Kendra looked at Brice. "If I want to marry Jack, then *I* will make that decision." He looked taken aback, as if he had not realized what an ass he'd made of himself. Turning to Jack, she noted how fast his smug smile disappeared with her next words. "And if I want to go to England, Jack, I don't need *your* permission."

When Jack started to speak, Kendra lifted her hand for silence. "Don't say a word, Jack, because I don't want to hear it. I didn't come here tonight to watch you two play tug-of-war." She grabbed her purse from under the table, then looked at both men in turn. "I hope you two have a wonderful evening. Together."

Brice and Jack stared, mouths open, as if neither believed she would actually walk out on them. Nevertheless, without another word, she turned her back on the two men and strode from the restaurant.

At once they followed, but were soon stopped by the frantic mâitre d' who cried out that they had forgotten the check. Kendra had a glimpse of Jack pulling out a credit card from his wallet, while Brice hesitated for the briefest of moments. His softly uttered, "Bloody hell," was muffled as the elevator door shut between them.

By the time Kendra made it to the ground level, her tears ran unchecked. This was not how she'd envisioned this evening to turn out. But then, how could she say good-bye, forever, to one man? How could she decide which man—which century—that would be? For weeks, she'd bemoaned that she'd never see Brice again. And during that time, Jack had returned to his old self, the man she thought she'd fallen in love with years ago. He wanted to marry her. She didn't want to hurt him. Certainly she owed him something as well?

And Brice? He had never offered marriage. He'd merely asked her to return with him. Would she be giving up her chance to be married and have a family of her own one day?

Kendra stepped from the elevator, not into the parking garage, but into the hotel lobby. Brushing the tears from her eyes, she went to the desk and asked one of the clerks on duty to call her a cab. Then, to avoid the curious stares of anyone loitering about the plush lobby, she stepped outside to wait. As the doors shut behind her, she turned and saw Brice and Jack emerge from the elevator. Having no wish to confront them, she fled into the night, ducking into the first doorway she came to.

A few moments later, both men shouted her name, but she remained where she was. They never saw her, though she could hear them talking, quite clearly. Jack told Brice to keep looking, while he got the car. "She's a sensible girl," he said, as his footsteps faded toward the parking garage. "She'll come out before too long."

Brice called out her name twice, then crossed the road, stopping beneath one of the many palm trees that lined the street. He walked up the block about halfway, calling out, then retraced his steps. He looked around, lost, and for the first time, Kendra realized what it must have been like for him to brave such a trip on his own. How different for him to come to her time, than for her to go to his. She knew something of the past, and once she'd discovered what had happened to her, it really hadn't been so bad. He, however, never knew what frightening thing to expect around any corner. Airplanes, automobiles, and anything else that moved. She'd seen it on the elevator, and God only knew how much adrenaline had rushed through him while sitting in the back of Jack's car. Not even Kendra's tales on board his ship of what life was like in her century could possibly have prepared him for what he'd experienced so far. And yet, here he was, alone in a strange land, all because he had wanted her. If that wasn't love, Kendra didn't know what was.

Still, after the scene in the restaurant, she felt both men could cool their heels a bit, and she allowed Brice to wander down the street looking for her, since Jack would soon be up with his car. As Brice passed a dark alley, a man emerged from its depths to watch him pass. Everything about the stranger pricked at Kendra's instincts. Short in stature, he had the broad shoulders and wide arms of a man who had nothing better to do than lift weights day after day, year after year. And the way his hair was slicked back and the manner in which he held his cigarette between thumb and forefinger as he watched Brice's retreating figure before falling in step behind him sent a chill up her spine.

Ex-con, Kendra thought immediately. "Bloody hell," she whispered. Glancing toward the parking garage exit, she hoped that Jack would come screeching out in his car as he normally did, but there was still no sign of him. What could be taking so long? The car wasn't parked that far away.

Pulling a small revolver from her purse, Kendra slipped out of her heels, and quietly crossed to the other side, careful to keep to the buildings for cover as she followed the con. Her stockings snagged on the rough cement, but she barely noticed. When the convict quickened his pace, gaining on Brice, she too, sped hers up, never allowing them to get too far ahead. Even so, the man's pace outdid hers, and he soon caught up to Brice. "'Scuse me, bud," he said. "You got a light?"

She saw Brice step back, apparently sizing up his opponent. Kendra wanted to scream at him to run, but she knew better than to frighten a con on the make. Instead, she edged her way closer, hugging the side of the building, keeping her gun trained on the thug.

"Light?" Brice echoed. "If you're requesting one to see by, might I suggest the hotel lobby across the street?"

"Huh?" the con said. "What're ya talkin' about?"

"You asked for a light. Or did I perhaps mistake your intent? You don't appear to need a light at all." Brice gave a pointed look at the man's cigarette.

"Well, whaddya know. So I don't," the thug said, taking a drag on his cigarette before flicking it into the street. "Just give me your wallet then. Okay?"

"Go to bloody hell," Brice replied, appearing his usual calm self, despite the pounding in Kendra's own heart as she edged closer still. What happened next came so fast, she had no time to think.

Like lightning, the con swung at Brice, punching him in the gut. Brice started to double over, but grabbed the thug's arm before the shorter man had time to pull back for another blow. The two struggled together, then fell to the ground, rolling upon the sidewalk. A flash of blue metal appeared suddenly in the convict's hand as he pulled a gun from his waistband. "You'll die for that, bastard," he said, pointing the revolver at Brice.

The sudden image of the man she loved lying dead in the streets of Miami hit her like a bucket of ice water. Kendra's own life flashed before her eyes, bleak and empty without Brice in it. She knew, then, with a startling certainty, that she could never live without him. Not in this world or his.

Rushing forward, she was on top of them, shoving her gun in the thug's ear. He froze at the sound of her voice. "You move one fraction, you bloody bastard, and I'll blow a hole in your head that'll ring clear through to China. Now drop the gun."

His weapon fell to the sidewalk with a clatter of metal on cement. For the briefest of moments, the three stood still as if frozen in time, until Kendra saw the con reach his other hand, slowly toward the weapon on the ground. "Don't move," she ordered, wondering where the hell Jack was.

The con looked up at her from the corner of his eye. "Look, lady. I was just gonna scratch my back."

"Try it, and it'll be the last itch you ever have." In warning, she shoved her knee into his back and pressed the gun to his temple.

"Okay, lady!" the con said just as the heavenly sound of wheels screeching from the parking garage met her ears. "Take it easy. I ain't moving."

Brice disentangled himself from the footpad, who remained as still as a statue for fear Kendra would use her weapon against him. He stood just as Jack's horseless carriage skidded to a halt beside them.

"What the hell's going on here?" Jack demanded from his open window.

Kendra glanced up. "What took you so long? You lose the car?"

Jack opened his door and jumped out. "No, I lost the parking ticket. You wouldn't happen to know where it is, would you?" Brice assumed they were talking about the slip of paper Kendra had placed in her purse.

"Sorry," she said, never moving from her position. "I didn't mean to jump on you. You couldn't have known this was going to happen anyway. Get your handcuffs, Jack." She looked up at Brice. "Are you all right?"

"Yes," he answered, thinking that, under the circumstances, Kendra appeared remarkably calm.

Jack started patting at the footpad's clothing, apparently searching for weapons. Finding nothing, he shackled the man's arms behind his back with a set of shiny metal objects. The handcuffs, Brice guessed, as he leaned against the side of the building.

"What have we here?" Jack asked, picking up the footpad's small pistol from the sidewalk. "A Saturday Night Special." He tucked the pistol into his own waistband, then lifted the thug to his feet. "Call a patrol unit, Kendra, so we can give this dirt-bag a ride to jail."

"Sure." Reaching into the open car door, Kendra grabbed a small, round object connected to the inside of Jack's car by a stiff coiled cord of some sort. Surprisingly, she spoke into it. "Sixteen-thirty-seven."

"Sixteen-thirty-seven," came a crackled echo from the interior of the car.

"We need a transport unit at the Miami Landmark Hotel. One in custody."

"Ten-four, sixteen-thirty-seven. You code four?" Apparently it was not an echo. Someone was talking to Kendra through the car. Whatever they were saying, however, sounded much like a gibberish of numbers and words.

"That's affirmative," Kendra replied. "Code four."

"Ten-four. ETA for transport approximately five to ten."

"Ten-four."

Kendra replaced the round object in the car, then looked up at Jack as he shoved the footpad into the back seat.

"Nice work, Ken," Jack said. "I'm just gonna have a look in this con's wallet and see who we got. Hmm, Christopher Murtag," he read aloud. "Wasn't there a B.O.L. out on him last week at briefing? Wanted for murder out of Palm Beach, I think. Too bad you're not working homicide anymore, Ken. It'd be a good stat, catching a murderer. And you could write the report instead of me."

Kendra gave him a small smile. "I've got to go find my shoes," she said. She crossed the street and picked up her shoes from the doorway where she had left them. Slipping them on her now ragged, stockinged feet, she returned at a leisurely pace and calmly listened while

Brice informed Jack of what had occurred. "In short," Brice said, after relating the facts, "Miss Browning saved my life."

"That makes us even," Kendra told him. "Besides, you did a pretty good job on your own. I just happened to be near enough to help."

Before Brice could comment, another horseless carriage, this one white with a blue stripe, pulled up alongside them, and a uniformed man emerged and took Murtag from Jack's car into his. Jack handed the weapon to another uniformed man. "Book that into evidence, Tony," he said. "And run a wants check on him in case he's the one Palm Beach's looking for in that murder they had last week. If it is, have dispatch notify their detective assigned to the case."

"Sure thing, Sinclair." Tony took the pistol and placed it in his trunk, then told his partner to radio in the check on Murtag. When he looked up, he noticed Kendra for the first time and smiled. "Hey, Browning. Haven't seen you in a while. Heard you're working juvenile, now."

"You heard right," she said.

A few moments later, the other officer poked his head out the window. "Hey, Sinclair. Dispatch just confirmed that warrant on Murtag."

Jack reached over and patted Kendra on the back. "Guess that's number two for you since you've been back, and you weren't on duty for either one." He turned to Brice, and said, "She was one of the best."

Brice regarded Kendra. Once more, she appeared calm, self-assured. "This is what you used to do before you met me?" When she nodded, he added, "I can certainly see why your life is so fascinating if this is how you spend your days . . . and nights."

Kendra gave him an exasperating look. "It's not like this all the time. Trust me."

Jack grinned. "Don't let her fool you, Brice. She was a top homicide investigator. Why the last guy we arrested, a serial killer, was because of her. But then you probably heard all about that. She said she got her information from England when she was on vacation with you."

"No, I hadn't heard," Brice informed him.

"You ever hear of Sean Clyde Parker, the Debutante Murderer?"

"The name sounds vaguely familiar, but I doubt I know of him."

"Never know," Jack said, "The guy's from Great Britain too."

"And you apprehended him?"

"Yeah. He's in jail now. Gonna be arraigned tomorrow. Interesting case, though," he continued, waving to the officers as they drove off. "Surprised you haven't heard of it. This Parker fellow was under investigation for murder in another state, but they could never pin it on him. And then there was this 'whither thou willest'—"

"Do what thou wilt," Kendra supplied.

"Yeah. That's written over the door at the murder scene. But the guy disappears for a while, and just when you think he's vanished from the face of the earth, he reappears here in Miami. But he won't be doing any disappearing for awhile. Unless he can come up with a million dollar bail. And since his assets are frozen, I doubt that'll happen."

"Do what thou wilt?" Brice asked, his interest piqued.

"Yeah. Kendra said that she guessed some guy had read about the Hell-Fire Club and some cult-type murders styled after it in nineteenth-century England. Figured we were dealing with some psychotic history buff who got off on copy-catting some ancient cases."

Brice looked at Kendra for clarification.

"I thought," she said, "that perhaps a very deranged person might have read about the murders at Hawthorne Woods in some history book and committed some of his own in the same manner."

"I see," Brice answered. It all made sense. At one time he had thought the murderer in his own time must be a lord, but if he were repeating the history of the Hell-Fire Club—or twisting it, rather, for his own deranged beliefs—it would stand to reason that whoever this madman was, he had adequate knowledge of the Club's history and so must be educated. A self-styled historian perhaps?

The only man Brice knew who had a passion for all things historical was Hawk. Though the murders happened on Hawk's land, and Hawk did have quick access to the general area around the Druid's Cave via his secret passage, Brice refused to believe it was him. No. It most definitely was *not* Hawk. Besides, he had been with him the night they found Luci.

Jack walked up to where Kendra still leaned against his car. "Hey, you're cold," he said, noticing her shivering.

"No. I'm just shook up. That's all."

"You?" Jack chuckled.

"They could've killed him," she whispered.

Brice wanted to tell her he was fine, they were fine, but Jack took off his coat and threw it around her shoulders despite the warmth of the night.

Jack stroked her cheek tenderly. "But they didn't. Your friend is fine. You did a great job." A single tear fell to her cheek. "Hey, Browning. No tears. Remember?"

Kendra nodded and looked away, but Jack turned her face toward his. "I'm sorry about tonight," he said softly. "We were just getting along so great lately, I thought—"

"I know," she replied wistfully.

"About three years too late, huh kiddo?"

Kendra nodded and smiled, her expression bitter-sweet. Reaching out, she touched Jack's face. "I'll always love you," she whispered.

When Jack lowered his face to hers for a kiss, Brice stepped back into the shadows and turned away. Somewhere in the distance, a loud keening sound echoed the bittersweet song in his heart. A foghorn, he recalled. But it had warned him too late, for the ship that his heart had sailed in on had already dashed to pieces upon the rocks.

Jack's kiss was tender and full of longing. "You're going to England?" he asked softly.

She nodded. They'd been partners for so many years, they could read each other like a book. They had to in their profession. His profession now. "I'm sorry. I didn't know until now. I'd never have hurt you this way," Kendra said.

Jack put his fingers upon her lips. "I know, sweet-heart. But love is funny sometimes, isn't it?" She nodded. "Does he love you as much as you love him?"

Kendra turned away, wiping the tears from her eyes. She didn't know the answer. "I know I'll be happy. And well taken care of."

"Then that's good enough for me. You have a wonderful life, Browning. And show those Bobbies a thing or two about police work while you're there."

"I will," she said, as he kissed her forehead, then stepped back. "What about your ring?"

"I bought it for you. Keep it to remember me by."

"I can't. It's too expensive."

"Have Frankie return it tomorrow."

Kendra, sensing it would ease his pride to not see her take off the ring, gave him one last hug. "Oh, Jack. I'll always remember you."

"I know," he said, stroking her hair. He pressed his cheek against her head, then pushed her away. "Now go. Unless you two want a ride home."

"We'll walk. And thank you, Jack. For everything."

"You're welcome," he said, stepping around to the driver's door.

She watched him drive off, not moving until the red tail lights faded into the night. Brushing the last of the tears from her face, she turned and found she was deserted. "Brice?" she called out with concern.

"Here," he said, stepping from a darkened doorway.

"Oh. For a moment I thought you'd left."

"Without saying good-bye?" he asked, an odd note to his voice.

"Let's go home. We have an early day tomorrow."

Brice studied her for a moment, then held his arm out for her. In silence, the two strolled up the street, each lost in their own private thoughts.

When they arrived at Kendra's apartment, Kendra said, "I'm going to call Frankie and let her know I'm going back to England with you."

Brice stopped her before she picked up the phone and taking her hands in his, absently fingered her ring.

"Let's not disturb her tonight. Shall we?" He kissed the backs of her hands, hesitating but the slightest of instances when his lips touched her left hand, his gaze resting upon the solitaire diamond. He drew her to him, then led her into the bedroom.

Their clothes lay scattered in their wake, down the hallway and ending at her bed where Brice settled himself on top of Kendra. Bracing his hands on either side of her head, he lifted himself and stared down at her, his dark, turbulent gaze unreadable.

"Kiss me," she said, wondering why he was so still when she was burning to feel him inside of her.

But instead of doing as she requested, he dropped to his side, grasped her left hand, and holding it against the pillow over her head, plucked Jack's ring from her finger. After tossing it onto the bedside table, his mouth crashed down on hers, and he kissed her with an urgency that bordered on frantic, as if she'd been lost to him, and he'd only just found her.

The next morning, she awoke to a perfect, sunny day. Her eyes drifted open, blinking against the bright light pouring through her bedroom window. Sighing, she stretched and rolled over, only to discover that Brice had already risen.

A smile crossed her face at the memories of the night they had spent together, and then a touch of bittersweet sadness invaded her thoughts at the realization that she would never again wake up in this room. Forcing herself from the comfort of her warm bed, Kendra rose and looked out the window. Outside, the crystal blue sky made a perfect backdrop for a flock of pelicans that drifted high overhead in their typical circular pattern, wings shining silver as they angled toward the sun.

This was where she had lived all her life, and the view from her window was one of the many things she loved about Miami. She wanted Brice to see it. To share the beauty of nature with her. "Brice," she called out. "Come look at the pelicans."

There was no answer.

Curious as to what he might be doing, Kendra grabbed her robe and slipped it on as she went to the living room. "Brice?"

He wasn't there. Nor was he in the kitchen.

A mild sense of panic took hold of her when she noticed the deadbolt was unlocked. Throwing the door open, she stepped onto the porch and looked down the steep stairs, then took them two at a time until she stood upon the sidewalk, frantically looking up and down the street.

She flew back up the stairs, not even bothering to shut the door as she ran into the house and to her bedroom to dress. Only then did she notice the note lying on her bedside stand. Grasping it as if it were a life raft, she sank to the bed to read.

My darling Kendra,

   Never in my life have I wrestled so long with a decision such as the one I must make tonight. I did not realize until now how selfish I was being in asking you to give up all you have ever known, merely to come with me and live a life that would be filled with uncertainties. I could never make the promises to you that Jack could, and so it is with great sadness that I bid you farewell.

   Your faithful servant,
   Brice

18

Although it took her no more than a few seconds to read the brief note, she stared blindly at it for several minutes. Then, in a fit of anger, she crumpled it up and threw it against the wall. "You bloody bastard!" she shouted. "You bastard. How could you do this to me. How?"

Sinking to the floor, she picked up the wrinkled paper and smoothed it out, holding it against her breast. "Why?" she whispered.

Perhaps a minute passed by, perhaps more, before she realized the telephone on her nightstand was ringing. She picked up the receiver. "Hello?" Her voice sounded hollow, as if it belonged to someone else.

"Ken? It's me, Frankie. You do know your front door's been standing open for the past fifteen minutes? I saw it when I went to get my paper."

"Is it?"

"What's wrong?"

"He's gone."

"Brice? He just got there."

"I know. But he's gone," she sobbed.

"Don't move. I'm coming over."

A few minutes later, Frankie walked into Kendra's bedroom. Kendra looked up from her seat on the floor wondering if Brice was halfway around the world by now.

"What happened?" Frankie asked.

Kendra handed her the note.

Frankie scanned it, then said, "What does he mean by he 'could never make the same promises that Jack could'?"

"Jack asked me to marry him last night."

"And?"

"All Brice did was ask me to return to his time with him. He can't marry me because I'm a commoner. I could never be more than his mistress."

"He *said* that?" Frankie asked incredulously.

"Well, no, but—"

"Oh, bull. A man doesn't travel through time to look for the woman he loves just to make her his mistress."

"Well, Brice did."

"I don't believe it."

"It doesn't matter anyway. He's gone. He's left me."

"So?"

"So?" Kendra repeated dully.

"So what are you going to do about it? Just sit here?"

"What do you mean? What else is there to do?"

Frankie shook her head. "First off, get dressed. You can't do much in your bathrobe. And rinse your face off. You look like hell." Frankie threw open Kendra's closet, then tossed a blouse and jeans to her.

"What are you doing?" Kendra asked as Frankie removed her silk ballgown from the closet as well.

"Getting you ready for a trip."

"Trip?"

"You love him, don't you?"

"Yes."

"Well, don't you think if he came halfway around the world to meet you, he must love you too? And coming in this direction couldn't be an easy feat for a man who's never flown."

"No, it wasn't," Kendra said, putting on the clothes Frankie picked out. "He told me *and* Jack that he was scared to death of flying."

Frankie stopped and gave Kendra a penetrating look. "There's only one thing I know that would force a man to do something like get on a plane twice in as many days when he's afraid of flying. And it seems to me, the least you could do is meet him halfway and remind him."

"Remind him?"

"That he loves you and you love him. Men can be dense that way sometimes. Look how long it took Jack to ask you to marry him. And *he* lives in the same century."

A smile broke out on Kendra's face, then faded. "But Brice is already gone. By the time I get ready and book a flight, he'll be there. And I don't know how many nights might be left in the portal."

Frankie shook her head in exasperation. "You forget you're talking to the woman picked best travel agent by *Miami Today*. Now go wash your face, grab a few things and meet me downstairs in ten minutes. It's early yet. We'll have you in England faster than you can say Timeswept Travels, Frances speaking."

Frankie rushed out, leaving Kendra standing in her bedroom, looking around at her belongings, wondering what to take and what to leave behind. Finally, grabbing a large tote bag, Kendra neatly rolled up her ballgown and stuffed it inside, then the matching slippers. There was really nothing else left to take except her family photo album and a Polaroid snapshot of her and Frankie taken last year at a New Year's party. After slipping the picture inside the photo album and that inside the tote bag, Kendra grabbed her fanny pack, purse, and keys, then ran out the door.

Precisely ten minutes later, Kendra, out of breath, walked in Frankie's door.

"In here, Ken," she called out from the back room she used for her office.

Kendra left her things by the door before joining her friend. "Any luck?" she asked, leaning over Frankie's shoulder to look at the computer screen, while Frankie typed away on the keyboard.

"Yep. We got the only flight not fully booked. It leaves an hour later than Brice's."

"We?"

"You don't think I'm letting you wander around there alone, do you?"

"But—"

"No buts. You're my best friend. The sister I never had. The least I can do is see you off. You got your things?"

"Yes. By the door."

"Grab them and let's go." Frankie pulled an overnight bag from her closet, then threw some underwear, a pair of jeans and a sweater in, while she waited for their tickets to print.

Frankie's driving rivaled that of Jack's but Kendra barely noticed. "Do you think we'll get there in time?"

"I hope so. But just in case we get pulled over, you better tell them you're on a case or something."

Thankfully, they were not pulled over, and made it to the airport in record time.

"I checked all the flights," Frankie told her on the way. "You were originally booked on Brice's flight."

"I was booked on a flight?" Brice *had* intended on taking her with him. But what made him change his mind?

"We'll arrive at Heathrow only an hour later than Brice. And if you factor in that I know modern day London, and he's probably as lost there as he was here, we should make even further gain. Now where is it we're supposed to go?"

"To Hawthorne Manor. I think. All I know is that the taxi driver told me they give tours there a few times a day. That's the only way I know how to get into Hawthorne Woods to the Druid's Cave. At least from the twentieth century. There's probably another way, but I don't want to chance not being able to find it."

"Definitely best to stick with what you know," Frankie replied as they walked up to the ticket counter.

As they stood in line behind several people, a man ran up to the counter, pushing aside whoever was next. "I need to get the next flight out," he said, sounding British and very out of breath. "My agent should have reserved a seat for me."

"I'm sorry, sir," the clerk told him. "But you'll have to wait in line. There are several people ahead of you."

"But—"

"Please, sir. But don't worry. There are plenty of seats."

The man, tall, dark-haired with a full beard, appeared mollified as he took his place at the end of the line. Frankie leaned over to Kendra and whispered, "Pushy fellow, isn't he."

Kendra, however, hardly noticed, her attention focused more on all she had to discuss with Frankie before they parted: about what to do with her belongings once she left and perhaps a way of contacting her later to let her know all had worked out. The latter problem deserved ample consideration, and she pondered over it during the majority of the flight to England.

By the time their plane touched down at Heathrow, Kendra thought she had taken care of everything except how she might contact her friend later, if the need arose.

Frankie suggested it would probably not be a good idea to do too much century-hopping. "What if the portal stopped working? You wouldn't want to get stuck in the wrong century," she'd said.

The point was a valid one, Kendra decided.

As they walked through the airport, Frankie pulled her into a souvenir shop to make a purchase. "It'll only take a second," she promised, when Kendra voiced her concern about wasting time. It was nearly three in the afternoon, and she had no idea when the last tour at Hawthorne Manor might be.

Kendra waited near the front of the booth looking at the postcards on a revolving rack. One in particular caught her eye: Great Homes of England. The picture on the front was divided into squares showing several different mansions. She recognized two from her sojourn in the nineteenth century. One was Blackmoor Hall, the other the earl of Winterowd's home. Another postcard showed the picturesque dower house, Briarwood. Kendra turned it over and read the following caption: "At one time, Briarwood was used as the dower house of Blackmoor Hall, before the current duke opened it to the public as a museum."

"Briarwood," Kendra whispered, flipping the card over to look at the picture once more. "Of course. That's how I'll get a message to Frankie." Kendra took the two postcards to the register.

"Put those on my bill too," Frankie said.

As they walked through the terminal to the exit, Kendra gave Frankie the postcards.

"Planning on writing to someone?" Frankie asked.

"Yes. You. But not on those. They're merely to remind you of where I'll be going and how I plan on getting in touch with you. I figure in six months I should know one way or the other if I'm going to stay." *Or rather if Brice will have me or not,* she added silently. "Either way, I'll leave word for you at Briarwood. That's the museum on the postcard that used to be the dower house."

"You're going to leave a message for me one hundred and how many years in the past?"

"Sixty-six. Unless I come back," Kendra added with a sigh. "Then I'll be waiting there, myself."

"But how're you gonna leave a message?"

"I haven't worked that part out yet. But whatever it is, it'll be at the museum at Briarwood. Somehow, I'll make sure you know what it is."

"*This* I gotta see," Frankie said, as she hailed a taxi outside the terminal. "I'll make sure I mark my calendar," she added as they got in.

"Hawthorne Woods," Kendra told the cabby.

Frankie handed a paper bag to Kendra. "This is what I bought at the airport. My going-away present to you. Who knows what kind of medical care you'll get."

Opening the bag, Kendra found a large bottle of aspirin. Laughing, she slipped it into her fanny pack. "It'll be a lifesaver, I know. Thanks."

"I only wish there was more I could do."

Kendra reached out and grasped Frankie's hand. "You've done so much already. I'll miss you."

"I know."

Twenty minutes later, their cab pulled into the gated drive of Hawthorne Manor. "You ladies want me to wait while you go on the tour?"

Kendra looked at her friend, who shrugged. "Sure. At least one of us will need a ride back."

Frankie glanced at her watch. "Three-fifteen. We made good time. It looks like the tour's just started."

About two dozen tourists waited on the steps of Hawthorne Manor, slowly filing in as a guard stood watch at the door. "Do you see him?" Kendra asked, as the taxi stopped by the front doors. Only a handful of people remained on the steps, and by the time they got out of the cab, those too had entered.

"I wasn't close enough."

"Do you think we'll have to take the tour? Maybe we can just slip to the back gardens, jump the wall and catch Brice there. I don't want to miss him."

Frankie shook her head. "He can't go anywhere until midnight anyway," she reminded her, as they approached the front doors where a uniformed guard stood sentinel. "So let's just do this right so we don't get kicked off the grounds before we've had a chance to get to the Druid's Cave. Brice can find his own way."

"I hadn't thought of that."

The women paid for their tickets, then followed the group into the hallway and up the stairs to the gallery where the tour guide, a young woman dressed in a white blouse and gray skirt, began speaking about some of the paintings on the wall. Kendra paid little attention, having seen everything long before it had faded with age, concentrating instead on each of the tourists in the group.

"I don't see him anywhere," she whispered, standing on tiptoe to see over the heads of the people in front of her.

"That's because he's not there," Frankie whispered back. "We beat him here."

"How do you know?" Kendra asked, still unconvinced.

"Because he's coming up the stairs now."

19

Brice, angry that he could not circumvent the guard and walk straight to the woods, strode up the steps to the gallery two at a time. He had hoped to be safely ensconced at Botolf's cottage until midnight, but that was not to be, unless he could get through this bloody tour. Nearing the top of the steps, he paused at the sight of a familiar looking face. Frankie. And beside her, with her back to him, stood Kendra.

As Kendra turned around, her gaze meeting his, time stood still for an endless moment, allowing him to see the hurt and betrayal in her eyes. Even so, he would not allow it to affect him. He knew, even if Kendra did not, that what he was doing was right.

"Miss Wendall," he said, bowing over Frankie's hand. "Once again, a pleasure to see you."

"Or perhaps a shock?" Frankie answered, easily resisting his applied charm.

"I'll admit to a moment of surprise. But only because I find I'm still so unfamiliar with . . . these changed times."

When Frankie smiled, letting him know she held no ill will, he turned to Kendra. "Miss Browning," he said, bowing when she refused to extend her hand. "I did not expect to see you here."

"I'm coming with you," she said.

"I regret to inform you otherwise."

"Why?" she challenged quietly, her green eyes sparking with anger.

Though he had no wish to hurt her, he knew it was the only way. "You don't belong here."

"Why not?" she said, this time with less conviction. "Because my blood's not blue enough?"

Brice steeled himself against the pain he knew his answer would bring. "Yes, if you must know the truth."

Her eyes glistened, and she turned her face away. The tour group began to file past the gallery to the hallway that led to the bedchambers. When he would have moved past her, she stopped him. "Please," she begged.

If hearts could break, he was certain his was doing so. "No," he replied succinctly.

Kendra looked to Frankie for assistance, but found none forthcoming when her friend took sudden interest in the paintings of some of Hawthorne's ancestors. Kendra wiped her tears. "You can't stop me," she finally said. "I'm coming back, whether you like it or not."

"You will stay in your own time, Miss Browning. You belong here. Not there." With that, he walked past her to follow the group to the bedchambers, though it was the hardest thing he had ever done.

"What am I going to do?" Kendra asked Frankie.

Frankie shook her head. "I've never seen two blinder people in my life. He wants you, but for some reason is unwilling to admit it. And you want him. But I can't make up your mind for you."

"You're right," Kendra said, swinging her tote bag over her shoulder with new determination, before striding down the hallway. "And I'm not going to let him make up my mind for me either. You coming?"

"Wouldn't miss it for the world," Frankie said, catching up to her.

Kendra entered the chamber and stalked up to Brice. "I've decided to finish the tour," she said in a no-nonsense tone.

"As you wish."

"Where are we?" she asked.

"In Hawk's bedchamber."

The tour guide confirmed this when she announced in her refined English accent, "This chamber is best known for the sixth earl, Lord Hawthorne, Hawk to his friends. The earl, as any historian can tell you, had two passions: the first being the study of history, about which he contributed several meticulously researched works over his lifetime; the second being women, which is what many believe led to his being given such a name as Hawk by his peers."

She waved her hand across the space of the room. "Lord Hawthorne often brought his mistresses into his rooms via a secret chamber that leads to an underground catacomb of passages, one of which leads into the forest beyond the garden walls to an area known as the Druid's Cave that many believe to be haunted. More than one person is surmised to have lost his life wandering aimlessly in the tunnels below, unable to find their way out."

Their guide pointed to a mahogany-paneled wall to the right of a marble fireplace. "It is a well known fact that because of this secret chamber Lord Hawthorne lost his life as well. But not, however, because he became lost, since he knew every twist and turn. Ironically, he was killed in a duel by his good friend the duke of Blackmoor, after Blackmoor caught his affianced lover in bed with Lord Hawthorne. The earldom passed on to a distant cousin, since Hawthorne left no male issue."

Brice chuckled loudly, receiving a few dark stares from some of the other tourists, including Kendra.

"You didn't kill him, did you?" she asked, aghast.

"How could I?" he replied. "What she's saying doesn't signify. I have no fiancée."

Frankie cocked an eyebrow at that. "Make sure you tell this Hawk fellow."

"What about Lady Caroline?" Kendra asked, trying to sound casual.

"I believe she said, 'affianced *lover*'? Lady Caroline? An amusing thought."

"I know *I* was laughing," Kendra muttered, feeling foolish for bringing up Lady Caroline. The woman was too much of a paragon to ever consent to being anyone's lover before her marriage vows were spoken. But if not her, then who? "You haven't caught Lord Hawthorne with your lover?"

He did not answer, instead gave her a look that told her she was being silly.

The tour guide motioned for everyone to circle around the paneled wall so that she might continue on with her narrative and yet afford everyone a view. "Here, through this secret door, is where Lord Hawthorne often met his lovers, and on that fateful night, Blackmoor's lover."

The woman sprang the catch allowing the door to swing open. A cool draft swept into the room, bringing with it a musty scent of damp earth. "What the earl could not have known was that someone had informed the duke of his fiancée's rendezvous that night, and he followed her here, to catch her in the embrace of his best friend. The rest is history," she finished, closing the door. "Blackmoor killed Hawthorne the next morning in a duel. Some even suspect he killed his lover, since she was never again seen from that day forward.

"Now, if you'll follow me into the next room, I'll show you a secret stairway that leads to the servants' quarters."

Kendra started to follow, until she realized that Brice no longer stood beside her. She turned in time to see the mahogany panel swing silently shut. Flying to the door, Kendra tried to open it as she'd seen the tour guide do. Nothing happened.

Frankie came up beside her. "What's the matter?"

"He's gone. He did it again. The bloody bastard left me again." Kendra pounded on the wall with her fist. "I can't believe it. You bastard! I hate you. Do you hear me? I hate you."

On the other side of the panel, Brice stood quietly, holding the door shut until he heard Kendra's and Frankie's footsteps fade from the room. Closing his eyes, he tried to forget the hurtful words she had thrown at him and the pain in her voice. He could not blame her for hating him. He hated himself for what he was doing. But he knew she belonged in her own time, not his. He could not allow her to sacrifice her life to be with him. She had saved *his* life, by God! Why had it come into his mind that she *ever* needed him? With a heavy heart, he pushed himself away from the door and trudged down the dark passageway.

✳   ✳   ✳

Frankie wiped the tears from her friend's eyes. "Don't waste your time on him. He's not worth it."

Kendra allowed Frankie to lead her from the room. They bypassed the tour group, and returned to the front of the house. Outside, it had begun to rain. Fitting weather, Kendra thought as she stepped out the doors, allowing the rain to soak her through.

Frankie pulled her jacket over her head. "Come on, Ken. We'll get a hotel room and catch a plane home tomorrow."

Kendra didn't move. "I don't want to go home."

"You have to," Frankie said, leading her down the slick marble steps.

Kendra, oblivious to everything, stepped into the path of a man flying up the walkway and only just missed being slammed into when Frankie grabbed her arm and yanked her back.

"Wasn't that the guy at the airport?" Frankie asked. "The one who was rushing to buy a ticket?"

Kendra's only glimpse of the man was when he nearly mowed her down—she had a vague recollection of dark hair and a beard, plastered down by the rain. She didn't have time to notice if he was the same man, nor at the moment did she really care.

"It's hard to believe he was in such a hurry just to catch this tour," Frankie said, drawing Kendra to their waiting taxi. "Probably missed half of it by now. Oh, well. I'm cold and wet, and I want a hot meal and a hot shower. How 'bout you?"

"Sure," Kendra replied absently.

A few hours later, Kendra sat on the bed in their hotel room, flicking through the channels on the television's remote control while Frankie showered. After a while, she tossed the channel-changer down, then lay back on the bed, uninterested in any of the programs.

The cultured voice of a British newscaster filled the room. "Scattered thundershowers are expected to last the rest of the week . . ." Kendra barely heard, her mind being at least a hundred or so years away.

She glanced at the radio clock on the bedside. Ten. Brice must be hiding in the catacombs. Two more hours and he'd be home. She imagined him sitting before the hearth in his study, his gleaming black Hessians propped up on a footstool before the fire, perhaps holding a glass of brandy in his hand as he stared into the flames, thinking about . . . Lady Caroline, of course. "Damn you, Brice," she whispered.

Frankie, wrapped in a towel, emerged from the bathroom. "How're you doing?" she asked cheerily, padding over to the edge of the bed to sit with a bounce on the mattress.

"Fine."

"Oh good, the news." Frankie leaned over and turned it up. "Hey, Kendra? Isn't that the guy Jack was investigating back home?"

"Hmm?" Kendra glanced at the television without interest to see several men in suits standing on the steps of some building, where a TV reporter stood interviewing one of them. "Where?"

"They just showed him. Watch. Maybe they'll show him again."

Instead, Kendra's eyes drifted shut, an image of Brice coming to mind. He reached out to touch her.

"Look!" Frankie cried. "That's him!"

Kendra sat up in bed. "Who?" she asked, thoroughly confused.

"The man from the airport!"

"What on earth are you talking about?"

The television newscaster flashed onto the screen.

"So far," the newsman said in his staid English accent, "the Miami Police have no idea as to the whereabouts of their escapee, Sean Clyde Parker, the man they call the Debutante Murderer, although authorities believe he may have fled the country. One source tells that Parker claims to have emigrated from Great Britain. However, a recent check with Scotland Yard shows no such person in their records. And now, the Royal watch with Emma Hastings—"

Frankie turned off the television. "What do you think?"

"You can be certain, once they knew Parker escaped, they'd have every airport on the alert."

"Well, you have to admit they kind of looked alike."

"Who?"

"Parker and that rude guy at the airport."

Kendra threw herself back on the pillows. "I seriously doubt it." At the sight of Frankie's hurt look, she said, "I'm sorry, I had my mind on other things at the time and didn't pay any attention. Do you really think it looked like the guy?"

"Yes."

"Then I'll call Jack now. Okay?"

"Sure. Whatever."

"What time is it back home?"

Frankie glanced at the clock. "It's ten here. That makes it five there."

Kendra dialed his office.

The division secretary answered. "He probably won't be back today. He's gone out to check on a lead. Is there something I can do for you?"

"I'm in London right now and just heard the news about Parker. My girlfriend swears to me that a guy she saw at the airport and later, here, looks just like him. I thought I should let Jack know."

"I'll leave a message for him, but I doubt it's the guy. We just got a tip that Parker was supposedly spotted getting out of a taxi just this afternoon. That's where Jack's at now."

"Well, let him know anyway. Okay?"

"Sure thing."

Kendra hung up the phone and smiled at Frankie, who was combing out her wet hair. "Parker was spotted this afternoon in Miami. Jack's looking for him. By the time we get back, he'll be in custody again."

"It gives me the creeps to think a killer's out there on the loose."

"Well, if it makes you feel any better, there are a lot more than just Parker running around out there. I wouldn't worry too much. Jack's a good cop. He'll get the guy eventually."

Long after the two women went to bed, Kendra stared up at the dark ceiling, fingering the moonstone hanging around her neck. As the seconds ticked by into minutes, Kendra's depression festered into a burning raw anger. The worst part about this whole situation, she realized, was that she couldn't even tell Brice that she was mad at him.

"Like hell, I can't," she said, sitting up in bed. The radio's clock glowed, as did the moonstone hanging on her necklace. Twelve-o-one. Brice had no doubt passed through the portal and was on his way to Blackmoor Hall by now.

"You bloody bastard," she whispered to the dark. "I'll be damned if I let you get away with that."

In the pouring rain, Brice traipsed through the muddy woods toward Blackmoor Hall. By the time he reached his home, he was soaked to the bone. He pushed open the front door and headed straight for his study. A servant, undoubtedly sent by the ever-watchful butler, scurried in and stoked up the fire, then slid out, almost unnoticed.

Unbidden, Brice's gaze strayed to the small marquetry box on the mantle. Moving to the hearth, he reached out and traced the smooth, inlaid rose as he'd done each night since he'd found the box in her room after she'd returned to her own century. Unlike those other nights, tonight he opened the box and stared at the once yellow rose, pale and fragile with age. She'd kept it by her bedside. Cherished it, the maid had told him.

And now it was all he had left.

Lifting it gently, he held it up and breathed in what faint scent remained on the dried petals, then carefully laid it back in its box. Closing the lid, he carried it to his desk and locked it in a drawer. He would not think about her again. He couldn't if he hoped to retain his sanity.

After pouring himself a brandy, Brice slumped into his favorite wing chair, propped his muddied boots up on an andiron, and stared into the fire. Images of Kendra danced in the flames, haunting him, teasing him. He picked up his brandy, but she was there, in the golden reflections in his glass. Her presence was everywhere. She would always be here, in this room. In this house.

"Brice?" Alethea stood in the doorway.

"Come in, Grandmère."

Alethea, dressed in a nightgown and wrapper, moved to his side, then looked around the room. "Where is she? You did bring her back?"

"I left without her."

"But why? I thought—"

"I did that which I thought best," he said curtly. "She doesn't need me."

When his grandmother placed her hand on his shoulder, he flinched. "Is that what she told you?"

Brice swirled his drink, then took a long swallow. The liquid burned a raw path down his throat. "She didn't need to. I saw it with my own eyes."

"I am very sorry. I—"

"Your sympathy is wasted, Grandmère. What's done is done. And now, I should like to be alone for a few moments before I leave."

"You're leaving tonight? Where?"

"To town. I have some preparations to make before I finalize and announce my betrothal to Lady Caroline. I shall stay in London until then." He expected some argument on his grandmother's part. There was none.

"Lord Hawthorne is expecting us tomorrow for his mother's birthday party. You know what a big event it is for her. She's likely to have fits if at least half the *ton* doesn't show up for her first event of the little season."

"I don't know when I'll return. I make no promises." He must get out of this house. Away from her memories.

"I shall leave you, then."

The door clicked shut behind her and the room once more began to whisper Kendra's name. He hurled his glass of brandy into the dying fire, where it shattered against the grate, igniting for an instant into a brilliant blue flame, before dying down, leaving only smoldering gray coals to warm his soul.

The minutes on the clock-radio silently changed as time refused to stand still. "Frankie," Kendra whispered. Then a little louder, "Frankie?"

"What?" came the sleepy reply.

"Wake up. We're going to Hawthorne Woods."

Frankie shot up from her pillow. "We're what?"

"I'm going back. You're going to help me."

"But he left you. You said you hated him."

"I know."

"But—"

"Get dressed." She turned on the light.

Frankie flopped back down on the bed and groaned.

"When was the full moon?"

"What do I look like, a lunar calendar? Why do you need to know that?"

"Because the portal only stays open for three nights. One before the full moon and one after. I can't wait another day to try again. Tonight's the last night. I'm sure of it."

Reluctantly, her friend got out of bed and drew on a pair of jeans. "What if, when you get there, you change your mind? What if it's not going to work?"

"We'll use our rendezvous point at Briarwood Museum. Okay?"

"You're crazy. You know that, don't you?"

"Crazy, and angry as hell."

"Six months is a long time."

"I'll take my chances. If I can't make him love me in six months, I'll come back the very next time the portal opens."

"You're lucky your best friend's a rich travel agent who likes you very much—otherwise, you'd find yourself stuck in England with no way to get home."

"I'll pay you back, somehow."

"I don't want to be paid back. I just don't want to see you hurt."

"Then help me get to the Druid's Cave."

Frankie gave her a flourishing bow. "I'm at your command."

"Good," Kendra said, grabbing her tote bag. "Call a cab."

20

The rain continued in a steady downpour as
Kendra slid out of the taxi just outside the locked gates
of Hawthorne Manor. Frankie followed, after telling the
cab driver to wait.

He shrugged, turned on the interior light and pulled
out a book from beneath his seat.

Frankie looked up at the high stone wall that surrounded the grounds. "Are you sure there's not some
easier way into the woods?"

"Not this close to the Druid's Cave, which happens to
be on the other side."

"Why would anyone go to the expense of building so
much wall?"

"If Brice killed Hawk in a duel as the tour guide
insisted, I couldn't imagine the new earl would be overly
fond of his neighbor."

"I hope they don't have any guard dogs."

"They didn't last time I was here at night. I'll just
have to take my chances." After glancing back at the

parked cab, Kendra motioned for Frankie to follow her. "If we head east, it'll bring us even closer. I don't want to climb over it so near to the front gates where someone might drive up and see us."

"Do people still live in that mausoleum?"

"I'm guessing so, since the night I returned, they were giving a party. Better safe than sorry though." They walked until they came to a large oak, its massive trunk blocking some of the view from the gates. "This is as good a place as any."

Frankie cupped her hands to give Kendra a boost up, since the wall was not the sort Kendra could easily jump over. Although she slipped on the rain-slick stones, losing her grip a couple of times, with Frankie's help she made it to the top, sporting only a scraped ankle and a few broken fingernails.

Straddling the top of the wall, she looked down to the other side. A bolt of lightning ripped across the sky, illuminating everything around her. The grounds were empty, deserted as far as the eye could see. To the east, she could make out the dark outline of the forest. Beyond that lay her destiny.

"Well, I guess this is it," she said, looking back at her friend. A roll of thunder rumbled across the sky.

Frankie lifted Kendra's tote bag up to her. "You're gonna change, aren't you?" she asked, squinting against the fat raindrops that splattered against her face.

"When I get to the Druid's Cave."

"I was going to say write sometime, but I guess that's not an option." She brushed at her eyes, but Kendra couldn't tell if she was wiping away the rain or perhaps tears.

"Remember, six months at the Briarwood Museum. Okay?"

"Okay."

They stared at each other for a long moment, before Kendra dropped to the ground on the other side, thinking she was glad it was raining, since it covered her own tears as well.

The wind whipped at her wet hair, stinging her face. Thankfully, her discomfort lessened when she entered the woods, the ancient oaks offering some shelter against the thunderstorm. Even so, by the time she reached the Druid's Cave, her teeth were chattering and she contemplated not putting on her gown after all. But the thought of running into someone from the nineteenth century while dressed in a pair of tight blue jeans was enough to make her brave the minor discomfort of changing into her ballgown.

Anticipation mingled with fear the moment she stepped between the portal stones to await her fate. What if she went to the wrong time? How would she know? More importantly, would the Druid's Light know? Her frantic thoughts were soon replaced by disappointment when nothing happened. The wind, however, drove the rain into every crack and crevice of stone, and it wasn't long before she was chilled through.

Frustration washed through her the longer she waited. When a bolt of lighting sheared the night, she realized nothing had changed. She was still standing, like a fool, between two monolithic stones while the rain turned everything around her to mud.

Before she had time to contemplate what she might do next—since the taxi was most likely gone—a crack of thunder boomed overhead, echoing off the stones around her. Startled, she dropped her tote bag, then smacked her head on the great rock while bending to retrieve it. As if that wasn't enough, she stepped on the

hem of her gown and promptly fell to the ground in a
heap of wet silk and mud.

"Wonderful. Just wonderful," she muttered, climbing
to her feet and futilely trying to brush some of the ooz-
ing slime from her gown.

Refusing to accept defeat, she stood there a few minutes
more, having gone too far to give up now. But again, nothing happened. Finally admitting failure, she grabbed her
bag and stepped from the portal, letting the rain wash the
mud from her clothes and the heartbreak from her soul.

Aimlessly, she wandered from the Druid's Cave, not
even noticing when the rains lessened to a mere sprinkle.

"Here now! Don't go that way."

Kendra froze at the sound of the gruff voice.

"Now look, miss," he continued, in a more congenial
tone. "I ain't got all night. Let's go."

An answering giggle, then a very feminine, "I'm coming. Just give me a moment," told Kendra that she'd not
been seen yet. Quickly, and as quietly as she could manage, she backed away from the voices. Thinking she
could hide at the Druid's Cave, she aimed in that direction, but found, to her horror, the two woods wanderers
were heading that way as well. She ducked behind a
large tree trunk when the pair nearly overtook her.

"Don't know why I put up with this, time after time,"
the man grumbled as he and the woman passed within
inches of Kendra's hiding place. "Especially here of all
places in miserable weather such as this. It's haunted, it
is. Heard it said over and over, but nobody listens."

She peeked around the base of the tree, then stared in
shock at the sight of the two as they continued on, oblivious to her presence.

The woman, wrapped in a cloak and hood, her long
gown trailing on the forest floor, put her hand on the

man's shoulder. "Think of how grateful his lordship is to you, and how lonely he would be if not for your dedicated services."

"A lot o' good it'll do me if milord's mother finds out what I've been doin' all these years. Why 'is lordship can't take care o' business in London like other gents confounds me. Got to smuggle 'em in through the forest so 'er ladyship don't see. Now mind yer step, milady, I've no wish to be carrying you the rest of the way."

From her position, Kendra watched as the two continued in a westerly direction through the trees. It took her a moment to realize what she was seeing—none other than one of Lord Hawthorne's infamous mistresses being smuggled to his bedchamber by way of the secret tunnel. But where was the entrance? They bypassed the cave, and curious, Kendra followed at a safe distance, hoping to catch a glimpse of this secret and yet—at least in the future—well-known passage.

After several minutes' walk, to Kendra's dismay, the pair did not disappear into any mysterious tunnel or hole in the ground. Instead, the man, looking around to ensure they were not being watched, led the woman, now blindfolded, from the trees to the summerhouse, a small but elegant building, situated well away from the manor at the edge of the woods.

Kendra decided that the tour guide must be wrong, because Lord Hawthorne obviously did not entertain women in his room as she'd said, but in the summerhouse, which in Kendra's mind made more sense. His mother was not as likely to walk in unannounced, especially in this weather.

Her curiosity satisfied, Kendra turned away and headed toward Blackmoor Hall, and her wet, muddied gown and sodden tennis shoes—she'd forgotten to put on the matching kid slippers—grew colder the longer she traveled. After about fifteen or twenty minutes, her limbs frozen and teeth chattering, she finally saw the roof of Blackmoor Hall emerge through the trees. Eventually, the forest thinned, to reveal the great house in all its splendor.

In spite of the cold, she stood for a few moments and simply stared at the mansion. It was just as she'd remembered. She had dreamed about this place for so long, pictured herself walking up the wide steps to the front door. As she reminisced, a figure emerged from the far side of the house—a man on horseback. He flew down the road, toward her.

Frightened by the way he rode his horse, as if the hounds of hell were at his heels, Kendra stepped back into the trees, afraid to be seen. Not until he had passed did she realize it was Brice, and by then, it was too late, for he'd disappeared into the night.

Why had he left in such a hurry? And to where? Shivering, she decided the answers could wait until after she thawed out in a hot bath. With her heavy skirts gathered up, she ran to the house and pounded on the door.

The speed with which it was answered surprised her as the butler swung the door open, then took a step back in shock. "Miss Browning! What—" He cleared his throat and, once more, he was his usually staid self. "I trust your voyage from the Colonies was a pleasant one?" he intoned, stepping aside for her to enter.

"At least I didn't get seasick this time." She stood, dripping, in the middle of the foyer looking around. Home, she thought. I'm home.

Alethea, book in hand, emerged from the library, then stopped and stared in disbelief. "Kendra?" she whispered.

"Grandmère." Smiling, Kendra took a step forward, intending to wrap her arms about the dear woman. Not wanting to get her wet, she stopped.

Alethea, however, had no such concerns and closed the distance between them, hugging Kendra fiercely. "My dear girl. I knew you would come back." Pulling away, she studied Kendra's face. "Will you stay this time?"

"I want to. It's just that—"

"Never mind," she said, sensing Kendra's reluctance to talk in front of the butler. "We can continue our discussion after you get out of these wet things. You will catch your death." To the butler, she said, "Have a hot bath drawn at once."

By the time Kendra had bathed and changed, she was yawning profusely, and Alethea, insisting that they wait until the morning to talk, retired to her own bedchamber.

It was late afternoon before Kendra stirred, and only then because of the odd feeling that she was being watched. A quiet giggle confirmed her suspicions, and she opened her eyes just enough to see two cherubic faces staring intently at hers, each with grins that would put any Cheshire cat to shame.

Tommy nudged his sister. "She's wakin'."

Through her lashes, Kendra saw Bonnie study her closely. "No, she's not," the little girl said after a moment.

"Yes, she is. I saw 'er eyes move."

Bonnie giggled with delight.

Kendra remained still as the two bent closer. When they were just inches from her face, her hands shot up and wrapped them in a bear hug. "Got you!"

The children, squealing with laughter, tried to squirm free, then froze at the sound of Jenny's voice. "There you are, you little ruffians." She wagged her finger at them from the doorway. "Didn't I tell you both to wait 'til Miss Browning had wakened?"

Bonnie looked down, but Tommy was not about to admit guilt. "We did," he announced. "I saw 'er wake up myself."

Jenny, hands on hips, tried to look sternly at the two, but the twinkle in her eye gave her away.

Kendra laughed. "They're fine. Really."

"Well, then," Jenny said, "You two mind yer manners, and don't stay too long." To Kendra, she asked, "Will you be wantin' somethin' hot to drink?"

Kendra eyed the children. "A pot of chocolate, and three cups, I think." Her request was met with rousing cheers as Jenny left to do her bidding.

"I can't believe how big you two have grown," Kendra said, hugging them once more.

When she let them go, Tommy puffed his chest out proudly. "I can read."

"You can?" Kendra pretended great surprise as Tommy nodded in affirmation.

Bonnie tugged on the sleeve of Kendra's nightdress. "I can sing my ABCs."

"Oh my! What a good girl."

"And she can spell cat, too. Spell it."

Bonnie looked at her with wide serious eyes. "Cat. C–A–T."

Tousling the youngster's blonde curls, Kendra blinked back the tears, thinking how, if not for a stroke of fate, these two beautiful children would be fending for themselves alone on the street, or worse yet, under that horrid Grimly's thumb. "And where, might I ask, did you two become so smart?"

"At school!" they both shouted proudly.

"School? Why you're not old enough for school."

Tommy took offense. "Yes, we are. Aunt Jenny takes us every time she goes to town to 'elp 'er grace out at the Browning Orph'nage and Shelter for Ladies. There's lots o' boys and girls there now and she lets us play with them when there's no lessons."

"The Browning Orphanage and Shelter for Ladies?" Kendra was touched that the women of the Ladies' Charitable Society would name the place after her.

"Aunt Jenny says if we learn to read, we won't 'ave to sweep no chimneys anymore. And our children won't 'ave to neither."

"That's right," Kendra said. "If you go to school and learn all you can, why you can do most anything you want. Sail ships, teach other children, open your own shop. Whatever you want to do."

The children spent the next hour drinking chocolate and showing off their singing talents with songs they had learned at the shelter, only leaving when Jenny returned and chased them away.

After Kendra dressed, she went in search of Alethea, finding her in the drawing room. "Good afternoon, Grandmère."

"I trust you slept well, dear?"

"Yes. Until two goblins came and woke me up."

Alethea smiled. "They were so excited when Jenny told them you were here. I quite imagine that they couldn't wait to see you."

After kissing Alethea on her cheek, Kendra sat down beside her on the settee. "I saw Brice ride off last night, just as I was arriving. Do you know where he went?"

The older woman sighed softly, and shook her head. "Last night, he called me Grandmère. He's so very stubborn, my grandson. He has gone to town to speak with Lady Caroline's father about the betrothal."

"Betrothal?" Her heart sank as she tried to picture Brice with Lady Caroline. "Did you talk to him? Before he left?"

"Yes. But he wouldn't say much—other than I am not to expect him home until after he is well and betrothed. Still, I wouldn't worry overmuch. Now that you are here—"

"Worry?" Kendra nearly shrieked. "He jilted me twice! The man's insane! Of course I'm going to worry." She began pacing the room. "What a fool I was to think he could possibly drop every value ingrained in him since birth to consort with a commoner like me."

"You mustn't say such things."

"It's true and you know it."

"Kendra. Dear. Please calm yourself. Your beautiful clear nimbus is turning a nasty shade of greenish brown."

"Because I'm sick. For the first time in my life, I know what I want, and when I finally have the guts to go and get it, it's snatched from beneath my nose."

"And what is it you want, dear?"

"Why, Brice, of course! I love him. I love every stiffly formal bone in his body. I love how mad he used to get when I called him Monty. And I love how he always calls me Miss Browning. And—" Kendra stopped her pacing and looked at Alethea in surprise. "I love him, and I'll be damned if I let him marry some other woman because of his faulty sense of duty."

Rising from her seat, Alethea grasped Kendra's hand. "That's the Kendra I have come to know and love. You must never give up. No matter what. But realize that once the announcement's made, Brice's 'faulty sense of duty' shall make it very difficult for you. He would never willingly hurt Lady Caroline by formally announcing his betrothal to her and then crying off."

It was true, and Kendra knew it. "Do you have any idea when he plans to do that?"

"He didn't say. I can only hope that you're successful in your endeavor."

They were interrupted by the entrance of Cecily. "Kendra!" she cried, running into her arms. "Grandmère told me you were here. I vow, I was sorely tempted to go and wake you myself, had you not arrived so late."

"Hello, Cecily. How are you?"

"Simply lovely! Peter's asked me to marry him, but I intend to wait until next season before I accept, assuming we're still in love. Would you like to see the gown I'm wearing to Hawthorne Manor tonight? You shall go, shan't you? It's his mother's birthday. We attend every year."

"I'm not sure."

"I missed you so, dear cousin," she continued. "Brice has been a veritable monster since you left. It's hard for me to recall how much I used to miss him when he was away for so long. Now, sometimes, I find myself wishing for him to return to his ships and sail around the world."

"Cecilia, dear," Grandmère admonished. "How you do go on."

Cecily grinned, not in the least daunted. "I do apologize. But now that Kendra's returned, he'll be his old self, I'm sure. Even so, I *do* hope he gets home in time to take us tonight."

But Brice never came home.

For the remainder of the day, Kendra's inner self wavered between joy and despondency—joy at being with the people she had come to love as her own family, and despondency at not knowing what would become of her and Brice.

Outside, the weather mirrored her own emotions:

sunny one moment, overcast the next. By the end of the day, the clouds won the battle, sending a steady rain down to claim its victory.

As the drops pelted to the earth, Kendra's depression was complete, and when it came time to leave for Hawthorne Manor, she claimed a headache and stayed behind.

Brice helped himself to the brandy in Hawk's study, then took a seat before the fire. Hawk was speaking animatedly about the latest discovery made by an English archaeologist from an Egyptian dig, though Brice barely heard a word he said. He simply nodded in agreement, while he sipped his drink and lost himself in the flames dancing on the hearth.

Where was Kendra now? he wondered. With Jack? Then again, what did it matter? She was not here, with him. And he, after tonight, would be betrothed to the lovely Lady Caroline—a woman of impeccable heritage, he reminded himself. But Caroline did not have laughing green eyes, and hair the color of a harvest sunset. But she knew how to give a dinner party, and was accepted at court, he added in an attempt to console himself.

"Brice?"

"Yes, of course," he answered, absently.

Hawthorne looked down at him, his expression one of concern. "I say, are you all right?"

"All right?"

"Perhaps this is not the best night to go through with your plans. There shall be other parties this winter."

It took Brice a moment to gather his thoughts and figure out what his friend was trying to tell him. "No. Tonight. It must be tonight."

Hawk took Brice's glass and refilled it. "I should think that on this night, the night you are about to become the happiest of men, you would act accordingly."

"I was merely thinking . . . "

"About Kendra," Hawk filled in. "Might I suggest that you finish up your thinking about her *before* you announce your betrothal to the fifty or so guests that shall be arriving this night?"

"You may," Brice said, taking the proffered drink. "As long as you realize that I am not the first man to think of one woman before I wed another."

Hawthorne sat down in the opposite chair facing Brice. "True, but most men do not look as if they are facing a life sentence in Newgate when they willingly walk into matrimony. There is no one forcing you to marry Lady Caroline. Put off announcing the betrothal for a time."

"No. I will make it tonight. I have put Caroline and her family through enough these past two years by avoiding a firm commitment."

"Perhaps because you did not want the marriage?"

Brice glared at his friend. "Is it not time you joined your guests?"

Hawk merely laughed. "Since they are my mother's guests, I need not hurry. You are an expert at parrying questions, but I shall not let that one pass quite so easily."

Brice lifted his glass in a mock toast. "And I shall not answer. There is no need, since after tonight the point of your question will have no practical significance. Now if you will excuse me, I must leave to find my future bride."

Kendra, still dressed in her finery, stared out the library window, watching the rain splash against the diamond panes of glass.

"Bloody hell!" she said, rising from her seat. What if Brice showed up at Lord Hawthorne's to announce his betrothal? Hawk's mother would invite only the crème de la crème of society—the perfect place to announce such a thing. And she knew, just as Alethea had explained, that Brice would never cry off once the announcement was made.

Running from the room, she called out for the butler to have a carriage brought 'round. Jenny came flying down the hall at her summons and Kendra hurriedly explained that she'd decided to go to the party after all.

By the time her carriage pulled into the drive at Hawthorne Manor, Kendra's nerves had stretched taut, ready to break with the slightest touch. Pulling her hood over her head, she ran up the wide stairs. Once in the house, she nearly threw her cloak at a footman before skidding to a halt and proceeding at a more demure pace, just as another footman opened the doors to the salon where many of the guests stood about the large mirrored room.

Her heart started to race when she saw that everyone had gathered around a central point, presumably to listen to someone speak. It was Brice, and standing next to him was Lady Caroline and her parents.

As Kendra crossed the sleek marble floor toward the salon, she was reminded, oddly enough, of the moment Brice was mugged in Miami. If she didn't reach him in time, she'd lose him forever. Then, as now, time seemed to fragment, and she felt as if she moved in slow motion, unable to stop the course of events from occurring.

21

Kendra's footsteps echoed across the room, matching the cadence of her heart. Brice took Lady Caroline's hand in his, then turned to the guests as the young woman's father said, "Friends. Tonight, I have the pleasure of announcing—" He stopped at the sound of her approach. Several of the guests turned around to see who was interrupting their private gathering.

At first, Brice just stared in silence, then slowly, several heartbeats later, he lowered Lady Caroline's hand to his side and took one step forward.

"To announce . . ." her father continued, apparently flustered by this turn of events.

Hawk cleared his throat loudly, then finished, "The arrival of Blackmoor's cousin, Miss Browning, from the Colonies."

Strangely, after Kendra's pulse returned to normal and she was able to tear her gaze from Brice, her main concern was for Lady Caroline, who for some reason, didn't seem the least bit hurt or angry as she rushed forward to greet Kendra.

"Miss Browning," she said, with genuine affection. "I am so glad that you have decided to return. You shall be staying this time for awhile?"

"I hope so." Was she only imagining Lady Caroline's look of relief?

Suddenly Kendra was surrounded by a dozen or so people, mostly the women she had worked so closely with during the opening of her shelter, all wishing her well, and expressing their joy that she had decided to return. Smiling at all of them, she searched the room for Brice, finding him in a deep discussion with Lady Caroline's father. She could tell nothing from his face, and wondered if he were angry with her. Not having the courage to face him just yet, she allowed the ladies to sweep her into the ballroom where dozens of guests danced to a lively minuet.

Spying Alethea amidst a group of matrons exiting the salon from a different set of doors, Kendra started toward her, but was stopped by a hand upon her arm. Lord Parkston smiled knowingly at her, his grip firm while his eyes held a dark glint of something she could not quite decipher.

"Ah, Miss Browning," he said, rubbing what appeared to be razor burn on his newly shaven face. "A pleasure to see you here again after so long an absence. I was beginning to wonder what made you spirit away so suddenly?"

"The fair winds and a sailing ship," she quipped, with a pointed look at her arm.

He released it, but made no move to let her pass. "Might I have the pleasure of this dance?"

Before she had a chance to answer, Cecily called out to her from but a few feet away. "There you are, dear cousin. I have been searching far and wide, and here you are in the ballroom." She stepped neatly between them, linking her arm through Kendra's with nary a look at Parkston. "I vow that if I don't get some fresh air, I shall swoon. Is it not stifling in here?" she asked, pulling Kendra through the crush of guests to the veranda doors.

"Thank you for your timely appearance," Kendra said, once they were out of earshot of the hated viscount.

"'Twas nothing. I daresay that man's soul is as black as night. It fairly emanates from him."

Kendra eyed her young friend speculatively, thinking of Alethea's talents. "Can you see it?"

"See what?"

"His soul?"

Cecily thought for a moment. "His soul? Goodness no. But when I look at him, compared with . . ." she glanced around the room, then nodded in the direction of her beau, "With Peter, well, there is almost a black cloud that hovers over Lord Parkston. It is not really there, of course, but sometimes it seems so."

"Do you know what I think? I think that you've inherited your grandmother's powers and don't even know it."

The younger woman cocked her head in thought, then smiled. "Perhaps you are right."

"Look around the room, and tell me what else you see."

Cecily did, her gaze resting on Hawthorne, who strode from the salon to stand alone near the steps to the ballroom. Just then, Brice approached from the opposite direction, but on seeing Hawthorne, he turned on his heel and left whence he'd come. Hawk, in turn, moved the other way.

Cecily shook her head. "No, it is no use. For I look at Hawk and see a dark cloud behind him as well."

"Behind Hawk?" Kendra eyed the golden-haired man, whose usually angelic face appeared taut. Lady Caroline approached him, and it softened.

Cecily sighed. "It's gone. See. I cannot even get that right. Hawk could be a monster, or Gabriel himself, come down from heaven, and I would never know. I haven't Grandmère's powers after all," she said as they stepped from the ballroom, the cool air hitting their faces. Though it was no longer raining, above them the moon disappeared behind a thick bank of clouds, giving warning that the inclement weather still threatened.

The two women stared silently out into the garden, each lost in their own thoughts until, after several minutes, a footman interrupted their communion with a slight cough meant to garner their attention. Kendra noticed a folded note upon the salver he held. "Miss Browning," he intoned.

Taking the note, Kendra waited for him to leave, then opened it.

Meet me in the master's chambers. Urgent.

It was unsigned, but Kendra thought she recognized the bold script, wondering what Brice could possibly want to discuss with her in Hawk's chambers of all places, unless perhaps her interruption of his betrothal announcement? It was, with all the guests mingling about, the only private area in the mansion.

She excused herself to Cecily.

As Kendra headed up the stairs toward Lord Hawthorne's bedchamber, she tried to picture Brice and Caroline together. They were all wrong for each other. Brice needed something more in his life. Something that only she could give him. Her love.

The sound of her skirts rustling as she walked seemed strangely loud in the silence of the hallway, away from the noise of the many guests below. Finding Hawk's chambers with ease, since she had been up here only yesterday, on a guided tour no less, she rapped on the door, which pushed open at first touch. After peeking inside the dimly lit room, she called out softly, "Brice?" then stepped in.

No one was about. A single wall sconce lit the room, casting gyrating shadows across the paneled walls. A dull glow emitted from the hearth where the fire had long ago burnt to embers.

Everything appeared much the same as it had but a day ago in the twentieth century, right down to the secret door which stood ajar a few inches. The only difference was that the silk wall hangings, bedding and Aubusson carpet appeared richer, newer. Something else that had not been present in the future, she noted, was the table near the fireplace, littered with artifacts that appeared ancient even for this time.

Curious, she stepped into the room to take a closer look. Many of the items had dirt upon them, as if they had only been recently excavated. She saw tarnished silver coins, and shards of rust-colored pottery, much like some of the artifacts she had seen in the museum at home. Her eye strayed to a small terra-cotta fawn. Dancing on one hoof, it was blowing a slender double flute. She could almost hear the clear piping, and she reached for the exquisitely wrought piece.

"Do not touch!" an angry voice cried out from behind her. Spinning on her heel, she saw Lord Hawthorne, his brows drawn as he slammed the door shut and rushed forward. He pulled her hand away. "Do you realize what you could have destroyed? It's irreplaceable!"

She took a step back. "I'm sorry. I wouldn't have picked it up." He seemed to calm down when she stepped away from the table. "Are these Roman?" she asked, looking down at the items that, had she bothered to notice, were all meticulously placed on the table, each with its name neatly printed on a slip of paper beneath it.

"Yes," he said, stooping to carefully straighten a label that had slipped from place. "I am preparing these for display at the museum. They are the culmination of my life's work. Civilization at its finest."

"I had forgotten your love of history." Her sudden recollection of that fact reminded her of a conversation between Brice, Jack and herself, on the streets of Miami. Jack had just finished telling Brice of the Debutante Murderer's capture, and what had led to his solving the case. *A history buff.* She backed toward the door, wondering if history were repeating itself—more than a century earlier.

What had Brice told her, so long ago? An aristocrat. At one time, he thought the murderer had to be a nobleman familiar with the area. My God! She'd seen, just last night, a servant leading a lady to the summerhouse from the area of the Druid's Cave. What was it the tour guide mentioned? And Brice, too? The string of mistresses and insatiable sexual appetite the earl had attempted to hide from his domineering mother?

And what of Cecily's sighting of the dark cloud hovering over him this evening? Was he hiding behind his seemingly angelic face?

No. She refused to believe it. Lord Hawthorne, Hawk, had always been the perfect gentleman, befriending her early on when she had needed a shoulder.

He looked up suddenly, one golden brow raised as he crossed his arms stubbornly. She took another step back. "Do not think to leave now," he said.

Kendra stopped and tried to look casual. "Why, whatever do you mean, my lord?"

He cast her a skeptical look before eyeing his precious artifacts once more, apparently to ensure all was in order. "If you're thinking to have me try to talk sense into Blackmoor's thick skull, it's too late. I have failed in that endeavor."

"Failed?" Kendra asked, glancing over her shoulder to see that she had backed not toward the door as she'd hoped but toward the open panel in the wall. What was he talking about?

Hawk raised up to his full height; the single wall sconce threw eerie shadows across his face. "I shall probably rue for the rest of my life that I failed to speak my feelings to him when he first told me of his intentions to marry Caroline. I would have forsworn all other women for her. Never shall I find another that compares. The blasted man deserves what fate has in store for him." He gave her a peculiar look. "That *is* why you're here, is it not?"

"Me? But I thought—" Before she had a chance to finish, a strong draft coming from the passageway snuffed out the light just as the secret panel slammed into her back, sending her sprawling into Hawthorne's arms.

Her scream had not even sounded when the bedchamber door burst open, spilling light into the room from the hallway beyond. A tall, broad-shouldered figure stood silhouetted in the doorway.

"Brice!" She could have fainted with relief. Until he stepped into the room and she saw his steel-cold glare. Only then did she realize Lord Hawthorne's arms were about her.

Another figure appeared in the doorway, but she paid little attention as she extricated herself from Hawk's grasp. "I don't know what happened. Someone pushed me."

Brice folded his arms across his chest. "Someone? When there is no one else in the room?"

Kendra pointed at the open wall panel. "They must have come from there."

Brice looked at the passageway, then turned his withering stare to Hawthorne. "One more in the endless line of beauties to whet your appetite?"

"See here," Hawk said, taking a step forward. He stopped when he noticed the other man in the doorway. "I say, what are you doing here, Parkston? I suggest you leave, at once."

Brice glanced over his shoulder to see his long-time enemy, too furious to care that Parkston was the man he suspected of sending those pirates to attack the *Eterne*. The event had nearly cost him his life, but was that any worse than what Hawk was guilty of? A lifetime of trust, shattered at the sight of Kendra in his arms in a darkened room. "What does it matter who witnesses this event? I shall use him for a second." The words were out before he even realized it.

Parkston had bent down to pick something up off the ground. When he rose, he nodded his head. "I would be honored."

Kendra, her green eyes glittering with disbelief and anger said, "You can't be serious. Hawk's your friend."

"No longer. Name your second, Hawthorne."

Hawk's face paled, undoubtedly because the man couldn't fire a pistol in a straight line if he tried. "No. You must listen to Kendra, er, Miss Browning. I only came up here because she asked to meet me. I have a note . . ." He stopped, apparently realizing how incriminating his words sounded.

"Do you indeed?" Brice said, taking a step toward him. "Is this your revenge because you were in love with Lady Caroline? Had you told me two years ago—"

Kendra moved between them. "Stop it! I don't know

what's gotten into you, Monty, but you're acting like a fool."

"Remove yourself, Miss Browning," he ordered.

"I'll do no such thing. Not until you agree to leave peaceably."

"And I shall do no such thing until I receive satisfaction."

Kendra snorted in disbelief. "Satisfaction? For what? I'm not a piece of property you can toss around indiscriminately until you feel the need to take up with me when and where it pleases you. You gave up that right when you left me. Twice I might add."

Brice refused to admit that Kendra was right. But she was. Even so, he was certain he'd rather be dead than see her with another man. "Your second," he said again, quietly.

"My God, Monty! Don't you see what's happening? The tour guide's prediction."

"You heard me, Hawk," he said, ignoring Kendra. He didn't want to think about anything the tour guide had said. What he wanted was to be done with this so that he could leave. He still needed to speak with Lady Caroline privately about why he was crying off. Despite this latest turn of events, he knew he could not marry Caroline, and he wondered, had he not been so blind to Hawk's apparent desire for the chit, if his former friend wouldn't have seen fit to stay away from Kendra. But he'd seen Kendra's arms around Hawk, too. He'd seen them both, though he wished to God it was not true.

Parkston sauntered into the room just then, taking a position against the wall. Brice ignored him, sensing that he was enjoying their discomfiture. He looked at Hawk instead, noticing his pale, but determined face, and the shock written upon Kendra's.

"Brice," she said, "stop and think about what you're doing. Hawk is your friend."

"Is he my friend? Then what is he doing with you, up here, alone?"

"Yes?" Parkston quipped.

Hawthorne pulled a slip of paper from his pocket. "I only came because Miss Browning sent me this. I assumed she wanted to discuss your relationship with Caroline."

"But I didn't send it!" Kendra cried.

Brice grabbed the note. *Meet me in your chambers.* He crushed it in his fist, then threw it into the hearth. After a moment, it flared up, until nothing was left but ash. The flame died and with it what was left of his hope. The handwriting had been decidedly feminine.

"You have to believe us," Kendra said. "I received a note, too. I thought it was from you, but found Hawk up here instead."

Parkston laughed. "Clever, Hawthorne."

The earl narrowed his eyes. "I did not send the note."

Brice looked at Kendra. He wanted to believe her. More than anything in the world, right now, he wanted—needed—to believe her. "Where is it?"

She turned her hands palm upward and stared into them. "It was here. I swear." Looking around, she pointed at Parkston. "Why don't you ask him?"

Brice didn't even turn his way. He couldn't. His heart had shattered with the betrayal of the two people he cared most about. Glancing at the clock on the mantle, he saw it was nearly half-past eleven. Lady Caroline would be waiting for him below stairs, and he wanted to tell her their betrothal was not to be, before her father did. "If you will excuse me, I have an appointment to keep." He turned, and strode to the door. "As for tomorrow morning, Lord Hawthorne . . . "

Kendra watched as he hesitated at the threshold, his quiet words ringing with lethal finality. Again she was reminded of the tour guide's prediction—or rather her dire warning: that the duke of Blackmoor would kill his friend in a duel. She realized at once that Hawk was not the source of danger she'd sensed. Her instincts had never been wrong, having saved her hide more than once on the streets of Miami. But what had frightened her so, if not Hawthorne?

Her eyes lit on Parkston. He was rubbing at his face just above that pointed goatee he always wore, as if his skin still irritated him. The man infuriated her, but she was more worried about Brice's broken pride, and his misguided challenge. "Brice, wait! You'll kill him! And all over a misunderstanding. You can't let this happen. Besides, you're not betrothed to me. She said it was your fiancée! Think about what you're doing!"

Brice remained where he was, his back to them, as if he were waiting to hear something that might change his mind. She knew if he left all would be lost unless she could somehow convince him of Hawk's innocence.

Frantically, she looked to Hawthorne, who shook his head. "If he wants pistols at dawn," Hawk said, "so be it."

She glared at Parkston, who leaned casually against the wall, seemingly pleased by this latest turn of events. "Give me the note," she demanded, holding out her hand.

"I fear I know not what you're talking about."

Brice left the room. She stared at the empty doorway, realizing then how things would seem to him. His best friend, with the woman he . . . loved. "Wait!" she cried.

"Let him go," Hawk said, moving to the hearth to pick up the poker. "And you, Parkston," he added, over his shoulder, none too kindly, "you may leave as well. All of you. Please, just go."

"Stop," Kendra said. When the viscount turned toward her, she added, "Give me the note."

"Note? Ah. You mean this scrap of paper I found upon the floor." He held it out and took a step forward, but before she could grab it, he crumpled it tightly in his hand. "Why is it so important?"

Behind her, Hawthorne apparently sought to ease his frustrations by shoving the poker into the hearth, again and again, stoking the fire until its flames rose up, warming her back. Returning her attention to Parkston, she was about to demand the note's return once more, when she was suddenly mesmerized by the play of shadows and firelight upon the viscount's face. She realized then that she had seen him somewhere before—or someone very much like him—and tried to remember why that seemed suddenly important. Quickly, her mind went over each of her encounters with him. First on the *Eterne* on the day she arrived in London; later when she had run off and he had offered his assistance. Of course she'd seen him at various balls and soirees throughout the season before she had returned home, but she knew it was something more.

"*You* wrote those notes. Didn't you?"

From the corner of her eye, she saw Hawthorne, poker in hand, straighten in sudden interest.

"Me?" the viscount answered, his hand rising to his chest. "Whatever makes you say that?"

"Yes, Kendra?" Hawk asked, moving forward.

Then, suddenly, she knew. Parkston's face. It had been partially sunburned when she had first seen him on the *Eterne*, as if he'd recently shaven a beard that he'd worn for quite sometime. And now, the way he was rubbing the irritated skin on his jawline, as if once again he'd only just shaven the beard from his face and was not quite used to the feel of it.

He was the man in the airport! The man who'd insisted he must be on the very next plane to England. And the man who had run into her on the steps of Hawthorne Manor after she'd left the tour. Which meant that he was the man Frankie had seen on the news!

"You're him!" she said, astounded that she'd not realized it sooner. "You're the Debutante Murderer."

"And you," he said in a low voice, "should have stayed in Miami like a good little detective."

He took one menacing step toward her and she backed up, only to see Hawthorne moving toward her, the poker raised over his head. Screaming, she scrambled for the door. Parkston lunged at her, grabbing her around the waist, slamming her against his chest as he spun toward Hawk, using her as a shield.

The feel of cold, smooth metal pressing against her neck told her that Parkston held a gun to her.

Lord Hawthorne, poker still raised, moved slowly toward them. "Let her go."

"One more step and she's dead," the viscount said. He moved his pistol to her temple.

Hawk lowered his arm, then dropped the poker. It landed with a thud, scarring the Aubusson carpet with black dust.

Slowly, with Kendra ensconced firmly in his grip, Parkston sidestepped toward the open panel in the wall. "I regret that I must leave your mother's party so soon, Hawthorne, but I find that I have pressing engagements in another time." He laughed diabolically at his own sick humor. "Oh, and do not try to follow, or your sweet friend will discover what it feels like to have her head filled with lead."

Kendra tried to remain calm. All thoughts of disarming him fled when Parkston pulled her into the dark corridor of the secret passageway. Just before he slammed the panel shut, she had a glimpse of Hawthorne running from the room. Suddenly, the pitch black engulfed her, and fear took over.

Parkston spun her around and pushed her forward, keeping the gun pressed firmly in her back. "If at any time I feel you distance yourself from this pistol, I will not hesitate to fire. Is that understood?"

"Perfectly."

"Then we shall get along famously. Please move forward at a steady pace until we reach the lantern I have left burning. At our arrival, I want you to slowly pick it up, and continue forward as directed."

Kendra closed her eyes, not being able to see anything anyway, and took a deep breath, before proceeding forward, her hands outstretched in case she should run into anything. Thankfully, the passageway ran straight with no sudden turns or stairs. She decided that time was on her side, and her best course lay in complacent cooperation—for now.

After what seemed an eternity, but was in reality little more than a minute or two, the blackness faded to gray and soon was replaced by a warm glow that emanated from around the now visible corner.

When they reached the lamp, Kendra stopped and slowly lifted it as instructed. She was not so foolish as to try to escape in such a narrow and confined space that, as she held the lantern aloft, revealed nowhere to hide amidst the cobwebs and unfinished siding. Occasionally they passed a doorway that led to some unknown chamber, but Kendra noticed they were all barred, which precluded anyone from entering. The passageway, she realized, extended the full length of the house, which was considerable.

Eventually, they reached a hallway branching out to the left and right that intersected their path.

"Straight ahead?" she asked, pausing to glance quickly down each corridor.

"Yes."

She continued on, the feel of the gun at her back a constant reminder that she must keep her wits about her, concentrating on nothing but watching for the opportunity to escape. Had Hawthorne run off to find Brice?

Would Brice put aside his anger to come looking for her? she wondered as Parkston nudged her toward a steep staircase leading down. Recalling the coldness of Brice's gaze as he left the room, she found herself praying that Hawk would find him in time and convince him of the danger.

The narrow steps seemed to descend forever, and Kendra noticed a distinct change in the air around her when they reached the bottom. Cold and damp. Instead of wood, the walls were cut from the earth itself and she hesitated when she realized they were underground.

Parkston impatiently pushed her forward with his gun. "Keep to the right," he said.

"To the right?" She looked down the rough-hewn corridor and saw more than one tunnel leading away.

"Yes. No matter what, turn to the right. That will eventually take us to the summerhouse, and to the forest beyond."

"Where are we going?"

"To the Druid's Cave," he replied.

"But the portal's closed."

"For some, perhaps. Those who haven't embraced the black arts. Now move on."

Slowly, Kendra did as he asked, careful not to walk too fast, in hopes that someone might come to her rescue before they made it to the portal and another time. Recalling the dire revelations of the tour guide: "Lord Blackmoor killed Lord Hawthorne the next day. Some even suspect he killed his lover, since she was never seen again from that day forward."

Kendra wondered if it were at all possible to change history.

22

Brice stood on the front steps, just out of the rain, waiting for his carriage to be brought 'round. Suddenly Lord Hawthorne burst through the doors toward him, then leaned against a column, gasping for breath.

"Kendra," the earl said, between gulps of air.

Brice cast him a cool glance, then looked out to the night. A bolt of lightning ripped across the sky, illuminating the horizon. "I had already cried off to Lady Caroline's father, even before Kendra met you in your chambers. There was no need for your display—"

Hawk shook his head. "Parkston's got her!" he shouted over the thunder. "He wrote the notes."

"A very nice try—"

"No! He took her. Pistol," he managed, all the while fighting for breath.

An inkling of fear crept up Brice's spine and he turned to the man who had been his friend since youth. True, at one time he had the momentary suspicion that

Hawk might have had something to do with the murders at the Druid's Cave, but that had died a quick death when he realized Hawk could no more kill a person than Brice could deny his own heritage, part Gypsy or not. But when he had received that hastily scribbled note telling him to go to Hawk's chambers at once, and had seen Kendra in his embrace, a lifetime of friendship could not stop the jealousy that flared to life within him. And yet, who had written the note?

"What are you saying?"

Lord Hawthorne, having recovered somewhat, replied, "Parkston grabbed Kendra after she accused him of writing the notes . . . and of being the Debutante Murderer. Threatened to shoot her if I followed."

In one long step, Brice closed the distance between them, grasping his friend's arm. "Followed? Where? Where did he take her?"

"Into the catacombs, but from there, I don't know. You know as well as I do, he could go almost anywhere from there. The man is mad. Said something about a pressing engagement in another time."

"Another time?" That inkling of fear exploded, almost paralyzing him. "We have to go to the Druid's Cave. At once!" Brice pulled his greatcoat tighter about him as he flew down the stairs. The storm was getting worse.

A muffled thud, followed by, "Damn!" brought Brice to a halt.

He glanced over his shoulder to see Hawk sprawled out on the ground. "What happened?"

The earl tried to stand, then winced in pain as he put weight on his right foot. "I slipped on the steps. I think I sprained my ankle." Despite his injury he tried to walk. It was no use.

"Never mind. There is no time to wait, and you can't be any help injured as you are. Not at the Druid's Cave."

"What is Parkston's plan? "

"There isn't time to explain." Brice paused an instant, then grasped Hawk's arm, intending to apologize.

The earl pushed him away, forgiveness already in his eyes. "Go!"

"Wish me luck," he said, before racing down the graveled path toward the gardens and the woods beyond.

"I always have, my friend."

Kendra knew why Parkston's instructions were so explicit, always keeping to the right, for the last part of their journey was made in total darkness, the lantern having given out long ago. She made her way by running her right hand lightly along the rough wall so that she knew when they had reached another turn. Everything smelled of damp earth, and Kendra began to feel as if she were buried and might never emerge.

Thankfully, they eventually reached the stairwell that ascended into the summerhouse, or rather she tripped on it, banging her shin quite severely.

Parkston shoved the pistol against her back. "Up the steps and be quick about it. The door at the top is unlocked."

When they emerged from the summerhouse into the pouring rain, Kendra took a deep cleansing breath, rejuvenating her senses in the night air. It cleared her thoughts, and though her fear threatened to consume her, she was better able to keep it at bay. "Where are we going?" she asked, hoping to pause long enough to look at her surroundings.

"Move," he said. "To the forest. The Druid's Cave."

Once more he pushed her forward, but Kendra, hoping to stall for time, pretended to stumble, falling to the ground on her hands and knees.

"Get up, you fool," he shouted against the wind.

Slowly she rose to her feet, allowing herself enough time to covertly glance around her, primarily back at the house which stood like a solitary beacon in the rain, its windows aglow with light. For an instant, she thought she saw someone running from the house, but before she could be certain, Parkston reached down, grabbed the neck of her gown and yanked her up.

They continued several yards farther, but this time, Kendra tripped for real when the skirts of her sodden gown wrapped about her legs.

Parkston had no sympathy. He grabbed her shoulder and spun her around, his eyes—maniacal eyes—bored into hers. "One more move like that and I won't think twice about killing you."

"I'm sorry," she said, hoping to buy some time. "It's the dress. It's hard to move in it when it's so wet."

"That is easily remedied," he said. "You can take it off."

She had no wish to parade through the forest in her chemise with a mad man at her heels. "I'll manage."

Once in the woodland, he slowed his pace, apparently no longer fearing they'd be seen since the forest covered their progress, and the wind, howling above the treetops, prevented anyone from hearing them at all.

"Why are you doing this?" she shouted back over her shoulder.

He grabbed her arm, careful to keep his weapon trained on her. "You're the detective. You figure it out."

"Because what I said was true?" When he failed to answer, she said, "You're the Debutante Murderer. And since you're so familiar with the Druid's Cave, I gather you murdered those women in this century as well."

"Bravo, my dear. Your power of deduction is quite good, though not perfect."

"You mean I'm wrong?"

"Not in the least. I merely thought an intelligent young woman such as yourself would realize the dangers of jumping through time. Had you stayed in your own century, you might have lived to see what the future brings. Instead, you chose to meddle in the past. For that I must kill you."

"You'll never get away with it," she told him, knowing full well that he could and would if he made it to the Druid's Cave.

"On the contrary, Miss Browning. Had you not chanced to come to the nineteenth century, then returned with information that only someone from this century could possibly know, I would have been able to return to your era and live the life I have painstakingly built for myself. You see, it occurred to me that people are intrigued by the past. Why, the paintings that used to hang in my gallery alone brought me a fortune when I took them to your time. And my dear wife's ruby necklace, one that had been in her family for generations, brought me more money than I could spend in a lifetime.

"Everything was ready for the day I left the nineteenth century permanently. All that money, waiting for me in preparation for the time I had to leave when things around here became too—how do the police in your time say it? Hot?"

He led her around a particularly thick growth of underbrush, all the while heading due east. An eerie mist spread across the ground in spite of the rain beating down on the forest floor.

"Unfortunately," he continued, "you have ruined all that for me with your meddlesome ways. I was happily conducting my black magic, careful to leave no witnesses to the sacrifices I had to make, to be able to leave through the portal whenever necessary, until you came along with your twentieth-century police training. I was even safe when Luci escaped. Through an art similar to hypnosis, I knew she'd never recognize me. What I don't understand," he said, stopping her for a moment, "was how you arrived here in the first place? I was not aware of another portal when I chanced to run across the moonstone I took from that old wizard Baldalf."

"Botolf," she corrected. "And I got here by drowning in the Atlantic. You ought to try it sometime."

"How did you get here?" he asked, waving the gun before her. "And just where did you come across the moonstone? You did use a moonstone, did you not?" he asked, his tone accusatory.

"How else? But I'm surprised yours worked for you," Kendra said, recalling Botolf's words that the moonstone found her, and not the other way around. For a moment, Kendra thought she saw Parkston's face flush with anger, but before she could dwell on it, the great dolmens that guarded the Druid's Cave materialized through the dark. Time was running out. Grasping at straws, she said, "I understand they are very particular about who they allow to pass through time."

"Are you telling me," he asked, "that you have no difficulty using yours? That you can do so at will?"

She sensed this was a sore subject with him. Taking a chance, she said, "Of course. Anytime. Can't you?"

He stopped to pin a withering glare on her but didn't answer.

"It must be tough not to be able to travel through

time without first stopping to dabble in the black arts," she taunted. "What a waste."

His grip on her arm tightened as he placed the barrel of the gun beneath her nose. "Perhaps," he hissed. "Had I not lost my moonstone in the future, I might have prevented much bloodshed. Then again, once I discovered the power entailed me, I doubt I would have changed my ways." His eyes sparkled with fury and interest. "Can you choose any century, any date you want to travel to?"

"Any date?" she echoed, realizing that he could easily escape without anyone knowing where or when he had gone to. At least between the two time periods she'd traveled through, Jack knew who to look for in one century, and, in the other, Hawk did, and perhaps Brice.

"Yes," he said, pulling her toward the portal. "Once I . . . dispose of you, I shall establish myself in a new time. Then again, perhaps I shall take you along. What say you to the year 1509? I have always been fascinated by the way Henry VIII tired of his wives and disposed of them. You could scream all you want, but with women being nothing more than chattel in those days, no one would listen. Yes," he said, scratching his chin with the gun, "that just might do."

"You can go to hell, Parkston."

He laughed. "To be certain. But not before my time." He dragged her to the portal. "Now it's a question of power and choice. Should we land in your century, you die. The Renaissance and you live. There is but one problem. If the moonstone takes us, it chooses the time."

"How do you usually pick your time?"

"Through sacrifice."

"You'll have to find another guinea pig, Parkston," she said, digging her heels into the ground. "I'm not a virgin." She couldn't let him pull her between the stones.

Her strength, however, was no match, and inch by inch, he dragged her toward the portal, its gaping mouth looming open like a pit of hell.

Just then, lightning struck overhead, illuminating a figure through the opening of the two stones.

"Brice!" she screamed, as Parkston pulled her in.

"*You!*" Parkston cried. "This is all your fault. Had you not survived the attack on your ship, I'd be free of all of you."

"A pity I could not accommodate you," Brice said, his voice as quiet as a knife slipping from a sheath. "Perhaps next time, you—"

"Next time? There shall be no next time for you, Blackmoor." He pointed his weapon at Brice's chest.

Thunder rumbled, shaking the very ground beneath them, and Brice lunged toward Parkston, grabbing for the gun.

"Run, Kendra. Now!" he ordered, but she stood frozen, unwilling to leave him. As the two men struggled for the weapon, she was knocked to the ground. They fell on top of her, pinning her helplessly beneath them. Suddenly a shot fired, and she flinched away, smashing the back of her head on the rock face, and then there was nothing but stillness. No movement, no sound save the patter of raindrops upon the ground and the relentless weight on top of her.

Afraid to move or speak, Kendra wondered who'd been shot. She dared not breathe.

After a moment the heaviness lifted from her and someone pulled her from the ground. "Kendra?"

She opened her eyes. "Brice?"

He pulled her into his embrace. "My sweet Kendra,"

he whispered, his lips brushing her ear. Still holding her, he stepped from the portal into the cleansing rain.

"Parkston?" she asked.

"Dead."

She breathed a sigh of relief. The nightmare was over. "How did you find me?"

"Hawk told me what happened."

"He didn't send me the note. Parkston did. I think he was hiding in the secret chamber and pushed me into Hawk's—"

"I know," he said, burying his face in her wet hair. "I know. I was a fool."

"The duel?"

"Is no more."

She laid her head against his chest, but then after a moment looked up at him. Her cop instincts took over. "Show me Parkston's body."

He pointed through the portal to the other side where Parkston lay in the mud, a dark stain seeping across his rain-soaked chest. She approached him, then leaned down to check his pulse.

After assuring herself Parkston was truly dead, she asked, "The gun?"

"I have it."

"Good."

It struck her that this was it. The turning point in her life. "I guess I can go back now. Well, in six months when the portal opens again." She saw him look up, as if wrestling with a major decision.

He said nothing. Though she willed him to, he didn't, and the hope that he might ask her to stay in his time faded with each second. After a minute, she turned away.

Why had she ever worn that damned necklace? Just as she reached for the moonstone, intending to rip it from her neck and fling it into the night, she heard, ever so softly, her name being called. She stopped but didn't turn around until she heard it again, this time louder.

He stood in the same place, though facing her now. "When the portal opens again, let me come with you," he said.

Her heart gave a little lurch. "What?"

"To live. I need you. I cannot live without you."

"Why?" she asked, needing to hear the words she had dreamed about for so long.

"I love you." He took a few steps toward her.

This time, her heart tumbled in her chest and she flew into his arms. "I love you so much. But I—"

He silenced her with a kiss, and when he finally pulled away to look lovingly into her eyes, she could see the pain his decision had cost him. He was sacrificing his own life for hers, forsaking the love of his grandmother and sister to be with her.

"No," she said, finally. "I can't let you do that."

"Because of Jack?"

It suddenly occurred to Kendra that Brice felt threatened by Jack. "That's why you left? You thought he and I . . ."

He nodded. "You were from the same world."

"He has nothing to do with this. I can't let you give up your life, your family, for me. And what of Lady Caroline?"

"Hawk will look after them. And her. He loves her. I was a fool not to see it before." Then Brice did what she had never expected. Keeping her hand firmly in his, he kneeled to the ground. "I love you, Miss Browning. Make me the happiest of men. Do me the honor of becoming my wife."

Kendra thought of all her dreams, her wish that she'd

hear him say those very words. And now that he had, she couldn't accept. Just yesterday, she was willing to give up the life she knew to live in Brice's world, with only a slim hope that she might win his love. And now, when he was willing to leave his world for hers, she couldn't do it.

She shook her head. "No," she said, feeling the tears mist her lashes. She closed her eyes against the pain. "Not in my century. You might be happy for a time, but—"

"Then stay with me in mine. As my wife."

Her eyes flew open, though she was afraid to believe she'd heard right. "In yours?" Was he truly willing to marry her in his own time in spite of her less-than-blue blood?

Brice stood and drew her to him, lifting her chin with his knuckle. "Would you mind so very much?"

"Not much," she said, then smiled as the tears spilled down her cheeks. "Would you?"

"I didn't ask before, because I thought you would rather stay in your own world. That's why I left you. You have so much."

"No. I don't. Everything I love is in yours. You, Grandmère, Cecily. I love you all so much." She brushed at her eyes, then buried her face in his chest, sobbing. "I wasn't sure how I'd live without you."

"Without me, Miss Browning?" he whispered, lifting her face to kiss the tears away. "Not in this or any other time. I love you."

Epilogue

Frankie parked the rental car just outside the gates of the museum, pleased to see no other vehicles in the secluded parking lot. More privacy to look around, she thought, as she locked the car door and strode to the storybook cottage named Briarwood. It was just as Kendra had described it, shaded by two ancient oaks, surrounded by a profusion of flowers, all in bloom.

Almost hesitantly, she pushed open the front door, hearing a bell tinkling somewhere within, announcing her presence. A gray-haired man emerged from a room to the right and smiled kindly at her.

"Have you signed in, madam?" he asked, pointing to a register on the table by the door.

"No. Not yet."

"Please do, then help yourself looking around."

"Thank you." Taking the pen in hand, she signed her name, Frankie Wendall, then printed her address right below it.

The gray-haired man picked up the book, and after

putting on a pair of spectacles, read her name. "Wendall," he muttered to himself. "Wendall?" He looked up at her and lowered his glasses to the end of his nose. "Would that be Frances Wendall?"

"Yes." She smiled, looking around the room. It was just as Kendra had told her.

"Wendall," he muttered as he shuffled from the room. "Oh my!"

Frankie paid little attention, more interested in the display of delicate teacups upon a tea cart. Then, spying an oddly placed porcelain bowl set on the floor near the tea service, she laughed at the memory of when Kendra had told her about soaking her feet in the herbal remedy that Alethea had brewed.

Recalling that her friend had slept upstairs, Frankie moved to the steps but stopped when a deep voice called out behind her.

"Mrs. Wendall?"

Frankie turned to see a tall dark-haired man dressed in casual slacks and a light pullover sweater standing in the doorway leading to what she guessed was the kitchen. "Brice?" But no, it wasn't him, she realized a moment later. Although with a few minor exceptions, he could certainly be Brice's double. She smiled questioningly.

"You *are* Mrs. Wendall?"

"Yes. Well, Miss Wendall, actually."

He smiled. A devastating smile. "Allow me to introduce myself. I am Grayson Montgomery, duke of Blackmoor. I'd say I was expecting you, but that would not exactly be the truth."

Frankie couldn't help noticing that this man, obviously one of Brice's descendants, was looking at her in much the way a man thirsty for a drink eyes a glass of cool water.

Finding her voice, she managed, "Expecting me?"

"Yes. If you would care to accompany me, I have something to show you."

A few minutes later, he was escorting her through the rear door of Blackmoor Hall, then leading her upstairs to the gallery. "You were friends with a Miss Browning?" he asked.

Amazed to see so many fine works of art outside of a real museum, she could only nod. He stopped and pointed up. "The sixth duke and duchess of Blackmoor, and their family."

Frankie's jaw dropped. Though she'd told herself that she'd always believed in Kendra's story, somewhere in the back of her mind doubt had always lingered. Until now. For there before her in a life-sized portrait were Kendra, Brice, and two lovely children. The boy, about ten, was dark like Brice, while the girl, perhaps six or seven, favored Kendra's fair coloring.

Grayson nodded toward the boy. "That is Grayson, the seventh duke of Blackmoor, my namesake and great-great-grandfather. Beside him is his sister, Frances Wendall Montgomery."

Frankie's eyes misted over at the touching tribute her friend had made to her. Kendra had said she would find some way to repay Frankie for helping her return to the past. But never had she expected this.

The duke moved away, allowing her a moment of privacy. When she could gracefully look at him without blubbering, he crossed the room and pointed to another picture. "This is a work that her grace had specially commissioned from a miniature she carried with her."

Frankie moved to a smaller portrait of two women and thought for a moment she had stepped before a mirror with Kendra standing beside her. "Oh my God!" she whispered, amazed. "It's all true, then. Isn't it?"

"I have to admit that I still think of the family legend as more of a fairy tale." He watched her intently. "Even so, each heir to the dukedom was raised with explicit instructions to prepare for this day. My daughter, however, assured me it was true. She's a romantic at heart."

"Your daughter?" she asked, feeling a strange disappointment that he was married.

"Carys Kendra Montgomery. At nine, she's very opinionated, and since she was named after her ancestor, she insisted that the story had to be true."

He glanced once more at the portrait and then at Frankie, almost as if he did not quite believe what he was seeing himself. "If you will follow me, I have some things you might be interested in looking over. A box of journals and such. They're in the attic."

As they strode from the gallery, Frankie caught sight of a portrait hidden in shadow that she had missed on her way in. It was of a woman, a very beautiful golden-haired and blue-eyed woman, in modern dress.

"Who's this?" Frankie asked.

Grayson stopped and returned to her side. "My wife. It was painted about eight months before our daughter was born." He stared up at it, a fond expression in his eyes. "She died about five years ago."

"I'm sorry," Frankie said quietly.

The sound of running feet echoing down the gallery broke the duke's sadness and he turned just in time to catch a golden-haired girl as she jumped into his arms.

"Papa! Papa! Have you come to see the picture I drew?" Suddenly the girl looked at Frankie, noticing her for the very first time. At once, her eyes grew round as saucers. "It's her! I knew she'd come. I knew it."

He kissed her cheek. "You did. Miss Frances Wendall, if I may, this little urchin here, is Carys."

Frankie couldn't help the smile that lit her face. "How do you do?"

"I'm fine, thank you," the little girl said, slipping from her daddy's arms to grasp Frankie's hand. "Can you stay for dinner?"

"I don't know," she answered, wondering what Grayson thought of the impromptu invitation. She looked to him, and he nodded in answer, his dark eyes holding the promise of—should she decide to stay—something more to come. Much, much more.

Let HarperMonogram Sweep You Away!

~~~~~~~~

Simply Heaven by Patricia Hagan

New York Times *bestselling author with over ten million copies in print.* Steve Maddox is determined to bring his friend's estranged daughter Raven home to Alabama. But after setting eyes on the tempestuous half-Tonkawa Indian, Steve yearns to tame the wild beauty and make Raven his.

Home Fires by Susan Kay Law

Golden Heart Award-Winning Author. Escaping with her young son from an unhappy marriage, lovely Amanda Sellington finds peace in a small Minnesota town—and the handsome Jakob Hall. Amanda longs to give in to happiness, but the past threatens to destroy the love she has so recently found.

The Bandit's Lady by Maureen Child

Schoolmarm Winifred Matthews is delighted when bank robber Quinn Hawkins takes her on a flight of fancy across Texas. They're running from the law, but already captured in love's sweet embrace.

When Midnight Comes by Robin Burcell

Time Travel Romance. A boating accident sends detective Kendra Browning sailing back to the year 1830, and into the arms of Captain Brice Montgomery. The ecstasy she feels at his touch beckons to Kendra like a siren's song, but murder threatens to steer their love off course.

And in case you missed last month's selections . . .

Touched by Angels by Debbie Macomber

From the bestselling author of *A Season of Angels* and *The Trouble with Angels.* The much-loved angelic trio—Shirley, Goodness, and Mercy—are spending this Christmas in New York City. And three deserving souls are about to have their wishes granted by this dizzy, though divinely inspired, crew.

Till the End of Time by Suzanne Elizabeth

The latest sizzling time-travel romance from award-winning author of *Destiny's Embrace*. Scott Ramsey has a taste for adventure and a way with the ladies. When his time-travel experiment transports him back to Civil War Georgia, he meets his match in Rachel Ann Warren, a beautiful Union spy posing as a Southern belle.

A Taste of Honey by Stephanie Mittman

After raising her five siblings, marrying the local minister is a chance for Annie Morrow to get away from the farm. When she loses her heart to widower Noah Eastman, however, Annie must choose between a life of ease and a love no money can buy.

A Delicate Condition by Angie Ray

Golden Heart Winner. A marriage of convenience weds innocent Miranda Rembert to the icy Lord Huntsley. But beneath his lordship's stern exterior, fires of passion linger—along with a burning desire for the marital pleasures only Miranda can provide.

Reckless Destiny by Teresa Southwick

Believing that Arizona Territory is no place for a lady, Captain Kane Carrington sent proper Easterner Cady Tanner packing. Now the winsome schoolteacher is back, and ready to teach Captain Carrington a lesson in love.